THE WICKED
DIE TWICE

THE WICKED DIE TWICE

A Slash and Pecos Western

WILLIAM W. JOHNSTONE

AND J. A. JOHNSTONE

PINNACLE BOOKS
Kensington Publishing Corp.
www.kensingtonbooks.com

PINNACLE BOOKS are published by

Kensington Publishing Corp.
119 West 40th Street
New York, NY 10018

PUBLISHER'S NOTE

Following the death of William W. Johnstone, the Johnstone family is working with a carefully selected writer to organize and complete Mr. Johnstone's outlines and many unfinished manuscripts to create additional novels in all of his series like The Last Gunfighter, Mountain Man, and Eagles, among others. This novel was inspired by Mr. Johnstone's superb storytelling.

ISBN-13: 978-0-7860-4380-4
ISBN-10: 0-7860-4380-6

First Kensington hardcover printing: October 2020
First Pinnacle paperback printing: February 2021

10 9 8 7 6 5 4 3 2 1

Printed in the United States of America

Electronic edition:

ISBN-13: 978-0-7860-4381-1 (e-book)
ISBN-10: 0-7860-4381-4 (e-book)

CHAPTER 1

When Town Marshal Glenn Larsen reined up in front of the jailhouse on Dry Fork's main street very early on a Sunday morning in early July, a cold stone dropped in his belly. He could tell by the look on the dark, craggy face of his deputy, Henry Two Whistles, that trouble was afoot.

As the older man, clad in a three-piece suit that hung a little loosely on his lean frame, stepped out through the jailhouse door, a fateful cast to his molasses-dark eyes was undeniable. Not that Two Whistles was ever all that given to merriment. He was three-quarters Ute from southern Colorado Territory, and he was true to the stoic nature of his people.

As he closed the jailhouse door and turned to face Larsen reining up before him on the marshal's sweat-lathered coyote dun gelding, the old man rested his double-barreled Parker twelve-gauge on his right shoulder.

"Anyone hurt . . . killed?" Larsen asked before Two Whistles could say anything, the marshal's voice pitched with dread.

Two Whistles frowned curiously, deep lines wrinkling

the dark-cherry tone of his forehead and spoking around his eyes.

Larsen canted his head toward his back trail. "I was on my way back to town last night when I met three Milliron Ranch hands. I thought it was a mite odd to see Milliron hands heading back out to their headquarters so early on a Saturday night, and said as much. They told me that Talon Chaney and 'HellRaisin' Frank Beecher had come to town, an' were sort of makin' all the stock hands homesick. They decided to cut out early and avoid gettin' caught in a lead storm."

Two Whistles gave a grim, stony-faced nod. "That damn Cut-Head Sioux is with 'em, too—Black Pot."

"Gabriel Black Pot," Larsen said as he swung down from his saddle. "Yeah, they mentioned him, too. He's an aptly named son of the devil, ain't he? There ain't one thing that ain't black about him, especially his heart."

Henry pursed his lips. "How bad, Henry?"

The old deputy lifted and lowered his left shoulder. "Not bad. This time. They came in late yesterday afternoon. Been holed up at Carlisle's place. All the ranch hands and everyone else in town know 'em well enough by now that they cleared out of Carlisle's as soon as Beecher's bunch bellied up to the bar."

"Not great for business, are they?"

"At least no one's dead. Not yet. They slapped around a couple girls, made 'em dance with 'em while Carlisle played the piano, but they was drunk when they rode into town, so by ten, eleven o'clock, they went upstairs an' passed out with a couple of Carlisle's doxies."

"That was nice of them." Larsen sighed. "When I heard they were here, I expected the worst."

Two Whistles's thick-lipped mouth rose in a grim smile.

"That would likely happen today, when they get goin' again. As Carlisle tells it, they're flush. An' it don't look like they're gonna let any of that stagecoach money burn holes in their pockets."

The three killers, along with the rest of their twenty-man bunch, recently ran down a stagecoach hauling treasure from Deadwood to Sundance. They raped the women aboard the stage, killed the men, including the jehu and the shotgun messenger, stole the gold and the ranch payroll in the strongbox, and ran the stage off a cliff.

The gang split up the gold and separated.

Larsen had been surprised that Chaney, Beecher, and Black Pot had had the gall to show their faces in any town so soon after a holdup, but in a town so close to the scene of their crime most of all. On the other hand, he wasn't all that surprised. Those three killers in particular had reputations for being spitin-your-face brazen about their wicked ways.

Maybe they felt they'd earned the privilege. They were known to have killed three deputy U.S. marshals and a couple of sheriffs who'd tried to run them to ground over the years, and double that many bounty hunters who'd hounded the gang for the bounties on their heads.

They probably hadn't hesitated to head to Dry Fork because they knew an unproven town marshal and his just as unproven, old-man, half-breed deputy were manning the jailhouse these days. Glenn Larsen and Henry Two Whistles had both been working out at the Crosshatch Ranch up until only seven months ago, when the rancher they'd worked for, Melvin Wheelwright, died suddenly from a heart stroke. His family had sold the ranch to an eastern syndicate, and that company's head honcho decided to hire an entire new bunkhouse of hands, despite every one being as seasoned as any other thirty-a-month-and-found cowpuncher anywhere in the territory.

Funny folks, those tailor-dressed syndicate men, most of whom were foreigners, of course. Maybe that was the explanation right there. . . .

Two of those hands given their time, a sack of grub, and one horse each to ride away on were Larsen and Two Whistles. Henry had been the Crosshatch cook since his bronco-busting days had gone the way of the buffalo, leaving him with a rickety left hip and a pronounced limp in cold weather. Larsen and Two Whistles had gotten to be good friends over the four years they'd worked together at the Crosshatch, even though Larsen now being only twenty-seven and Two Whistles somewhere in his fifties (though he'd never said where exactly) were separated by nearly thirty years in age. It just seemed natural that, when the two lone wolves left the headquarters and neither had anyone else in their lives, and nowhere else to go, that they'd ride nowhere together.

The nearest town was Dry Fork, so they'd headed there for a drink or two to drown their sorrows. It just so happened the town had been in need of a new marshal and a deputy and, since no one else had seemed to want the dangerous jobs, here the two former Crosshatch men were now, sporting five-point town marshal's stars.

Not only had a job been awaiting Glenn Larsen, but a pretty girl, as well. The first moment he'd lain eyes on the mercantiler's comely daughter, Tiffanie Bright, he'd tumbled head over heels. To his astonishment, it had turned out that she'd felt the same way about him, so against Tiffanie's family's wishes, they'd been hitched inside of two months. Now they had a neat little frame house, which her father had staked them to, on the corner of Main Street and Third.

Larsen was eager to head home to his pretty wife now, as he'd been away for the past three days, looking for the two men who'd stolen stock from a local feed barn, and he knew Tiffanie was worried about him.

First things first.

"All right," he said now, sliding his Winchester carbine from his saddle sheath. "They're over at Carlisle's, you say?"

"That's where they are, all right. Carlisle's swamper has been keepin' me updated. I wasn't gonna make a move on 'em till you showed up. Not unless they started shootin' up the place anyways. I didn't even show myself, knowin' that would only provoke 'em."

"No, no, I'm glad you didn't. Hell, Bill Tilghman wouldn't make a play on that bunch solo. An' there's no point in provokin' 'em and risking other folks' lives."

"So you're sayin' I ain't just a coward?" Henry gave a rare smile.

"No more than me, anyway." Larsen gave a droll chuckle and slowly, quietly jacked a round into his Winchester's action, as though the three brigands might hear the metallic rasp from all the way over at Carlisle's Saloon, two blocks away. "I wouldn't go it alone against them three. I sure will be happy to have them under lock and key— I'll tell you that much, Henry. When I took this job, I didn't think I'd be facing the likes of Talon Chaney!"

Again, Larsen chuckled. It was a nervous chuckle. He had the jitters, all right, and no mistake. His knees felt a little spongy, and his hands were sweating inside his buckskin gloves. He hadn't felt this nervy since the night before his wedding.

Tiffanie.

He sure hoped he made it through this morning in one piece, so he could see his lovely bride again. Thinking of her, of walking over to their little house on the corner of Main and Third, and sitting down to breakfast with her, after he had the three killers under lock and key, calmed his nerves a bit.

He kept her image in the back of his mind, and the image of their peaceful, cheerful, sunlit morning kitchen, as well, as he said, "All right, Henry. Let's do this. Me, I'm ready for breakfast."

"Really?" Henry said as they walked east along the main street, keeping to the boardwalks on the north side. "I couldn't eat a thing. In fact, I feel a little off my feed." He winced and pressed a hand to the middle-aged bulge of his belly.

"Truth be told, I was just jawin'." Larsen glanced at the older man walking beside him. "Right now, just the thought of food makes me a little ill."

"Yeah," Henry said.

As the two men walked along, spurs clanging softly, boot heels scuffing the worn boards of the sidewalk, Larsen saw that the street was deserted. That was strange. It was almost eight o'clock.

Normally, there would be some wagon traffic at this hour. Housewives would be strolling toward Mergen's Grocery Store for fresh eggs and cream. Children would be tramping in small groups toward the schoolhouse on the town's west end, bouncing lunch sacks off their thighs, the little boys triggering tree branch guns at each other or at imaginary Indians, the little girls whispering delicious secrets and giggling.

At the very least, a shopkeeper or two would be out sweeping the boardwalks fronting their stores, or arranging displays of their goods.

There was nothing but soft morning sunshine, a few

small birds darting here and there, the light morning breeze kicking up little swirls of dust. Otherwise, the street was deserted.

Larsen didn't even see one of the town's mongrels heading home after a night in the countryside or hunting along the creek, a dead rabbit in its jaws. Occasionally, he saw a face in one of the store windows as he passed—a shopkeeper stealing a cautious glance into the street before letting a curtain drop back into place and scuttling back into the shadows, wary of catching a stray bullet.

Word had gotten around, of course.

Three of the nastiest killers ever to haunt the North Platte country were in town. Folks had learned that the three killers were at Carlisle's, and that the town's two unlikely lawmen, Glenn Larsen and Henry Two Whistles, were going to make a play on them. . . .

Larsen and Two Whistles stopped on the corner of Main Street and Wyoming Avenue, and turned to face Carlisle's standing on the adjacent corner, on the other side of the main drag. It was a sprawling, white-painted, clapboard, three-story affair with a broad front porch. Larsen had never thought the place had looked particularly menacing. Just another saloon—one of three in the little settlement of Dry Fork, though the largest and the one with the prettiest doxies, as well as the best cook. Magnus Carlisle wasn't known to water down his whiskey, either, so his saloon and "dance hall," which was mostly just a euphemism for "whorehouse," was favored by men who could afford his slightly higher prices.

Now, however, Larsen would be damned if Carlisle's didn't look like a giant powder keg sporting a lit fuse.

He turned to his deputy. "You ready, Henry?"

"No," Two Whistles said, staring without expression at the saloon across the street.

"Yeah," Larsen said. "Me neither."

Squeezing the rifle in his hands, Larsen stepped into the street.

Larsen and Henry approached Carlisle's, whose porch and front door faced the street corner, the front of the building forming a pie-shaped wedge. A large sign over the porch announced simply CARLISLE'S in ornate green letters outlined in red and gold. Larsen felt his heart picking up its pace. The young man who had been sitting tipped back in a chair near the saloon's louvred front doors dropped the chair's front legs to the floor with a quiet thump and rose slowly.

That was Eddie Black, the curly-haired young swamper who had been relaying information about the cutthroats to Two Whistles at the jailhouse.

Eddie moved forward, and as the two lawmen stepped up onto the boardwalk fronting the porch, he came quickly down the broad wooden steps, eyes blazing anxiously. He was of medium height and skinny, and he wore a black wool vest over a white shirt adorned with a red cravat stained with beer and the tobacco juice he emptied from the saloon's brass spittoons.

He was "a little soft in his thinker box," as the saying went, and he sported a bushy thatch of curly red hair. He wasn't really as young as he seemed; Larsen had heard he was somewhere in his thirties. But his simple-mindedness made him seem much younger.

Breathless, he stopped before the two lawmen and said, "You gonna take 'em down, Marshal?" He grinned delightedly but also a little fearfully. He was fairly shaking with excitement.

Larsen and Two Whistles shared a glance, then the marshal said, "Well, we're gonna give it a try, Eddie. You'd best wait out here, all right?"

"Oh, don't you worry! I know who them fellas are!" Eddie scampered off to the left along the boardwalk and crouched down behind a rain barrel at the big building's far front corner. He looked cautiously over the top, as if he were expecting hell to pop at any second.

The young man's anxiety increased Larsen's. He shared another look with Two Whistles, and saw that the swamper's demeanor had had a similar effect on the normally stone-faced Ute. Henry's eyes were a little darker than usual. He was also a little pale, and sweat beaded his forehead, just beneath the brim of his black bullet-crowned hat.

Larsen adjusted the set of his own tan Stetson, then, opening and closing his hands around his rifle, he and Henry started up the porch steps. There were around a dozen steps, but it felt like a long climb. Finally, the lawmen pushed through the batwings and stepped into the saloon's cool shadows.

CHAPTER 2

"*Damn!*" a voice exclaimed.

Jerking his rifle up suddenly, Larsen turned to see Magnus Carlisle standing behind the bar just ahead and on the marshal's left. The man had been rolling a quirley, but apparently the two lawmen's sudden appearance in the front entrance had spooked him. He'd dropped his rolling paper and tobacco onto the polished mahogany bar top.

Larsen gave a soft sigh of relief and lowered the rifle.

Glaring at Larsen and Two Whistles, the portly, bespectacled saloon owner said, "You scared the hell out of me!"

Keeping his voice down, Larsen said, "Didn't you hear us comin' up the steps?"

"No!"

Larsen hadn't realized that he and Henry had been walking almost as quietly as two full-blood Indian braves on the warpath, but apparently they had. He glanced at Henry, who shrugged and gave a wry quirk of his upper lip.

Turning back to the saloon owner, Larsen said, "They still upstairs?"

"Yep," Carlisle said darkly, looking over the tops of his

round, steel-rimmed spectacles. "Been there all damn night. You sure took your own sweet time getting here."

Larsen felt his face warm with anger. "I got back to town as quickly as I could, Mr. Carlisle," he crisply replied. And he nearly killed his horse doing it, he did not add. "Which room are they in?"

"Third floor. The big room all the way down on the end, right side of the hall. It overlooks the street. You better hope like hell they didn't see you walking over here." Carlisle narrowed an anxious eye and said, "They could be layin' in there waitin' for you."

"We'll handle it," Larsen said as he and Two Whistles walked along the bar, heading for the broad staircase at the room's rear. The young marshal hoped he'd sounded more confident than he felt.

Carlisle followed them, running a hand along the bar. "Take no chances, Glenn. If they get past you, they'll come down here and tear into *me*. There won't be enough of me left to bury!"

"Keep your voice down, Mr. Carlisle," Larsen said levelly, keeping his own voice just above a whisper.

"Shoot 'em through the door! Just shoot 'em through the door!"

As both lawmen stopped at the bottom of the stairs, Two Whistles turned to the saloon owner and said, "Don't they have a couple girls up there?"

Carlisle stared at him thoughtfully and blinked. He looked a little sheepish. "Yeah, I reckon they do. Claudine and Sally Jane. Still, though, fellas, shoot 'em through the door. Please! Don't take no chances. Claudine an' Sally Jane would understand!"

Larsen and Two Whistles shared a cynical glance and then started up the stairs.

Behind them, leaning forward and pushing his pudgy right hand against the bar top, Carlisle rasped, "Shoot 'em through the door! Don't take no chances! Hell, they'll burn the whole town down! You know how they are!"

Larsen whipped his head back to the frightened man and pressed two fingers to his lips. Carlisle just stared up at him, looking anguished. Turning forward again, Larsen and Two Whistles kept moving slowly up the stairs, keeping their eyes forward. At one point, Larsen's right spur jingled. He stopped, glanced at Henry, and then the two men wordlessly, quietly removed the spurs from their boots and left both pairs on that very step.

Spurless, they resumed their climb, crossing the second-floor landing, then continuing to the third floor.

Slowly, quietly, almost holding their breaths, they made their way down the third-floor hall, which was dingy and sour-smelling and lit by only the one dirty window at the far end. As they walked side by side, Larsen holding his Winchester up high across his chest, Two Whistles holding his Parker the same way, the marshal kept his eyes glued to the last door on the hall's right side.

He pricked his ears, listening.

The building was as silent as a tomb. There were still no sounds on the street. It was as quiet as Sunday morning when the whole town was in either of the two churches—the Lutheran or the Catholic.

A door clicked on the hall's right side. The lawmen stopped suddenly.

Larsen's heart quickened as he turned to see a near door open. A girl, dressed in a thin cotton wrap, stepped into the hall; then seeing the two gun-wielding men before her, she stopped and gasped, her eyes widening.

"What in holy blazes is goin' on?" she said way too loudly. Her words echoed around the previously silent hall.

"*Shhh!*" both Larsen and Two Whistles said at the same time, pressing fingers to their lips.

The girl looked as though she'd been slapped.

Larsen dipped his chin to indicate the door at the end of the hall. The girl turned her head to stare in that direction, then, appearing suddenly horrified, apparently remembering the three killers on the premises, stepped quickly back into her room and quietly closed her door.

Larsen stared at the last door on the hall's right side. He prayed it didn't open. Somehow, he had to get those three killers out of the room without getting the doxies killed. If the killers learned that the law was on the way, they might use the girls as human shields. Or they might just start shooting, and the girls would die in the crossfire.

Larsen couldn't wait for a better time. There might not be a better time. He had to arrest the cutthroats as soon as possible. No citizen was safe as long as the three cold-blooded killers were running free. Now was the best time to take them down, when they were either still asleep or groggy.

The two lawmen shared another fateful look, then resumed their slow, deliberative journey.

Finally, they found themselves standing in front of the door at the end of the hall.

Larsen tipped an ear to the panel. The only sounds issuing from inside the room were deep, sawing snores.

He looked at Henry and arched a brow, silently asking, *Too good to be true?*

The deputy gave a noncommittal shrug.

Holding his rifle in his right hand, aiming it just above the knob, Larsen placed his other hand on the knob and turned it very slowly. He winced when the latching bolt retreated into the door with a click.

A loud click. At least, to Larsen's nervous ears it was loud.

One of the three snoring men inside the room abruptly stopped snoring and groaned.

Larsen's heart thumped.

He shoved the door open and stepped quickly inside and to the left. Henry stepped in behind him to pull up on his right side, aiming the shotgun straight out from his right shoulder. Inadvertently, Two Whistles kicked a bottle that had been lying on the floor in front of the door. The bottle went rolling loudly across the wooden floor to bounce off a leg of one of the four beds before the two lawmen.

The bottle spun, making a whirring sound.

Henry looked down at it, stone-faced.

Larsen sucked a silent breath through his teeth, aiming his Winchester out from his right side.

One of the three men, each occupying three of the four beds in the room, lifted his head from his pillow. He was a shaggy-headed man lying back down on a bed ahead and against the right wall. The man sat partway up, but he didn't open his eyes. He merely groaned, then rolled onto this side, lay his head back down on his pillow, groaned once more, yawned, then resumed snoring softly.

Henry glanced sheepishly at Larsen, who gave him a look of silent scolding.

Returning his gaze to the three killers, Larsen looked them over.

A vacant bed lay to his hard right. The other three beds were filled. The two girls lay in each of the two beds on Larsen's left, each with one of the other two killers. The near girl appeared to be asleep, lying belly down beside a man with long coal-black braids and clad in a pair of threadbare long-handles. He also lay belly down. He and the girl were only partly covered by a twisted sheet.

The man with the black braids would be the Cut-Head Sioux, Black Pot.

The man beyond him, in the bed abutting the wall overlooking the street, was Talon Chaney himself. The second girl lay with Chaney, sort of wrapped in his thick arms. No sheet covered them. They were both naked. The girl was not asleep. Her blue eyes peered out through her tangled, tawny hair. They were bright and wide open, cast with terror and desperation. Silently, she begged Larsen and Two Whistles for help.

Something told Larsen she hadn't slept a wink all night.

He couldn't blame her. Not one bit.

Chaney, who had close-cropped hair and a patchy beard on his blunt-nosed face, lay sort of spooned against the girl from behind, his thick, tattooed arms wrapped around her. His face was snugged up tight to the back of her head, his nose buried in her neck. With each resounding exhalation, the outlaw made the girl's hair billow up around his nose and mouth.

Larsen shifted his eyes to the right, to the third killer lying alone in the bed beside Chaney and the girl's bed. That would be Hell-Raisin' Frank Beecher—shaggy-headed, tall, hawk-nosed, crazy-eyed, and with a silver hoop ring dangling from his right ear.

All three were sleeping like baby lambs.

However, these three lambs had guns close to hand. In fact, the room resembled a small arsenal. At least two pistols apiece were buckled to each of the brass bed frames, within an easy reach of each killer. Sheathed bowie knives also hung from bed frames. Rifles—two Winchesters and a Henry—leaned against the walls, also close to each bed. Boxes of shells littered the room's single dresser cluttered with women's underfrillies.

Three piles of tack were carelessly mounded here and there, including saddlebags likely stuffed with the money these three had taken off the Sundance stage.

The room might have looked like an arsenal, but it reeked of a whore's crib in which three drunken men who hadn't bathed in a month of Sundays had been well entertained.

Larsen chewed his lower lip. How were he and Two Whistles going to get the two girls out of here without arousing the three killers? Maybe he should try to get all of the weapons out of the room first. . . .

He nixed that idea. With so many guns and knives littering the room, it would take too long. Doubtless, one or more of the killers would wake up and begin the foofaraw. Larsen would try to get the girls out first. If the killers woke up in the process—well, then there would be trouble.

One thing at a time.

The marshal leaned close to Two Whistles and whispered very softly into the older man's right ear, "Cover me. If one or more of them wakes up, blast 'em."

The old Ute gave a slow, single nod, keeping his eyes on the room.

Larsen started forward, stopped, and turned back to Two Whistles to whisper in the man's ear again: "But wait till I'm out of the way. And the girls, too."

Two Whistles gave a grim half smile.

Larsen stepped forward. He walked past the girl asleep belly down on the bed with Black Pot. He crouched over the girl lying fully awake, eyes glazed with terror, beside

Talon Chaney. He aimed his rifle at Chaney with his right hand and extended his left hand to the girl.

"Come on," he mouthed.

The girl glanced at Chaney curled against her from behind.

She looked at Larsen, beetling her brows, terrified to move.

Larsen crouched lower and said into her left ear, his breath making her blond hair flutter a little, "If he grabs you, I'll shoot 'im." He rose slightly and waggled his fingers at her again.

The girl drew a breath, steeling herself, then, sitting up, slowly lifted her left hand.

Chaney groaned, muttered incoherently.

The girl stopped and whipped her horrified eyes at the man beside her.

"Keep comin'," Larsen whispered.

She turned to the lawman again. She continued to stretch her hand toward him, sitting up. Larsen closed his hand around hers and gently pulled her out of the bed. As she rose away from Chaney, the killer's right arm slid down her side to the bed. He turned his face into his pillow and muttered, "Wh . . . where you . . . goin' . . . sugar . . . ?"

The words were badly garbled. The killer was likely still drunk.

Good.

The girl rose, the long tendrils of her blond hair dancing across her slender, bare shoulders. Larsen stepped aside to let her pass behind him. As she padded on tiptoes out of the room, Larsen looked around at the three killers surrounding him.

All three were still sawing logs.

He glanced at Two Whistles aiming the shotgun into the

room, gave an expression of "So far, so good," then moved to the cot on which the other girl slept beside Black Pot.

Larsen dropped to a knee beside the girl. The chubby brunette was snoring softly into her pillow.

Larsen placed his hand on her right arm, which hung down over the side of the bed.

Instantly, she lifted her head and opened her eyes, which were cast with the same terror as the other girl's eyes, and said much too loudly, "Oh, God—please don't hurt—"

Gritting his teeth, Larsen clamped his right hand over her mouth.

She stared over his hand at him, wide-eyed, the light of understanding gradually filling her gaze. Larsen looked over her at Black Pot. The man shifted a little but only grumbled into his pillow, then resumed snoring.

He didn't wake.

Neither did the two other killers. Snores continued rising so loudly that they almost made the marshal's ears ache. The stench in the room nearly made his ears water.

To the brunette before him, Larsen whispered, "Very slowly, get up and leave the room."

She nodded quickly.

Larsen pulled his hand away from her mouth.

Glancing behind her at Black Pot, the girl slid her body, clad in a thin, torn gown, out of the bed. The bed squawked and jounced. Still, Black Pot snored deeply into his pillow.

The girl placed her bare feet on the floor beside Larsen, glanced up at him with a look of extreme gratitude, then shook her hair back from her face and tiptoed past Two Whistles and out of the room.

Larsen looked around at the three killers. He couldn't believe his luck. They were still asleep.

He still couldn't believe his luck when, ten minutes later,

he had placed his and his deputy's handcuffs on all three killers, cuffing their hands behind their backs. None so much as stirred through the entire process.

Still, they slept like baby lambs.

Trussed up baby lambs. Only, baby lambs didn't snore nearly as loudly as these three unconscious killers.

Now all the two lawmen had to do was get them over to the jailhouse and turn the key on them. That shouldn't be hard at all. All three men were defenseless. Chaney and Beecher were naked. Black Pot was clad in only threadbare longhandles.

Larsen stepped back over to Two Whistles, who had been covering him with his Parker, and looked over his handiwork.

The two lawmen smiled at each other in deep relief.

CHAPTER 3

"This soft life you two old cutthroats are living is gonna get you both killed!"

The woman's voice, albeit a familiar one, made Jimmy "Slash" Braddock sit bolt upright in the bed he'd been sound asleep in. "Huh . . . *wha* . . . ?" he said, blinking sleepily, automatically waving a hand toward where he usually kept a pistol within an easy grab.

His vision focused, and his heart warmed. He lowered his hand. A smile played across his lips as he stared into the jadegreen eyes of the woman he'd finally worked up enough gumption to propose to. He'd even done it sober, a fact that still amazed him.

"Huh . . . *what* . . . ?" Jaycee Breckenridge good-naturedly mocked him as she stared into Slash and his partner's sleeping quarters at the rear of their freighting office, one hand on the pine plank door. She smiled that smile that made the whole universe want to dance. In fact, still half-asleep and mildly hungover, as usual, Slash's middle-aged ticker was dancing a jig inside his rib cage.

The ring on a finger of Jay's hand holding open the door caught the morning light angling through a window behind

Slash, and glinted like sunlight off a high mountain lake. That had been Slash's dear mother's wedding ring. Studded with diamonds and rubies, it must have cost his pa a pretty penny. Slash had given the ring to Jay to wear as an engagement ring until their wedding in the fall.

"I'm cooking you boys up a good breakfast for the trail," Jay said as Slash's partner, Melvin Baker, who'd been known as "The Pecos River Kid" in their recent former outlaw days, stirred in his own bed on the other side of the braided rug from Slash.

Slash preferred to be called Jimmy these days, though it was hard for him and his partner to remember to call each other by anything but their old outlaw monikers. They'd put their outlaw days behind them for keeps, and they'd just as soon no one in their adopted hometown of Camp Collins, Colorado, know of their dark history as bank and train robbers of some celebrity and more than a little disrepute.

"Come on, Pecos," Jay said. She also had trouble calling them by their given names, since she'd known them both during their outlaw years, had even been the common law wife of a man, the dearly departed and legendary Pistol Pete Johnson, from their own gang. "You boys are burnin' daylight. Didn't you say you were supposed to be on the trail headed to Dry Fork by eight o'clock? Well, it's pushing toward seven thirty. Myra and I are cooking you up a nice, big breakfast for the trail."

"You are?" Slash said. Sniffing the air, he smelled the savory aroma of bacon and coffee. His empty belly stirred despite the overabundance of tangle-legs he and Pecos had indulged in last night, at the saloon Jay owned right here in Camp Collins—the House of a Thousand Delights.

"We've been cooking and banging pots around for the

past forty-five minutes," Jay said, chuckling. "I'm surprised you didn't hear us."

"So am I!" both Slash and Pecos said raspily at the same time, exchanging incriminating glances from either side of the braided rug.

"Like I said," Jay said, "this soft life you two old cutthroats have been living is going to get you killed one of these days, especially if you keep riding for that old reprobate Bledsoe." She wagged her head, not liking their employer, Chief Marshal Luther T. Bledsoe, one bit.

But, then, no one did like that old, pushchair-bound human coyote. . . .

"Hurry up, now," Jay said. "Myra and I will be filling plates in three jangles of a doxie's bell!"

With that, she gave Slash a flirtatious wink, flashed him another one of her million-dollar smiles, and pulled the door closed.

Slash leaned back on his elbows, staring at the door.

Pecos gave a caustic chuckle. It was then that Slash realized his former partner-in-crime and current-partner-in lawdogging—yeah, lawdogging of all things!—was sneering at him from Pecos's bed on the room's other side.

"What?" Slash grunted.

"You two with all your mooncalf eyes."

It was then that Slash realized he'd been smiling at the closed door, though of course it hadn't been the door he was smiling at but at Jay's lovely visage still emblazoned on his retinas.

"You're just jealous," Slash grouched as he tossed away his covers and dropped his stockinged feet to the floor. "You got your drawers in a bunch because you can't have the woman you're pinin' after, because the woman you want is too good for you, not to mention far too good *looking* to give you a second look, ya big, ugly ape. *Not to mention* that she's old Bleed-Em-So's assistant."

"Bleed-Em-So" was the nickname given long ago to their employer, Luther T. Bledsoe, due to his uncompromising and ruthless lawdogging ways that weren't often all that more upstanding than the ways of the outlaws he'd spent most of his adult life bringing to justice. In fact, Bledsoe had pretty much blackmailed Slash and Pecos into working for him—unofficially and off the record, taking on assignments the Chief Marshal deemed too dangerous for his bona fide deputy U.S. marshals. If the two former cutthroats hadn't accepted the job he'd offered, after resigning from the train-robbing business, he'd more or less threatened to hang them.

In exchange for their agreement to work for him, he'd offered them an amnesty—but one that would promptly be revoked if they ever crossed him or decided to stop working for him, which for all intents and purposes would amount to the same thing.

The apple of Pecos's eye was Bleed-Em-So's assistant, Miss Abigail Langdon, a big-boned Viking queen of a gal with long lake-green eyes, like a cat's eyes, and the thickest, goldest hair Slash had ever seen. She was a big gal, but no gal ever wore her size better or in a more beguiling, fairy-tale-like fashion. A fella with a good imagination could picture Miss Langdon with her golden locks in braids tumbling down from an iron helmet, her cheeks painted for war, her supple, shapely body clad in furs and leather, and with a shield in one hand, a war ax in the other.

"If you made a play for that cat-eyed beauty, Bleed-Em-So would throw a necktie party in your honor and play cat's cradle with your ugly head!" Slash laughed.

"That ain't true. You know he treats her like he would

a favorite niece. Bleed-Em-So would want her to find a righteous, upstanding man to walk her down the aisle!" Pecos chuckled as he, too, tossed his covers back and dropped his long, longhandle-clad legs over the edge of his bed.

"Hey, what's your boot doing over here on my side of the room?" Slash picked up the boot in question and whipped it at his partner. It bounced with a thump off the big man's right shoulder.

Sitting on the edge of his bed, Pecos jerked his head up and tossed a lock of his long gray-blond hair back over his shoulder. He glared at the smaller-boned, darker of the two cutthroats and said, "Ow, dammit—that hurt!"

"Oh, quit caterwauling, ya Nancy-boy!"

Pecos rose up off the cot to his full six foot six inches and clenched his ham-sized fists at his sides, red-faced and ready to fight. "You do that again, I'm gonna take that boot and shove it up your—"

Someone knocked loudly on their bedroom door, and yet another female voice yelled, "You two stop roughhousing in there and get out here! Didn't Jay tell you we're about to shovel up the grub?"

This voice was a little higher pitched than that of Jaycee Breckenridge.

That would belong to the young former outlaw girl who now pretty much ran the freighting business even when Slash and Pecos weren't out risking life and limb for Chief Marshal Bledsoe—Myra Thompson. Myra was only in her early twenties, but she'd been around the block a time or two, had good business sense, and had a no-nonsense pragmatism to equal that of the most persnickety banker.

Between her and Jaycee Breckenridge, who in her early forties was Slash's junior by roughly ten years, the two women made sure Slash and Pecos remained (relatively) sober during working hours and kept to a solid workaday schedule, whether they were running their new freighting company in northern Colorado or running down bad guys for Bleed-Em-So and Uncle Sam.

"Yes, Myra," both Slash and Pecos replied through the door, sheepish as schoolboys who'd been caught dropping garter snakes through the half-moon in the girls' privy door.

Five minutes later, the two stumbled out of their room and into the living and kitchen area of their shack. The main office was at the very front. Myra had a room off of the front office—a long lean-to addition she didn't spend a whole lot of time in, since she was always filing or cleaning or wrangling the hostlers in charge of the wagons and mule teams in the barn, or going over books or shipping orders, or trying to make sense out of the cash receipts Slash and Pecos brought back from freighting runs.

She was in the kitchen area of the shack now, just then scooping potatoes out of a cast-iron skillet onto two large stone plates while Jay stood at the range, scrambling eggs in the popping bacon grease.

"There they finally are," Jay quipped. "Drink a little too much last night—did you, boys?"

"It was that card shark from Denver," Slash said, walking up to his betrothed and wrapping an arm around her waist. "He kept buying us good Kentucky bourbon because apparently he didn't think he was fleecing us badly enough without it." He gave a caustic grunt and planted a kiss on Jay's neck.

Jay and Myra chuckled.

"Thank you mighty kindly, ladies," Pecos said, walking over to Myra, crouching down and planting a brotherly—or, given their age difference, a *fatherly*—peck on her cheek. "You sure didn't have to go to all this trouble for me an' Slash."

He gave his partner a cold look and added, "Especially for Slash."

Myra blushed and grabbed Pecos's hand before he could pull away from her. She smiled up at the big, blond galoot. At least, he was a galoot in Slash's eyes, though Slash reckoned his partner wasn't nearly as ugly as Slash always told him he was. Melvin Baker was tall and blond—well, gray-blond these days—and broad-shouldered, with pale-blue eyes the ladies found quite alluring.

Slash just liked to get under the bigger man's skin because—well, because they had a relationship similar to that of quarreling and constantly roughhousing beloved brothers, and since Pecos was bigger, Slash thought the bigger man should be able to take the abuse. He just plain liked trying to rile the big man, if the truth be known. He attributed the desire to the ill-behaving boy remaining inside him despite the gray in his own thick dark brown hair, which he wore down over his collar.

Myra didn't seem to think Pecos was at all ugly. In fact, in the year or so they'd been operating the freighting business together—her, Slash, and Pecos—it had become more and more obvious that the young woman was positively smitten by the big, blond galoot. She turned to watch him now as he plucked a strip of bacon piled on a plate on the table. She grinned as she admonished him with: "Pecos, you mind your manners and wait till the rest of us are seated!"

"I'll be hanged if that ain't great bacon, and it sure tastes good after a long night in which I got my pockets turned inside out!"

"Come over here and get your plate," Myra ordered him, lacing her voice with a crispness that was not heartfelt. "I put potatoes on it for you. I know you like a lot of potatoes, so I fried extra . . . with onions and peppers, just the way like them." She blushed as he walked over and crouched down to accept the plate and give her another peck on the cheek.

"Thank you, honey. You're gonna make one of the young men in town a fine wife someday."

"Oh, you!" she said, and turned around to face the counter to hide the look of vague frustration that had tumbled across her eyes. She didn't want any of the young men in town— several of whom had come calling on her here at the freight yard a time or two. She wanted the big man right before her.

"Ain't that right, Slash?" Pecos said, taking his plate to where Slash stood with Jay, so Jay could shovel eggs onto it from the cast-iron skillet in which she'd scrambled them.

"Ain't what right?" Slash asked.

"Ain't Myra gonna make a right good wife one of these days?"

Slash looked at Myra again. She kept her back to them as she buttered the toasted bread on the counter before her.

"I reckon that's right," Slash said.

Jaycee glanced at Myra then, too, and, sensing the turmoil inside the younger woman, gave her arm an affectionate squeeze. Jaycee shot Slash a conferring look. Slash only shrugged.

"I'm gonna sit outside and eat on the porch," Pecos announced, when he'd piled bacon over his potatoes and eggs, and had accepted a slice of toasted bread fromMyra.

"I'll join you," Myra announced, and quickly filled her own plate.

When she and Pecos had stepped out the side door, where there was a short stoop facing the freight yard corrals and barn and blacksmith shop to the west, Slash set his plate down on the table and dragged a chair out with his boot.

As he did, Jay turned to him from the range, with her own filled plate, and said, "That big galoot is going to break that poor girl's heart, Slash. Isn't there something you can do about it?"

CHAPTER 4

"Ah, hell, I don't know what to do about him," Slash said. "Pecos, he don't seem to realize his effect on Myra."

Jay set a piece of toast on her plate, then moved to the table, shaking her copper hair back from her face. She wore a formfitting cambric day frock printed with a wildflower pattern and an apron. The simple dress was a stark contrast to the richly colored velveteen gowns she usually wore at work, managing the Thousand Delights.

This morning, she wore her hair down, and it shone with a recent washing and brushing. She wore no rouge on her face, like she usually wore at night at the popular watering hole, gambling parlor, and whorehouse.

All in all, it was a softer, more domestic look for Jay—one that Slash very much liked on her.

Jay sat down across from him, reached across the table, and squeezed his hand. Gently, she said, "Maybe you should talk to him. Explain it to him—how Myra obviously feels about him."

"Ah, heck, Jay—you know women are always fallin' in love with that big galoot. Big he may be, but he's a charmer with his soft voice and his easy way with women."

"So what are you saying?"

"Maybe we should just let it run its course. How's he supposed to keep the girl from tumbling for him when so many others have in the past?"

"But he's going to break her heart, Slash. She's had a tough time, having such a lousy upbringing, then getting enmeshed in that outlaw gang." In fact, it had been Slash and Pecos's own gang she'd gotten enmeshed in. When Bledsoe had sent the two former cutthroats out to run their old gang to ground, the gang, led by a couple of young firebrands who'd double-crossed Slash and Pecos, had sent the pretty young Myra back to distract them and kill them, though obviously and fortunately for Slash and Pecos, she hadn't managed to pull it off.

In fact, Jay herself had intervened. If not for Jaycee Breckenridge's help, Slash and Pecos would have been crowbait.

"And now . . ." Jay turned to the open side door through which she and Slash could hear Pecos and Myra chatting and chuckling together.

"And now she's got her feelings all wrapped around that big, old cutthroat out there on the porch," Slash finished for her, pausing with a forkful of eggs and potatoes to stare out the open door and into the brightly lit yard. "All right, I'll talk to him on our way to Dry Fork. That's a three-day ride, so we'll have plenty of time to powwow about it. Maybe we can come up with a plan to cushion the blow for her. That big, old reprobate is too damn old for her. I wonder what she's thinkin'."

Jay swallowed a mouthful of the succulent vittles and smiled sweetly across the table at Slash. "At that age, they don't think. They just *feel*. Don't you remember?"

"Um . . . well . . . yeah, of course I do . . ." Slash kept

his eyes on his food and kept shoveling it into his mouth, trying to keep the lie from showing on his face. At least, he thought it was a lie. Back when he'd been Myra's age, he'd been so busy stomping with his tail up, chasing women as opposed to falling in love with them, as well as robbing banks, stagecoaches, trains, and anything else that housed or carried money, that he really hadn't taken time to fall in love.

Or maybe he hadn't been capable of falling in love back then.

But he was now . . . wasn't he?

He glanced up at Jay studying him a little too quizzically for his own good comfort. He was in love with her, wasn't he? Wasn't that what he felt for her? Or did he really know what love was even now in his yonder years . . . ?

"Slash," Jay pressed him, "you have been in love before, haven't you?"

"Of course, I have." He chuckled as he shoved more food into his mouth, returning his gaze to his plate. "I mean . . . yeah . . . time or two . . ."

"Slash?"

He felt his shoulders tighten. He didn't like the serious tone of her voice. It meant they were going to have a conversation about something important, and Slash Braddock was a man who preferred to focus on frivolous things.

Steeling himself, holding his freshly loaded fork in front of his mouth, he said, "Yeah, Jay?"

"You do love me . . . right?"

"Of course, I do." Chuckling again, he reached across the table with his free hand and closed it around her own free hand. "Of course, I do, Jay. We're gettin' hitched, ain't we?"

She studied him. Her eyes were painfully serious, probing. They sort of made Slash shrivel up inside and start thinking that it was maybe time for him and Pecos to hit the trail for Dry Fork.

"Slash?"

"Uh-huh."

Jay canted her head a little to one side, narrowing one of her serious eyes. "You aren't getting cold feet, are you?"

"Me? Cold feet? Nah!"

Slash was genuinely astonished by the question. He'd made up his mind to marry this beautiful, copper-haired, hazel-eyed woman. He'd been in love with her—at least, in something very close to love, if he had any idea at all about the nature of love—since she'd been hitched to Pistol Pete Johnson. That had been years ago. He'd loved her beauty, which she still very much maintained even now in her forties. He'd loved her earthiness and practicality . . . the ease with which he found himself being able to talk to her, like no other woman ever before. He liked the way she wore a blouse and a tight-fitting pair of jeans . . . and the way she walked . . . the sound of her voice . . . her husky laugh . . . the fact that she didn't begrudge a man an off-color joke now and then and even told them herself . . . and several other things about her he'd best not think about lest he start blushing.

He really did, deep down, feel that he and Jay were soul mates. If he knew anything else about his often-mysterious self, it was that he could see himself growing old with Jaycee Breckenridge.

"Are you sure?"

"Certain-sure." Slash squeezed her hand a little harder and gave her a direct stare, which was not something that came easy to him, given his shy nature, especially around most women. . . . "I love you, Jay. I am not getting cold feet. Hell, they ain't even chilly!"

They both chuckled at that. Jay seemed convinced.

"All right, then," she said, setting her fork down on her empty plate. "You boys best get moving. It's almost eight thirty. When you get back, I thought we'd go over to that house Old Man Springer put up for sale last week. The one on the south edge of town, by the Poudre River?"

"A house?" Slash said. He'd had to clear his throat to get it out. For some reason, his vocal cords suddenly felt more cumbersome than they had a minute ago.

"Yes, a house." Rising from her chair and picking up their empty plates, Jay laughed as she looked around the cluttered, roughhewn cabin. "You don't think we're going to live here after we're married, do you? With *Pecos*?"

She laughed again.

"You better be talkin' me *up* in there and not *down*!" Pecos yelled from out on the porch.

Slash chuckled, but it sounded wooden to his own ears. "Oh, right, right. You'd get tired of smellin' his socks in no time—like I done twenty years ago." Slash laughed. Pecos cursed them both from the porch.

Then Slash said, "Let's go over and take a look at Old Man Springer's place just as soon as we get back from Dry Fork, darlin'." He winked.

She smiled, then as she dropped the plates in the wreck pan over the dry sink, she frowned over her shoulder at him. "Why is old Bleed-Em-So sending you boys to Dry Fork, anyway? I don't think you told me last night."

"Pickin' up some prisoners, is all. Transportin' 'em via jail wagon to Cheyenne, then via train to the federal building in Denver to stand trial."

"Is it dangerous?" Jay asked.

"Nah, this should be an easy one, for a change." Slash threw back the last of his tepid coffee, then rose from his chair. "In fact, it's so unimportant that the chief marshal only sent a letter this time, giving us the assignment. You know how if it's somethin' bigger and needs more explainin' we meet the old devil himself out somewhere?"

Slash shook his head as he plucked his black hat off a wall peg. "Not this time. The way I figure it, he didn't have some wet-behind-the-ears lacky deputy handy, so he decided to send me an' Pecos. That's all right. As long as the check don't bounce. Me, I'm ready for a nice, peaceful ride in the country, anyways. Maybe do a little fishin' up around the North Platte. Haven't done that in years."

"Yeah, I reckon this is just a little vacation for me an' Slash."

Pecos followed Myra back through the side door and into the cabin. Myra was carrying the empty plates of her and Pecos both. "We'll just have to take that load of dry goods up to Del Porter in Jamestown after we get back next week," Pecos continued, stretching and yawning, the ill effects of last night apparently lingering in the big man's bones.

"Want me to send a telegram to let Porter know about the delay, Pecos?" Myra asked, helpfully.

"Would you mind, darlin'?"

The pretty brown-eyed girl, gifted with a thick head of pretty auburn curls, beamed up at the big, gray-blond ex-outlaw. "I'd love to. Anything I can do to help out. You know that, Pecos."

"Thanks, darlin'." Pecos pecked her cheek again, and Slash thought the girl was going to squirm out of the red calico prairie dress she wore.

The two men said their goodbyes, both ex-outlaws hugging both women, for the four were like a family, after all, then headed out of the cabin through the side door, heading for the barn and their horses. They'd been instructed to ride up to Cheyenne to pick up the federal jail wagon from the barn behind the courthouse.

"Hey," Jay called from the side porch. "I know it's an easy job. Leastways, it sounds like one. But you know how you two manage to get yourselves into trouble no matter what?"

Both men, halfway to the barn, stopped and turned to her, grinning guiltily.

They glanced at each other. Then Slash said, chuckling, "I reckon we do, at that, sweetheart."

Jaycee Breckenridge planted her fists on her shapely hips and canted her head to one side, fixing them both with a pleading scowl. "Please, don't!"

"So . . . what do you think about that girl?" Slash asked Pecos an hour later as, astride their well-traveled mounts, they followed the Union Pacific rails north toward Cheyenne. The Front Range of the Rocky Mountains lumped boldly up on their left.

"What girl?"

"What girl?" Slash said with a caustic grunt. "Myra! Who the hell you suppose I'm talkin' about?"

"I don't know—I thought maybe you were referring to one of Jay's girls." Jay wrangled a stable of pretty doxies over at the Thousand Delights, and Pecos regularly partook of the lovely ladies' delights, although Slash refrained

for obvious reasons—namely, because he was fixing to
marry the madam.

"No, I'm not referring to one of Jay's girls. I know what
you think of them. It's obvious every time you walk into
the saloon and they tumble all over you, and you blush up
like an Arizona sunset." Slash chuckled, wagging his head.
"No, it's Myra, I'm talkin' about, you fool!"

Pecos scowled at him from beneath his tan Stetson. "Well,
what about her?"

"Can't you see she's done tumbled for you?"

"Tumbled?" Pecos frowned, pensive, disbelieving.
"For *me*?"

"Yes, for you." Slash stared at him in exasperation. "You
mean you really haven't seen it? The way she looks at
you and fawns all over you? Not like Jay's girls, but like
a girl who has rightly and truly, make-no-mistake *tumbled*
for you?"

"Pshaw!" Pecos said. "We're just pals, Myra an' me. Just
like Myra an' you!"

Slash shook his head again. "Boy, here I thought I was
the stupid one when it came to women." He gave a caustic
laugh as he stared straight ahead at the blond prairie rising
gradually toward where Cheyenne was laid out amidst
haystack buttes to the north.

Pecos continued staring at him skeptically as they rode
along the two-track maintenance trail hugging the shiny
iron rails. Slash rode a rangy Appaloosa, while Pecos
straddled a buckskin big enough, seventeen hands high, to
carry his bulk. "Stop insultin' me an' chew it up a little finer
for me, will you, Slash—before I haul you out of your
saddle and kick the stuffing out of both ends of you!"

Slash sighed. "Myra's gone for you." He spoke more

slowly, enunciating each word carefully. "She has fallen head-overheels, bloomers-over-her-head in love with you, you dunderheaded polecat!"

"Nah."

"Yes."

"Really?"

"Yes."

Pecos turned his head forward, staring off to the north, but he wasn't doing much seeing, only thinking.

They rode along in silence for close to ten minutes before Pecos turned to his partner riding beside him again and said, "Well . . . that just purely breaks my heart, Slash."

He looked genuinely pained. In fact, Slash wouldn't have put it past the big, tender-hearted galoot to let out a sob or two. Pecos had been known to bawl and even wail over women in the past, but mostly only over those who, having soured on his outlaw ways, kicked him to the curb.

"It purely breaks my heart, it does," he insisted.

"The point here, Pecos, is what are you gonna do so's you don't break her heart?"

"Well, I don't know," Pecos said. He thought again for a time, then said, "I'm way too old for her. I mean . . . I sorta see her like a younger sister or . . . even a daughter. She wouldn't want nothin' to do with an old man like me. Not *really*."

"You better let her down easy, or you're gonna have Jay on your behind. She feels right protective about Myra."

"Yeah, I know . . . I know," Pecos said, scowling miserably over his buckskin's head at the northern horizon.

"Well, you got some time to think about it." Slash gave a dry chuckle as he put his Appy into a trot. The ugly sprawl of Cheyenne bisected by two sets of railroad lines had begun to show itself on the fawn plain ahead, cradled by tall bluffs. "I gotta hand it to you, partner—you sure have a knack for getting yourself into women trouble!"

Booting his own mount into a faster pace, Pecos yelled ahead at Slash, instructing his dark-haired partner to do something physically impossible to himself.

Slash only laughed.

CHAPTER 5

A half hour later, the two former cutthroats crossed the Union Pacific tracks at Union Station and made their way down the clogged and muddy mire of Sixteenth Street, which served as Cheyenne's main drag.

They wended their way between traffic-ensnarled freight teams and ranch and farm wagons, and the foot traffic of blanket Indians and Chinamen leftover from the track-laying days, and passed the big Rollins House Hotel on the right side of the street.

The Cheyenne–Black Hills Stage was just then parked out front of the hotel, and there must have been a good dozen men and women piling onto it, and even a dog.

Several mustached men in bowler hats and cheap suits—likely drummers or gamblers—were taking seats on the roof, leaving the more comfortable seats inside the carriage to the ladies, though Slash silently opined that when it came to stagecoach travel, the words *comfortable* and *seats* should never be uttered in the same sentence.

He'd stick to his trusty Appaloosa, which he hadn't named, knowing that only debutantes and fools named horses, whereas Pecos, the gentle giant, had given his buckskin the unimaginative handle of Buck.

The Laramie County Courthouse sat three doors down, on the same side of the street, from the hotel. It was a large, square building constructed of native stone, and both the U.S. flag as well as the Wyoming territorial guidon rippled on a pole in the gravelly front yard in which only bits of sage and prickly pear grew. A broad wooden front porch ran the length of the building's front wall. Sheriff Hank Covington sat out in the yard fronting the porch, to the right of the veranda's stone steps.

The famous Wyoming lawman sat on a straight-backed, leather-bottomed chair, holding a quirley in one hand and a stone mug of coffee in the other. He had one long, broadcloth-clad leg crossed over the other one, and he was staring up the street to the north, sort of squinting against the light.

"Hidy-ho, there, Sheriff," Slash said as he and Pecos reined their mounts up to one of the two rod-iron hitchracks fronting the courthouse, flanked by stock tanks.

Covington didn't turn to face the newcomers. He just kept staring up the street as though at something with great fascination. He didn't wear a hat, and his silver-streaked black hair lay flat against his head. It glistened with barber's oil. He wore a thick, bushy mustache of the same color as his hair. His face was of the weather-beaten, red texture of men who'd spent their younger years in the great outdoors, which Slash knew that Covington had, for the man had worked on ranches for most of his life, after fighting as a soldier of some renown in the Indian wars before buying his own spread near Laramie.

"I say there, Sheriff Covington," Slash repeated, a little louder this time.

Still, Covington didn't turn to face the newcomers. He just sat with the quirley in one hand, holding his coffee mug on his knee with his other hand, staring up the street to the north. His five-pointed sheriff's star, pinned to his brown wool vest, glinted in the sunlight.

Slash and Pecos looked at each other curiously.

"Well, I'll be damned," Slash silently opined. "The poor old guy must have gone deaf, likely from all the shooting he'd done and been around, all the Indian war whoops he'd listened to up in the Black Hills country in the years before Custer got separated from his topknot in the Greasy Grass."

Slash waved his hand out to the left, hoping to catch the sheriff's eye. He raised his voice to a yell: "Hey there, Sheriff Covington! It's Slash an' . . . er, I mean it's, uh, James Braddock an' Melvin Baker. We're here to pick up the—"

"It's out back," Covington responded while keeping his gaze up the street to the north. The man lifted his coffee cup to his lips and sipped, then swallowed, worked his lips around a little, and returned the cup to his knee.

Slash and Pecos shared another curious glance.

Pecos hiked a shoulder. Slash did, as well.

Still deeply puzzled by the sheriff's demeanor, Slash reined his Appy out away from the hitching post and gigged it on down the street to the north. Pecos did the same with his buckskin. Both men, glancing curiously over their shoulders at Sheriff Covington, who kept his gaze fixed on something up the street beyond and over the former cutthroats now, turned their horses to ride down along the courthouse's north side to the rear.

"What you suppose that was all about?" Pecos asked.

"Hell if I know."

A long, low barn and a small corral flanked the courthouse, as well as its two two-seater privies. The barn stood beside a woodshed. What was of even more interest to Slash, however, were the three men standing around out front of the barn's two open doors. They all wore suits or parts of suits, and had deputy U.S. marshal badges pinned to their shirts or wool vests.

One, standing to the left of the doors, was tall and lean and sandy-haired, with a dome-like forehead.

The second one, standing near the right door, with his hands in the pockets of his broadcloth trousers, was short, stocky, and red haired. His face was a mess of tiny brown freckles.

The third, leaning back against the right door, was easily the largest of the three. He must have been Pecos's size, around six-six, but a little beefier than Pecos, with a prominent gut bulging out his fancy brocade vest. Red suspenders climbed up over his broad shoulders. He was as bald as an egg, and he wore a natty handlebar mustache with waxed ends.

Slash, being a former cutthroat, recognized all three men, though he'd never met any of them personally. He knew *of* them because as a man who had tried to stay ahead of such men for the better part of the past thirty years, he'd always felt it was in his best interest to get to know who the western lawmen were, to be able to recognize them on sight. Thus, either by hook or by crook, he'd come to know the first man—that lean one with the dome-like forehead—as Deputy U.S. Marshal Wendell Powell.

The second one, the stocky, freckle-faced one standing by the right door with his hands in his pockets and a mocking grin stretching his lips back from his crooked teeth, was Deputy U.S. Marshal Gaylord Thomas.

The big bruiser in the brocade vest and stylish if overly dandified mustache was Deputy U.S. Marshal George Wade.

All three, of course, worked for Luther T. *Bleed-Em-So* Bledsoe. The first two were somewhere in their forties, while Wade was around Slash's and Pecos's age. All three men, Slash knew, had an office in the courthouse, rubbing elbows with Sheriff Covington and Covington's four deputies.

Slash reined his horse up in front of the barn. Pecos reined his buckskin to the right of Slash. Slash and Pecos shared another dubious glance; then Slash leaned forward, resting his left arm on his saddle horn, and shaped a coyote grin with one half of his mouth. "Hidy, fellas. Fancy seein' all three of you here. You've come to help us hitch the horses to the jail wagon, have you? Well, then, let me thank you in advance for your help."

"Help?" Pecos gave a wry chuff and glanced at Slash. "Help, hell. Why don't we go on over to Mrs. Ray's Canary Café and get us some lunch while they do the dirty work? I mean, since they're here an' all . . ."

"That's a good idea," Slash said, keeping his grinning gaze on the three lawmen standing pugnaciously before them. "I do love Mrs. Ray's chili. Best you'll find this far from Texas, in my humble estimation."

"Right you are, Slash," Pecos said. "Right you are."

"You think you two are pretty damn smart, don't you?" asked the deep-voiced, broad-chested, bald-headed George Wade, taking two steps forward and swinging his arms at his sides. He wasn't wearing a gun rig. Nor a hat. In fact, Slash realized now that none of these three lawmen wore a gun rig or a hat.

Also, they had their shirtsleeves rolled up to their elbows. As though they'd prepared themselves to get down to a job of work. Rough work. Rough and tumble work, perhaps.

Pecos turned to Slash. "You know what I think, Slash?"

"What's that, Pecos?"

"I think these three fine, upstanding keepers of the peace have met us out here to stomp us around a bit."

"No!" Slash feigned disbelief. "Why would they do something like that to two such well-bred innocent fellers like ourselves?"

"Like I said," George Wade said, a little louder this time, glaring up at the two former cutthroats, "you two think you're pretty damn smart—don't you?"

"You worked it pretty well," added Wendell Powell, narrowing his deep-set, angry eyes beneath his bulging forehead. "Had the law on your trail for damn near thirty years—then *poof!*" He raised his hand, opening it suddenly, then letting it fall. "One stroke of the pen by none other than the U.S. President, and it's all wiped out."

"Not only is it wiped out," said the stocky, freckle-faced Gaylord Thomas, "but ole Bleed-Em-So awards you with commissions."

"*Unofficial* commissions," Wade put in, his angry flush rising from his clean-shaven cheeks into his egg-like head, "but commissions just the same. He threw you in with us— fellas who been keeping our noses clean for a good long time while we put men like you away in the federal pen or, better yet"—he shaped a cold smile, lifting his ostentatious mustache with its thin, waxed ends—"dropped you through a gallows floor."

"Just makes my neck sore thinkin' about it!" Slash quipped. "Don't it you, Pecos?"

Pecos winced and massaged his neck with his hand.

"All in all," Slash said, smiling at the three men glaring up at him, "yeah, I reckon we are purty smart. Even Pecos is smart in that way, I guess, if in few others."

"Thanks, Slash," Pecos said, glowering at him.

"Well, you ain't gonna get past us without takin' a lickin'," Wade said, thumping his big left fist into the palm of his right hand and gritting his teeth with every blow. "That, at the very least, you will get."

"Yeah," Powell said. "Nothin' like a long pull in the ole jail wagon with sore ribs." He grinned sadistically and glanced at his two cohorts, who chuckled.

"The jail wagon's in there, I take it?" Slash asked, lifting his chin to indicate the shadowy interior of the barn behind the three marshals.

"It's in there, all right," Wade said. "It's waitin' on you to hitch it up and head north."

"We won't overly delay you," Thomas assured them, taking two steps forward, then stopping, spreading his feet a little more than shoulder width apart, and planting his fists on his hips. "Wouldn't want you late pickin' up Talon Chaney."

He and the others snickered through their teeth.

"That right there oughta be punishment enough," Wade said, then spread his mustached mouth again in a delighted grin. "But it ain't. No, sir. We want to add our own."

"So let's stop wastin' time," Powell said, raising his fists and assuming a fighter's crouch, moving around, shifting his feet, feinting from side to side. "Climb down from those saddles and take your medicine, cutthroats!"

Slash looked at Pecos. Pecos looked back at him, one brow arched.

"Jesus, fellas," Slash said, turning back to his and Pecos's three would-be assailants, "I'm startin' to feel a whole lot smarter than I did even before we rode back here."

The three deputies looked around at each other, puzzled.

"Why's that?" Wade said, squinting one eye.

"Because you three are gonna hitch two horses to the jail wagon for me an' Pecos," Slash said. "All we're gonna do is sit right here an' watch. I might even have me a cigarette."

Again, the deputies looked at each other. Suddenly, they broke into laughter.

Laughing, Wade said, "Now, how in the hell do you think *that's* gonna happen?"

The other two were still laughing, as well.

Pecos shucked his big Russian from the holster on his right hip, cocked the hammer, and aimed the heavy, top-break piece at Wade. "Because you fools done left your gun rigs inside the barn. I can see 'em in yonder, hangin' over a saddle tree."

"Fellas," Slash said, sliding both of his own stag-butted Colt .44s from their holsters, one positioned for the cross-draw on his left hip, the other thonged low on his right thigh, "did you really think we were gonna just climb down out of these saddles and disarm ourselves so you could wallop the crap out of us?"

He aimed one revolver at Wendell Powell, the other at Gaylord Thomas. He clicked both hammers back at the same time and narrowed his eyes with menace.

The three deputies had stopped laughing. Suddenly, they

were sober as judges, their eyes quickly acquiring skeptical casts. They looked at the cocked revolvers aimed at them, and then at the no-nonsense faces of the men aiming them, and then at each other.

The skeptical casts to their eyes turned to apprehension.

"Now I think I know why ole Bleed-Em-So hired us on," Slash said. "His so-called bona fide lawmen are so stupid they probably can't find their backsides with both hands."

Wade stepped forward, bunching his face angrily and waving an angry finger at Pecos and Slash. "Put those pistols down, you fools. For better or worse, we're on the same side!"

Pecos said, "You take one more step toward this horse, Deputy Wade, and I'm gonna blow a hole through your chest big enough to drive a freight train through."

Wade's brows furled as he stared at the big hogleg in the big ex-owlhoot's right hand. "You wouldn't do it," the bald-headed federal challenged Pecos. Glancing at Slash, he gave a coyote grin and said, "Neither would you, Slash. Maybe a few years back, sure. But now that you're workin' on this side of the law—pshaw!"

"You can take a rat out of the well," Slash growled, his cold gaze on Wade, flaring one nostril, "but you can't take the well out of the rat. Once you get a taste for federal blood, it never quite goes away."

"All it takes is a little nudge," Pecos added in his own soft, menacingly resonate voice.

Wendell Powell shifted his feet nervously, working his lips together. He cursed and glanced at the other two bona fides. "I'll be hanged if they don't mean it."

"You'd best get to work, fellas," Slash said. "Pull that wagon on out here and hitch two horses to it. Live to see another day. You don't do it, you'll die howlin'. Me an'

Pecos will plant your own guns on you, make it look like you ambushed us."

"You were all riled up over Bleed-Em-So bringin' us on the federal payroll after all your years chasin' us that you just couldn't live with it, so you decided to turn us toe down. But since you're dumber an' slower, havin' fed at the public trough for way too long, we savvied the double-cross and got the drop."

The big, gray-blond cutthroat grinned and half turned his head toward Slash, saying, "Damn, we got it figured so well, Slash, I say we just go ahead an' do it. Let's turn these federals into sieves. I been waitin' to do it for years!"

He threw his head back and gave a wild, bizarre-sounding whoop.

"Hold on!" Gaylord Thomas held out his open hands. "Hold on! Just hold on!"

"Cold-blooded, kill-crazy devils," Wade gritted out through his teeth, spittle frothing his lips. "Same way you were ten, twenty years ago. An' ole Bleed-Em-So brought you into the fold." He gave his head a frustrated shake.

"It's such a nice, cozy fold, too," Slash said with a caustic grunt. "You boys best get to work. We wanted to be on the Bozeman Trail by now, headed to Dry Fork. We're burnin' good daylight. Go ahead an' drag that big rig out here and get 'er hitched, or you won't see sundown, so help me God!"

CHAPTER 6

Slash and Pecos grinned at each other while sitting their horses in front of the barn, keeping their cocked revolvers aimed at the low-down dirty lawmen as those very same lawmen pulled and pushed the jail wagon out of the barn and into the hay-strewn yard fronting it.

Doing so, and then roping a couple of horses in the corral to the barn's right, they muttered angrily amongst themselves and cast Slash and Pecos frequent, darkly furious and worried glances. Cursing at each other, as though blaming each other for their embarrassing predicament, they led two stout geldings out of the corral and hitched them to the federal jail wagon, which appeared to be an old Conestoga outfitted with an iron-banded cage over its old wooden bed.

The cage had a rear door.

An American flag ran up from just behind the driver's box, on the wagon's left side, to billow out in the breeze just above the cage. Along the low wooden side panels running the length of the wagon below the cage, official-looking black letters announced: U.S MARSHALS.

While the three so-called bona fide federals adjusted

the horses' hames and harnesses, as well as the straps and buckles, Slash glanced over at Pecos and grinned even more deviously than before.

Pecos arched a curious brow at him.

Slash swung his right leg over his saddle horn and dropped lithely to the ground. He walked into the barn and gathered up the three gun rigs from off the saddle tree, slinging all three over both shoulders. The three so-called bona fides were busy with the harnesses, so they didn't see what Slash was doing.

Slash walked out of the barn, grinning up at Pecos, who only frowned curiously at him.

Chuckling under his breath, Slash walked over to one of the two-hole privies standing in the brush, a scrawny hawthorn shrub twisting between them, about fifty feet from the barn. He grinned at Pecos as he stepped inside the privy, his shoulders draped with the three bona fides' gun rigs. He came out a few seconds later without the gear.

Pecos stared at him dubiously from his buckskin's back.

Slash brushed his hands together, chuckling, and walked back over to his horse. The three bona fides hadn't seen him go into the privy. They were still working on the harness straps and buckles.

"Nice work, gentlemen," Slash said, leading his Appaloosa over to the back of the wagon. He tied the reins to a bar at the rear of the cage. Pecos walked his buckskin over, swung down from the saddle, and tied his reins to another bar at the rear of the cage.

"Much obliged, fellas," Pecos said.

He and Slash, having holstered their revolvers now that the three bona fides had finished slaving for them, transferred their saddlebags and war bags, which they'd filled with trail supplies back in Camp Collins, under the jail wagon's front seat.

The three bona fides stepped away from the two horses they'd hitched to the wagon. The lawmen were sweating in the midday sun. They still looked a mite on the sour side, but George Wade gave a devilish grin as he said, "You two enjoy your ride up to Dry Fork, now, hear? It's gonna be a whole lot more peaceful than your ride *back* to Cheyenne . . . with Talon Chaney, Hell-Raisin' Frank Beecher, and Gabriel Black Pot ridin' in that cage behind ya there."

He grinned at the iron-banded cage.

"Hmmm," Pecos said, climbing up into the driver's box, over the wagon's left front wheel. "Don't believe I've ever heard of them three gents."

He sat down on the leather-padded seat and untied the reins from the brake handle as the three bona fides stood side by side and several feet apart, discussing the three former outlaws with customary disdain and mockery. "None too sociable, are they?" Pecos asked.

The three lawmen glanced at each other, chuckling like overgrown schoolboys with a dirty secret.

"No," Powell said, snorting. "None too sociable."

"Nope," chimed in Gaylord Thomas, wagging his head and brushing a streak of sweat from his freckled left cheek. "No, them three I wouldn't invite home to supper. You two have a good time haulin' their nasty hides back to Cheyenne. A real good time!"

"In fact, if you make it in one piece, and don't get skinned alive and dumped along the trail between here an' Dry Fork, we'll buy you a drink and a bowl of chili," added Wade, giving the shoulder of Wendell Powell a comradely slap.

"We're gonna hold you to that, George!" Slash assured the men from where he sat on the driver's seat beside Pecos. He pinched his hat brim to the three lawmen as Pecos disengaged the break and slapped the ribbons over the backs of the two stout geldings in the traces.

"Bye, now!" Pecos said with a smile.

But when he glanced at Slash, he wasn't smiling at all. Neither was Slash. Slash had thought this was going to be a nice ride in the sun. He thought he'd do a little dreamy fishing on the North Platte. Now, he was beginning to wonder.

Talon Chaney.

Hell-Raisin' Frank Beecher.

Gabriel Black Pot.

Hmmm.

As Pecos put the wagon up through the empty lot beside the courthouse, heading for the main street, Hank Covington stepped out from the courthouse's front corner. The lawman looked at Slash and Pecos and then at the three sweaty deputy U.S. marshals milling around outside the barn.

The sheriff turned back to Slash and Pecos, scowling, looking positively crestfallen. He was deeply puzzled why the two ex-cutthroats appeared to be in such good health. He'd known good and well who the former outlaws were going to run into back at the courthouse barn. He'd been quiet as a church mouse, but he'd probably been cutting up like a drunk Irishman inside.

Until now.

"See ya later, Sheriff!" Slash yelled with a wave. "We'll tell the chief marshal you said howdy!"

"It was nice talkin' to ya, Sheriff," Pecos said, grinning. "Let's do it again real soon."

Covington just stood scowling at them.

"Hey!" one of the three bona fides shouted behind the jail wagon. *"Where's our guns?"*

At the same time, seventy miles north, in Dry Fork, Town Marshal Glenn Larsen stared through the cell door bars at Talon Chaney and said, "Get back. Now, Chaney!"

He felt a little chagrined at the tremble he heard in his voice.

Chaney was squeezing the bars of his cell door in his large,beefy hands. On the back of his left hand was the tattooed silhouette of a buxom naked woman. Chaney gritted his teeth as he squeezed the bars so hard that the knuckles of his darkly tanned hands were nearly white.

"Just a second, Marshal," Chaney said in a voice pinched with strain. "Just tryin' to see if there's any give in these bars."

Larsen glanced at his deputy, Henry Two Whistles, who sat near Chaney's cell in a Windsor chair, between the row of four cells running along the rear wall of the small stone jailhouse and Larsen's desk abutting the front wall. Holding his double-barreled shotgun across his bony thighs, the old deputy drew a deep breath, glowering at the savage outlaw.

Turning back to Chaney, Larsen yelled, "Knock it off! Take your hands down off those bars, Chaney!"

"Just give me one more second," Chaney said again in his strained voice.

"Chaney, dammit, if you want this coffee, remove your hands from the bars and step back away from the door!"

"All right, all right!" Chaney dropped his hands from the bars and grinned sneeringly through the cell door at Larsen. His big, broad face was still red from exertion. "I think I found me some give in that iron, Marshal. You might want to look into it. I got me a feelin' that iron is purty old. How long has this old jailhouse been here, anyways? I'm guessin' for the past thirty years or so . . . ?"

"Step back away from the door," Larsen ordered the man in a voice of strained patience. He held a fresh, smoking cup of black coffee in his left hand, the key for Chaney's cell in his right hand. Both hands trembled slightly. He didn't think it was noticeable. Not to anyone except himself, that was.

Knowing his own fear was humiliating enough.

Chaney raised his hands and thick, muscular arms in supplication and took three steps straight back away from the cell door. "All right, all right, Marshal. I'm just sayin', if you get the wrong prisoner in here, I mean one who really wants out of this cell—well, you might have a problem. I think a fella strong as myself could pry them welds loose. Them welds is old and weak. You pry one loose and then they're all gonna go, and . . . you got trouble."

The tattooed outlaw with close-cropped brown hair shrugged. His square, severely featured head could have been crudely chipped out of solid granite. Chaney grinned, eyes slitting devilishly, as he glanced around at the three other cells on his right—two of which were occupied by none other than his two partners in savagery—Hell-Raisin' Frank Beecher and Gabriel Black Pot.

"I don't know if you're safe," Chaney said in a soft, menacing voice to Larsen. "You might want to look into all this old iron in these cells. That's all I'm sayin'."

"Keep that Parker on him, Henry," Larsen said out of the corner of his mouth as he slowly turned the key in Chaney's door. He so much as flinches, you empty both barrels into him."

"Don't worry, Marshal," Two Whistles said, aiming the double-barreled barn blaster straight out over his right knee. "I got you covered. Don't you worry about nothin'." He lifted his leathery, brick-red left cheek in a sly grin, though Larsen knew that the old man was as afraid of these three devils as he himself was.

"Easy, old man," Chaney said, glaring at Two Whistles. "Don't let that gut-shredder go off by accident, now, hear?" He smiled again. If the devil smiled, that smile would be the twin to Talon Chaney's smile. "If it was to go off, you might hit the young marshal here by mistake."

"Shut up, Chaney," Larsen said as, staring cautiously through the bars at the thick-set, muscular outlaw, he slowly opened the door. Fear weighed heavy in him. The hinges squawked, giving Larsen a start, making his heart quicken.

Chaney sensed the young lawman's terror, and grinned his seedy grin.

Larsen slid the door open just far enough to stick the coffee cup through it, which he did as he bent his legs, crouching, and set the cup on the floor. He withdrew his hand, then quickly slammed the door closed. Just as quickly he turned the key in the lock, throwing the bolt home. As he did, he couldn't help looking at the welds at the bar joints. He knew it was what Chaney had wanted him to do, but he couldn't help it.

Suddenly, there didn't appear to be a whole lot of quality iron holding these three mad dogs at bay. The bars of the cells looked as insignificant as party bunting.

The killers must have read his mind. All three were laughing at him through the steam rising from their coffee cups.

"That's right, young Marshal, sir," said Gabriel Black Pot, standing in the next cell to the lawman's left, Chaney's right. "Them bars can't hold us. Nope, they sure can't. We'll be out of here soon." He grinned as he lifted his chin and slitted his black eyes with open mockery. "*Very* soon!"

"And when we get out," said Hell-Raisin' Frank Beecher, standing at the door of his own cell, which was the one just beyond Black Pot, holding his steaming coffee cup in both hands, "we're gonna talk to you about what you did to us the other day."

Larsen knew the oddly effeminate killer—a tall, lean, shaggy-headed man missing the end of his nose and his entire left ear—was referring to Larsen and Henry leading all three killers to the jail from Carlisle's place, naked, wearing only handcuffs.

The three men had stumbled through the dusty streets, still half-drunk and badly hungover. They hadn't said much then. But they'd said plenty when they'd woken up in their respective cells and remembered the humiliation of half the town having come out of the shops and houses—men and women of all ages, including some children who'd been walking late to school—to stare and mutter amongst themselves and for small groups of men to break out in jeering laughter.

Several dogs had barked at the naked, bleary-eyed trio. One had run up behind Black Pot and nipped the half-breed in his left calf, making him jump, stumble, and fall.

Larsen had not intended to humiliate the three killers. Now he regretted that it had played out the way it had. At the time, however, he'd seen no other way. After he'd gotten the handcuffs on all three while the three had slept in the whores' crib upstairs at Carlisle's, he certainly hadn't been about to uncuff them so they could dress. There was no way they could have gotten dressed wearing the cuffs, so there had been nothing else he could have done.

Given the killers' reputations and all the guns in the room, he'd had no choice but to cuff them then and there.

If they'd been anything less than what they were—three cold-blooded killers who had been murdering and raping and stealing to their hearts' content all over northern Wyoming and southern Montana for the past several years—he would have let them dress before leading them off to jail. As it was, all he'd wanted to do was to get them as quickly over to the jail as he could, and the only way he could have done that was just what he'd done—lead them naked through the streets of Dry Fork.

What he hadn't counted on was half the town coming out to watch and jeer.

That had been unfortunate. He'd thought the citizens of Dry Fork above such shenanigans. Or, if not above it, at least smart enough to not tease coiled rattlesnakes, which was what these men were. But they'd watched and they'd laughed, and there'd been nothing that Larsen and Two Whistles could have done to stop it, for their attention had been on the killers. So now here they were with three very angry, cold-blooded killers bound and determined to get free of their cells and murder not only Larsen and Two Whistles but the whole damn town of Dry Fork.

Larsen just hoped—no, he *prayed*—that that jail wagon got up here from Denver soon. He wouldn't rest, much less sleep, before Dry Fork was free of these devils.

"We won't just be talkin' about what you did, young marshal," Black Pot assured Larsen, pressing his big, round, brown, hawk-nosed face up close against his cell door, "we'll be showin' what happens when you embarrass me an' my friends . . . in front of the whole town, no less!"

"We're gonna kill you slow, Larsen." Chaney shifted his gaze from the young marshal to Two Whistles, still sitting in the Windsor chair and holding the double-barreled Parker straight up from his right thigh. "And the old man, too. *Real slow*. The whole town is gonna hear you two wail before they get what's comin' to *them*, too!"

Larsen glanced at his old deputy. Two Whistles gave a taut half smile. He was putting on a brave face, but Larsen saw the lie in it. Only a few months ago, Henry had been slinging hash out at the Crosshatch. He'd done that for the last ten years. Larsen himself had been repairing fences and shifting beef on the hoof from one pasture to another, and burning brands into dirty hides every spring.

Now here they both were, holding three savage killers for the U.S. marshal in Denver. Three of the nastiest killers Larsen turned to Chaney and said, "Look . . . about that, uh . . . the other day. I didn't mean for it to . . ."

He let his voice trail off when the front door of his office opened suddenly.

CHAPTER 7

Larsen whipped his head around, half suspecting that the rest of the three killers' gang was here to bust their brethren out of the lockup.

The young marshal felt a brief relief when he saw his pretty wife poke her blond head into the office. Her cornflower-blue eyes twinkled when they landed on Larsen himself. The former Tiffanie Bright wore a sun-yellow day dress with a matching felt hat that complemented the gold curls of her hair tumbling across her slender shoulders. In her white-gloved hands, she clutched the handle of a wicker basket covered with a red-and-white checked oilcloth.

"Glenn, honey, when you didn't come home for lunch, I thought I'd bring a basket over here for both you and Henry. I know how . . ."

She let her voice trail off as Talon Chaney put his blunt face up close to the bars of his cell door and gave a high, shrill whistle of appreciation. "Good Lord, Marshal—is that *your* gal?"

Black Pot howled, then pressed his own hawk-nosed

face up close to the bars. He stuck his tongue through the bars and waggled it lasciviously.

"Now, that there, gentlemen," intoned Hell-Raisin' Frank Beecher, "is a balm to these sore eyes and battered soul. Come closer, honey—let me get a better look at you. I do declare, you're purty as a summer peach!"

"An' just as ripe!" added Black Pot.

"Oh, she's fine, Marshal," Chaney whooped. "You did right well for yourself. Look at *that!*"

Larsen hurried over to his young wife, meeting her a few feet in front of the door. "Tiffanie, my God," he said, grabbing her shoulders and gently pushing her back toward the door. "What're you doing here? I told you not to come over here. At least, not while . . ."

"Glenn, honey," the young woman protested, "you didn't come home for lunch like you said you would, like you always do . . ."

When Larsen got Tiffanie ushered back out the door and onto the small boardwalk fronting the small, stone jailhouse building, he drew the door closed behind him. He could still hear the yips and yowls issuing from the cells inside the building.

"Come back in here, little lady," Black Pot called. "Let's see what kinda goodies you're packin'!"

"Them's the marshal's goodies, Black Pot, you cad!" remonstrated Beecher in his oddly effeminate voice.

"I don't see no reason why the marshal shouldn't share!" Chaney howled.

A collective roar of laughter pressed against the door behind Larsen.

"Honey," Larsen said, frowning down at his young wife, whose pale cheeks had turned as red as apples, "I told you

those men were savages. I didn't want you to see . . . or
hear that."

"I'm sorry, Glenn, but when you didn't come home . . .
Glenn, you have to eat something. You haven't been eating;
you haven't been sleeping. Not since you threw those
three . . . *animals* . . . in your jail. It's not healthy, Glenn!"

"I'm sorry I missed lunch, Tiff. I reckon I got distracted." Larsen scowled at the closed door behind him.
"I meant to be home at noon sharp. You certainly didn't
need to . . ."

"Oh, Glenn, I wanted to bring you and Henry something. Poor Henry's probably getting as little sleep as you
are, and he has no one to cook for him."

"I tell you what," Larsen said, glancing at the door
again, glad that the prisoners inside had piped down a little,
"let's you and me go on home and eat this fine lunch of
yours in that swing out back." Smelling the succulent
aromas of the fried chicken wafting up from beneath the
oilcloth, the young marshal led his young wife east along
the street, in the direction of their neat little house. "When
we're done, I'll bring Henry his share and give him some
time off to eat it. You know how he likes to eat his lunches
down by the creek."

By "the creek," Larsen had meant Dry Fork Creek that
ran along behind the jailhouse. It was mostly just a sandy,
gravelly arroyo except during the springtime snowmelt,
but it was filled with shrubs that the birds liked to flutter
around in, and Henry liked to watch the birds and hear
them sing.

They didn't see much after that, until they were safely
ensconced in their backyard, behind their little frame house
on the corner of Main Street and Third, which was practically the far east end of Dry Fork. The town didn't sprawl

much beyond a single square mile, if that. The yard had several small transplanted trees and shrubs, offering some privacy from the other, mostly log shacks and sheds flanking it, haphazardly situated on their own trash-strewn lots. Beyond those shacks and sheds was wide-open, gently rolling prairie on which Larsen could hear coyotes yammering every morning and evening.

Tiffanie, uncharacteristically dour, set a leg of fried chicken, a hardboiled egg, and a dill pickle on his plate.

Larsen didn't feel much like eating, but for his wife's sake he made himself bite into the leg, which was crispy on the outside and juicy on the inside, cooked exactly how he liked it. Still, because of his own dark mood, the meat tasted like boot leather. Sitting beside his wife on the little love seat swing that he had built himself and hung from an oak branch with two strong ropes, just outside their backdoor, the young lawman glanced at his pretty wife.

"I'm sorry for forgetting to come home for lunch, Tiff," he said gently, chewing, then taking a sip of his coffee. She had set the pot and two cups on a small table fronting the swing. "I reckon those three devils just got me distracted, is all. Besides, I sorta hate to leave Henry alone with them. Afraid he might go to sleep, an' . . ."

Tiffanie swung around to him, her golden curls flying. "Oh, Glenn, I'm not angry at you!"

"You're not?"

"Of course not!"

"Well, you haven't said two words since we left the jail—"

"Glenn, I'm just so worried for you! Those men are . . . well, they're savages! More wolf than man!"

Larsen set his half-eaten chicken leg down on his plate and wrapped his left arm around his wife's shoulders, drawing her close against him. "It's only for another day or so, Tiff." He pressed his lips against her head. "The deputy U.S. marshals should be getting here from Denver any ole day now. They'll haul those savages away in cuffs and leg irons, and then we'll be done with them."

"Until the next batch comes along."

"Oh, no . . . now, Tiffanie. This is a quiet, little town, all in all."

Tiffanie stared down at her plate. Larsen saw that she hadn't eaten even as much of her lunch as he'd eaten of his. "Glenn . . . ?"

"Yes, honey?"

"What would you think about quitting the marshal's job? No, wait!" Before Glenn could open his mouth to object, Tiffanie turned to him with her anguished blue eyes and placed two fingers against his lips. "Let me finish."

Larsen pulled his mouth corners down.

"Why don't you accept my father's offer and go to work for him in his mercantile store?"

"Ah, Tiffanie, I'm no shopkeeper."

"Oh, Glenn, you're no lawman, either!"

"What's that supposed to mean? I'm wearing this star right here." Larsen brushed his thumb against the five-pointed, nickel chased badge on his shirt. "That means I'm the law, Tiffanie!"

"Oh, you know what I mean, Glenn. You're a cow-puncher. A ranch hand. You're . . ."

"You mean I'm weak," Larsen finished for her, anger growing in him, a feeling he didn't like one bit. He'd rarely felt anything but unrestrained love for his bride, and he hated the burn of animosity he felt growing at her stinging words. Words that had lashed him deep—deep down to the core of his manhood.

She squeezed his arm. "Not at all! That's not what I meant!"

"Yes, it is." Feeling like a sulky schoolboy, Larsen crossed his arms and stared down at the plate on his lap. "What's worse . . . I fear you're right."

"Oh, Glenn, that's not what I meant. You're a good, nice man. A very polite young man. A lawman needs to be . . . he needs to be, well . . ."

"Go ahead and say it—a lawman needs to be tough. He needs to be fearless."

"You are tough and fearless."

"Oh, stop patronizing me, Tiffanie. You know that ain't true. I know it most of all. I've never felt so weak and ter-rified in my whole life." He swung his right boot forward and kicked a rock. "Hell, every time I look at that damn Talon Chaney, all my insides shrivel up in a big ole ball in my belly."

Tiffanie clutched his arm again, squeezing tighter. "Whose *wouldn't*? Like I said, he's more wolf than man!"

"I gotta ride it out, Tiff." Larsen kicked another rock. "I'm sorry, Tiffanie. You married the wrong man, I reckon. I gotta see this through. I gotta keep the job for at least a year. Then . . . who knows . . . ?" He smiled weakly. "Maybe I'll grow a spine by then, and men like them in that jail won't turn my knees to putty. If not, I'll accept your pa's generous offer. I'll become a shopkeeper."

"Oh, Glenn," Tiffanie said. "I married just the right man for me." She turned full around to face him, reached up, and slid a lock of his longish light brown hair back from his right cheek. "I'm sorry. I shouldn't have said anything about quitting your job. I love you, honey. My love is un-conditional and undying. Because of that, you and I will both get through this. *Together*."

She smiled, showing all her snow-white teeth, then, holding both their plates so they wouldn't tumble from their laps, she stretched up to plant a warm, heartfelt kiss on her husband's cheek.

Glenn Larsen suddenly felt better about everything.

Until, that was, the back door of the house opened and Talon Chaney poked his granite-like head out into the yard, his eyes popping wide as he exclaimed, "Hello there, love-birds! Can we join the party?"

Earlier, just after Glenn Larsen left the jailhouse with his lovely wife, Henry Two Whistles rose angrily from his chair. He faced the three laughing and hollering savages, and said, "Shut up!"

They didn't seem to hear him. They kept laughing and howling.

Two Whistles stomped his high-topped, mule-eared boot on the floor. "Shut up, I said. Shut up, damn you!"

That time they heard him. They all looked at him, sobering gradually.

Talon Chaney arched his brows in surprise. "Well, well, the old dog-eater done told us to shut up, fellas. I reckon we'd better do as he says, since he's wielding that big ole Parker an'all." He slid his eyes to the big, braided half-breed in the cell beside his own. "Uh . . . B.P., you don't mind me callin' one of your own a dog-eater, do ya?"

"Nah, that's all right," said Black Pot, grinning, showing a mouthful of rotten teeth. "I won't take it personal." He snickered.

Two Whistles kept his face stony, but he felt angrier than he thought he'd ever felt before. He kept remembering the look on young Tiffanie Larsen's face when those three prisoners had started laying into her with their goatish comments and insults. He doubted the poor girl, brought up right in a good family, had ever been confronted with talk like that in her entire life.

Two Whistles planted the shotgun's butt plate on his hip. He walked over to the desk, removed the ring of keys from the second drawer down on the desk's right side, and walked over to Talon Chaney's cell. He looked at Chaney, who stood about two feet back from the door, staring at him skeptically.

"What, uh . . . what's goin' on?" the prisoner asked.

Two Whistles poked the key in the lock. His hand shook. He looked at Chaney. He glanced at Black Pot, then at Frank Beecher. Both men stood in their cells facing Two Whistles, scowling curiously at the old Indian deputy.

The old man knew he shouldn't do what he was about to do, but his fury was a raging fire within him. He was tired of these three killers. He was tired of them for both himself as well as for his young friend, Glenn Larsen. He was tired of them for all of the citizens of Dry Fork, most of whom he knew were sleeping little better than himself and Glenn, wondering if the human wolves would bust out of this little jail and go on one of their savage rampages.

It was time to shut them up once and for all.

He gritted his teeth as he turned the key in the lock. The bolt ground back into the door. The door hinges squawked as the door hung loose in its frame.

"What're you doin', you old dog-eater?" Chaney asked, smiling uncertainly.

"Gonna give you a chance."

Two Whistles stepped straight back. He opened the outside door, leaving it standing wide so that a rectangle of buttery midday light angled into the office. The deputy broke open his shotgun and plucked out one of the wads. He held up the wad to show the three prisoners. He dropped the wad, which plunked onto the jailhouse's rough stone floor and rolled around beside the old deputy's right boot.

He snapped the Parker closed, then walked over and sat down in the swivel chair at Larsen's cluttered desk. He turned to face the three prisoners standing just inside their cells. He turned again, leaned the shotgun against the desk, to his right, then turned back to face the prisoners.

"There's your chance." Two Whistles gave a grim smile, slitting his dark, angry eyes. "Go ahead." He canted his head toward the sunlight. "Make a run for the door. You have a chance. I'm old and slow. I only got one wad. If you can make it, you're free. One by one, you're free."

Black Pot said in a high-pitched, wheedling voice, *"Wha-at?"*

"Chaney first," Two Whistles said. "Then Black Pot. Then Beecher. One by one. I'm giving you a chance."

All three prisoners stared at him through their cell doors.

He could tell they were thinking about it.

Could they run fast enough? Could they outrun the old man's slow reflexes?

Could they outrun buckshot?

Two Whistles stared at Chaney, who had now moved up to squeeze the bars of his cell door in his hands. He grinned with challenge through the bars at the old deputy, head down, his chin resembling a stone spade. His brown eyes were wide and round and glassy.

"Go ahead." Two Whistles canted his head toward the open door. "Give it a try." He smiled again. "What's the matter, Chaney? You *afraid* of this old dog-eater?"

Chaney stared back at him with the same expression as before.

"Go ahead," Beecher whispered from his own cell. "Make a run for it, amigo!"

Black Pot just stared at Chaney, grinning expectantly. He was making a soft, hissing sound through his rotten teeth.

Chaney opened and closed his fingers around the bars of his unlocked cell door. He stared at Two Whistles. The old deputy stared back at him, his challenging grin remaining on his lips.

Finally, Chaney stopped opening and closing his hands. He jerked them back, pulling the door closed, latching it.

"Not this time, old man," he said, scowling angrily now, knowing he'd been made to look the coward.

A figure moved in the doorway to Two Whistles's right. He turned to see Eddie Black step into the jailhouse, carrying a large wooden tray covered with a blue-and-white checked oilcloth. Eddie looked at Two Whistles and said, "Dinnertime, Henry."

"About time!" Black Pot complained. "My belly feels like a big rat's been gnawin' on it!"

Eddie hiked a shoulder as he started into the room. "Café's been busy. Ma MacDonald said prisoner food comes last."

"Oh, she did, did—"

Talon Chaney cut himself off abruptly.

Two Whistles had just gained his feet to let Eddie feed his prisoners, but now, following Chaney's surprised, delighted gaze, he turned to the door. His heart banged against his ribs.

Two men had just dashed through the open office door. The second man slammed the door with a *bang!* The first man ran up and grabbed Eddie Black from behind, raising a pistol to the swamper/gopher's head and clicking the hammer back.

Eddie screamed and dropped the tray.

The man behind him shouted, "Drop the thunder stick, old man, or he buys a bullet!"

CHAPTER 8

"No, no, no, no, no," Pecos said, his voice quavering with the jolts of the jail wagon. "You're too damn quiet. You been too damn quiet for two whole days now and it's continued way too deep into the third one!"

Slash, sitting beside his long-time partner on the jail wagon's leather-padded driver's seat, turned to the bigger man as he exhaled smoke from the quirley he'd taken his time building and had just lit a minute ago. Slash frowned beneath the brim of his black Stetson. "Say *what?*"

"You haven't insulted me in over an hour. In fact, I don't think you've said anything since noon when you said, 'Hey, Ugly—stop the wagon. I gotta water a sage bush.'"

"So?"

"Something's wrong. You're brooding about something."

"No, I ain't."

"Yes, you are."

"No, I ain't. Leave me alone. I wanna smoke in peace."

"You worried about leaving Jay alone in Camp Collins with that handsome town marshal friend of hers—Cisco Walsh."

Blowing twin plumes of smoke out his nostrils, Slash

turned to Pecos again, scowling. "No, I ain't worried about leaving Jay alone with Cisco Walsh!"

Pecos smiled with satisfaction and aimed his gaze out over the bobbing heads of the horses in the traces. "Yeah, you are. Sure enough. That's it."

"No, it ain't," Slash protested. "What does Walsh have that I don't have?"

"Well, he's taller. He's better looking. He has a better personality, though that ain't saying much. Hell, a rattle-snake has a better personality than you, Slash." Pecos chuckled dryly. "He takes a bath more than once a month. Visits the barber weekly. And he sure as tootin' dresses better! How old are them duds you're wearing, Slash? Ten, twelve years old . . . ?"

"Oh, shut up, you big, ugly galoot!"

"There—now that makes me feel better! Yessir—now we're gettin' somewhere!"

Pecos laughed and stared up the winding two-track trail they'd been following since leaving the little settlement of Wheatland, heading northeast into the high, barren desert of eastern Wyoming, where nothing grew in the chalky alkali except rocks and prickly pear. At least, that's how it seemed. Not much appeared to live out here, either, except the occasional coyote, buzzard, and jackrabbit.

Pecos turned back to his partner, narrowing one skepti-cal eye. "All right, it ain't Walsh. If it was Walsh, I'd have gotten a bigger reaction out of you. So . . . what is it? It's gotta be somethin' concerning Jay."

Slash glared at him, narrowed his dark eyes, and opened his mouth to give the bigger man another tongue-lashing. But then, just as quickly, he closed his mouth, squirmed around on the seat as though he had ants in his pants, and looked out to the east, away from Pecos, toward a couple of small, flat-topped buttes humping up against the far horizon.

Pecos knew his old partner in crime well enough to know that Slash was about to speak. At least, Slash would mutter a few colicky words within the next five minutes or so. He was like a volcano that way. He grumbled and smoked a while before the big explosion. Pecos had been right. Something was weighing on the mind of Slash. Now Slash, so uncomfortable under the weight of his worries, was considering lightening the weight a little by talking it out.

That meant it had to be a heavy burden, indeed, for Slash Braddock was the most tight-lipped fellow Pecos had ever known. At least he was when it came to discussing what was on his mind or in his heart.

Patiently, Pecos waited. It was getting late in the day, so he scanned the dry wash falling away on his left for a good place to set up camp for the night. A rattlesnake lay coiled in the shade of a small bitterbrush shrub, along the lip of the wash. Pecos was considering stopping the wagon and shooting the snake for supper when Slash finally spoke. "I got cold feet."

The snake slithered out of Pecos's mind like the last fog burned off by a hot morning sun. Pecos turned to his partner and said, "You do?"

Slash filled his lungs noisily and stared at the right hitch horse's spotted rump. "Yep."

"About the weddin', you mean?"

"Yes, of course, I mean the wedding," Slash snapped. "What in hell else does a fella get cold feet about?"

"All right, all right. Don't take it out on me!" Boy, Slash really was feeling colicky. His hair trigger was filed down shorter than usual. If he was a gun, a whispered breath would have fired him off by now.

Pecos waited. Slash would talk it out in his own good time. Slash was not a man to be rushed. Pecos knew it could be hours before his taciturn partner vented his spleen about his cold feet, and he was correct. It wasn't until two hours later, when they were camped in a small grove of dusty cottonwoods on the bank of the wash, with the sun down and the first stars pricking to life, that Slash finally continued the conversation.

As he tossed away the plate from which he'd just scrubbed the last of his cooked beans with a baking powder biscuit, he said, "She's talkin' about a house."

"A house."

Slash refilled his coffee cup. "Correct."

Pecos spooned up his last few beans and chewed, thinking. He nodded. "Oh, right. A house. One for you two to live in. Well"—he chuckled—"you weren't thinkin' you were going to live in the freight yard shack with me an' Myra, were you?"

Slash sat back against his saddle, raised one knee, and rested an arm over the top of it. "I reckon I hadn't gotten that far."

Pecos chuckled again. "Well, how far had you gotten, Slash? I mean, you did finally manage to work up the oysters to ask her to marry you. What were you thinkin' would happen after that? After you two were married, I mean."

"Like I said, that's as far as I got. It took so much out of me to finally ask her to hitch her star to my wagon, that once she said yes, I was so relieved to have all of that over and done with, I just stopped thinking about it. All of it.

The whole thing. I hadn't gotten beyond the wedding. In my head, I'm sayin'."

Slash sipped his coffee, swallowed, and continued. "I didn't think about the house or livin' together, just her an' me? Just the two of us. Man and wife. We gonna walk to church together every Sunday? Am I gonna be able to go to a saloon when I want to? Have a drink with you—just you an' me out alone? Or am I gonna be tied to the house? An' speakin' about the house—I reckon that means I'll be a house owner, then, too, right?"

"Yeah, if you buy a house, that'll make you a house *owner*, all right, Slash."

Pecos suppressed the laughter he felt boiling up inside his chest. This was no time to laugh at Slash. For Slash, this was serious business. What might have seemed obvious about the situation to Pecos was all new to Slash. For Slash, his married life was a puzzle that was all coming together so he could get a better idea of the complete picture it shaped and colored. Pecos could see by the fear in his partner's eyes and the slight tremor in his voice that he was having a crisis of spirit. Of heart. Of courage.

Slash Braddock had faced entire posses, laughing while the bullets cut the air around him. But the thought of marrying and settling down with a woman in a *house* frightened him like nothing else ever had in his life.

"I reckon I'll have a yard to keep up. A garden to grow. I'll have to keep paint on the damn house."

"Yep, yep. That's what goes with home ownership, Slash. You're right."

Slash cut his suspicious eyes at Pecos, furling his dark brows. "Are you laughin' at me?"

Covering a chuckle bubbling up from his throat, Pecos sipped his coffee, sighed, smacked his lips, and gazed soberly back at Slash. "Nope, I'm just tryin' to work my mind around what you were thinkin'."

"I told you—I wasn't thinkin'. At least, not beyond the wedding."

"Well, hell, you don't want to live with me the rest of your life—do you, Slash? You said it yourself—I smell bad. And I snore loud."

"That's for sure!"

"Believe me, if it was me—if I had a good woman who had accepted my proposal of marriage, I wouldn't have a single second thought of skinning out on you and thanking my lucky stars for the escape, to boot!"

"Yeah, well . . ." Slash scowled down at the fire.

"Marry the woman," Pecos said, gently. "Buy the house. Sure, you'll have to keep it up. Sure, you won't be able to live like you live now—drinkin' an' whorin' and playin' cards all hours of the night an' day. You'll be a *homeowner*. You'll have to stay home and rock in your chair and talk to your wife and tend your garden. But think of what you'll get in return."

Slash looked at him expectantly.

"You'll get Jay," Pecos said, smiling warmly into his old friend's eyes. "*Jay*. You *love* her, Slash. I know you do. Without her, you'd just get old alone . . . which is what's more than likely gonna happen to me."

"You?" Slash scoffed. "You've been with more women than I've ever talked to! You're just goin' through a dry spell . . . if you don't count Myra, of course."

"I ain't countin' Myra," Pecos said, testily. "She's too young for this old buzzard." He wished she wasn't. He liked Myra plenty. But she was too young, and there you had it.

"Yeah, well, Miss Langdon ain't too young."

"She's plenty young, too, but . . ." Pecos chuckled and absently tossed a rock side-armed into the wash, listening to it bounce across the gravelly bed. "That's too much woman for me."

"Hell, that's too much woman for the two of us put together!"

"Besides, she ain't the marryin' type. She's the kinda woman who likes her life without a man. She's the kinda woman who likes a job *instead* of a man. I reckon I can't blame her. Would you want to be married to either one of us, Slash?"

"Hell, we practically been married for the better part of thirty years!"

They laughed at that, but they both knew it was true. It had been a good marriage, too, though neither man would admit that, of course. They preferred to pretend they were enemies. Pecos wasn't sure why men got embarrassed about how they felt about each other. He supposed he loved Slash. He alsosupposed that Slash loved him back. Neither, of course, would admit as much, much less to each other.

Hell, slow Apache torture couldn't have forced it out of either of them.

But there it was.

Maybe that was the cause of Slash's cold feet as regards his marrying Jay. Or one of the things, anyway. The main thing, Pecos knew, was that Slash was basically a lonely, solitary soul. He didn't want to be. He loved Jay. He wanted to be with her for the rest of his life, into his old age, probably right up to his death. He didn't want to die alone.

On the other hand, it was hard for Slash to be with anyone for more than a few minutes at a time. With anyone except Pecos, that was. But even Pecos had to give his old friend plenty of room to be silent and brood and moon around about stuff only Slash knew about.

"I reckon it's time for us to divorce each other, pard," Pecos said. "Time for you to hitch your wagon to Jaycee Breckenridge." The big ex-cutthroat stared out over the wash. It would be pitch-black in another twenty minutes. The rolling prairie stretched away beyond the wash, silent and still. There weren't even any coyotes yammering. Not yet, anyway.

"Don't worry," he added, pensive, Slash's own brooding mood infecting him now, too, "I'll be along soon. Least-ways, I hope I'll find a good woman soon. It sure would be funny if you, a love-'em-for-a-night kinda fella, ended up the married one and I ended up in some Odd Fellows Home of Christian Charity, babblin' to myself, goosin' the butt of the old ugly spinster who ran the place, and gettin' slapped for my trouble."

When Slash didn't say anything, Pecos turned to him. "Wouldn't it?"

But Slash had retreated into himself again. He sat with one leg up, one arm draped over his knee, his coffee cup now empty, staring out across the dry arroyo. He was wondering, worrying, brooding.

"Oh, well," Pecos said, a deep yawn coming over him. "It'll all work out. Me, I'm gonna go water some prickly pear, then go to sleep. I'm a sleepy fella."

He didn't know if Slash had heard him or not. Slash didn't say anything. He just stared off toward the eastern horizon on which stars were glittering like expensive jewels.

Pecos heaved his tall, brawny frame up, dusted off his pants, then wandered off in the darkness. He glanced at where the wagon sat to his right. The four horses—his and

Slash's and the two-horse hitch—stood idly where they were tied to the picket line Slash had strung between two cottonwoods. Pecos's buckskin was staring off to its right, toward the south, while the other three stood with their heads hanging, appearing ready to call it a day.

Pecos stopped near where the arroyo swung toward the south, unbuttoned his trousers, and got a stream going. He sighed, rocked back on his heels. He tipped his head back, closed his eyes.

Behind him, one of the horses whickered softly.

Somewhere out across the arroyo curving around from behind Pecos's left shoulder to angle off in front of him, drifting south, another horse snorted. The sound had been clear in the silent night, above the trickle of Pecos's water stream.

Quickly, he got himself put away and buttoned up.

He moved back to the camp. "Slash," he said, keeping his voice low and reaching for his Colt revolving rifle, "I think we got company."

He looked around, frowning. Slash wasn't sitting where he'd been sitting just a few minutes ago.

"Slash?"

"Down here."

Pecos looked into the arroyo. Slash stood on the bottom of the wash, holding his rifle low in one hand, staring south.

"We got company," Pecos whispered.

"I know."

CHAPTER 9

Colt rifle in hand, Pecos scrambled down the bank and into the wash as fleetly as possible for a man of his size.

He ran crouching through the deep sand and loose gravel to a small island in the wash tufted with sage and short brown grass. Slash had moved onto the island and was crouching behind a rock. He had his own Winchester carbine in his gloved hands, and he was staring across the broad wash toward the south.

Pecos crouched beside him. "Who is it, you think?"

"I don't know, but I see a fire." Slash jerked his chin toward the low bank rising on the wash's southern edge. A small fire flickered under a cottonwood over there, on the lip of the bank.

"Was it there before?" Pecos asked, keeping his voice down. The night was so quiet, sound would carry far.

"If so, I didn't see it till just a minute ago."

"Someone followin' us?"

"Maybe." Slash shrugged. "On the other hand, could just be some fellow pilgrim."

"I reckon we're not gonna get any sleep till we find out if that pilgrim is friend or foe."

"That's what I was thinkin'." Slash raked a thumb across his jaw and chewed his bottom lip. "I reckon we could pull our picket pin and move a little farther along the trail."

"Too dark."

"Yeah."

Pecos placed his hand on his partner's shoulder. "Let's check it out. Probably a cowhand. Most he'll likely do is offer us a cup of mud. We got some leftover beans, so maybe this will all go friendly-like."

Slash gave a wry snort. "I like the rosy way you look at things, pard."

"Yeah, well—come on, you cynical cuss. Why don't you swing around to the north and I'll swing around to the south . . . just in case?"

"That's better."

As Slash straightened to a crouch and drifted off to the north, Pecos drifted south, moving as quietly as possible through the sun-scorched brush, keeping an eye on the fire but looking widely around it, as well. The fire could be a trap. On the other hand—why would it be?

The two former cutthroats were just that—former. On the other hand, there was likely a bounty hunter or two . . . or even a lawman or two . . . who hadn't heard the news. Someone might have seen Slash and Pecos in Cheyenne or even in one of the little backwater towns they'd passed through after leaving Cheyenne, like Chugwater or Wheatland, and recognized them. Maybe the person of topic even had an old wanted dodger in their saddlebags, or remembered one from a Western Union bulletin board and decided to up their life's ante . . .

That was the trouble with the outlaw way of life. It

stayed with you, dogging your heels like a hungry coyote, even as you walked the straight and narrow. . . .

Pecos swung wide to the south, finally climbing up out of the wash about fifteen minutes after he'd left Slash. He couldn't see Slash to the north because by now it was too dark. There was still a little light left in the sky, but it didn't help much down here on the ground.

Atop the wash's southern bank, he dropped to a knee and looked around carefully. Someone might be waiting for him in the brush over here. He couldn't see the fire because of the brush and scattered, gnarled dwarf cottonwoods and cedars standing between Pecos and the mystery camp. Also, he thought the camp lay around a slight bend to the northeast. He was probably about a quarter mile south of it. Slash was probably that same distance north of it by now.

Pecos took his time looking around and listening. Slash was likely doing the same. They'd been chased from one end of the country to the other for so long that they both had cultivated a keen sense of caution. They'd also acquired sharp senses. Continuing to look around, his eyes now having adjusted to the dark, Pecos listened, as well.

There was only a faint breath of a breeze making the short grass rustle. Far away to the north, probably from a jog of buttes he'd seen in that direction before the sun had set, a couple of coyotes were yammering. Pecos could barely hear the sounds when the breeze ebbed.

No other sounds came to his ears from close by.

Slowly, making no sudden movement that could be picked up easier by the eye than slow ones, Pecos began working his way north. He kept a few feet back from the lip of the wash, meandering through the widely spaced trees, careful not to kick stones or break blowdown branches.

In a few minutes, he could see the fire's wan glow before him, partly obscured by brush. He took several more steps, swinging his gaze from left to right, then back again, occasionally turning full around to see behind him. He held the Colt revolving rifle down low, where the light from the stars or the fire wasn't apt to reflect off of it.

When he figured he was roughly twenty feet from the camp, he stopped and called, "Hello? Anybody here?"

Slash yelled from somewhere ahead, "Pecos, get down—it's a trap!"

Pecos dropped like wet clothes from a line.

Rifles cracked. A bullet screeched over him. He rolled and saw a lap of flames from a rifle barrel. The bullet ricocheted shrilly off a near rock. Pecos gained a knee, raised the rifle, aimed at where he'd just seen the rifle flash silhouette a man, and fired. He fired again . . . again.

To the north, two other rifles spoke. One was Slash's, for that one's report came from dead ahead, on the other side of the fire. The other report came from the east.

Slash fired two more times and then started cursing in typical Slash fashion, bellowing a string of nastiness that would have made the devil blush. A few seconds later, Pecos knew what had caused his partner's tantrum. Hooves thudded away to the east, dwindling quickly.

Slash's bushwhacker had gotten away.

Pecos's, however, had not. Pecos had heard a clipped grunt just after he'd fired his last shot. He'd also heard the crunching thud of a body hitting the turf.

Pecos pushed ahead and stopped at the edge of the firelight.

"Slash, you all right?"

Slashed stepped out of the shadows on the other side

of the fire. He was punching fresh cartridges into his Winchester's load gate and glowering angrily. "Yeah, I'm fine. That son of a buck got away. I think there were two. Did you get the other one?"

"Yeah."

"Dead?"

"I don't know."

Pecos moved up to the fire. It had burned way down. Nothing lay around it except boot tracks from the man or men who had built it. Pecos lifted a burning branch from the fire, held it aloft.

"I think he's over here."

"Well, be careful. He might be playing possum."

"I don't think so." Pecos leaned his rifle against a tree and drew his Russian .44. He turned away from the fire and, holding the burning branch above his head, walked slowly through the brush, the branch in his left hand, the Russian in his right hand. He clicked the big gun's hammer back.

It took him a while, but the light from his branch finally landed on the body of the man he'd shot. The bushwhacker had scrambled several yards away from where Pecos had dropped him. Pecos saw the crimson glow of bloodstained brush in the man's wake.

"You got him?" Slash called behind his partner.

"Yeah." Pecos waved the branch.

Slash moved up to stand beside him, staring down at the dead man lying belly down atop the small cedar he'd bent over when he'd finally given up the ghost. Pecos kicked him over. The man was of average height, maybe forty. He'd lost his hat and his head was nearly bald. Long, thin sideburns ran down both sides of his long, craggy face. His open eyes stared up at Slash and Pecos, glowing eerily in the light of the burning branch. The light also glinted off of one silver front tooth.

He wore dusty trail garb, including a denim jacket against the night's chill.

He wore a pistol in a holster on his right hip. His rifle, a Sharps carbine, lay where the man had first fallen.

Pecos glanced at Slash. "You recognize him?"

"Nope."

"Me neither."

A horse whinnied to the east. The whinny was followed by a nervous whicker.

"That would be his mount," Slash said.

Pecos dropped to a knee and went through the dead man's pockets, finding a wallet filled with ninety-seven dollars in crisp bank bills. He found a comb and a receipt for two boxes of .45-70 cartridges from a gunsmith shop in: "Camp Collins," Pecos said, glancing up at Slash staring down at him.

"What's the date on it?" Slash asked.

Pecos studied the receipt. "The twenty-first. Same day we left town."

"You suppose this fella and his partner followed us all the way from Camp Collins . . . to kill us?"

"Must've."

"Could be a coincidence."

"You don't believe in coincidences any more than I do, Slash."

"Anything on him identify him?"

"Nothing. There's no ID in his wallet. Just them fresh bills. I'm betting there were a hundred in there before he bought those cartridges and maybe trail supplies."

"Let's check his horse."

It took them a few minutes to run down the dead

man's horse. The mount—a dapple gray gelding—was understandably nervous. It had heard gunfire, probably smelled blood, and the two men moving toward it were strangers.

When Slash finally grabbed the reins, Pecos unsaddled the beast, then went through the gear. All he found were two burlap sacks filled with trail supplies and saddlebags with some cooking gear and an extra change of clothes. Nothing to identify the owner. The horse, however, had a brand low on its left wither.

"Tumbling Box H," Slash said, running a gloved finger over the blaze.

"That's a spread near Camp Collins," Pecos said. "Up the canyon toward Horsetooth Rock."

"Yep."

"What the hell?"

"That's a puzzle. Why would Tumbling Box H riders want to trim our wicks?"

"You haven't insulted any Tumbling Box H riders lately—have you, partner?"

"Not that I remember." Slash took a step back and stared at the horse. "I've seen this mount before."

"Really?"

"Yeah, I know I have. See that dark ring around its left eye? I've seen that before, made note of it. It's a peculiar mark. I just can't remember where exactly I've seen it before, but I've seen this horse before, all right."

"Well, think about it. Where did you see it, Slash?"

"I'm tryin', an' I can't remember."

"Try harder."

Slash gave an angry chuff. "I'm doin' the best with the gifts God gave me."

"Not encouraging!"

"It'll come to me. Just give me some time. You know how you remember things as soon as you stop trying to remember 'em?"

"No."

"Well, it's true. Just shut up an' leave me alone, and it will come to me."

Pecos glanced back toward where they'd left the dead man. "In the meantime, what are we gonna do with the dead fella?"

"Hell, leave him."

"Not bury him?"

"You think he would have buried you if he'd killed you?"

"Fair point."

Slash turned to gaze off toward the north. "What I'm wonderin' about is the other fella. If they wanted us dead bad enough, he might come back."

"One of us is gonna have to keep watch for the rest of the night, I reckon," Pecos said with a sigh.

They both thought for a time.

Pecos said, "That other fella might circle back for the dead man's money. Maybe we'll catch him then."

"Where's the dead man's money?"

"On his carcass."

Slash stared at his big partner incredulously.

"What? You think I'm low enough to rob a dead man?" Pecos said in exasperation.

Slash laughed. "He was probably paid that money to kill us. So, I say it's rightly ours. Besides, even if it wasn't, what the hell is he gonna do with it now? Feed it to the coyotes that'll likely be chewin' on him by sunrise?"

Slash gave a frustrated groan and stomped off in the direction of the dead man. "Sometimes, Pecos, I really wonder about you. I really do!"

Suddenly, Slash stopped and turned back. "See—I told you I'd remember as soon as I stopped trying."

Pecos scowled. "Huh?"

"I just remembered where I've seen that horse before." Slash paused as if to build suspense.

"Well?" Pecos said. "You going to make me guess, or . . . ?"

"I've seen it tied to the hitchrack in front of Jay's saloon, the Thousand Delights!"

CHAPTER 10

"Hello there, pretty lady. Would you mind if this old border rascal bought you a drink?"

Jaycee Breckenridge lurched with a slight start.

"I'm sorry," said the tall, handsome, slim-hipped man coming up behind her to stand beside her at the long, horseshoe-shaped bar in the main drinking hall of the House of a Thousand Delights in Camp Collins. "I didn't mean to startle you."

"Oh, not all," Jay said, feeling a warm blush rising in her cheeks as she usually did when the handsome town marshal came calling on her, which he usually did sometime during the long night in the saloon/gambling parlor/brothel. "I was just . . ."

"Staring down into your coffee with a downright pensive expression on your ravishing features," the charming, bearded marshal finished for her, giving her a toothily appealing smile as he leaned on an elbow and turned his large body to face her. He was standing very close. So close that Jay could feel the heat of his long, tall body—the body of a rugged horseman, though Jay had only known the man as a lawman, first in Dodge City some years ago, before she'd been lovestruck by the old, unheeled catamount Pistol Pete Johnson.

"Was I?" Jay said with a self-conscious chuckle. "I hadn't realized."

"What were you thinking about, pray tell, lovely lady?"

The heat of her blush growing, Jay smiled into her half-empty coffee mug again, tucked a stray lock of her copper hair behind her left ear, and said, "Oh, I don't know . . . I was just I was just . . ."

"Thinking about that old outlaw you've gone and promised yourself to, no doubt," Walsh finished for her, clucking his disapproval. "And leaving all of us bachelors here in town all the sadder."

"Oh, please, Cisco. That's laying it on a little thick even for you—don't you think?"

Walsh blinked once, slowly. He stood so that his polished, silver, five-point town marshal's star, pinned to his brocade vest behind his black frock coat, lay about six inches from Jay's right breast. Jay noticed this and silently chastised herself for feeling a ripple of pleasure waltz its way up her back. "No," Walsh said, shaking his head. "I don't think I was laying it on thick at all. Please, let me buy you a real drink. Here, it's almost midnight, business is extremely slow, it being a weeknight, and you're still drinking coffee for heaven sakes."

Jay laughed. "I guess you're right. Bill, add a little brandy to my coffee, will you?"

"And I'll have two fingers of Four Oaks," Walsh said.

"Comin' right up, Miss Breckenridge . . . Marshal Walsh." Bill Tolliver was the only bartender working at this hour. Jay had kept two serving girls on in case business picked up when The Imperial, just down the street, closed its doors at twelve thirty. Both girls, however, were idly chatting with the thin crowd of customers sitting at tables around the large, well-appointed saloon.

As Tolliver poured a jigger of brandy into Jay's coffee, then set a glass of bourbon in front of Walsh, the marshal said, "I hear that old brigand has gone and left you here all alone. One of my deputies saw him and Pecos . . . uh, excuse me—*Melvin Baker*," the marshal corrected himself with a smile, knowing that the two ex-cutthroats were no longer using their nicknames, "leaving town a couple of days ago. On horseback as opposed to freight wagon."

Jay sipped her coffee and brandy. "Your boys don't miss a thing—do they, Cisco?"

"No, ma'am. I remind them to keep their eyes peeled. Never know what they're going to run into. Everything matters." Again, Walsh offered Jay an agreeable, vaguely flirtatious smile, then frowned as he asked with subtle probing, "Unexpected business?"

"Excuse me."

"What called them out of town. Not that it's any of my business, you understand. I'm just curious what could possibly have pulled Sla—er, *James* Braddock away from his lovely betrothed. Especially when he knows full good and well I'm waiting in the wings."

"Oh . . ." Jay hesitated, sipping her coffee and brandy again as she tried to come up with a believable lie. "Just, um . . . personal business. They wouldn't want me to bore you with it, Cisco."

"All right, all right. None of my business. Understood." The marshal sipped his bourbon again, then leaned forward over his glass but kept his brown-eyed gaze on Jay. "So, tell me, Jay . . . what were you thinking about when I walked up? You looked concerned. Worried. At the very least, you appeared perplexed. It can't be the business.

While it's a mite slow tonight, I know you make most of your money on the weekend. And even on slow nights, your girls upstairs—as polite and lovely as they are—are always busy with gentlemen callers."

"My, we're curious this evening, Marshal!" Jay intoned with friendly mockery.

"Not curious as much as, um . . . I'd call it *attentive*."

"Attentive? Oh, I see. All right . . . well, if you must know, I was thinking about Sla—er, James Braddock." Jay laughed at her own inability to call Slash by his given name. She shook her head, sipped her coffee, then set the cup back down on the counter. "He asked me to marry him, and I truly do believe he loves me . . . as I do him . . . but . . . I sense . . . I don't know, I sense . . ."

"A certain reluctance in taking that final step?" Walsh asked. Jay nodded. She been frowning down at the bar, but now she looked up at the tall lawman again. "Yes, a certain reluctance."

"Well, I reckon that's to be expected, isn't it?"

Jay frowned. "How so?"

"Oh, I don't mean that you're not a great catch. No, ma'am. Not at all. I don't think I've exactly hidden how I feel about you, Jay."

"Now . . . well, I'm flattered, Cisco."

"I just meant that the man's seeming reluctance to settle down is probably purely out of habit. I mean, he's never really settled down before, has he? Heck, he and Pec—doggone it, I mean, Mr. Baker," he laughed, "were running off their leashes for a good many years. The idea is probably so foreign to him as to be quite frightening. He wouldn't want to admit as much. He'd be afraid he'd risk hurting your feelings."

"I think you're right, Cisco." That did make her feel

better. The reluctance she'd sensed in Slash—or Jimmy or Jim or James or whatever in hell she was supposed to call him these days!—was probably just as the marshal had said. He felt anxious about settling down after so many years on the run. It probably had nothing to do with her, personally, at all.

"He'll come around." Cisco reached over and placed his hand on one of hers, gave it a reassuring squeeze. "If for some reason, he doesn't, however . . ." He arched a brow and gave her a vaguely sheepish, insinuating gaze.

Jay found herself tittering, flattered. "Oh, well, if you say so, Cisco."

"I do, indeed."

Just then Walsh swung his head around to the front door as four men entered the saloon. He turned back to Jay and, pushing back away from the bar, asked, "Jay, is there a room upstairs I could hold a private meeting?"

"Oh. Well, uh . . . upstairs?" She frowned curiously between the lawman and the four men who had just entered, recognizing one of them as Jason Hall, owner of the Tumbling Box H ranch outside of Camp Collins. She believed the three other men with Hall were Hall's foreman, Keldon Reed, and two Tumbling Box H ranch hands who came into the Thousand Delights from time to time when they could afford an hour or two upstairs with Jay's pleasure girls. "Of course," Jay said to Walsh. "I don't think anyone's in the billiard room. Help yourselves. You know where it is."

"Of course."

"I'll bring brandy and cigars if you like. "

"That would be wonderful. Please, put it on my tab, will you?" Walsh smiled his winning smile, then leaned forward to plant a warm kiss on her cheek. "Thank you, Jay. And please don't worry about that old outlaw of yours. The man may be many things, but he's not fool enough to pull out of marriage to a woman like you."

"Thank you, Cisco. I hope you're right."

"I know I am."

Walsh looked at Hall and the other men, then beckoned them with a toss of his head. Giving Jay one more parting smile, he swung around and started for the broad, carpeted staircase at the room's rear. Hall led his foremen and other two men after Walsh, all of them giving Jay a smile and a nod in greeting as they strode past her.

Jay smiled and nodded in return, then looked at the barman, who was reading a newspaper spread atop the bar before him. "Bill, give me a bottle of our best brandy and a handful of cigars, will you? How 'bout those rum-soaked Cubans I got in last week?"

"You got it, Miss Breckenridge. Why the frown?"

"What's that?"

Tolliver, a big, swarthy man with a boyish face and close-cropped, straight blond hair, smiled at her as he plucked a bottle of Spanish brandy off a backbar shelf. "You seem puzzled."

"Oh . . ." Jay had only vaguely realized her befuddlement. "I don't know—I guess I was just wondering why anyone would be holding a business meeting at nearly twelve thirty at night."

Tolliver shrugged as he set the open brandy bottle on a tray. Reaching for five goblets, he said, "Busy men meet at odd hours, I reckon, Miss Breckenridge."

"I suppose you're right."

When Tolliver had set five red-banded Cubans onto the tray with the bottle and the glasses, Jay lifted the tray from the bar and headed for the stairs. She climbed the stairs, careful not to trip on the hem of her long gown. When she gained the second-floor landing, she heard loud male voices thundering from somewhere down the hall. As she approached the door to the billiard room, which was the second door on the hall's left side, under the head of a snarling grizzly bear, she realized the commotion was occurring inside that very room.

Jay paused outside the closed door. The door wasn't latched, making it possible for her to hear voices more clearly now. Specifically, the rancher, Hall's voice, saying:

"That team will be hauling eighty thousand dollars in bullion, Walsh, and—"

"I know how much it will be carrying, Hall. I just don't want your men to—"

"Like I said, we'll all be there to make sure everything goes off without a—"

"At Horsetooth Station?"

"Yes, that's where I said we'd meet. We'll get back to you on the exact night. Now, look, Marshal, if you're getting cold feet, let me remind you of a little problem in your past. One that likely would not—"

Hall's voice stopped abruptly. It was as though someone had waved him to silence. Too late, Jay heard furtive footsteps moving toward the door. She stood frozen in shock a moment too long. In the next moment, someone drew the door open wide, and Jay found herself staring up at one of Hall's ranch hands—a tall man in his late twenties and with one wandering blue eye. His good eye stared down in silent recrimination at Jay, while the wandering eye glared at the tip of his nose.

"It's Miss Breckenridge," he said, turning to the table behind him.

The other men sat at a table on the far side of the room,

three billiard tables arranged around the room to their right.

Jay stepped forward, brushing past the cowhand with the wandering eye and fashioning her best toothy smile as she strode toward the table. Trying to ignore the anxious fluttering of her heart, she said, "Gentlemen, I'm sorry to keep you waiting. I've brought you a bottle of our best brandy— Spanish brandy, of course—and five rum-soaked cigars that arrived all the way from Cuba only last week!"

She knew she was speaking too loudly and with too much ebullience, but she couldn't help herself.

Calm down, Jay, she told herself. *It's not what you think it is. It is not what you heard!*

The men around the table studied her in troubled silence. The table was oval-shaped. Cisco Walsh sat at the left end. The rancher, Jason Hall, a small, gray, hard-eyed man, stood at the other end, his big cream Stetson overturned on the billiard table to his left. His face was still red from his previous anger. Between Walsh and Hall sat the foreman, Keldon Reed. The man who'd opened the door remained near the door, gaping at Jay.

They were all gaping at her, eyeing her suspiciously.

She could read their minds. *How much had she heard?*

Trying desperately to look nonchalant, Jay removed the brandy bottle from the tray. She tried to keep her hand from shaking but was not able. Her hand and the bottle shook slightly as she set the bottle on the table.

Had Walsh noticed?

She slid her eyes to his. His own eyes were on her hand just as she removed it from the bottle. A smile curled his upper lip, but his eyes looked stricken.

"Best brandy I serve," Jay said, her own stiff smile in

place as she set the five goblets on the table, one at a time so they wouldn't clink together in her shaking hand.

Calm down, dammit! Just calm down, Jay!

When she'd gotten each glass onto the varnished wooden table, she set the cigars down beside them. Folding the tray down in front of her, she stepped back and arched a brow at Jason Hall, whose own suspicious gaze was fixed on her, and then at Walsh. "Would you like me to pour?"

Hall looked at Walsh. Walsh returned the man's dark look, then lifted his gaze to Jay and widened his smile a little, but his lips could have been made out of plaster of Paris. They appeared about to crack and crumble onto the table. "No, that's fine, Miss Breckenridge. I'll pour. Thank you very much for your hospitality.

Jay glanced at the Tumbling Box H foreman, Keldon Reed, a tall, long-limbed man with a walrus mustache. He sat as though frozen in his chair, facing the far wall. His big, brown, rope-burned hands lay flat atop the table before him.

"All right, then—enjoy, gentlemen," Jay said, stepping back. "Whups!" She stumbled into a corner of the billiard table. Chuckling, she swung around and made her way past the cowhand with the unmoored eye to the door. The distance between the table and the door was only ten or fifteen feet, but the walk seemed to take a long, long time. The cowhand watched her, swinging his head slowly, tracking her with his good eye, and she was worried for a second that he was going to stretch his arms out and grab her.

She moved through the doorway and drew the door closed behind her.

She stopped just outside the door. Pressing the tray against her chest, she drew a deep, calming breath and released it slowly. It did nothing to calm her. She felt her heart pounding against the tray.

CHAPTER 11

Steering the jail wagon with a light hand on the ribbons, Slash sniffed the air.

He turned to where Pecos had fallen into a herky-jerky sleep beside him, his head shuddering with the wagon's bounce and sway over the rough two-track trail.

"Pecos, you smell that?"

"Huh? Huh?" The bigger ex-cutthroat lifted his head and poked the brim of his hat up off his forehead. "Smell what?"

Slash sniffed again. "That."

Pecos lifted his chin and sniffed. "I don't smell . . . *Oh!*"

"Yeah."

Pecos frowned at Slash. "Smoke?"

"I been smellin' it for the past ten minutes. The smell's been gettin' stronger. I thought maybe wildfire, but . . ." Slash looked around in all directions. "I don't see smoke. If there was a wildfire out here, with all this dry brush, we'd for sure see it, as strong as it smells."

"Let's not talk about wildfires. The only thing I hate worse than bein' ambushed is havin' to outrun a wildfire. Remember that one we had to outrun in Arizona?"

"At least it got that posse from Payson off our tails."

"Yeah, but if that fire had caught up to us, which it damn near did—man, those wildfires can run faster'n a mean ole grizzly bear!—we'd have been wishin' the posse had caught us instead. The only thing I can think of worse than hangin' is . . . holy moly—look at *that!*"

Slash had just pulled the jail wagon up to the top of a hill. Now he stopped the horses and stared ahead and down the other side of the hill, toward where Pecos was staring, the big man's lower jaw hanging nearly to his chest.

Pecos said, "Is that . . . is that *Dry Fork*?"

Slash thumbed his own hat back off his forehead. "I reckon it *was*."

What was left of the town sprawled in a shallow, brightly sunlit valley before them, roughly a half a mile away. Most of the town had been burned, and a few fires were still burning. Black smoke rose to hang in a stormy black cloud over the town, low enough in the valley that it couldn't be seen from far beyond it.

The fire must have started the previous day; most of the wooden buildings had already been reduced to smoldering rubble. A few buildings remained standing, but damned few. Most of even the outlying shacks and small, frame houses had either been burned or were still in the process of burning. Horses and other livestock that had likely been released from stock pens milled on the low slopes encircling the burned town—horses, cows, pigs, chickens, and even some goats.

Two churches bookended the small settlement. At least, Slash thought the large pile of rubble on the town's east end was . . . or *had been* . . . a church. He could still see the bell tower and the cross rising up out of the cupola, though both were now on the ground, partly burned and canted to one side. The rest of the smoldering ruins humped up blackly behind it.

A small fire burned in the brush behind the church, though most of the fuel feeding it appeared to have already burned.

The church standing on the town's west end hadn't been burned, though it was somewhat obscured by the sprinkling of willows and cottonwoods encircling it and the cemetery spread out on the hill below it, to the right of it. The church was a simple white frame structure with stone steps rising to the double doors. It also had a cupola, but no cross rose from it, unlike the church on the opposite end of the town.

Slash and Pecos shared a dark look.

Then Slash turned his head forward and slapped the ribbons over the geldings' backs. "*Hy-yahhh!*" he cried, putting the two beasts into a fast run down the slope toward the broad, shallow valley. "*Hy-yahhhh, you cayuses!*" Tied to the rear, the saddle mounts galloped along behind them.

The jail wagon rocked and rattled wickedly, its clattering so loud that Slash could barely hear beneath it the thudding of the horses' hooves. Beside him, Pecos held tight to the seat. Slash knew that Pecos was thinking the same thing he was thinking—the three prisoners had been busted out of jail by their gang. Once loose, they'd gone on a rampage and burned the town.

Following the trail, the wagon dropped straight down the hill and into the valley before swinging west and becoming the town's main street. Slash put the wagon up to the burned-out church. As he did, a wicked, pungent stench filled his nose, making his eyes water.

Beside him, Pecos lifted his arm to his nose and said in a muffled voice, "That's the stench of burned flesh, Slash.

I know that smell. Once you smell it, you never forget it. There was folks in that church when they burned it!"

Slash checked the team down in front of the church and gazed somberly at the ruins. Some of the fallen timbers were still smoldering. Squinting, looking closely, he thought he could make out the charred remains of humans amongst the heaped black and gray ashes and the remains of pews and ceiling beams.

The geldings whickered and shook their heads, not liking the stench any more than Slash and Pecos did.

Slash gigged the team ahead. As the wagon rattled slowly down the broad main drag, he and Pecos looked around at the burnt-out hulks of the business buildings on both sides of the trace. A couple were still burning, but they were all reduced to rubble. At least, the wood frame buildings were rubble. The adobe brick or limestone block buildings had been scorched black by the fires around them.

Slash's insides churned when he saw several dead men lying amongst the rubble. Several men and even a few women lay in the street. So did dogs and horses. Most of the men and women in the street hadn't been burned. They'd been shot and left to lie in their own blood pools.

An old lady in a dark brown dress and poke bonnet lay in the middle of the street just ahead. The handle of a wicker basket was still hooked over her right arm. She lay twisted on her side in death, eyes open, staring sightlessly at the ground.

"Whoa."

Slash drew the team to a halt. He handed the reins to Pecos, then leaped down from the wagon. He walked up to the dead woman and dropped to his haunches. He removed his right buckskin glove and poked a finger into the blood pool beneath the bird-like body. The blood was thick, almost of the consistency of jelly.

Scrubbing his finger off in the dirt, he looked up at Pecos scowling down at him from the driver's seat. "She's been dead since last night. Maybe earlier." He looked down at the old lady again. Brown eggs, some broken, lay scattered in the dirt around her overturned basket.

"Sorry, old woman."

Slash rose with a curse and climbed back into the wagon. As he put the wagon ahead once more, Pecos pointed and said, "Look. That's the marshal's office up the street, on the right."

Slash followed the man's gaze to the small, limestone structure a block ahead. A wooden sign over the door announced in simple, square black letters: TOWN MARSHAL. There was no porch, just a small boardwalk fronting the wooden door, which was open.

Slash angled the wagon over to the office. He grabbed his Winchester out from beneath the wagon seat and climbed down from the wagon. Pecos grabbed his sawed-off, double-barreled, twelve-gauge shotgun out from beneath the seat and slung its wide leather lanyard over his head and shoulder. The Richards was Pecos's weapon of choice—at least, for interior, close-range work. Outside, he preferred the Colt's revolving rifle and his Russian.

Slash had another gun, too—a pretty, pearl-gripped, over-and-under Derringer residing in his vest pocket. The hideout was his weapon of choice in tight situations and as a last resort. Now, however, he racked a live round into his Winchester's action and stepped up onto the small boardwalk fronting the marshal's office.

He glanced at Pecos, then nudged the door open wider with the rifle's barrel.

"Hello?" he called.

He stepped inside, looking around. As his eyes adjusted to the building's heavy shadows, he saw two men lying on the limestone floor near a large, cluttered desk abutting the room's far, front corner. Four steel-banded cages were lined up against the rear wall. All doors were open and all cells were empty, of course. After what he'd seen outside, Slash hadn't expected to find anyone in here. At least, no prisoners. He hadn't expected to find lawmen in here, either.

At least, not living, breathing ones. And he'd been right, it appeared.

The first man nearest the door lay belly down. His throat had been slit. He was younger than the other man who lay near the desk. The second man was maybe in his late fifties to early sixties. He had some Indian blood. He also wore a deputy town marshal's star. He lay on his back, staring wide-eyed at the ceiling. He'd been tortured with knives and then gutted. The floor around him was thick with a broad pool of blood. His passing had been painful; the man's lips were stretched back in agony from his teeth.

Three pairs of saddlebags sat atop the office's rolltop desk. Slash opened a flap and peered inside and widened his eyes at the gold coins and silver certificates stuffed inside. "Well, well," he said to himself. Likely the money the killers had taken off the Sundance stage.

"Jesus."

Slash whipped around with a start to see Pecos standing behind him.

"Dammit, you scared me, ya big galoot!"

"I thought you heard me come in."

"Well, I didn't." The burned town, the death, the poor dead half-breed deputy before him had frayed Slash's nerves. "Anybody alive out there?" He jerked his chin at the street.

"I didn't see nobody."

"One's alive—but I'm about it," said a man suddenly standing in the open doorway.

Both Slash and Pecos jerked with starts this time.

Their sudden movements startled the little man in the doorway. He stumbled backward, holding up his hands as though to shield himself from a bullet. "Easy, now, easy!" he cried, cowering like a whipped dog. He had greasy dark brown hair. He was relatively clean-shaven, maybe in his late forties, and he wore a dirty, soot-smudged, pin-striped shirt and an apron. "Don't hurt me, dammit. I didn't do nothin' but get my feed store burned to the ground by them savages!"

He looked desperately between the open hands he held up in front of his ash-smudged face and said, "You ain't part o' them, are ya? I didn't think so or I wouldn't have come out of hiding. I seen the U.S. MARSHALS sign on your wagon out yonder, an' I figured it was safe . . ."

"You're safe," Slash said. "We're with the marshals. We're here—leastways, we *were* here—to pick up three prisoners."

"Yeah, well, good luck!" the obviously terrified little shopkeeper cried, though it was partly a laugh, as well. Mostly it sounded like a strangled croak.

"Where are they?" Pecos asked.

The little man, whose pale face was badly pock-marked, gave another little strangled croak, then flinched and held a finger to his lips. He looked around fearfully, then, pushing Slash and Pecos back, he stepped into the marshal's office and closed the door. He latched it with a wince and then turned back to Slash and Pecos.

He was sweating, and a muscle beneath his left eye twitched wildly.

"I ain't sure where they *all* are. Maybe some left town. I don't know. B-but t-two of them loco savages are over at Carlisle's. After they were all through shootin' up the town—oh, Lordy, that went on all yesterday afternoon and most of the night. Shootin' and stabbin' an' laughin' an' killin' just for the sake of killin'. Oh, and what they did to the women. The *girls! The teacher from the school!* My God, they made a party out of it. Some o' the men tried to stand against 'em, but they were so fearful they couldn't shoot straight. They died first while the killers laughed! Some folks—they got away. Left town. Either on horseback or just runnin', nothin' but the clothes on their backs. Some folks holed up in the Catholic church, but them crazy loco savages burned it down! Oh, you shoulda heard the *screams from inside!*"

The terrified little man closed his hands over his ears and shut his eyes as though to quell the screams he was still hearing inside his own head.

Slash stepped forward and pried the man's hands from his ears. "Listen, Mr . . . what's your name?"

"S-Stanley D-D-Donovan. I hid in the communal cellar! I peeked up through the door . . . seen it all. Oh, Lordy, I'll see it . . . *hear it!* . . . for the rest of my life!"

"Easy, now, Mr. Donovan," Pecos said in his gentle, resonant voice. "You say two are still over at Carlisle's?"

"Yeah . . . y-yes . . . I seen 'em go over there early this mornin'. They didn't burn the place. They wanted the liquor an' . . . the-the g-girls. The girls musta been hidin' in there, but they still found 'em, all right. I heard the screams. Two . . . two of them killers are over there now. The two that busted the other three out. It's been quiet.

God only knows what's goin' on." Donovan stared up at Pecos hopefully. "Maybe they're asleep!"

Slash said, "The two who busted the other three out of the jail here are over at Carlisle's?"

"Th-that's right."

"Where are the three prisoners? The men we were sent to pick up."

"God only knows! They're off prob'ly still wreakin' havoc on the land somewheres!"

"What about the rest of the gang?" Pecos asked.

"I don't know. As far as I could tell, only two of the rest of the gang rode into town. M-maybe the rest is still on the way here. Oh, Gawddd!"

"Take it easy, Mr. Donovan." Slash took the man's arm and, stepping over the two dead men, led the little man over to the chair by the desk. He shoved Donovan into the chair and said, "You sit here out of sight. You'll be all right. Just rest, take it easy. Take some deep breaths. We'll be back for you soon."

Donovan shuddered and grabbed himself as though deeply chilled. He lowered his chin to his chest and sobbed.

Slash moved back to the door. Pecos had already stepped outside. He stood on the small, wooden boardwalk. Slash stepped out beside him. Both men stared off to the west, where a large, sprawling, white-frame building stood on a street corner, on the opposite side of the street from the marshal's office. A big sign running across the second story, above the first-story veranda roof, announced simply: CARLISLE'S.

Carlisle's was the only wooden building still standing on that side of the street. It had probably been sheltered from the flames of the rest of the burning town by the two adobe structures on either side of it and by its wide separation from the other wooden structures that had burned.

Slash glanced at Pecos. "Didn't I tell you this wasn't gonna be no picnic?"

"No."

Slash sighed as he turned back toward Carlisle's. "Yeah . . . well."

"Let's go," Pecos said.

Shouldering his Colt's revolving rifle, he stepped down off the boardwalk. Slash matched his stride as the two angled across the main street, heading for Carlisle's that stood, eerily silent and eye-achingly bright, in the midday sunshine.

CHAPTER 12

Slash looked up the street to the west, then down to the east, toward the burned church they'd passed. Nothing moved. Only smoke.

He and Pecos took the broad, high porch steps side by side. They confronted the batwings side by side, as well. They slid cautious glances around the frame, squinting into the dark interior.

They shared a questioning glance; then Slash pushed through the left door. Pecos followed through the right door. They each stepped to one side so the doorway wouldn't backlight them.

Slash scowled incredulously into the gloom, where a big man was dancing with a scantily clad young woman—a slender blonde with long, curly hair tumbling down her naked back. The man was even bigger than Pecos, and lantern-jawed. His hair was cropped close, and a two- or three-day growth of beard stubble darkened his broad face.

Slash's scowl deepened. He'd thought the two were dancing. He'd been wrong. The big man was the only one of the pair dancing. He was dragging the poor blonde around Carlisle's floor—back in the shadows, where tables had been cleared away to form a dance floor fronting a stage where bands had likely played during happier times. The girl's head was tipped forward against the big man's stout left shoulder.

Her bare, pale feet dragged across the floor puncheons. Asleep?

There was another man in the room, Slash saw. A portly man lay dead in front of the bar. Judging by the blood matting his shirt and the apron tied around his bulging waist, he'd been shot a good half-dozen times. He'd overturned a table and one chair when he'd fallen, and now lay on his back, glaring up at the ceiling.

The big, living man—the dancer—had his eyes closed as he moved slowly, sliding to and fro, his feet clad in high-topped, mule-eared boots. He hummed along with the waltz playing in his head. He wore only a bowie knife in a sheath strapped to his waist. A gun rig lay on a table nearby. The rig held three holstered pistols. A Springfield carbine lay on the table near the rig, as well as the man's feathered black opera hat, which lay crown down near three bottles, one half-empty, and four shot glasses, all empty.

The big man had his head down, a dreamy smile on his face as he danced. He and the girl could have been two lovers on their wedding night. Only, they weren't. Suddenly, having sensed the two newcomers' presence, the big man lifted his head and turned toward the batwings.

"Hey!" he said in a deep voice that echoed briefly around the cave-like, all-but-empty room. He released the girl's hands and pointed toward Slash and Pecos. "Who're you?"

The girl fell straight back away from the big man, her knees buckling. She dropped to the floor like a fifty-pound sack of potatoes and lay unmoving, crumpled, legs curled beneath her back. She stared toward the front of the room through wide-open, lake-blue eyes.

Dead. Had to be. She hadn't resisted the fall a bit.

She didn't appear to have been shot or stabbed. There was no blood.

Heart attack, maybe . . . *Death by terror.*

The big man stared down at her with mild surprise. He chuckled, then turned again, angrily, toward Slash and Pecos. He pointed again. "I said, *who're you?*"

With a calm he did not feel, Slash said, "We're the fellas that just killed you, friend."

The man's eyes snapped wide. His lower jaw dropped, his big mouth opened. "Oh, you think so—do you?"

He stepped forward, heading toward the gun-laden table before him.

Slash raised the Winchester to his shoulder, peeled the hammer back, and blew a .44-caliber round into the big man's chest. Dust puffed from the man's wool shirt and brown leather vest.

He grunted, flinched, but kept moving toward the table.

Slash shot him again.

The big man kept moving, albeit a little less steadily, toward the table.

Slash glanced skeptically at Pecos, then ejected the smoking cartridge from his Winchester's action, seated fresh, and shot the big man a third time. The man bellowed loudly, his voice thundering around the room. He reached forward and started to shuck a Remington revolver from one of the holsters before him.

"Time for the Richards," Slash told Pecos, stepping aside.

"Be happy to."

Pecos stepped forward, raising the double-bore,

sawed-off shotgun in both hands. As the big man, bellowing again, raised the pistol straight out from his right shoulder, the twelve-gauge thundered. It sounded like a keg of detonated dynamite. Rose-like flames and roiling smoke blossomed from both bores.

The big man gave a shrill cry and triggered the Remington into the ceiling as he ran backward and then to one side and flew, howling, over a table. He rolled over the table and hit the floor with another thundering boom. He gave another grunt, one more, then groaned as his life bled out from the twin pumpkin-sized wounds in his chest.

Slash spied movement at the rear of the room.

Jerking his head that way, he saw a man run down to the second-story landing. The man's gun rig was looped over his left arm. His shirt was unbuttoned, its tails out. He held a pistol in his right hand. Stopping on the landing and crouching to gaze down into the drinking hall, he raised the Colt and fired. The bullet sawed through the air between Slash and Pecos to slam into one of the batwings behind them, knocking it outward.

Slash stepped forward, raised the Winchester again, and fired.

The man on the landing cursed, wheeled, and ran back up the stairs. Slash wasn't sure if he'd hit him or not.

Slash hurried forward, pinching fresh cartridges from his shell belt and sliding them through his carbine's loading gate. Pecos close on his heels, he hurried up the stairs. He could hear the man's running foot thuds in the ceiling above his head.

Slash crossed the second-floor landing, turned, and took the last set of steps two at a time. He paused at the top of the steps.

"Get back!" he told Pecos, nudging his big partner back

and to one side as their quarry, standing in the middle of the dim hall, triggered his revolver twice.

Both shots flew over the staircase and thumped into a wall. The man turned and resumed running, taking long strides, scissoring his arms and legs. Slash raised the Winchester, but before he could plant the beads on the re-treating man's back, the man leaped straight through the window at the hall's far end.

Just like that—out of the darkness of the hall and into the sunlight, *gone!*

Only, Slash could hear him whooping wildly as he flew through the air outside the saloon, beyond the raining glass.

Slash lowered the Winchester and took off running. "I'm gonna get that son of a buck!" he shouted at Pecos running behind him, his big partner's steps sounding twice as loud as Slash's.

Slash gained the end of the hall and kept running. . . .

Right through what remained of the window.

A quarter second earlier, he'd seen the roof of the building next door to Carlisle's. He'd also seen his quarry crawling up and over the peak of the roof, disappearing down the other side. If he could make it, so could Slash.

Slash flew out of Carlisle's third-floor window like mortar from a Napoleon cannon. But a mortar with not enough powder behind it. Slash flew a few feet out away from Carlisle's—then down like a wounded duck. He'd forgotten until now that he was still clutching the Win-chester. He dropped it, inwardly wincing at the gun's mis-treatment. He had a feeling his own mistreatment was going to be worse.

A half second later, he was proven right.

Ufffghhhrrrrr! exploded out of him as he slammed onto

the roof of the adobe brick building beside Carlisle's. The roof was steeply pitched. Immediately, he began sliding down the rough wooden shakes. He tried to grab purchase, but there was nothing to grab on to.

What in the hell had the man who'd come before him grabbed?

A sickening feeling flooded his belly and loins when he felt his feet and then his legs drop over the edge of the roof. His head and shoulders slid down, down, down while he continued digging his gloved fingers into the shakes. Or trying to, but to no avail. His head and shoulders went over the edge, as well.

At the last second, he managed to close his hands around the edge of the overhang.

He hung there against the side of the brick shack, dangling, kicking his legs, trying desperately to swing them up and over the overhang. That wasn't going to happen. Something like that kind of an athletic, acrobatic feat hadn't happened in the past twenty years—not since he'd left his twenties, anyway, and probably a good bit longer ago than that. When he was a teenager growing up in Missouri, he'd once had to skin out of a parlor house in Blue Springs, when his pa had gotten word he'd become a regular patron of a pretty Mexican doxie. He'd made a mad, cat-like, successful dash across several rooftops, buck-naked, his clothes clutched in his arms. But that was years ago, and his father, armed with a solid oak pitchfork handle, had been hot on his heels.

Now he watched in horror as his old fingers slipped off the edge of the overhang. His heart slid up into his throat as his body plunged down the side of the adobe brick shack. Fortunately, a pile of shipping crates lay beneath him. He struck the crates with a grunt and a curse, fell, and rolled, the crates tumbling around him as he slid down the stack to the trash-littered ground.

"You crazy bedbug!" Pecos shouted at him, as the bigger ex-cutthroat ran past on the street, having taken the easy way out of Carlisle's. "If you've broken anything, I'm gonna shoot you!"

Groaning at the ache in his right ankle, Slash cursed his partner and said, "Thanks for your sympathy!"

But by then Pecos was gone, having dashed out of sight around the front of the brick shack, in hard pursuit of their quarry.

Slash rolled onto his hands and knees. His right ankle felt as though a railroad spike had been driven through it. But he didn't think it was broken. Just twisted. He heaved himself to his feet, glanced at his poor Winchester lying at the base of Carlisle's, near his hat. Not wanting to take the time to retrieve the abused rifle, he shucked one of his stag-gripped .44s and took off running painfully around behind the shack he'd so recently fallen from.

He stopped so suddenly that his bad ankle gave, and he dropped to a knee, falling forward. The move saved his life, for the gunman had just lifted his head above a stack of firewood abutting the back wall of the next low adobe brick building, twenty feet beyond the one Slash had fallen from. The man triggered a round, the revolver popping hollowly. The bullet whistled two feet above Slash's head. Slash raised his .44 as the gunman gritted his teeth and cocked his own Colt, then narrowed one anxious bright eye as he drew another bead on Slash.

Slash squeezed his .44's trigger. The bullet plowed into a log just beneath his assailant's head, blowing slivers in the man's face. Cursing, the man triggered his own Colt wide, the bullet screeching off a rock behind Slash. The gunman drew his head back, squeezing his eyes closed. He rose and ran, crouching—limping, too, it appeared—around the adobe building's far corner, disappearing down the side.

"Pecos!" Slash shouted. "He's over here!"

Slash grimaced as he heaved himself to his feet and ran to the adobe shack's rear corner, on the far side of the wood pile. He glanced around the corner and into the break between the adobe building and the burned-out hulk of a livery barn. He pulled his head back as the gunman triggered another round at him, the bullet screeching off the adobe inches from where Slash's face had just been.

"Hold it, you polecat!" Slash heard his partner yell.

Slash looked into the break again.

The gunman stood halfway between the rear of the adobe shack and the front, and about ten feet out away from it. He was turned to face the adobe shack, his gun rig still looped over his right arm, his Colt in his right hand. He whipped his gaze toward where Pecos was poking his head out from around the adobe building's front corner.

Slash stepped out from the corner. His .44 leaped and roared.

The gunman screamed and jerked backward, turning toward Slash as Slash's bullet plowed into his right arm. Blood instantly stained the upper arm of his unbuttoned cream shirt. Pecos extended his Russian and fired.

The gunman screamed again and whipped to his left as Pecos's bullet tore into his left arm.

"Dirty dogs!" The gunman gritted his teeth as he raised his pistol toward Pecos. He didn't get it level before Slash and Pecos each fired two more rounds, all four rounds cutting into the gunman's torso and sending him tumbling backward to lay in a writhing pile near the still-smoldering ruins of the livery barn.

He'd dropped his Colt and his gun rig on which two more Colts were holstered.

He lay on his back, grinding one boot heel into the turf. He pressed his shaking fingers into the ground to each side of him.

Slowly, Slash and Pecos moved toward him, Slash still limping on his bad ankle. He stared down at the dying killer. He was a small man—probably not much over five-and-a-half feet. Reed thin. No wonder he'd been able to make that jump. He was long-faced, ugly as a snake. Long, thin, sandy-brown hair slithered around his shoulders. He was pale and thin-lipped, and his eyes were a washed-out green.

"You de-devils kilt me," he grunted.

"Where's the rest of 'em?" Pecos asked.

"Go to hell!" the killer spat.

Guns popped to the west, a good distance away. A man hooted loudly, jubilantly. More guns popped.

Slash and Pecos shared a conferring glance.

Slash blew a hole through the killer's pale forehead; then he and Pecos hurried back toward the main street.

CHAPTER 13

Slash and Pecos stepped out of the break between the adobe building and the burned livery barn. They turned toward the sounds of sporadic shooting. It seemed to be coming from the church on the other end of town. From their position on the main street, they could see the church sitting alone on its own lot and up a slight rise to the north. A small cemetery fronted the church, on its right side.

Men were milling around the place, firing rifles into it. Smoke slithered up from around the building's stone foundation. Apparently, the men now firing rifles at the church had piled brush up around it and set it on fire.

"You suppose that's *our* curly wolves, do you?" Pecos asked, shouldering his Colt's revolving rifle, his sawed-off twelve-gauge hanging barrel down behind his back.

"There does appear to be three of 'em an' they do appear to be curly wolves, up to no good as they appear to be."

"Why do you suppose they're torchin' that church?" Pecos gave Slash a dark look. "You suppose there's more innocent folks holed up in there, like there was the other one?"

Slash's heart thumped. "Why else would they burn it?"

"Yeah," Slash said, raising his voice. "Why else?" He swung around and started limping back in the direction of the marshal's office. "Let's get the jail wagon!"

Pecos jogged past him, glancing over his shoulder at him. "How's your ankle?"

"It hurts."

"Serves you right."

"Go to hell!"

They untied their saddle mounts from the jail wagon, then climbed up onto the driver's seat. As Slash untied the reins from around the brake handle, the marshal's office door opened. Stanley Donovan peered out, squinting one eye. He looked to the east, then to the west, then at Slash and Pecos. "You get them two no-accounts over at Carlisle's?"

"They've done given up their ghosts, Mr. Carlisle," Slash said, clucking the two geldings into the street. "But there's more trouble over at the Lutheran church, looks like."

"You don't say?" Donovan said. "I bet that's the first time them words have been spoken. I'll just stay out of it!" The shopkeeper's eyes glinted fearfully as he quickly slammed the door.

Pecos gave a wry chuckle, then held tight to the seat as Slash hoorawed the team on up the street to the west. As he held the ribbons, he pulled his right-hand Colt from its holster and shoved it at Pecos.

"Reload that for me—will you, partner? I'm gonna need both my hoglegs, as I left my rifle back yonder."

"You're a damn lot of work!" Pecos grimaced as he lay his rifle down beneath the seat. "I'm using your shells, dammit." He reached over and thumbed six cartridges from Slash's shell belt. He flicked open the loading gate on

Slash's Colt, clicked out the empty shells, and replaced them with the fresh ones. He slid the loading gate closed, spun the wheel, then returned the revolver to Slash's holster.

"Don't you think you better slow down?" he said as they came up on the church and the cemetery fronting it, off the trail's right side. They could more clearly see the three shooters sauntering around outside the place, laughing, passing a bottle, and firing their rifles through the flames lifting around the outside of the building.

Slash could also hear the muffled cries of what could only be people trapped inside.

"Hell, no," Slash said. "Them folks inside must feel like roasts inside a Dutch oven!"

"Ah, hell!" Pecos said, bending down to pull his rifle up off the floor.

As Slash turned the wagon off the main trail and onto the trace that climbed the hill to the church, Pecos checked to make sure his rifle was loaded, then raised it high against his chest. "You're a crazy son of Satan," he yelled above the thunder of the gelding's hooves and the roar of the iron-shod wheels. "Always have been, always will be!"

"That's what my mother told me before I left swaddling clothes!" Slash laughed. "See if you can pink one of them nasty, low-down dirty dogs, Pecos!"

They were halfway up the hill, but so far, the three men ahead of them, staggering around, drinking and shooting and laughing, hadn't appeared to have seen the jail wagon barreling toward them. They were too drunk, and the noise inside the church, their own shooting, and the roar of the flames probably covered the wagon's lumbering din.

"Well, try to hold this hideous contraption steady, dammit!" Pecos barked as he rose to his feet.

"This is as steady as she gets!" Slash returned.

They were within a hundred yards of the church now. The wagon was bouncing so violently that Slash couldn't see clearly, but he did see one of the three killers turn toward him. The man's lower jaw sagged, and his eyes widened. He held a bottle in one hand, a rifle in the other. He staggered drunkenly backward, then turned toward the man on his right—a big bruiser with twin black braids and distinctly Indian features. The Indian had just fired his rifle into the church. Now he turned to see the jail wagon mounting the hill, and his own black eyes snapped wide.

Pecos spread his boots shoulder width apart on the floor of the driver's box. He aimed the Colt's revolving rifle over the heads of the lunging horses, and fired.

The white man before the wagon had been raising his own rifle. As the bullet cut into his upper left thigh, he stumbled backward, turning to his right and triggering the Winchester wild. No, not wild. The third man who'd been standing over there—a tall, thin, shaggy-headed man— gave a yelp and grabbed his own right thigh. He was holding a pistol and a bottle, but now he dropped the bottle and bent down to inspect his leg, cursing loudly.

"Damn, Talon!" he screeched, looking in glassy-eyed exasperation at the man now lying on the ground howling and holding his own wounded leg. "You *shot* me!"

With those two down, Slash aimed the geldings at the Indian. The Indian saw him coming and raised his own rifle. But the horses were right on him, so he threw the rifle aside and wheeled to run. Only, he was too drunk and too slow. The left puller barreled into his back, throwing him to the ground and then trampling him. Slash saw him on the ground, hammered by the hooves. Then the wagon passed over him and he was behind it.

Slash stopped the team to skidding halts, half turning them, half turning the wagon, kicking up dirt and gravel. The horses whinnied and shook their heads, not appreciating the fire. Slash leaped out of the wagon and hit the ground on both feet, forgetting about his ankle. His knees buckled and hit the ground.

"*Ow—dammit!*"

"You damn fool!" Pecos scolded him, leaping out of his side of the wagon, running around behind it, leveling his rifle on the three drunk, sorry-looking killers.

Slash straightened, holding both pistols now, stumbling forward. The Indian, who must be Black Pot, lay groaning on the ground, caked with dust, bloody from cuts the wagon's two horses had inflicted. His clothes—calico shirt trimmed with a beaded necklace, and black denims with high-topped moccasins—were torn. He was spitting and hissing like a leg-trapped bobcat. When he saw Slash limping toward him, his coal-black eyes glittered, and he reached for one of the two pearl-gripped pistols bristling from black leather holsters on his hips.

Slash crouched over him and rapped the barrel of his right Colt across the big Indian's left temple. "Ow!" the man squealed, clutching his head with both hands. He lay on his back, rolling from side to side and howling.

Quickly, Slash ripped both guns from the man's holsters and tossed them down the hill and into some brush. Pecos was already disarming the man who Slash assumed was Talon Chaney, a muscular beast with close-cropped brown hair and a head like a miniature boulder shaped by the chisel of some drunken, dark god. The man's eyes didn't appear to line up right. He was covered in tattoos.

The other man, who had to be Hell-Raisin' Frank Beecher,

lay parallel to the church's front step. He was clutching his wounded leg with both hands, howling, shaking his head and his dirty tumbleweed of long, curly hair. He was too preoccupied with his health at the moment to be an imminent threat.

Meanwhile, the fire from the brush was chewing into the church's walls. Men and women and children were screaming inside. A baby was howling.

Slash limped quickly past Pecos, heading for the front door. "Watch these vermin!"

"I got 'em!"

Slash hurried up the church's front steps. The church doors had been locked by shoving a stout two-by-four through the door's wooden handles.

"Christ!"

Slash holstered his Colts and yanked the two-by-four out of the handles. He pulled a door open and two men burst through the opening, nearly shoving Slash down off the steps. The men were coughing into the handkerchiefs they held over their mouths and noses. Smoke roiled through the opening around them.

"Come on out!" Slash yelled, waving his hand to clear the smoke, trying to see through the open doors. "You're safe! Come on out!"

He stepped back as several more men and women and a few children ran through the doors, bent over, coughing, sobbing, crying, the baby wailing in a young woman's arms.

Slash turned away from the doors and back to the prisoners. Pecos had them well in hand. Chaney and Black Pot, stripped of their weapons, lay side by side. Chaney was wrapping a bandanna around his wounded leg. Pecos was just then burying the toe of his right boot into Hell-Raisin' Frank Beecher's gut.

"I told you to keep your hands away from your hoglegs!" Pecos bellowed at him. The man flopped onto his back, wailing, and Pecos bent over at the waist, yelling, "You hard o' hearin', amigo?"

"I'm shot!" Beecher hollered. "I'm wounded! I'm bleeding! I need a doctor!"

"We oughta throw you into that church an' let you burn!" Slash yelled at the man, thrusting his arm and finger out to point at the church from which the dozen or so citizens of Dry Fork had emerged to gather in a group in front of the burning building, composing themselves. "Give me one good reason why we shouldn't do that? Give me one good reason why we shouldn't drill bullets through your ugly heads right now!"

He turned to look at Chaney and Black Pot. Chaney lay on his side now, propped on an elbow. He regarded Slash, grinning, as though Slash had just told him a joke he'd found royally amusing. Black Pot was sitting Indian style, still caked with dust, his eyes pain-pinched. But even the big Indian was curling half of his thick, chapped upper lip in a jeering grin at Slash.

Beecher, however, just held his bullet-torn leg in both hands and screamed, "Doctor! I need a doctor, damn you! I'm gonna bleed dry here!"

"Shut up!" Pecos told him.

"Don't mind ole Hell-Raisin' Frank," said Talon Chaney, slurring his words. "He never could stand the sight of his own blood!"

He and Black Pot laughed.

Slash cast his frustrated gaze at Pecos.

Pecos returned it, shook his head. "Well, we got 'em, anyway, partner."

Slash nodded. He looked at the church. It was nearly fully consumed and the wind from the fire was blowing against him. He turned to the people who'd been locked in there. Now they were making their way down the hill, heading toward the burned town by ones and twos and threes, looking like survivors of a very large and savage battle.

Or a massacre. Yeah, that's what this had been. A damned massacre.

Slash looked at the three killers. They were sweating and dirty. They smelled like something dead, like smoke and sour whiskey. Slash spat to one side. He ran a grimy sleeve across his mouth. "Let's get these animals into their cages, Pecos. And get the hell out of here."

Pecos turned to Beecher. "You heard the man."

"Go to hell!" Beecher said.

"Who the hell are you?" This from Talon Chaney, now sneering at the two ex-cutthroats. "The U.S. marshals sent a couple of *old men* to take *us* to Denver?"

Slash limped up before Chaney and Black Pot. "You two get your raggedy asses into that cage, or I'll shoot you both right here."

"You ain't gonna make it." Black Pot smiled knowingly and shook his head. "No, sir—you two old men ain't gonna make it. You don't know who you're dealing with, amigo."

"You got till the count of three to stand up," Slash told them, aiming his pistols out and down, clicking both hammers back.

"You too, Frank," Pecos told Beecher.

"One," Slash said, smiling coldly down at Chaney and the Indian. "Two . . ."

"All right, all right." Chaney grimaced, started to rise, then sat back down and extended his hand toward Slash. "I'm gonna need a hand, though. You done shot me good, old man. You crippled me!"

Slash narrowed an eye and aimed down the Colt's barrel, planting a bead on Chaney's forehead. In the dead center of the man's forehead, two inches above his wedge-like nose. He started to squeeze the trigger. Chaney slid his brown eyes toward Slash's trigger finger and snapped his eyes wide in terror. *"All right! All right!"* He pushed off the ground with a grunt, gaining his feet and glaring at Slash. "I'll be damned if you wasn't about to do it."

"I'd be damned if you're not right," Slash said with a grin.

"We're criminals," Chaney said, thumbing himself in his lumpy chest. "We got rights!"

"Not on this ride," Pecos said behind Slash.

Slash had just switched his gaze from Chaney to Black Pot, when the Indian gave a wild cry and sprang off his heels. He moved so fast and unexpectedly that by the time Slash got his Colts turned toward him, Black Pot's head was already smashing into Slash's chest and the Indian's long arms were wrapped around Slash's waist.

Black Pot slammed Slash over backward.

Slash triggered both Colts into the ground where Black Pot had just been sitting before he'd made that puma-like leap. With the big Indian full on top of him, Slash flew up off his feet and hit the ground with a loud *whuff!* as the air exploded from his lungs. Black Pot gave another wild cry and reached for one of Slash's Colts.

A shadow passed over Slash. Slash saw the butt of a rifle swing over him, making a soft, whistling sound before it connected with Black Pot's left temple, making a solid thumping sound. Black Pot flew off of Slash and crumpled up on the ground beside him. Out like a blown lamp.

Slash looked up at Pecos standing over him. Slash's brains were still scrambled from Black Pot's assault, but Pecos must have seen the expression on his face when Slash saw Frank Beecher run at Pecos from behind. Pecos wheeled, swinging his rifle again like a club.

"Oaf!" Beecher said, staggering backward and grabbing his own left temple. "Oh, oh, oh!" He turned full around, dropped to his knees, then fell facedown in the dirt.

Talon Chaney started toward Slash, but by now Slash had gotten his wits about him enough that he raised both his Colts again at the tattoo-laden monster before him. Chaney stopped, resting most of his weight on his good leg.

"Go ahead," Slash said. "Please, do it. I really want you to do it, Chaney. Take one step. I'm begging you."

Chaney glared down at him. He looked at the unconscious Black Pot, then at the unconscious Beecher. He returned his defiant gaze to Slash and held his hands up in surrender. "Not now," he said, and spat to one side. "I'll save it for later."

CHAPTER 14

Jaycee Breckenridge clutched the pearl-gripped, .32-caliber Colt Rainmaker to her breast and ran her thumb across the hammer. She pricked her ears to listen for sounds in the hallway outside the closed door of her third-floor suite.

So far this morning, the House of a Thousand Delights had been quiet, as it was most mornings. But a minute ago, she'd looked out the window to see Cisco Walsh making his way toward the saloon from the opposite side of the street, weaving through Camp Collins's early-morning traffic and puffing a fat cigar. He'd disappeared from the view from her window, and when he had—when she knew that he was mounting the front porch steps on his way inside the saloon/brothel/gambling parlor—she'd found herself hurrying over to her armoire and pulling out the small wooden drawer in which she kept the Rainmaker.

Now she sat in a brocade armchair by her unlit fireplace, clad in only her nightgown and velvet auburn robe, clutching the snub-nosed popper to her breasts. She could feel her heart beating against the pistol as she remembered

the conversation, almost word for word, she'd overheard the
night before through the billiard room door:

"That team will be hauling eighty thousand dollars in
bullion, Walsh, and—"

"I know how much it will be carrying, Hall. I just don't
want your men to—"

"Like I said, we'll all be there to make sure everything
goes off without a—"

"At Horsetooth Station?"

"Yes, that's where I said we'd meet. We'll get back to you
on the exact night. Now, look, Marshal, if you're getting
cold feet, let me remind you of a little problem in your
past. One that likely would not—"

That was when Hall's voice had stopped abruptly, as
though someone on the other side of the door, realizing
they were being overheard, had waved him to silence.

Jay wondered—had, in fact, wondered all through the
long, sleepless night—if Walsh and Hall knew that she'd
overheard their nefarious plans. They must have. She
remembered how her hand had shaken when she'd set
the brandy bottle on the table, and how when she'd
looked at Walsh, he'd been looking at her shaking hand.

Why else would she have been shaking—unless she had
just heard that Walsh had thrown in with a plan to rob
eighty thousand dollars in bullion routed from one of the
mountain mines through Camp Collins and probably to the
railroad several miles east? Cisco Walsh—the handsome,
dashing, brash, and upstanding western lawman himself!

Jay wondered how long he'd been riding on both sides
of the law.

She wondered if he knew that Jay was now privy to his
secret. She wondered what he would do about it if he was,

which he most certainly was. Would he try to kill her? Try to *have her* killed?

And what was she going to do to foil his robbery scheme? It had to be foiled. Not that Jay held herself up as some great upstanding citizen. After all, she'd once run with outlaws herself. But she couldn't allow that bullion to be robbed. She was a part of the legitimate business community here now, and she had to do her part to maintain law and order. Since she was likely the only one who knew about it, and of Walsh's betrayal to the citizens of Camp Collins, she felt the weight of her responsibility. . . .

Boots sounded on the stairs.

Clomp! Clomp! Clomp!

Slow, steady, echoing thuds. Each one followed by the trilling of a spur. It was almost as though he was trying to sound menacing. Trying to put the fear of God into her . . .

Almost?

Maybe that's exactly what he was doing. For it most surely was Walsh on the stairs. He usually paid her a visit in the morning at the Thousand Delights. But never this early and never upstairs, in her room. Since she worked late, she usually slept in and didn't go down for breakfast until ten or eleven. Sometimes Walsh would join her in the dining room off the saloon. Not every morning, but maybe once or twice a week.

He'd come early this morning, however *and he was coming all the way up to her room* because he was eager to find out if Jay really had overheard that telling conversation. He'd probably gotten as little sleep as Jay herself had, wondering what she knew. Wondering what she would do with the information if she did, indeed, know . . .

Boots thumped in the hallway, growing louder.

Spurs rang.

Her hands shaking slightly, Jay flicked open the Rainmaker's loading gate and checked the cylinder, turning it slowly, quietly, not wanting the faint clicks to be heard in the hall. When she saw that brass resided in each chamber, Jay flicked the loading gate closed. She gasped when the thudding stopped in the hall outside her door.

She gasped again, nearly dropping the pistol, when three light taps sounded on her door. Cisco Walsh's voice: "Jay?"

She drew a breath to calm herself. "Y-Yes?"

"Are you up?"

She paused, her mind working. "*Just* up. I haven't bathed yet, Cisco. What can I help you with?" Did her voice sound several octaves higher than usual, or did it just seem that way to her?

There was a discomfiting pause followed by his menacingly quiet, even voice: "Can I come in, Jay? I'd like a word."

A scream rose inside Jay's head. She looked down at her hand holding the Rainmaker. It was shaking. She closed her left hand over it, squeezing, trying to formulate a response. She could not let him into her room. That might be a big mistake. Maybe the biggest mistake of her life.

Maybe he was reading her mind, because before she could respond, he said, as though trying a different tactic, "I was wondering if you'd join me for breakfast."

Um . . . "It's a little early for me, Cisco. And I haven't bathed yet." She tried to think. She didn't want to see him today. She wasn't sure what she would say. She needed time to compose herself . . . to come up with a plan . . .

She was just too damn nervous!

"I have a rather busy day ahead, in fact," she said, speaking a little too quickly, though she couldn't get herself to slow down. "Perhaps later in the week . . . ?"

A pause. A *long* pause.

Then, Cisco's voice sounding a bit miffed: "Perhaps."

A floorboard in the hall squeaked. Footsteps thudded, dwindling, as the town marshal walked off toward the stairs.

Jay let out the breath she hadn't realized she'd been holding. Resting the revolver on her right thigh, she sank back in the chair, relief washing over her. It was a short-lived relief. As she heard Cisco's boots retreating down the stairs, echoing in the quiet building, Jay's heart picked up its rushed beating again.

What was she going to do about the robbery? Somehow, she had to stop it.

How?

Walsh was the law here in town—the man she would normally go to in such a situation. But he was the man who'd caused the situation. One of them, anyway.

Should she go to one of his deputies?

No. If he was planning the robbery, one or all of his three deputies might be in on it, as well. Possibly not, but it was not a risk she could take. If she wasn't careful, she was liable to get herself killed. She wasn't sure if Cisco was capable of murdering her to keep the robbery secret, but then she hadn't thought him capable of robbing a stagecoach, either.

Cisco Walsh—the brash, legendary, upstanding western lawman!

He and Jason Hall, a widely respected rancher, were

planning to rob eighty thousand dollars from one of the local mines.

Why?

Never mind that. They were, that's all.

And Jay had to do something to stop it.

She drummed her fingers on the arm of the chair. She so wished that Slash and Pecos weren't out on one of Bledsoe's assignments. She needed Slash here with her. He would help her figure out what to do.

Maybe she should contact the Chief Marshal in Denver. Perhaps the county sheriff . . . ? Maybe she should walk over to the courthouse this morning and get the whole troublesome issue off her chest.

The more her mind swirled and her palms sweat, she realized that she needed someone to talk to. She had few close friends, however. Jay was a good businesswoman, but her business interests hadn't left time for cultivating personal relationships with anyone except Slash, who'd been a friend of hers for many, many years. And Cisco, of course. He'd been an old friend, too. One whom she'd just learned was not really who she'd thought he was . . .

Her heart thudded at the whole improbable, confounding notion.

One face rose from the murk of her muddied thinking. Myra.

Next to Slash and Pecos, Myra Thompson was her closest friend even though Myra was years younger. Jay saw a lot of her younger self in the pretty, savvy young ex-outlaw girl. . . .

Myra was street-smart, wise beyond her years. She might have some ideas about what Jay should do with the devastating information she knew about Walsh and Hall, whether she should go to the sheriff or the marshal . . .

Jay herself was a little wary of all lawmen due, of course, in no small part to her own shady past.

Having decided what she would do first, she flung away her robe and dressed in a simple, salmon-colored day frock. She gave her hair a quick brushing, leaving it down so she could wear a hat, then grabbed the felt topper she wore around town, to give her some protection from the merciless Colorado sun. She shrugged into a brown leather vest, pulled on a pair of kid riding gloves, and moved to the door.

She stopped, looked back at where she'd left the revolver on the brocade armchair. Should she take the weapon? She shook her head. Too heavy and cumbersome. Opting for the Lady Derringer she kept in her underwear drawer, she retrieved the silver-washed, over-and-under popper, which didn't weigh much over a pound, and stuck it into her right vest pocket. It hardly made a bulge; not one that most people would notice, anyway. She doubted that Walsh or Hall would accost her on the street, but Jay wasn't one for taking chances. There was much about Walsh she didn't know. How could she be certain he wouldn't send some skulking brigand to drag her off and murder her?

She strode to the door again, opened it slowly, and poked her head into the hall. It was quiet and empty. No sign of the marshal. No sign of anyone, for that matter. Good.

She stepped into the hall, locked the door, pocketed the key, and headed off toward the hall's west end, where there was a door to a hidden rear stairway mostly used by housekeepers and Jay's sporting girls when they didn't want to be seen coming and going from their rooms. She dropped quietly down the stairs, glad to see none of the girls or housekeepers on it, preferring not to be seen leaving the Thousand Delights this time of the day, which was rare for her. She didn't want to appear furtive and arouse suspicion, or to have to parry questions.

The stairs let out into the kitchen, but the saloon's back door was only a few feet away. A couple of cooks were working at the range, but they had their backs to Jay, so she managed to slip out of the building without being seen.

"Good morning, Randall," she said to the young man who tended the Thousand Delight's feed barn and corral during the day. "Would you mind hitching the mare to my buggy for me, please?"

The young man had been tending the horses of two of Jay's overnight guests, a couple of cattle buyers from Chicago who were likely still asleep upstairs with their respective girls. He turned to Jay with a curious expression, which Jay countered immediately with: "And let's keep my little outing this morning just between you and me— shall we, Randall?"

She knew the young man to be the gossip rival of any women's quilting party, though she couldn't blame him. He no doubt got quite lonely working back here most of the day alone, only seeing customers briefly as they came and went.

"Oh, yes, ma'am—of course, Miss Jay. I won't say nothin' to no one." Randall ran a big, thick, dirty hand down the front of his pin-striped overalls that bulged over his considerable belly. He frowned at his pretty boss from beneath the floppy brim of his shapeless black hat, looking troubled. "I won't tell . . . er, I mean . . ."

Jay frowned. "You won't what, Randall?"

"I won't tell . . . I won't tell . . . um . . ."

Jay felt her frown grow more severe. "You won't tell who *what*, Randall?"

"Um . . . well . . . the marshal was back here a few minutes ago. He . . . um . . ." Randall toed a fresh horse apple.

Apprehension placed a cold hand against the small of Jay's back. "He what? Perhaps he asked you to let him know if I went anywhere today . . . ?"

Her heart thudded.

"Yes, ma'am," Randall said, looking sheepishly down at the scuffed toes of his boots. "He did do that, ma'am. He told me not to tell, but since you're my boss an' all . . ." Again, he let his voice trail off as he continued to toe the apple, looking severely consternated.

Jay caught her breath, then said, "Thank you for telling me, Randall. Please don't do what the marshal asked you to do, all right? I can't tell you why. I just don't want you to do it. If he returns and asks you whether I left, please tell him no. Will you do that?"

"Yes, ma'am. You're the lady I work for, so . . ."

"Right. I hate to ask you to lie, but under the circumstances it's important that you do. Now, please hitch the mare to my buggy. I'm in a hurry."

"Right away, ma'am!"

As Randall grabbed a rope with which to capture the mare in the rear paddock, Jay turned to face the barn's open doors, pressing her hand over her fast-beating heart.

CHAPTER 15

Jay took the most circumspect route possible between the House of a Thousand Delights saloon to Slash and Pecos's livery yard. For reasons that were now obvious after her conversation with Randall, she didn't want Walsh and his deputies to see her.

She took a backstreet from the saloon and drove east for nearly a mile before swinging across the main trail, near the now-abandoned army outpost, and heading north of town, approaching the livery yard on the town's northeast side from its rear.

She parked the buggy behind the main barn. The two hostlers were giving the barn a new roof, removing the old shakes and replacing them with new ones. Jay strode up along the barn's northeast side, looking for Myra but also peering north, making sure she hadn't been followed. She didn't like the fearful knot she'd been feeling in the pit of her stomach ever since she'd inadvertently eavesdropped on Walsh and Hall. She didn't like having to keep looking behind her back, wondering if her life was in danger.

"Jay?"

She swung around with a start. She'd been gazing north

while she'd walked, not realizing that she'd reached the front of the barn. Myra stood in front of the barn's open doors. A big mule stood behind her. She had her back to the mule and was holding the big beast's left front hoof up between her denim-clad legs. She held a hoof file in both gloved hands while gazing at Jay expectantly, brows arched in surprise.

"Oh, Lord!" Jay said with a relieved chuff, slapping a hand to her chest. "You gave me a start!"

"You gave me one, too!" Myra laughed a little nervously, then opened her knees to release the mule's hoof, which dropped to the ground with a thud. Straightening, she swiped her bare arm across her sweaty forehead—the sleeves of her checked work shirt were rolled up to her elbows—and said, "Where did you come from, anyway?"

"Behind the barn."

"Oh." Myra leaned forward a little to stare along the side of the barn toward the rear. She gave Jay a dubious look. "What were you doing back there?"

"Hiding."

Myra jerked her head back skeptically. "Huh?"

Jay stared toward Camp Collins proper, to the south. The heart of the town lay roughly a half mile from the livery yard. She didn't see anyone close around except Myra and the two hostlers pounding their hammers up on the barn's roof. A farm wagon bounced along a near street, a straw-hatted man in the driver's seat, a brown dog sitting beside him. That was the only movement on this side of town. "I didn't want Cisco Walsh or any of his deputies to see me."

"Why not?" Myra said with a laugh.

Jay stepped forward and squeezed Myra's left forearm. "I know this is going to sound crazy, but I think Cisco might be out to kill me." There, she'd said the words aloud for the first time, and a swell of emotion rose inside of her. She gave a single, involuntary sob, then clamped the back of her hand over her mouth.

Myra gaped at her. "Jay, you're serious!"

Paranoid, Jay looked around once more, then up at the two men working on the barn. One glanced at her skeptically. She canted her head toward the main cabin and freight office to her left. "Myra, can we . . . ?"

"Oh, sure, sure. Let's go over to the office."

She returned the hoof file to the barn, then walked back up past the mule standing obediently in place.

"What about him?" Jay said, canting her head at the sleepy-eyed mule.

"That's old Mordecai," Myra said, starting toward the office. "He won't stray far from the hay crib. He'll probably just stand there and sleep in the sun. I'll get back to him later."

"I'm sorry to interrupt," Jay said as she and Myra walked toward the office in the intensifying morning sunlight. She glanced at the two men on the barn. "You keep yourself busy over here, don't you, Myra?"

"Yeah, well, there's a lot to do, and Emil Becker didn't keep the place in great repair. That barn's been leaking for years, I'm sure." Becker was the old man whom Slash and Pecos had bought the business from. "There's too much work for the hostlers, so I help out with the mules when I can. I like taking breaks from the account books, which Becker didn't leave in much better shape than his buildings, and Slash and Pecos—"

"Aren't much better, I'm sure," Jay finished for her.

Myra said with a chuckle, "I suppose bank robbers don't have much need for accounting skills."

"Yeah, all they did with their loot was split it up and flee to Mexico."

They both laughed, but Jay heard the tightness in her own mirth.

As she and Myra mounted the office's front stoop, Myra said, "Would you like some milk? I bought some fresh from Mr. Sunday just an hour ago and stowed it away in the springhouse. Should be nice and cool by now."

Jay shrugged. "That sounds good." She hadn't had breakfast yet. She was too nervous to be hungry, but she thought the milk might do her some good.

"Why don't you wait out here, and I'll fetch it from the springhouse?"

Jay grabbed Myra before the girl could turn away. "Myra, do you think we could go inside?" She cast another nervous glance toward town.

"Oh, sure," Myra said, casting her own skeptical glance toward town. "Sure, we can. Go on in and I'll fetch the milk."

"Thank you, dear."

While Myra stepped off the stoop and walked around the office to the springhouse behind it, Jay stepped through the office's front door. There was a desk in here and several tables cluttered with account books and other office paraphernalia. Emil Becker had hung hides and animal skulls on the walls, as well as horseshoes and a pair of snowshoes that he likely used during his winter freight-hauling treks into the snowy mountains. Myra had done her best to clean the place out, but her main order of business had been getting the accounts in order for Slash and Pecos, who had brought in their own brand of chaos, which she, too, had to juggle.

Though they'd both wanted the freighting business to

be their main employment now that they were getting too old for robbing trains anymore, it had turned out to be more of a front for the unofficial lawdogging they were doing for Chief Marshal Bledsoe.

Jay pulled a chair out from the planks that served as a table running along the front of the room, beneath the window, and sank into it with a sigh. Boots thumped on the stoop, and Myra came with a glass bottle filled with creamy milk nearly as yellow as whipped butter. She set the bottle on the table near Jay.

"I have a couple of clean glasses in here," Myra said, and disappeared into the addition off the shack's east side, which was her private living quarters. She came back with two glasses and set them down near the bottle. "Hot out there already," she said, and popped the cork on the bottle. "I was ready for a break."

She glanced at Jay. Jay sat staring through the window before her, frowning.

"Here's your milk," Myra said, sliding the glass she'd just filled toward Jay.

Jay placed her hand on the glass but left it on the table. She continued to stare out the window. "Thank you."

Myra filled the second glass, then retrieved the chair behind her paper and ledge-littered desk. She pulled it up beside Jay and sank into it, studying Jay closely.

She took a couple of sips of the milk, then set the glass back down on the table.

"All right," she said, wiping her mouth with the back of her hand. "Why would the town marshal be out to kill you, Jay?"

"Sounds crazy, doesn't it?" Jay gave a dry chuckle and glanced at the young, brown-haired woman sitting beside her, regarding her skeptically. "Just hearing you say it makes me question my own sanity. But here's the thing, Myra." Jay turned around to face the younger woman. She placed her hands on the girl's knees. Keeping her voice low and secretive, she said, "I overheard a conversation between Cisco Walsh and Jason Hall last night, around midnight, in the Thousand Delights. I think they plan to rob a gold shipment at Horsetooth Station."

"When?"

Jay flinched with surprise. "What?"

"When do they plan to rob the stage?" Myra took another sip of her milk, then rested the glass in her lap. She regarded Jay seriously.

"You believe me?"

"Of course. Why would you make something like that up? I know you're not crazy. And I know how men are. Even *lawmen*. Walsh certainly wouldn't be the first crooked town marshal I've ever run into." Again, she sipped her milk, then brushed the mustache away with her hand.

Jay sank back in her chair, vaguely relieved that the girl believed her. Myra's believing her so quickly and easily was a little troublesome, though, too. That meant that Jay was, indeed, probably right. That she hadn't overheard wrong or been confused.

Walsh and Hall really were going to rob a gold run from one of the mines.

Now she had no choice but to do something about it.

"I don't know when," Jay said. "Some night this week is all they said. That's the problem. All I'm certain of is *where*—at Horsetooth Station."

"What're you going to do?" Myra asked.

Such a simple, direct question. But there it was.

"I don't know." Jay looked around at the cluttered, rough-hewn office and at the door flanking Myra's desk that led back to the ex-cutthroats' personal quarters. "I sure wish Slash and Pecos were here, though. I'll tell you that."

"I reckon what we need to find out is when this robbery is supposed to take place."

"Yes, but *how*?" Jay said.

"Right . . ."

Jay sipped her milk and pondered the problem. "Or, maybe . . ."

"Or what?" Myra asked.

"We could turn it over to the sheriff, let him take care of it."

"The sheriff isn't in town," Myra said, running a thumbnail around the milky rim of her glass.

Jay frowned at her. "How do you know?"

"Delbert told me."

"Delbert?"

"Delbert Thayer. One of Matt McGuire's deputies." Matt McGuire was the Larimer County Sheriff.

"Is that the . . . the . . . young man I've seen mooning around after you . . . ?"

Jay had seen a tall, skinny young man following Myra around the freight yard while she'd been doing her chores, his hat in his hands, or perched atop a corral, snapping lucifer matches to life on his thumbnail. Jay had thought she'd seen a badge on the young man's shirt.

"One and the same," Myra said with a weary sigh. "I met him in the post office and he's been doggin' my heels ever since. Wants me to go on a picnic or some such, as though I had time for such foolishness." She shook her head full of auburn curls in disgust. "Anyways, he told me the sheriff is away at some convention of mucky-mucks down in Santa Fe. While he's gone, he's seein' some sawbones down there about an ache he's been having in his belly. Won't be back for a while. So it's just Delbert and McGuire's two other deputies—both dumb as posts and useless as gophers, if you ask me—holding down the fort. Er, the courthouse, leastways . . ."

Jay chuckled as she stared at the girl. Myra was as pretty as they came, and it amused Jay that she had no time for the opposite sex. At least, none her age. It was the big, lumbering, and much older Pecos she'd set her hat for. In that way, as in so many other ways, Myra reminded Jay of herself back when she'd fallen for the mossy-horned old hoorawer, Pistol Pete Johnson. . . .

"What's funny?" Myra said, arching a brow at her.

"You and Delbert Thayer."

"Believe me, there is no *me and Delbert Thayer*. There is just *Delbert Thayer*, who comes dragging his heels over here from time to time, though I have given him absolutely no reason to do so."

"You're beautiful and he's in love with you," Jay said, reaching up to tuck a lock of unruly curls behind the girl's left ear. "You can't blame him for that."

"He's a young fool. He'll never make a man. McGuire made him deputy because McGuire's his uncle and Delbert's mother made him do it. McGuire lets him sweep out the office and tend the horses and occasionally collect county taxes, little more."

"Hmmm . . ." Jay was back to pondering her own situation. "I don't know how to do it, but somehow we have to stop that robbery, Myra. I . . . and now you . . . are the only ones who know about it. The people of Camp Collins need to know who . . . and *what* . . . Cisco Walsh really is."

"Much easier said than done," Myra said with a sigh. She leaned forward and placed her hand on Jay's. "I'll talk to Delbert. He's not as dumb as he looks, and if he can help me out, he'll tumble all over himself trying. He might have an idea how we can stop that stage robbery."

Jay studied her, thinking. She could wire the Chief Marshal in Denver, but it would likely take him a couple of days to send a man or two over this way. Also, ole Bleed-Em-So might figure it's out of his federal jurisdiction.

Hell, since he knew her own outlaw history, he might not even believe her.

"All right," Jay said, nodding slowly. "What other choice do we have?"

CHAPTER 16

"Do you want another card?"

"Huh?"

"Do you want another card?"

Pecos looked down at the cards in his hands. He and Slash were sitting in Carlisle's, sipping whiskey. Outside, a storm was brewing, so they'd decided to cool their heels overnight here in the burned-out town of Dry Fork.

"Nah."

"Well, I do."

"Give yourself one, then."

"All right, I will." Slash snorted with amusement and hit himself. He looked at Pecos sitting on the other side of the table, staring into the heavy shadows at the room's rear. "What do you have?"

"Huh?"

Slash gave another snort. It was a disgusted one this time. "What do you have?"

"I don't know."

"Let me see." Slash reached across the table and looked at his partner's cards. He glared at Pecos. "For a man who's not payin' much attention to poker, you sure filled out a nice hand for yourself!"

His straight wouldn't beat Pecos's full house. He slapped his own cards on the table. "I ain't gonna play cards with you if you're gonna win without even payin' attention, dammit!"

"Look at her over there."

"Hmmm?"

"Look at her."

Pecos's gaze was on the only citizen aside from Stanley Donovan that he and Slash had found still alive in Dry Fork. After they'd ridden back into town with the jail wagon and their three kill-crazy prisoners, they'd found her sitting on Carlisle's porch steps. She hadn't said a word when Slash and Pecos had pulled the jail wagon up in front of the saloon. She'd been beaten, obviously. Cuts marred her otherwise pretty, brown-eyed face. Her dark blue dress was badly torn, almost ripped off her body. Her thick, long brown hair was badly disheveled, with dirt, leaves, and weed seeds clinging to it.

She'd tried to run when she'd seen the prisoners, but Pecos had run her down, calmed her, and gotten her to go into Carlisle's, since that was about the only reasonable shelter left standing. She'd needed a roof over her head, for the storm had been brewing even then. She hadn't said a word then, and she still hadn't. She just sat alone at her table, a blanket wrapped around her otherwise bare shoulders. She sat staring down expressionlessly at the shot of whiskey and cup of coffee Pecos had set before her, having brewed a pot of mud on the saloon's potbelly stove.

While Pecos had tended the woman, Slash had dragged the four bodies out of the saloon, laying the aproned man and the doxie, as well as the two dead gang members, out in the back alley flanking the place. He didn't know what else to do with them. The rest of the dead folks in the town were still laying out exposed, and there was nothing to be done about that.

Slash and Pecos couldn't take the time and expend the energy that would be needed to gather them all and bury them. They'd have to let nature run its course, which, regrettably, meant leaving the dead citizens of Dry Fork to the predators. The killers deserved nothing better, but the innocent citizens did.

"What about her?" Slash said.

"She looks miserable. Poor gal."

"She'll come around."

"What do you suppose they done to her?"

Slash scowled across the table at him, through the smoke rising from his cigarette. "You know what they done to her."

Pecos turned in his chair to glare out the saloon doors at the jail wagon parked in the street, where they'd left it. Since the livery barn was gone, Slash had hobbled both geldings and his and Slash's horses in the lot beside Carlisle's, where they'd have a little shelter from the storm. The prisoners sat slumped in the wagon's steel cage, the wind blowing their hair, lifting street dust up around them as the storm settled over the town.

"I feel like going over there and shooting all three. Shooting them down like hydrophobic curs."

"Don't cheat the hangman, Pecos," Slash said, blowing a plume of smoke into the air. "He's gotta eat, too."

"Still, though," Pecos grumbled, "what's the point?"

"Like I said . . ."

"Yeah, I know what you said," Pecos said. "Hangman's gotta eat, too."

"You wanna play another hand?"

"No, I'm not in the mood for cards. How can you be?"

"What do you mean?" Slash asked.

"The whole damn town—well, most of it, anyway—is dead! Buildings burned." Pecos looked at the young woman still staring down at her whiskey. She didn't appear to have touched either of her drinks. "Women savaged . . ."

"Hey, where's Donovan?"

"I seen him tryin' to run down a horse when we were pulling back into town. I think he wanted to get a long, long way away from those three out there." Pecos hooked a thumb over his shoulder, indicating the jail wagon. "He's probably to the next county by now."

Slash sucked on his quirley, blew out another smoke plume.

"Nothin' really gets to you, does it?" Pecos said, giving Slash a hard, critical look. "I mean, a whole town has been sacked and you just sit there, playin' cards, smokin' your quirley, and drinkin' your whiskey."

Slash raised his shot glass. "Whiskey helps cut the smell." He threw back the last of the shot and poured out another one.

"A whole town burned, murdered," Pecos said, wagging his head slowly as he stared at the table.

"Here," Slash said. "Have some more whiskey. Make you feel better." He refilled his partner's glass.

Pecos gave him another hard stare and said with a sigh, "You're cold, Slash."

"Not really," Slash said. "Just used to it."

"Hey, you in there!" Talon Chaney shouted from the jail wagon. "You gotta bring us in outta the rain. It's startin' to come down hard out here!"

Slash and Pecos shared a chuckle.

Slash grabbed his shot glass and rose from his chair. "I'm gonna go out and enjoy the rain. I always did enjoy a summer storm."

He sauntered out the batwings and stood on the covered porch. The rain was coming down hard. It looked like a gauzy curtain dropping at an angle over the black mounded ruins of the town. It was as dark as dusk. Lightning sparked in the swollen bellies of cloud the color of bruised plumbs.

"Yeah, this is a good one," Slash said above the hammering rain and crashing thunder, smiling out into the street.

"Come on!" Chaney bellowed. He and his two fellow prisoners slumped against the onslaught, the rain thrashing them, pouring off their heads and shoulders. "This ain't right! At least take us into the jail!"

"You're gonna stay right where you are!" Pecos yelled back at the man. He'd come out to stand beside Slash, his whiskey glass in his hand. "Maybe it'll wash your sins away. I don't think so, but it's worth a try!" He chuckled.

Slash stepped over to his left and slumped into one of the several chairs arranged haphazardly around the porch, where they'd been occupied by the town's loafers in happier times. Before Talon Chaney et al. rode into town. "Yes, sir," he said, smiling at the storm. "I do like me a summer storm."

Pecos sat in a chair beside him, turning it around to face him, then leaning forward and crossing his big arms across the back of it. "Slash, what're we gonna do about that poor girl inside?"

"What do you mean?"

"Well, we're pullin' out tomorrow, correct?"

"Yeah."

"We can't just leave her here. Not in the state she's in."

Slash looked into the street again, this time with a pensive expression.

"I'll go with you."

The unfamiliar female voice behind them jerked them both around.

The young woman stood just outside the batwings, staring down at them. She held the blanket, shawl-like, around her shoulders.

"Good Lord!" Pecos rose from his chair. "Here, here, little lady. Come over here and sit down."

She stood where she was and said again, "I'll go with you. You're going to Denver, right?" She must have overheard them talking. "I'll go with you to Denver. That's where I'm from. I don't have anyone there anymore, but at least it's home." She gazed out into the street at the jail wagon and hardened her jaws, as well as her eyes. It's . . . it's better than this."

"Yeah, I'll say it is," Pecos said.

"They'll be comin' with us, too," Slash warned the young woman, whom he figured to be in her early to mid-twenties. She didn't look as pale as she had before. In fact, she even seemed to have some color in her naturally pale cheeks.

She stared at the jail wagon and said tonelessly, "I got nowhere else to go." She turned to Pecos, then to Slash, and said in a hard, demanding, frightened tone, "You'll keep them in there? You'll keep them caged? You won't ever let them out?"

"No, ma'am," Pecos said. "They won't be gettin' out of that cage till they're in Denver. My word's bond on that. You can ride along with us. It won't be a comfortable trip, but we'll keep you safe, all right." He gestured at the chair. "Come over here and sit down."

She looked at the chair, drew a breath, then walked over and sat in it.

"What's your name?" Slash asked.

Staring out at the rain, she said again in her low, flat voice, "Jenny. Jenny Claymore."

"I'm Sla—er, I mean, I'm Jimmy. This big, ugly critter is Melvin."

"Jimmy and Melvin," she said. It wasn't a question. It was as though she were trying out the names on her tongue. She turned to them and with that bland expression again, she said, "Not Slash and Pecos?" She arched one brow skeptically.

Slash looked at Pecos. Pecos looked at Slash.

Smiling sheepishly, Pecos said, "We left them Slash an' Pecos days behind. You can call us Jimmy an' Melvin."

"Now you drive the U.S. marshal's jail wagon . . . ?"

"We do, indeed," Slash said, dragging out his makings pouch to roll another cigarette. "We've moved up in the world, me an' Melvin have."

"Melvin and I have," Jenny Claymore said.

Slash glanced at her, the drawstring of his makings sack in his teeth. "Huh?"

"I am . . . was . . . the schoolteacher here in town. *Melvin and I have moved up in the world.*"

"Oh," Slash said, glancing at Pecos again. "Well, Miss Jenny, since you're already back to work, you must be feelin' better."

"No," she said flatly, staring out through the rain and the storm-battered cage in the street. "After what those animals did to me . . . to this town . . . I don't think I'll ever feel *better* again."

"Here." Slash held out his shot glass to her. "Drink that. Make you feel better."

She took the glass and threw back the entire shot. She lowered her chin, squeezed her eyes closed, swallowed, and shook her head. She leaned forward to slam the glass down on the floor at her bare feet. Raising her head, she ran her hand across her mouth, then rubbed the hand dry on what remained of her dress.

She whipped her head to Slash. "Didn't do a thing."

Slash grimaced at her. He reached tentatively out toward the girl, not sure he should be making this intimate gesture after all she'd been through, but deciding to go through with it anyway, though it made him feel awkward and uncomfortable. He placed his hand on her shoulder, gave it a light squeeze.

"Give it time, Jenny."

He jerked with a start when she turned to him suddenly. He thought she was going to slap him, punch him, tell him to get the hell away from her. But she did no such thing. Her face crumpling, she sobbed, grabbed his arm, and squeezing it desperately with both hands, pressed her head against his shoulder. She wailed an animal-like wail that lifted the short hairs on the back of Slash's neck. He sat frozen in his chair, looking down at the girl bawling as she ground her face into his bicep.

He sat stiffly, tensely, not sure what to do, what to say.

He looked up at Pecos leaning back against the front of Carlisle's, and silently asked his partner for help.

Pecos smiled at him, as though to say: "All's well, Slash. Just ride it out."

Jenny lifted her head sharply and with a terrified gasp when one of the prisoners gave a loud whoop above the roar of the storm. The other two whooped and howled, as well, and then Talon Chaney shouted, "Well, hello there, Marshal! Ain't seen you in a while!"

Slash rose from his chair. Pecos pushed off the wall. He and Pecos shared a conferring glance, then walked up to the top of the porch steps, staring out into the street. A figure was moving toward Carlisle's from their right. The man moved slowly inside the buffeting gray curtain of rain. He walked with his arms hanging straight down at his sides, as though they were too heavy to lift. As he walked, he dragged the toes of his boots, and his knees bent precariously with each step, as though the strain of each step threatened to send him sprawling into the muddy street.

Something shiny shone on his shirt.

Jenny gasped and slapped her hand to her mouth. "Marshal Larsen," she said in a plaintive, tragic voice.

The man approaching Carlisle's and the jail wagon in which the prisoners yipped and yowled like moon-crazed coyotes took one more halting step before he fell forward into the mud and lay in the street as though dead.

CHAPTER 17

"Whoa!"

Slash hurried down Carlisle's steps and ran into the muddy street that had nearly become a river. Lightning forked over the burned-out town. Thunder crashed like cymbals. The rain lashing at him, instantly drenching him and sluicing off the brim of his black Stetson, Slash dropped to a knee beside the man who'd fallen in the street.

Beneath the storm he could hear the three human coyotes yipping and yowling in the jail wagon.

Pecos knelt on the other side of the fallen man and said, "Is he dead?"

"I can't tell."

"Let's get him into the saloon."

Slash grabbed the man's left arm, Pecos grabbed the man's right arm, and they pulled him up out of the mud. Immediately, the man began moving his head and muttering. He'd been badly beaten, his eyes swollen nearly shut, and his lips had been smashed and cut. Dried blood was caked on them, mixed with the mud of the street.

The former cutthroats each draped an arm of the beaten man around their necks and half led, half dragged him up the saloon steps. Slash could hear him groaning, grunting. Jenny Claymore held one of the batwings open as she stared in horror at the poor, beaten man whom Slash and Pecos led across the porch. Slash stepped through the open left door as Pecos bulled through the right one.

"Let's get him into a chair," Pecos said.

They led him over to their own table. Pecos kicked out a chair, and he and Slash eased the man into it. Slash retrieved a glass from the bar and splashed whiskey into it. He held it up to the beaten man in the chair.

"Here, son. Take a sip of that." He thought the whiskey would bring him around.

The man opened his swollen eyes to slits. He looked like a large, drowned rat, though Slash suspected he was fine to look at under all that mud and bruising. Slash figured he was in his late twenties. He was clean-shaven with short dark brown hair, and he wore a store-bought, three-piece suit. The mud-caked, five-pointed star pinned to his vest had the words TOWN MARSHAL engraved on it, though Slash could barely read the words for the mud.

The man raised his muddy right hand. He seemed to have trouble getting it to the glass, so Slash shoved the glass into it. The man closed his thumb and fingers around the glass, brought it to his lips, and sipped. He sipped again, again, and again, and then threw back the rest of the shot and swallowed.

He gritted his teeth, shook his head.

"Christ, she's dead!" he wailed, throwing his head back.

"Who's dead, son?" Pecos asked.

The young man lowered his head and sobbed.

"His wife," said Jenny Claymore, standing before the young town marshal, between Slash and Pecos. "He must mean his wife—Tiffanie."

The man sobbed for a couple of minutes while Slash and Pecos and Jenny Claymore stood looking down at him, helpless. Finally, the young marshal brushed his sleeve across his battered mouth and turned to stare out the window to his left, at the jail wagon obscured by the heavy wedding veils of falling rain.

"Animals," he grunted. "They beat me while Tiffanie screamed. They dragged her . . . inside."

He closed his eyes, gritted his teeth as the remembered images assailed him. "They dumped me in the ravine behind the house. I couldn't move. They beat me so hard, took my gun . . . beat me with it. I could hear them whooping and hollering. I could hear Tiffanie screaming and then . . ."

He sobbed, squeezed his eyes closed. "Then . . . slowly . . . her screams tapered off. I musta passed out . . . then woke up and I could smell the smoke . . . felt the heat of the fire."

He sobbed again, his head bobbing.

Again, he scrubbed a muddy sleeve across his mouth, sniffed, and said, "I . . . I tried to climb out of the ravine. I wanted to get to the house . . . to save her . . . but I passed out. Just came to when I felt the rain . . ." He sniffed, gritted his teeth again, and wailed, "*Oh, God—she's dead and I let them kill her!*"

"No, no," Slash said, patting the young man's back. "It wasn't your fault. Like you said, they're animals. Nothin' you could have done."

"I should have shot them while they slept, right here at Carlisle's! Shouldn't have even taken 'em into custody. Should have just shot 'em like the wild dogs they are!"

"No, you were just doin' your job," Pecos told him.

Slash looked at Pecos. "I think we'd best get him upstairs,

get him into a bed. He needs rest. Should have a doctor look at him, but . . ."

They both knew the doctor had hightailed it earlier, when the rampage had started, or he was dead along with the others who'd gotten caught in the killers' pillaging of Dry Fork.

"I'll look around and see if I can find some food," Jenny said. "I'll bring something up to him, try to get him to eat."

"Good idea," Slash said with a grunt as he and Pecos lifted the marshal out of the chair.

They helped him upstairs, moving slowly. He barely put any weight on either foot. He was injured, weak, and exhausted. They led him down the hall to a half-open door. Slash peered inside, making sure it was unoccupied. It was. Neither he nor Pecos had checked up here for survivors of the rampage, but they hadn't heard any noises, so they'd assumed everyone who'd been in the building— aside from the dead man and the dead whore they'd found downstairs—was either dead or had pulled out.

Judging by this empty room, anyway, it appeared they'd been right.

They gentled the marshal onto the rumpled bed. A half-filled thunder mug was stinking up the room, so Slash set it down the hall aways. When he returned to the room, the marshal was muttering, "Keep a lookout . . . rest of the gang . . ." He'd grabbed Pecos's arm and was squeezing it. Or at least trying to.

"What's he saying?" Slash asked.

"Something about the rest of the gang."

"What're you talkin' about, Marshal?" Slash stood over the man lying wet and muddy on the badly rumpled, sour-smelling bed. "You think the rest of the gang will come for those three outside?"

The marshal looked up at Slash through his swollen lids. "Two did," he croaked out. By the way he was wheezing, his ribs must be badly bruised or broken. "They must have split up after the robbery. Two of the others got word . . . came here to spring those three. You'd best . . ." He winced as pain spasmed through him. Lightning flashed in the window flanking the bed. "You'd best assume the others will get word and come for 'em, too."

"How many in the gang?" Pecos asked.

"At least twenty, I'm told."

Pecos started counting on his fingers.

"That leaves fifteen, you idiot," Slash told Pecos, who, flushing with embarrassment, dropped his hand to his side.

Pecos glared at Slash.

The battered marshal looked up at them dubiously. "Are . . . you . . . two . . . marshals . . . ?"

"Yeah," Slash said. "Don't we look like it?"

Larsen just stared up at him. His battered face made any kind of expression nearly impossible.

"We'll explain later," Pecos said. "We'll leave you to sleep. Say . . . you want us to help you out of them wet clothes? You'd feel a whole lot better dry."

The young man's head shook slightly. "I'm too sore. I'll just lay here for a while, try to get my strength back. I'll wrestle out of them when I'm able."

"Sounds good." Slash drew a quilt over him. "We'll be back up to check on you in a while."

Footsteps sounded in the hall—a light tread. Jenny appeared in the doorway holding a steaming bowl in her hands. A thick piece of brown bread poked up from one side of the bowl. The schoolteacher came into the room, looking at Larsen and saying, "I found some canned stew, heated it up. If you feel like eating . . ."

"Not now." Larsen glanced at a chair by the bed. "Just set it there, will you, Miss Claymore?"

"Of course." She set the bowl on the chair.

As she straightened, Larsen reached out and gently grabbed her hand. "Are you . . . are you . . . all right?"

She compressed her lips, trying to smile. It didn't work. She nodded, and tears glazed her eyes. "I'm all right. Better shape than you."

"I doubt that," he said, staring up at her knowingly.

She patted his hand holding her own. "I'm sorry about . . . about Tiffanie. She and I were friends. I'm going to miss her."

"Me too," he said tightly, lifting his dark eyes to stare up at the ceiling.

Jenny patted his hand again. "It wasn't your fault, Glenn."

"Yes, it was." Larsen removed his hand from between hers and stuffed it down beneath the quilt.

"No . . ." the teacher insisted.

Pecos took her arm. "Come on, Miss Claymore. We'll let the marshal sleep."

She let Pecos lead her to the door. As she did, she kept her concerned gaze on the miserable-looking marshal. Slash followed them out into the hall and closed the door behind him.

Miss Claymore walked down the hall ahead of them, toward the stairs. Slash could hear her sobbing quietly, one hand to her mouth.

"Nasty situation," Pecos said through a sigh.

"About as nasty as I've ever seen, and we've seen a few."

"I reckon we'd best assume the rest of the gang could show up any ole time and try to spring those three wolves from the wagon."

"I reckon we'd better."

They moved off toward the stairs.

Later that night, after the storm had rolled and grumbled and flickered off to the northeast, Slash laid out a game of solitaire at his and Pecos's table in Carlisle's and said, "Maybe we oughta roll that wagon up closer to the saloon so we can keep a closer eye on it."

Pecos sat near the batwings, which he'd nailed back so he could see outside. He sat to one side of the doors, facing the opening in his chair, his Colt rifle and Richards coach gun resting across his knees. They'd lit only one lamp in the whole, big, cavern-like place, so anyone outside would have trouble seeing in.

"I can see it just fine," Pecos said.

"Can you see 'em in there—them curly wolves?"

"No, they must be sound asleep or too miserable to move around much. But they're in there."

Slash squinted down at the cards in the weak light that was mostly shadows, a quirley smoldering in one corner of his mouth. "How can you be so sure?"

"Think they found a way out?"

"Wouldn't put it past 'em." Slash laid a queen of spades down on a king of hearts. "Maybe their gang came and sprung 'em."

"Without makin' a sound?" Pecos gave a snort. "They'd need dynamite to blow that iron door open. We'd hear a dynamite blast, Slash. Even from here. Even *you* would from here!"

"All right. Just remember it's gonna be your ass on the block if they ain't in that wagon tomorrow," Slash said, laying a ten of spades on a jack of hearts. "I hate to think about what ole Bleed-Em-So's gonna do to you. I can already hear you hollerin'!"

Pecos looked through the doors and yelled, "Hey, curly wolves—how you doin' out there? You need a warm blanket, a hot meal? Maybe some whiskey?"

Silence for a time. The only sound was the dripping of the rain from the saloon's eaves.

Slash had started to turn in his chair, apprehension growing in him, when the wagon creaked as one of the three sodden devils stirred. The man groaned, hacked phlegm, and in a voice quaking with a sodden chill, told Pecos to do something physically impossible to himself.

"There—you satisfied?" Pecos said to Slash. "Snug as three bugs in a rug."

Slash turned back to his game with a relieved sigh. "I'm just sayin' it don't hurt to check from time to time."

Footsteps sounded on the stairs at the back of the room. Slash turned that way to see Jenny coming down from the second story. She was a slender silhouette in the near darkness, one hand on the bannister. The weak light touched her hair and made the outer strands shine like amber. Slash and Pecos had hauled buckets of hot water upstairs for her, so she could take a bath and wash her hair, and change into some clean clothes. She'd intended to crawl into a bed up there afterward.

"Couldn't sleep, honey?" Slash asked her.

She shook her head as she strode out from the bottom of the stairs. She grabbed her coffee cup off the table she'd occupied earlier, walked over to Slash's table, and splashed some of his whiskey into her cup.

She took the cup to the potbelly stove in which a fire burned against the damp chill, and filled the cup with coffee that had been smoldering there for a while. It tasted like tar, but Slash was used to burned coffee. In fact, he preferred it. Maybe it conjured his younger, wilder cut-throat days, when they'd carelessly burn coffee in remote outlaw lairs, though he'd never been in a situation as wild as this one. He just wasn't young enough to appreciate it anymore, he supposed.

Jenny returned to Slash's table and sat down across from him. She'd changed into a nice, stylish dress with a white shirtwaist with puffy sleeves and a long, pleated skirt. One of the doxie's outfits, most likely, though not overly enticing even though it complemented Jenny's trim, buxom figure nicely. Because of the current circumstances, Slash discreetly kept his eyes off her figure, however. At least, he didn't let them linger.

"Thank you for the bath, fellas," she said, and blew on her coffee.

"Feel better?" Slash asked her.

Sort of hunched into herself, she shook her head. "No, just cleaner. But only on the outside. I feel soiled deep down to my core."

"It'll pass," Pecos said from the nailed-open batwings.

She turned to him and said sharply, "Oh, really? How would you know?"

"I reckon I wouldn't," Pecos said with chagrin, and returned his gaze to the street.

"I'm sorry," Jenny said.

"Don't be," Slash said. "That dumb old catamount deserves a tongue-lashing from a woman from time to time. He don't take it serious when I do it."

Jenny took another sip of her whiskey-laced coffee. "Do you think they'll come? More . . . like . . . them . . . ?" She peered out the night-dark window flanking Slash.

Slash laid another card down. "If they do, you'll be safe.

Me an' Pecos have stood against steeper odds than them an' come out a little rumpled and sore maybe, but otherwise little worse for the wear."

Pecos turned to him from the batwings. "It's *Pecos and I,* you damn fool." He glanced at Jenny. "He's worse than a Georgia mule. You can't teach him anything."

"I wish I could sleep," Jenny said. "But every time I close my eyes . . ." She gave a shiver and held her coffee up close to her chin.

"You need more whiskey in your coffee." Slashed added an extra jigger of busthead to her mug. "See, that's a trick you learn with age."

She fought back a genuine smile, tucking her lower lip under her upper lip. "Thank you for your wisdom, Slash."

"Jimmy."

"*Slash,*" she said with quiet insistence, looking at him over the rim of her cup.

Slash gave a hangdog shrug and laid down another card.

Pecos laughed.

CHAPTER 18

Jay was standing at the bar the next morning, sipping her first cup of coffee, when Cisco Walsh walked into the Thousand Delights. Jay drew a sharp breath, held it, steeling herself for what would come.

In the backbar mirror, she watched the town marshal doff his hat as he stepped through the swinging doors. Brushing a lock of his thick, wavy, nicely barbered hair back from his left eye, Walsh looked around briefly before his gaze fell on Jay standing at the bar before him. He must have just that morning polished his large, silver, five-pointed star, for it glinted brightly on his freshly brushed, fawn leather vest as he moved toward the bar, his serious gaze pinned on Jay.

The silver star looked larger than usual, for some reason.

But, then, so did Walsh.

Jay felt her spine tighten.

She'd known, of course, that she'd have to talk to him eventually. She couldn't hide from the man forever. Her world was a small one. It consisted almost solely of the Thousand Delights. She couldn't hide upstairs in her suite forever. She had to come down and run the saloon and her girls, and oversee the kitchen, as well as the gambling layout, and of course, Cisco would eventually enter the place and they would . . .

Do just what they were about to do.

Speak.

Still, despite knowing their meeting was inevitable, Jay's heart raced and her palms grew moist.

She kept her eyes on the marshal until he bellied up to the bar beside her, on her right. Then she lowered her gaze to her coffee mug. Chicken flesh rose across her shoulders and down her back. Walsh set his brown bowler hat on the bar, drew a deep breath. She could smell the mint of his shaving balm and his hair tonic, feel the threatening heat of his body next to hers.

He said just loudly enough for Jay to hear above the soft conversational hum of the breakfast diners, "Don't you think we'd better talk about this?"

Jay lifted her gaze, looked at Walsh in the mirror. Somehow, it felt safer to look at him in the mirror as opposed to confronting him directly. "What's there to say, really, Cisco? I overheard your conversation with Hall. I know it and you know it. How can you defend it?"

"I can't."

The reply startled her. "What?"

"I can't defend it."

The morning barman, Grant McMichael, came up holding a pot of coffee. "Coffee, Marshal?" he asked in his customary affable tone.

"No," Cisco brusquely replied, keeping his hard, level gaze on Jay now as he turned to face her, resting his right elbow on the edge of the bar.

Jay saw a vaguely hurt, vaguely puzzled expression pass like a fast-moving cloud over the barman's face as he muttered something inaudible, nodded, glanced curiously at Jay, and then carried the pot over to the two customers standing on the opposite side of the bar.

"Then what is the point of us having a conversation?" Jay asked, her own voice low and tight.

"You never know," Walsh said, "it might save your life."

Now she turned to him, her heartbeat quickening. "Are you threatening me, Cisco?"

Suddenly, he smiled. It almost looked warm. It almost looked genuine. "No, you know how I feel about you, Jay." He paused, his smile in place. "I'm going to offer you an opportunity."

"An opportunity."

"Yes."

"Go on."

"I'll cut you in . . . in return for your silence. When the job is done, we'll both have enough to money that we can shed this backwater, louse-infested village—together."

"Together?"

"How does San Francisco sound? I've been offered a job with the Pinkerton's out there."

Jay stared at him in astonishment. "You actually think that I'd—"

"Why stay here? Honey, pardon me for saying so, but you're not getting any younger. This is a big place to run, to keep up. You can't continue to carry the load of the Thousand Delights forever. Of course, there's Slash, but . . . please, you're not really, serious considering marrying him, are you?"

"Yes, Cisco," Jay said. "I am. I'm going to, in fact."

"Do you think he really loves you?"

"Yes."

"That wild old scalawag! Ha!" Loudly, Walsh slapped the bar and seemed oblivious of all the heads swinging toward him. "He's incapable of love. Oh, he might *think* he loves you, but that old train robber and whoremonger has a heart like granite. Me? I think he's just scared of growing old alone. Even if he did love you, Jay, how long do think it would last? How long do you think it would be before he got shifty feet, started to miss the excitement of the robbery and the chase to some outlaw camp in the mountains? Or the pretty little señoritas down Mexico-way?"

Jay just stared at him, biting her tongue, anger burning inside of her.

Cisco continued. "Slash Braddock has never sunk a picket pin in his entire life. Neither has Pecos. Those two might be putting on a good show, running their legitimate freighting business while working for Bledsoe, but how long do you think *that's* gonna last?" He leaned toward her, his lips smiling but his eyes flashing with mockery. "Those two are outlaws, Jay. Through and through."

"I guess it takes one to know one—doesn't it, Cisco?"

"Shut up!" Walsh looked around. Leaning closer to Jay, he grabbed her arm and gave it a painful squeeze. "Keep your voice down, dammit!"

Raising her voice even louder, Jay said, "You're not going to get away with it, Cisco. I won't let you. You're a wolf in sheep's clothing, and it's time the people around here know about you!"

"Damn you—I told you—"

"Go to hell!" Jay slapped his face hard. The sharp crack sounded like the report of a small-caliber pistol. She jerked her arm free of Walsh's grip and backed away from him, looking around the saloon and yelling, "Everyone needs to know that Marshal Walsh is planning to rob a gold shipment from one of the mines. Which shipment, I don't know.

But it's going to happen in the coming week, and it's going to be a big haul—eighty thousand dollars in gold bullion!"

Walsh moved heavily toward her, his eyes aflame with fury. "Stop, Jay. I'm warning you!"

"He's in cahoots with Jason Hall! Spread the word!"

"Damn you, Jay!" Walsh bounded off on his boot heels. He lunged forward, wrapping both his hands around Jay's throat and bulling her backward. The carpeted floor came up to strike her hard about the head and shoulders.

Her ears rang.

Her vision blurred.

She blinked up at the blurry vision of Cisco Walsh straddling her on his knees, lips stretched back from his teeth, both hands wrapped around her neck, trying to choke the life out of her. He was doing a good job of it, too. It seemed that the harder Jay tried to wrestle the marshal's hands from her neck, the deeper his thumbs dug into her throat, pinching off her wind.

Her head swelled until she thought it would explode.

From far away came pounding sounds. They grew louder and louder.

"Jay!" someone yelled. A young woman's voice. "Jay! Open up! Let us in!"

Jay opened her eyes just as Walsh's demon-like image evaporated before her. She sat up, drawing a deep breath, surprised that the air moved down her throat and into her lungs so easily. She blinked, still feeling panic rush through her. It began to diminish as she looked around and saw that she was in her bed in her suite upstairs at the Thousand Delights.

She was not in the saloon.

Cisco Walsh was nowhere to be found. She was alone. Safe in her own bed . . .

. . . with someone pounding on her door.

"Jay!" Myra Thompson yelled, whacking the door two more times, hard. "Please open the door!"

"Coming," Jay croaked out. She still felt as though she'd been strangled.

As she threw her covers back and dropped her feet to the floor, she cleared her throat and yelled more clearly this time, "I'm coming, Myra! Everything's fine! I'm coming!"

The pounding stopped.

Jay shrugged into a powder-blue housecoat. She stepped into her soft wool slippers. Tying the robe at her waist, she moved out of her bedroom and into the parlor of her suite. She unlocked and opened the door.

Myra Thompson stood before her, eyes glassy with terror. She stepped forward and placed her hands on Jay's shoulders, crying, "Jay! *Are you all right?*"

"Yes, yes, Myra. I'm fine. I'm sorry—I was just—"

"I was about to kick the door open," said the tall young man whom Jay just now saw standing to Myra's left and a little behind her. "I was gonna give it one big whack with my boot, tear it right on out of its frame!" He lifted his foot to display the boot of topic. "We figured you was bein' murdered in there, ma'am . . . judgin' by the awful sounds!"

Jay shook her head, embarrassed. "I'm so sorry I worried you both. I was dreaming, though . . ." She turned to look into her suite, half expecting to see Cisco Walsh standing in a corner or disappearing behind one of the heavy velvet draperies hanging over the windows. "It still seems so real."

"I'm glad it was only a dream. And I'm glad you woke up when you did. I was about to have Delbert kick your door in!" Myra laughed.

Jay saw several girls standing outside the doors to their rooms, staring toward her with concern. She held up her hands and said, "It's all right, ladies. All is well. I was just having a dream, is all. Go back to bed."

Judging by the dim light in the hall, it was still early. At least, by doxie standards.

"Glad to hear you're all right, Miss Jay," one of the girls said, then quietly closed her door.

"Come in, come in," Jay said, beckoning Myra and the tall young man into her suite. When they'd stepped inside, the young man holding his bowler hat in his hands and now looking rather bashful and uncomfortable, Jay closed the door and smiled up at him.

She extended her hand. "You must be Delbert."

"That's right, ma'am," he said around a mouthful of prominent teeth, proudly giving Jay's hand a resolute shake. "Deputy Sheriff Delbert Thayer at your service." He glanced at Myra. "Miss Myra an' me, we're—"

"Friends," Myra finished for him a little too energetically, rising up and down on the balls of her scuffed, boy-size stockmen's boots. She wore her customary workaday attire—blue jeans, cotton shirt, boots, and round-brimmed felt hat. She wore a denim jacket against the morning chill. Her curly auburn hair tumbled about her shoulders.

Thayer was in his early twenties—a tall, gangling young man with buckteeth over which his lip stuck out, and a long-nosed, slightly coyote-like, but not unattractive face. Light brown freckles were splashed across his nose and cheeks. His sandy hair was very straight and thin, and he wore it down over his ears. It showed the line where his hat had been. He wore suit pants, a pin-striped, collarless shirt to which his deputy sheriff's badge was pinned, and suspenders. An old-model Remington revolver was strapped to his right hip.

He nervously turned his hat in his hands and said, "Miss Myra says you think the town marshal's gonna hold up the stage!"

"Shhh!" both women said, holding fingers to their lips and grimacing.

"Oh," the boy said, flushing a little and glancing at the door. "Sorry. I, uh . . . sometimes don't realize how far my voice carries. It was a problem at home."

"That's all right," Jay said with a nervous chuckle. "I doubt anyone heard. It's just that I want to go to pains to keep this as quiet as possible until we can figure out what to do about the, uh . . . the *situation*."

Especially after the horrible dream she'd just had. She couldn't get the dream image of Cisco's demonic face out of her head, nor the pain and suffocating feeling of his hands around her neck.

"That's what I'm here to help you do, ma'am," Delbert said. "I came here on Myra's request, and I stand here in an official capacity."

Jay frowned up at him. "Official capacity?"

"That's lawman talk," Myra said with a weary sigh. "Del loves to speak the language. He means he's here to offer advice."

"*Official* advice, Miss Myra," Delbert said, frowning at her, vaguely indignant. "I'm a deputy. Says so right here." He brushed his thumb across his badge. "I know what I'm doin'. Uncle . . . I mean, *Sheriff* McGuire . . . always says so. Why, just the other day, before he left town, he told me I got one heck of a bright future." He glanced at Myra and a pink flush rose in his pale, freckled cheeks. "He told me I should find me a good woman an' settle down because I was gonna be workin' for him—"

"All right, Del, all right!" Myra intoned. To Jay she whispered behind her hand, "He does like to go on, Delbert does."

"I do tend to go on," Delbert allowed to Jay, "but I am good at what I do. Deputy work an' such."

"Shall we have a seat?" Jay said, not sure that it had been such a good idea to bring the young man, who was obviously infatuated with Myra and still wet behind the ears, into the fold. But here he was now, so . . .

Jay led the three into the parlor area of her suite. "Please . . . sit anywhere."

As she herself sat on one end of a couch abutting the wall to her bedroom, Myra took the smaller sofa on the other side of the coffee table from Jay. Delbert considered the armchair at the end of the coffee table, but then chose to sit on the small sofa with Myra, who drew her mouth corners down when she saw him coming. The young man flushed, slid a little closer to Myra, not quite touching her but almost, then set his hat on the table, folding his long arms across his skinny knees.

"I'm sorry," Jay said. "I would offer you coffee, but I always take mine downstairs."

"We're fine, Jay."

"Yes, ma'am," Delbert said. "I'm fine. I don't touch the stuff. The sheriff told me it'll turn my hair black." He grinned, showing his buckteeth, and snorted a laugh. His laughter sounded like a mule braying.

Myra rolled her eyes.

"Anyway . . ." Delbert cleared his throat and looked at Jay. "Would you like to tell me exactly what you overheard, ma'am?"

"Please, Delbert—call me Jay."

He grinned again. "Only if you'll call me Del."

"Del, it is." Jay leaned forward, resting her elbows on her knees, and entwined her hands together. She related the conversation she'd overheard between Walsh and Hall as best she could remember, which she thought was pretty well, then arched a brow expectantly at the young sheriff's deputy sitting across from her.

"By *golly!*" Del said. He whistled as he leaned back in the sofa and wagged his head from side to side in unabashed delight. "It sure enough sounds like hell's about to pop an'—"

"Shhh!" Jay and Myra beseeched him at the same time.

Lowering his voice and flushing with embarrassment, Del said, "It sure enough sounds like just what you said— the marshal an' Mr. Hall are fixin' to rob a gold shipment!"

"It does, indeed," Jay said. "What do you propose we do about it?"

"Hmmm." Del scrunched up his face to gaze at the ceiling. He twisted his lower lip between his thumb and index finger and said, "I think what I'd best do is send an official telegram to Uncle . . . pardon me, I mean *Sheriff* McGuire in Santa Fe. He'll be down there till next week, seein' a sawbones about some aches an' pains he's been havin'. My ma says it's all on account of Aunt Polly's cooking, but—"

"Del!" Myra snapped at him, giving his knee a whack with the back of her hand, cutting him off.

"Oh! I'm sorry." Del waggled his head around miserably. "How I do go on!"

"How you do!" Myra cajoled him.

"Here's what I'm gonna do," Del said, returning his serious, official gaze to Jay. "I'm gonna send a telegram to the sheriff. Sort of consult with him on the matter, don't ya know. He'll probably cable me right back, me bein' one of his top deputies an' all."

Again, Myra rolled her eyes. Jay suppressed a mirthful snort, not wanting to offend the young man.

"I'll tell him what you told me, and we'll see what he says."

"All right," Jay said. "I guess that's as good a place to start as any."

"Oh," Del said. "Do you know when this holdup's supposed to take place?"

"No," Jay said. "All I know is that it's going to happen this week, and it's a shipment of eighty thousand dollars in gold bullion."

"All right, all right," Delbert said, ponderingly. "If it's a stagecoach, I sure hope it ain't carrying passengers. Wouldn't want any innocent bystanders hurt—you know, in the event of a lead swap after the authorities become involved in the matter."

"Lead swap?" Myra asked.

"You know—a *shoot-out*. Not unexpected when we're dealing with as much money as Miss Breckenridge says will be rollin' out of them mountains. Men fixin' to steal that amount tend to get reckless . . . downright savage in their veniality."

"Savage in their *what*?" both Jay and Myra asked at the same time.

"Savage in their *veniality*," the young deputy said, grinning proudly. "I got that out of the *Police Gazette*. I'm a regular subscriber, don't ya know!"

"Great," Jay said, sitting back in the sofa, smiling but feeling crestfallen. "Just great."

CHAPTER 19

Slash felt something warm against the side of his neck. A warm breath.

He chuckled in his sleep, dreaming that he was in a warm doxie's cozy bed. "That tickles, darlin'."

There was a soft snorting sound.

"Go back to sleep, darlin'. Slash is too sleepy to play."

Something cold and rubbery touched his neck. That woke him, his eyes snapping wide, remembering instantly that he was not in a whorehouse but on the step of Carlisle's in Dry Fork. He turned to his right . . . and stared into two cinnamon-colored eyes set close together atop a long, gray, black-tipped snout.

The coyote's pupils contracted. The bristled lips rose above sharp white teeth, including two impressive fangs.

Slash jerked his head back and gave a shrill yell that he was immediately embarrassed by. It sounded womanish—girlish—even to his own ears.

"I ain't dead, you smelly, mangy, louse-infested vermin!"

The coyote yipped with its own start, lunged backward, twisted around in a blur of quick motion, and leaped down off Carlisle's steps and into the street. It bolted off to the east so fast as to resemble a large gray bullet, quickly disappearing in the murky gloom of a soaking wet dawn.

Slash had been so startled by the nosy beast that he'd dropped his rifle, which he'd been holding across his thighs when he'd drifted into his nap maybe an hour or so ago. Now he bent to pick it up from a step below him, wincing as his stiff, old spine grieved him. It felt as though it would snap like dry kindling. This cold, wet weather didn't set well in an old man's bones.

"What's the matter, you old devil?" called one of the prisoners in the jail wagon. "That coyote think you was dead? Well, you're *gonna be* dead. You're gonna pay for makin' us stay out here all night without even a blanket and no tendin' for our wounds. That wasn't the only coyote on the prowl last night. A good half-dozen of 'em circled this wagon several times, sniffin' an' snortin' an' growlin' through the bars!"

"Stop your caterwaulin', Chaney," Slash said, using his rifle as a cane with which to help hoist him to his feet.

Behind him, a floorboard squawked, and Pecos said, "You all right, boss?"

"I'm all right," Slash said with a groan, planting a hand on his hip and leaning backward to stretch his spine. "Who screamed?"

"Never mind." Pecos snorted.

"Coyote thought I was one of the dead citizens of Dry Fork," Slash said. "You'd scream like a girl in pigtails, too, if you woke to see a coyote eyein' you like breakfast." He grimaced, shaking his head. "Foul-smelling breath, too! Nasty!"

"They probably been suppin' on the town overnight."

"Yeah, I heard 'em."

"Come on in for a cup of coffee. I got a pot brewin'.

Then I reckon we'd best hitch the horses to the wagon and start south." Pecos turned and walked back into the saloon.

Slash turned to the wagon. In the misty gray light he could see the three prisoners sitting on the wagon's near side, glaring at him like hungry zoo animals.

"I'll be in shortly," Slash yelled to Pecos. He moved down off the steps and started walking toward the wagon. "I'm gonna have me a little talk with the clientele."

"Just don't cheat the hangman!" Pecos yelled back at him.

"I know, I know," Slash said, striding toward the wagon, his rifle on his shoulder. "Hangmen gotta eat, too."

"So do federal prisoners," Hell-Raisin' Frank Beecher said. He sat to the right of Talon Chaney, who sat between Beecher and Black Pot. "I believe you overlooked supper last night. How 'bout some breakfast?"

"Yeah, how 'bout breakfast, you old toad!" said Black Pot, shoving his face into a gap between the bars. He had his hands wrapped taught around two of the iron bands.

Slash jerked his rifle down off his shoulder and rammed the butt against Black Pot's left-hand fingers. *"Owww!"* the half-breed yowled, jerking both hands back and clutching the injured one in the healthy one.

"That there's what I came out here to talk to you about," Slash said, glancing from Black Pot to Chaney and Beecher, who both wisely removed their hands from the cage's iron bands.

The three looked like a trio of half-drowned rats. Their clothes were still wet from the downpour. Their hair was only starting to dry. Blood shone through the bandages wrapped around Beecher and Chaney's leg wounds. They were tired, hungry, miserable, and madder than the proverbial old wet hen.

"What'd you come out here to talk to us about?" Chaney asked through a searing glare. "Breakfast? I'll have four eggs over easy, a pile of bacon, a mess of fried potatoes with onions, and six buckwheat cakes!"

"You'll get breakfast," Slash said. "A meager one. But you'll get breakfast . . . as long as you're nice. You understand?"

"As long as we're nice?" Beecher laughed his effeminate laugh. "We're outlaws, you old coyote. You're taking us to Denver to hang us. How can you expect us to be *nice*?" He laughed through his teeth and slid his lunatic-bright eyes to his two compatriots to his left.

"Because if you ain't nice, you won't be fed. You won't get your slop bucket emptied, neither." Slash looked at the wooden pale in the wagon's far corner. "Now, see here," the old ex-cutthroat added, "I want you to be on especially good behavior when that young schoolteacher comes out here."

"What young schoolteacher?" Chaney sneered.

Slash glared back at him, suppressing the fire of rage burning behind his heart. "The one you so badly abused." He drew a deep, calming breath. "But, then, you abused so many, you probably don't remember."

Beecher turned to Chaney and snickered through his teeth.

Chaney grinned.

Black Pot snorted.

"Now, she's gonna be ridin' along with us, see? In the wagon here." Slash canted his head to the driver's seat.

"Who?" Black Pot said, still holding his injured hand. "The teacher is?"

"That's right. She wants to go to Denver. So we're gonna take her there."

Beecher grinned and whistled, rubbing his hands together.

Slash switched his gaze to the effeminate hell-raiser. "If any of you says anything off-color to her, or even looks at her in a way I don't like, or *does anything in general* that I think might *remotely* offend her, I'm gonna . . ."

Slash switched his rifle to his left hand. Fast as lightning, he drew his right-side Colt, aimed, and fired between the bars. The blast thundered around the town, echoes ringing off the jail wagon's bars.

Beecher slapped his hand to his left ear, eyes wide with shock. Blood dribbled down from beneath the hand clamped to that side of his head.

"What the *hell* . . . ?" said Black Pot.

Both he and Chaney turned to Beecher.

"Did he shoot you, Beech?" Chaney asked him.

"Yes, he shot me!" Beecher glared in enraged exasperation at Slash, who smiled at him through the smoke curling up from his Colt's barrel. "He shot my ear!" He looked at Chaney and removed his hand from his ear. "Take a look!"

Chaney looked at Beecher's ear. "Damn, he shot your earlobe right off!"

"The whole damn thing?" asked Beecher.

"Most of it. All you got left is a bloody little nub!"

Black Pot stared at what was left of Beecher's ear in hang-jawed awe.

Beecher covered the ear with his hand again and bent forward at the waist. "Damn, that burns!" He looked at Slash. Rage flared again in his eyes.

He opened his mouth to speak but closed it when Slash cocked the Colt again and said, "Consider very carefully what you say next, Frank."

He aimed at Beecher's other ear.

Beecher just glared at him. The outlaw's eyes appeared ready to leap out of their sockets. All three prisoners glared at Slash, but they kept their mouths shut.

"We understand each other now?" Slash asked. "You're not gonna say a word to the teacher, understand? No leers or lewd gestures or anything even close." He paused and looked at Beecher again. "Right, Frank?"

Beecher just glared at him, his chest rising and falling heavily as he breathed.

Slash put some steel in his voice as he said again while aiming down his Colt's barrel, "Right, Frank?"

Beecher flinched, glanced away. "All right, all right . . . yes, yes. Butter won't melt in my mouth."

Slash switched his gaze as he aimed the Colt's barrel at Talon Chaney. "Right, Chaney?"

Chaney held Slash's gaze for about five seconds before he said, "All right, all right."

Slash slid his gaze, as well as the Colt, to Black Pot. "Right?"

"Sure, sure. If you say so, you old—"

Slash squeezed the Colt's trigger.

Black Pot leaped nearly a foot up off the wagon's floor as Slash's bullet ricocheted off a bar in front of the half-breed, then echoed off one to his left and then off another band at the front of the cage, behind Beecher and Chaney, who lowered their heads and clamped their hands over their ears.

"Yes! Yes! Yes!" Black Pot wailed. "For the love o' God!"

"Christ Almighty!" Chaney exclaimed, staring at Slash as though at some savage beast of the wild. "You ain't even half-right in the head!"

"No, I'm not." Slash holstered his Colt. "You remember

that. Now, if you'll excuse me . . ." He swung around and began heading back toward the saloon. "I'm going to go enjoy that first cup of morning coffee."

"Don't forget our breakfast!" Chaney shouted behind him.

Slash stopped, half turned, and glared back at the man. He draped his right hand over his Colt.

Chaney flushed, winced. "Please."

Slash smiled and continued to Carlisle's. He climbed the porch steps and stopped. Jenny Claymore stood just outside the batwings, holding a stone mug of steaming black coffee. She gave Slash a coyote smile, glancing at the jail wagon and then shifting her gaze back to Slash again.

"Here you go," she said.

"For me?"

"For you."

Slash smiled as he accepted the cup. "Why, thank you, Jenny."

She moved up close to him, rose onto her toes, and pressed her lips to his cheek. "Anytime."

Slash flushed and moved on into the saloon, where Pecos sat drinking coffee and smoking a cigarette. "You know what, Pecos?" Slash pressed his hand to the warm, moist spot Jenny's lips had left on his cheek, and said, "I don't think this is gonna be such a hard trip, after all."

Pecos glanced at Jenny moving into the saloon behind Slash, and laughed.

Jenny continued walking on down the bar to a door at the rear, to the left of the stairs. "I'll have breakfast out in five minutes," she said.

Slash frowned at her retreating back, then sniffed the air. "Is that . . . bacon?" he asked Pecos.

"It is, indeed. She found some bacon and eggs, an' she's even makin' biscuits."

"I'll be damned. I didn't know schoolteachers could cook." Slash sat down in his chair. "I guess I thought that was why they became schoolteachers."

"Shows how much you know about the world, Slash," Pecos said, taking a deep drag off his quirley.

"Don't start in on me," Slash said. "Besides, you're just jealous, knowin' I'm likely the only one of us who's gonna get kissed by a purty girl today."

Boots thudded on the stairs. Slash and Pecos turned to see the young town marshal, Glenn Larsen, dropping slowly toward them. Larsen appeared to be moving considerably better this morning. He was dressed in clean duds, as well—a white shirt buttoned to the collar, and blue denim trousers that were just a tad too short in the legs. He wore brown boots, suspenders, and a dark brown, bullet-shaped, round-brimmed hat.

"Well, I'll be damned," Pecos said. "Look at that."

Slash said, "Good mornin', young marshal. I see you survived the night. Look some better, to boot. Even found some clothes that almost fit you."

"A sheepherder kept a room here and a set of fresh clothes. These are his. He's a little shorter in the legs than I am, but they'll do. I'll shop for new ones in Denver."

Slash and Pecos shared a curious look.

"Denver?" Pecos asked.

"Yes, Denver." Larsen came to the bottom of the stairs and stopped. With one hand on the newel post, he cast Slash and Pecos a hard, determined look and said, "I'll be riding with you. I want to make damned good and sure those three devils make it to Denver and swing for what they did here. For what they did to my wife."

Pecos glanced at Slash, then grabbed a mug off the bar and filled it with coffee. Turning to the young marshal, he said, "Mud? It ain't very good, but it's black."

CHAPTER 20

Larsen walked across the saloon and accepted the mug of coffee from the bigger of the two lawmen. At least, he assumed they were lawmen. They were with the marshal's service, anyway, though neither wore the customary moon and star of a deputy U.S. marshal.

"Thanks," Larsen said.

The big man, whom the smaller, darker man called Pecos, said, "You sure you feel well enough to make that journey, Marshal?"

"I'm well enough." Larsen himself wasn't sure. But he was going to make the journey, all right.

Besides, what else did he have to do? He had nothing left here in Dry Fork. Nothing but ashes. His wife and his best friend were dead. He hadn't seen Henry's body, but he knew Henry was dead. The killers had bragged to him about their handiwork with knives, torturing the poor old man to death before they'd strolled over to Larsen's house, jumped him, dragged poor Tiffanie inside, and . . .

He squeezed his eyes closed.

The big, blue-eyed man with long, thin gray-blond hair smiled warmly and squeezed his arm. "Why don't you sit down?" He glanced at the table he'd been occupying with the other man he'd heard the bigger man call Slash. "That old snake don't bite. Leastways, his fangs are so dull it don't hurt much."

Larsen turned to the table and sat down in a chair across from the man called Slash. Slash stretched his right arm across the table, offering Larsen his open hand. "James Braddock. That big drink of foul-tasting water is Melvin Baker."

Larsen frowned, puzzled. "I thought I heard . . ."

"Yeah, I know, I know," Slash said. "In a past life I was known as Slash and he was known as Pecos, and I'll be damned if we can get used to callin' each other by our straight-and-narrow names."

Larsen stared down at his coffee, mentally perusing the wanted dodgers filed in his office. "Slash . . . Braddock," he muttered. As two particular circulars clarified in his mind's eyes, he glanced first at the man sitting across from him and the bigger man still standing by the potbelly stove. "Slash Braddock and the Pecos River *Kid* . . . ?"

Slash grimaced, cut a quick look at Pecos. "Yeah, that's us, all right. I reckon our reputations still precede us, partner."

Larsen heard himself give an amused snort in spite of his mental and physical torment. "Why, I used to read about your exploits in magazines and dime novels . . . back when I was a kid."

"Whoa, now," Pecos said, holding up the hand that wasn't holding his coffee mug. "That'll be enough of that. If you ain't careful, you're gonna go an' make Slash an' I feel old." He gave a snort of his own and sipped his coffee.

"You're going to go and make *Slash and me* feel old,"

Jenny corrected the big ex-cutthroat as she came out of the kitchen with two steaming plates in her hands.

Slash chuckled.

"Doggone it," Pecos said. "I thought I had it right that time!" He flushed as he took another sip of his coffee.

"Here's breakfast," Jenny said. "Mr. Carlisle kept a well-stocked kitchen." She set a plate down in front of Slash and one at the end of the table nearest Pecos. Turning to Larsen, she said, "I'm glad to see you're up and around, Marshal Larsen. I'll bring you a plate right away. I made plenty."

Larsen removed his hat, dropped it on the table near his coffee. "Please don't call me 'Marshal' no more, Miss Jenny," the young man said with a weary sigh. "How can a man be marshal of a town that don't even exist anymore?"

Jenny drew her mouth corners down and nodded. Tears glazed her eyes. She drew a breath, suppressing her emotion, and turned and headed into the kitchen. "Just the same, I'll fetch you a plate."

"I'm really not hungry," Larsen said to her back.

"You have to eat." Jenny continued into the kitchen.

She brought the plate out a few minutes later and set it down in front of the grieving lawman. "Eat as much as you can."

"All right." Larsen looked up at the young woman, whose face was badly bruised, one eye partly swollen. His heart ached for her. He knew what she'd been through. She was lucky to be alive. "How 'bout you, Jenny? How are you doing?"

She stood by his chair, her hand on the back of it, leaning toward him. She cast her gaze out the window, and a flush of rage rose into her cheeks. "About as well as I can. I'm so sorry about Tiffanie, Glenn. She loved you so very much."

"Yeah," Larsen said, choking back a sob and staring down at his plate as a fresh wave of emotion threatened to swamp him. "Well . . . she's gone. And I'm gonna make sure those three dogs get to Denver. I'll be riding along with"—he glanced over at the two ex-cutthroats just then finishing their plates—"Slash and Pecos. Just to be sure," he added. "I just have to make sure they hang for what they did to Tiffanie and you and Henry and all the rest of the town."

Jenny nodded. "I understand. I'm coming, too."

Larsen frowned. "You are?"

She shrugged. "Can't stay here. I came from Denver. My father and mother are dead, and my sister and brothers have moved on, but it's the only place I have to go to. They have some private girls' schools there. I figure maybe I can get a job there."

"Are you . . . are you sure you can . . . ride?" he hesitated to ask her.

She drew a calming breath. "I can ride. Just a little sore is all. But I can ride. I have to."

"I'm sorry it didn't work out with . . . with . . . well . . ."

The young teacher shook her head quickly. "The less said about that situation, the better." She glanced at Slash and Pecos. "I'll fill a couple of grub sacks for the trail."

"You best eat, too, darlin'," Slash said.

She scowled down at Larsen's plate. So far, he'd only managed to break the yoke on one of his eggs resting on a pile of nicely browned potatoes. "I don't have much more of an appetite than the mar—er . . . I mean, Glenn . . . does, I'm afraid."

She swung around and disappeared back into the kitchen.

Larsen figured she was mostly wanting to keep busy, so she didn't ruminate on what had happened. He understood. Maybe that's what he in part was doing, as well.

Larsen forked some egg and potato into his mouth. He swallowed. He was sure it tasted good, but he couldn't detect any taste at all. It was a small bite of food, but it settled in his belly like poison. He tossed his fork down onto the plate, slid his chair back, and rose from the table.

"You should eat," Pecos told him over the steaming rim of his coffee mug. "Gonna be a long ride."

Larsen grimaced, shook his head. "My, uh . . . my deputy . . . ?"

"We left him in your office," Slash said a little guiltily. "With another man. We figured if we started buryin' folks, we'd be here forever "

"I understand. It's his gun I want."

Larsen set his hat on his head and strode across the room and out through the batwings. He stopped at the top of the porch steps and stared at the jail wagon parked on the street before Carlisle's. He looked at the killers. Sitting back against the jail wagon's far barred wall, two stared back at him. Hell-Raisin' Frank Beecher appeared asleep, head down, chin against his chest. Chaney elbowed him, and Beecher raised his head.

All three gazed in silence at the town marshal, whom they'd beaten, whose wife they'd ravaged most brutally, whose citizens they'd terrorized and butchered . . . whose town they'd burned. They stared at him without expression, their eyes flat and dull. They could have been three dogs or wildcats imprisoned over there in that wagon. Not the least bit of shame. But, then, there was nothing more savage than a savage man. That was a breed all unto itself. . . .

Larsen walked down the porch steps. He turned east

and angled across the street, passing the burned-out hulks of buildings, the sodden piles of ash and charred wood. His boots made sucking sounds in the mud. He approached the fire-scorched stone building that housed his office. He paused in front of the door, steeling himself. He could already smell the sickly sweet stench of death. His guts twisted.

Grimacing, he drew a deep breath and pushed through the door.

He stopped just inside and looked around. Eddie Black lay belly down a few feet inside the office. His throat had been cut. He lay in a large dark red pool of his own semidried blood. Two broken plates littered the floor. The food was gone. Apparently, the killers had taken time to eat their dinner meals—probably while they'd tortured Two Whistles. Henry lay just beyond him, near Larsen's overturned chair. The poor old half-breed was covered in blood. They'd cut him to ribbons, torturing him slowly before they'd finally slit his throat.

Henry lay on his back, staring at the ceiling. An expression of incomprehensible pain and terror still shaped itself on his mouth. The death stench lay thick and heavy.

"Jesus."

Larsen hurried forward, stepped around Eddie Black's blood. Quickly, Larsen removed the holstered Colt Lightning and cartridge belt from around Two Whistles's waist. He cinched it around his own waist, then walked over to the gun cabinet on the far wall. Two Winchester carbines remained in the rack, the chain over which had been unlocked and removed by the killers. They'd taken back their own revolvers and rifles, which Larsen had hauled out of Carlisle's after he and Two Whistles had jailed Chaney and the other two outlaws. Larsen grabbed one of the carbines.

He plucked a box of .44 cartridges from the bottom drawer of his desk, and stepped over his deputy and around Eddie Black as he made his way back to the door.

He stopped and turned back to the dead men. He considered a burial, but nixed the idea. The ground was too wet. It would take too long. Besides, he didn't think he was physically capable. The beating had taken a lot out of him and left him with miserably aching ribs. The elements and the predators would have to suffice for Henry and Eddie Black. Larsen really didn't see much difference, anyway.

Worms or coyotes?

The erosion of time and the elements would have to suffice. As for Tiffanie, she'd been consumed by the fires that had leveled their house. There was nothing left of her to bury or to be desecrated by the carrion-eaters.

His stomach churning against the stench and the grisly sight inside the office, Larsen hurried out the door. He stopped and drew a deep breath, then another and another. He loaded the carbine from the cartridge box, jacked one into the chamber, off-cocked the hammer, and lowered the rifle to his side.

He walked back toward Carlisle's, grimacing at the ache in his ribs. He hoped he could sit a saddle. He would have to. He couldn't stay here. Besides, he owed it to Tiffanie and Henry to make sure their killings were avenged. He wanted to see Chaney, Black Pot, and Beecher hang from the neck until they were dead. Somehow, he had a feeling that when he watched them die, Tiffanie and Henry would rest a little easier.

He was nearly to Carlisle's front steps when he stopped and turned toward the jail wagon. He'd sensed the killers' eyes on him. He hadn't been imagining it. All three stared at him through the bars. He'd hoped they'd at least have those blank looks again. He'd hoped they wouldn't be smiling. But that's what they were doing, all right.

They were smiling at him. Mocking him. Mocking his pain and his grief over his wife and his best friend's killings.

It was too much for Larsen to suppress. The anger was overwhelming.

He dropped the carbine and the cartridge box, and hardening his jaws, he turned and strode toward the wagon. His pulse throbbed in his knees. He clenched his fists at his sides until he thought the knuckles would burst through the skin. He kept seeing his burned house all but leveled to nothing but black ashes. He kept seeing Henry lying butchered in the office. He kept hearing Tiffanie's screams . . . her wails . . . her pleas for help that was not going to come . . . .

He heard the killers' laughter as they'd disrespected and murdered her.

And he saw growing larger before him, as he approached the barred wagon, the faces of the killers curling their lips and narrowing their eyes at him. Making light of him and of what they had done.

As Larsen came to a stop six feet from the wagon, a vague unease passed over the killers' eyes. Chaney was the only one with a faint smile still curling one side of his mouth. And now the outlaw's mouth straightened as the dark-eyed devil known as Black Pot elbowed him, alerting the gang leader to possible trouble. They each in turn glanced at the Colt Lightning holstered in the black leather holster on Larsen's right leg.

"What were you smiling about?" he choked out through a knot of tightly bound emotion residing just south of his vocal cords. He had his chin down, eyes wide, and he could feel several veins throbbing in his forehead.

"What's that?" asked Frank Beecher.

"You heard me," Larsen said. "What were you smiling about?"

He shuttled his gaze back and forth across them. All three stared back at him, their eyes now stonily defiant. Finally, Chaney let out a chuckle. He turned to grin at Black Pot, who smiled then, too.

Larsen couldn't help himself. Suddenly, Two Whistles's Colt was in his hand. He raised it, hearing the three clicks as his thumb drew the hammer back. His hand shook. He steadied it with the other one, dripped his chin again, and narrowed one eye as he aimed down the barrel at Chaney's head.

"Hold on now!" Chaney said, holding up his hands, palms out. "Just hold on, now, Marshal." He looked around Larsen toward Carlisle's and said, "Trouble over here! You two better get this young marshal back on his leash. He's actin' crazy!"

Larsen heard two sets of footsteps and knew the two former outlaws, Braddock and Baker, were moving toward him.

"I have to do it," Larsen yelled at the two men moving toward him from behind, squeezing the revolver so tightly he could hear the handle cracking. "I can't help myself! Why should they live after what they did to my wife . . . to Henry . . . ?"

Braddock moved up on his left and stopped.

Baker moved up on his right and stopped.

Mildly, Braddock said, "You do what you have to."

CHAPTER 21

Larsen glanced at Braddock out of the corner of his eye and furled his left brow. "Huh?"

"Go ahead," Baker said on his other side. "If anyone has the right to send these three ugly polecats to hell, it's you, Marshal." A slight pause, then in Baker's deep, resonant voice and slow western drawl: "Go ahead."

Larsen felt a smile curl his own lips as he aimed down the Colt's barrel at Chaney.

"Hey, now!" the outlaw protested, holding his hands straight up above his shoulders. "You can't shoot a jailed prisoner. It's against the law!"

"You're gonna die," Larsen told him. "You smiled. You mocked my wife. You mocked what you did to her. I saw what you did to Henry. Why should you live? Give me one good reason!" His voice cracked at the end of the exclamation.

All three killers looked anxious now. All three held their hands up in supplication. Chaney's eyes were wide and bright with fear, his face mottled red and floury white.

Larsen began to pull back against the Colt's trigger. It was a satisfying feeling. Relief was coming. . . .

A hand rose up from right beside him. A pale female hand. The hand closed down over Two Whistles's revolver, pushed it back down to Larsen's side. He turned to see Jenny Claymore standing just off his right shoulder, regarding him with an expression of concern mixed with her own horror and grief.

She shook her head, sniffed. A tear rolled down from her left eye.

"That's who they are." She tossed her head toward the wagon. "It's not who you are."

"Ah, hell!" Larsen lowered his head and sobbed.

Jenny pressed tight against him, wrapped her arms around him, hugging him, rocking him gently in her arms.

"Ready to go?" Pecos asked Larsen and Jenny Claymore an hour later.

He was leading two saddled horses toward Carlisle's—his own buckskin and a horse he'd caught and saddled for Larsen—a big roan gelding that must have broken out of one of the barns or corrals during the fire.

Slash was still inspecting the jail wagon's hitch. He'd harnessed the two geldings to the wagon and tied his own Appaloosa to the back. His rifle lay on the driver's seat. He'd stashed the saddlebags containing the killers' stolen loot beneath the seat. The gold and certificates would be returned to their rightful owners after the jail wagon party reached Cheyenne. Jenny had stowed several bags of trail beneath the seat, as well—enough for the three-day ride back to Cheyenne, where they'd abandon the wagon and catch the train for Denver.

While Slash and Pecos had readied the horses, Larsen and the young schoolteacher had waited together on Carlisle's front steps. Jenny had packed a carpetbag; it rested beside her left thigh. She and the young marshal sat close together, legs touching, quietly lending comfort to each other in this time of incomprehensible tragedy for both of them. They looked badly battered, but Larsen's face was in worse shape than the girl. Both of his eyes were badly swollen, and his lips were cracked and occasionally oozing fresh blood, which he brushed away with his sleeves. His own carbine leaned against his left leg; his bullet-crowned hat was on his head. It was large and black, like a crown of mourning.

Larsen nodded. "Ready."

He winced as he tried to rise, dropped back down to the step.

"You sure?" Pecos asked the young man, whose ribs must be grieving him miserably.

"Yep." Larsen grunted as he heaved himself to his feet.

Jenny rose to stand beside him, looking up at him. "Are you sure, Glenn? We can stay here. I'll stay with you . . . until you're ready to travel. We don't have to leave now."

Larsen looked from the young woman to the jail wagon. The previous anger passed over his swollen eyes once more, his bruised cheeks flushing, and he turned back to her. "I have to."

She heaved a breath, nodded. "All right." Larsen touched her arm. "Can you?"

Jenny nodded. "Yes, I'm not in that much pain. At least, my body isn't in that much pain."

Larsen pursed his lips. "Yeah . . ."

He took the roan's reins from Pecos and turned to the horse. Slash had walked over from the wagon, and now he picked up Jenny's bag from the step. He took her arm and led her over to the wheeled jail.

As he did, Pecos swung up onto Buck's back and rode over to the wagon. He gave the three killers a cold, dark look, silently cautioning them against saying anything to the girl they'd savaged. The three outlaws just stared up at the big man blankly, with customary subtle defiance and vague mocking. No doubt in deference to what Slash had done to Beecher's ear, they kept as silent as church mice as Slash helped the young woman up onto the wagon's seat. The seat was padded with leather, but Slash had further softened it for the girl's comfort with a folded quilt from Carlisle's.

Slash walked around the front of the team and climbed onto the seat beside Jenny, who sat stiffly, staring straight ahead, her hands in her lap, her carpetbag at her feet. Slash released the brake and turned to Pecos, who was riding up beside him.

"Ready," Slash said.

"All right," said Pecos. "I'll ride ahead, hold the point, and swing off the trail now and then to make sure we're not bein' shadowed."

"Good." Slash narrowed one eye as he turned to look up the street to the east, where Larsen sat the roan, silently waiting, looking straight off to the east, wary of the killers' gang making an appearance. "He gonna be all right, you think?"

"I don't know," Pecos said, and nudged his buckskin ahead. "I reckon we'll just have to see."

He booted Buck ahead. As Slash gigged the two geldings and the wagon on down the street, Pecos rode up beside Larsen and stopped. "Why don't I ride point and you ride drag? That way we can keep a better eye on things—front and back."

"Do you think they'll come?" Larsen wanted to know. "The rest of the gang, I mean."

Pecos shrugged. "I reckon it depends on how valuable they see them three back there. I can't imagine they'd risk their own lives to spring Chaney and the others, but, then . . ."

"Maybe they're just as bad as Chaney and the others."

"There you have it. Some of these outlaw gangs are powerful loyal to each other."

Larsen gave a grim smile and glanced at Slash pulling the wagon up behind him and Pecos. "I reckon you two would know a thing or two about that, wouldn't you?"

Pecos gave a sheepish shrug. "Anyways, if they come, I doubt they'll be shy, so we'd best know they're comin' before they get here . . . if you get my drift."

"I get it." Larsen reined his horse away from Pecos and the oncoming wagon. "Drag it is."

"Stop and rest as often as you need to," Pecos said as he booted Buck on ahead.

"I won't need to," Larsen fired back.

"Determined young feller," Pecos said to himself as he pulled away from Larsen and the wagon. He just hoped the young lawman didn't pass out and tumble out of his saddle, because he sure looked like he could.

As Pecos trotted Buck eastward, the burned town dropped away behind him, and the open prairie spread out before him—a gently rolling desert of short, fawn-colored grass, widely scattered ponderosa pines, prickly pear, bitterbrush, and sage. The smell of the sage on the warm morning breeze was a relief after the death and burn stench of the town.

Looking around, Pecos could see for a long way. Out here, men would have to crawl nearly a mile to sneak up on him and his party. The two-track trail they were following meandered off ahead, narrowing and foreshortening into the distance as it became one silver line snaking off toward a distant jog of low hills. A mile or more away, it disappeared over those hills backed up against the bright horizon that shimmered like water.

The wagon rattled behind Pecos, its heavy, iron-shod wheels thundering over chuckholes. Occasionally, Pecos glanced behind to see Slash and the young woman sitting side by side. Slash leaned forward, elbows on his knees, keeping a light hold on the reins. His black hat hid his eyes. The girl sat to his right—straight-backed and grim-faced, staring straight ahead.

Behind them, the motley trio of killers slumped back against the bars, shaking and grimacing against the roughness of the ride.

Twenty minutes later, Pecos topped the line of hills. He stopped and looked around at the mottled gray, green, and brown landscape falling away beyond him in all directions. Occasional rocky outcroppings rose from the prairie, and stone dykes slanted like the backs of half-buried dinosaurs.

Nothing living moved out there. Not even a coyote or a jackrabbit. Occasionally the wind lifted a dust devil, swirled it for a time, then dropped it.

Pecos started down the hill, heading toward a scattering of boulders a hundred yards beyond the hill. He'd just reached level ground and was rounding a bend through the rocks when he saw two horseback riders sitting on the trail ahead of him, another hundred yards beyond.

"Whoa," he said, pulling back on Buck's reins.

He raised his left hand, palm out, and he heard the wagon's incessant clattering dwindle to silence, as Slash said quietly, "Whoa, whoa, hosses . . ."

Pecos glanced back at his partner. Slash was staring beyond Pecos.

"Who do you suppose they are?"

Jenny sat even more rigidly when her own eyes found the two riders.

Beyond the wagon, Larsen said, "What're we stopping for?"

When neither Pecos nor Slash said anything, he galloped up from behind the wagon and drew to a halt beside Pecos. By now, he'd seen the two riders. He and Pecos blinked against the dust catching up to them.

"Two from the gang?" Larsen asked Pecos.

"That's be my wager, the way they're just sittin' there."

Both riders appeared to be holding rifles across the bows of their saddles. One turned to the other one. Pecos thought he could see his mouth move as he said something. Then they each raised their rifles in one hand and triggered shots at the sky. They gave a whoop and a holler, and then reined their horses sharply off opposite sides of the trail, and batted their heels against the mounts' ribs. They were bounding into fast gallops—one to the northeast, the other to the southwest.

Pecos cursed and turned to Slash. "I'm going after one o' them coyotes! Keep the wagon here!"

Pecos spurred Buck into an instant gallop up the trail and then angled off to the northeast, after one of the two fleeing riders.

"Hold on, dammit!" Slash bellowed behind him.

"I'll go after the other one!" Larsen shouted. Beneath the rataplan of Buck's hooves, Pecos heard Larsen's horse whicker, followed by the thunder of the roan's galloping hooves.

"Hold on," Slash called again. "It's probably a trap, you two dunderheads!"

Pecos barely heard and was only vaguely listening to

the last of his partner's admonition. If these two were part of the gang, it was best to thin their ranks as soon as they could, before the others joined them. The rider was about a hundred and fifty yards ahead of Pecos, but Buck was chewing up the ground at a nice clip, gradually closing the gap.

Ahead, horse and rider dashed off across the prairie, trailing a ribbon of tan dust. Occasionally, the rider turned to glance back over his shoulder as though making sure Pecos was following. Horse and rider rose up the near side of a rocky dyke, then disappeared down the other side.

Pecos galloped to the bottom of the dyke, and stopped.

The fleeing rider's dust was still sifting. An eerie silence settled over Pecos and Buck. Pecos stared at the crest of the sandstone dyke. He did not hear the beat of hooves beyond it.

He swung down from the buckskin's back, shucked his Colt's revolving rifle from its scabbard, and adjusted the leather lanyard from which his Richards double-barrel hung barrel down behind his back.

"Stay, Buck."

Pecos walked forward, up the dyke. The closer he drew to the crest the lower he crouched until he dropped to his knees, tossed his hat down, and crabbed to within a few feet of the top. He lifted his head to peer down the other side.

Nothing but fawn desert beyond a dry wash sheathed in scrub.

He was sliding his gaze to his right and along the middle distance when something moved to his left. He turned back to it, saw the hatted head and the rifle of the man crouched behind a rock topping the next rise beyond the one Pecos was on. Pecos pulled his head down, catching only a brief glimpse of smoke and flames stabbing from the rifle's barrel.

The crash of the rifle vaulted, echoing.

The bullet ripped up gravel in front of Pecos and a few inches to his right.

He lifted his head for another look, pulled it down again when he saw the rifle aimed at him.

There were two more blasts, the bullets slamming into the dyke with screeching wails.

Pecos held his head down, expecting another blast or two.

When none came, he lifted his head, as well as his own rifle. He aimed down the barrel, drawing the hammer back, ready to fire. He stared at the rock from behind which his ambusher had fired at him. The man did not reappear. At least, he didn't reappear from behind the rock.

Hooves thudded distantly.

A few seconds later, the horse and rider bounded up a rise beyond the rise from which the man had flung lead a minute ago. This rise was higher than the one before.

Pecos aimed the Colt at the man's back, raising it to allow for the man's climb while also trying to compensate for windage. It would be a hard shot from this distance of probably two hundred yards and with the horse and rider jouncing as they galloped up the ridge, slanting slightly to the right. The man glanced back over his right shoulder as Pecos pulled the Colt's trigger.

The bullet plumed dust just off the right rear hoof of the fleeing rider's horse. The man jerked his head back forward.

Pecos cursed, snapped the hammer back again. He aimed, fired.

A second and a half later, the bullet tore up dirt off the horse's left rear hoof.

Again, Pecos cursed. He fired two more rounds, both falling short of the fleeing rider. Then the man topped the rise and disappeared down the far side.

Guns crackled to the south.

Pecos turned his head to see two riders galloping hard about five and four hundred yards, respectively, away from Pecos's position. One was pursuing the other. It was Larsen pursuing the second gang member. Pecos watched as the fleeing rider triggered a pistol back toward Larsen, who rode low in the saddle, keeping his head below the head of the roan.

Larsen was bound and determined. Despite the lead the man he was pursuing was triggering at him, he did not waver but kept after his quarry in a straight line across the desert. The man he was chasing suddenly dropped into what appeared a shallow canyon, out of sight.

"No," Pecos told Larsen. "Stop, now. Stop!"

But the Dry Fork town marshal kept going until he'd dropped into the canyon and out of Pecos's sight. For a short, eerie time, silence. Like a held breath.

Guns thundered—several of them, triggered fast and with determination. A wicked barrage.

A horse whinnied shrilly.

"Ah, hell!" Pecos heaved himself to his feet and ran down the dyke toward Buck.

They'd caught the young marshal in an ambush!

Chapter 22

Glenn Larsen booted his roan into a ground-eating gallop straight south across the Wyoming desert.

The man he was chasing had swung his own mount from the west to the south, and Larsen felt himself and the roan closing on him gradually. Larsen hunkered low in the saddle. He'd lost his hat in the chase, and his hair blew around his head in the hot wind. His ribs cried out against his crouched position and against the jarring of the hard ride, but the young marshal only gritted his teeth and endured it. The man he was chasing was among the gang of the three killers in the jail wagon. He'd helped rob the stage, rape the female passengers, murdered the men, and driven the stage and team off a cliff and into a canyon.

He was one *of them*. He was here to spring his kill-crazy partners. For that the man would either be taken to Denver for trial, or he would die. Larsen would not allow those killers of his wife and of Henry and of the entire town of Dry Fork to be set free so they could continue their plundering, pillaging, and raping like a band of savage, sword-wielding barbarians from the Dark Ages.

Ahead, Larsen's quarry suddenly dropped out of sight.

It was as though the ground had swallowed him. Larsen saw only the man's sifting tan dust. The young marshal stared straight out over the horse's poll, looking for the man ahead of him. Doing so, he didn't see the sudden drop-off until too late. The horse gave a shrill whinny as the ground suddenly disappeared beneath it, and the horse and rider were tumbling down into a canyon.

Larsen cursed and kicked free of his stirrups.

The horse gave another terrified scream as it and Larsen plunged toward the incline ten feet beneath them. The horse struck first and rolled, kicking up the chalky alkali dust that rose like a clinging white blanket. Larsen hit the incline a quarter second later and rolled down the steep hill. He was vaguely aware of the horse rolling to his right. He was more aware of the crackle of guns, of bullets striking the slope around him.

Trap, he thought. *I rode right into their trap like some shaggy-headed, bucktoothed army recruit fresh out of Jefferson Barracks.*

He and the roan struck the bottom of a sandy wash at the same time. Giving another exasperated whinny, the horse rose, dust and sand streaming off it and billowing around it. The saddle now hung beneath it, as did Larsen's sheathed carbine, well out of reach. As the horse ran off down the wash to the west, seemingly unhurt but only frightened, Larsen rolled up against a hummock in the wash's center. He'd taken a brief glance ahead of him, had seen at least three shooters triggering rifles at him from the bank on the wash's far side, maybe fifty yards away.

Too close. Too damn close.

On the other hand, since he had only his revolver now, they were too far away for him to be able to return fire with much accuracy.

And his ribs were barking at him loudly, causing him to grind his back molars and suck sharp, painful breaths through gritted teeth.

"Damn fool move, Glenn," he berated himself, keeping his head down as more bullets hammered the top of the hummock. "Damn fool move! You're not thinking clearly!"

His physical pain and his mental agony had clouded his mind. He could not get Tiffanie's screams out of his head. For Chrissakes, they'd just started a life together! They'd intended to raise a big family and grow old together! And they would have, too, if not for those savages, just like the ones throwing lead at him now!

He fumbled Henry's Colt from the holster on his right leg, glad that it hadn't fallen out during his tumble. Pressing his back against the hummock, he cocked the revolver and waited for a gap in the shooting so he could return fire. If he could take out one of his ambushers, possibly two, he might have a chance of getting out of the mess he'd gotten himself into.

When the gap he was looking for came, he half turned, leveled the Colt over the top of the hummock, picked out a target, and fired. He saw through his billowing powder smoke that he'd missed cleanly, for the man had seen his move and pulled his head back behind some brush fringing the lip of the wash. Besides, Larsen's ribs ached too badly for him to adequately steady his shooting hand.

They resumed triggering lead at him. As they did, he crabbed to the northeast side of the hummock and dared a look around the edge. He winced when he saw the ambushers spreading out. One dropped quickly down the ravine's bank, landed flat-footed on the bed of the wash, and before Larsen could draw a bead on him, dove behind a rock about six feet out from the wash's bank.

The man was to Larsen's left. Glenn could tell now from the sounds of the continuing gunfire from the other two men that they were moving to the southwest. Soon, they too would drop into the wash and continue firing, pinning him down, until they'd surrounded him and turned him into a sieve.

He pressed his back against the side of the hummock, rested the Colt in his lap.

Odd how he felt no fear. In fact, what was he feeling exactly as the bullets kept coming toward him, spanging off rocks, plowing into the top of the hummock within inches of his head, blowing sand in his hair?

Relief?

His torment would soon be over. He hadn't gotten the three killers to Denver, but that was all right. Maybe the two former outlaws, Braddock and Baker, would. They'd have to beat tall odds, but maybe they could do it. If not, well . . . Larsen would no longer care because he'd be dead. If there really was a Heaven, like all the sky pilots talked about, he'd join his beloved Tiffanie there. Maybe Henry, too. He could apologize to both of them for the stupid, tragic mistake he'd made, hauling the three killers alive to his jail when he could so easily have shot them all as they'd slept and saved the lives of most of the town. . . .

Larsen frowned curiously as the gunfire tapered off. At least, the near shots did. They were replaced by the reports of more distant rifles. A man on the wash's bank howled. There was the thud of a man dropping to the ground.

"Benji, we got trouble—pull out!" another man shouted from the lip of the wash somewhere to the west.

"What the hell's goin' on?" came Benji's reply. Benji must be the ambusher who'd dropped into the wash with Larsen and was hunkered behind the rock.

"Two are shootin' from the northern ridge!" the first man shouted. "Fall back! Fall back!"

Larsen had seen it by then—puffs of smoke rising from the ridge behind him—the ridge over which he'd ridden the roan so carelessly, so stupidly, right into the killers' trap. The bullets weren't landing near him. The shooters up there had to be Braddock and Baker. In fact, squinting his swollen eyes, he could see Braddock's black hat just above the barrel of the rifle on the ridge to Larsen's left, and the high-crowned cream Stetson over the barrel of Baker's Colt's revolving rifle to the young marshal's right. The two men were spaced about fifty yards apart and really giving Larsen's attackers hell.

"Hold up, Duke!" Benji yelled. "Cover me, dammit!"

Larsen turned his head to peer around the left side of his covering hummock. Benji just then bounded up from behind his boulder and ran back toward the ravine's bank. He was a short, stocky man with dark skin and shaggy black hair. He'd just reached the bank when Larsen angled his Colt around the hummock, cocked the piece, aimed, and pulled the trigger.

The Colt barked and bucked.

Benji howled a curse and, half turning toward Larsen, grabbed his right leg. The young marshal's bullet had plowed into the back of it. Gritting his teeth, revealing several gaps in his smile, Benji started to raise the Henry rifle in his hands. Larsen clicked back the Colt's hammer, aimed again, and triggered that second round through Benji's chest, just above the open, skin-exposing V of his partly unbuttoned, pin-striped shirt.

Benji flew backward against the bank. He grunted and groaned as he slid down the face of the bank to sit on his butt at the bottom of the sandy wash. He stared wide-eyed at Larsen, his dark brown eyes glazed with shock. He looked down at the blood bubbling up from the hole in his chest. He brushed at it with one gloved hand. That hand flopped down to his side.

The shooting had stopped. Larsen could hear the fast thuds of a galloping horse dwindling quickly to the south. One of the three shooters had gotten away.

Larsen glowered against his misery as he heaved himself to his feet. He stumbled over to where Benji sat, dying.

"How many of you are there?" Larsen asked, raising the Colt and aiming it at the dying man's forehead. "How many have come?"

Benji's eyes were slow to focus on the young man aiming the Colt at him. A faintly mocking smile pulled at the corners of his wide, thick-lipped mouth inside a dusty, shaggy black beard. "Oh," he wheezed out. "Oh . . . they'll *all* be here . . . soon. We protect . . . our . . . own s-see?"

He broadened his jeering smile at Larsen.

"G-good . . . luck," the man added.

The young marshal drilled a finishing round through the man's forehead.

He lowered the gun and turned to stare at the opposite ridge. He could see neither of his two benefactors. As he began making his slow way back across the ravine, heading for the other side, hoof thuds rose on his left. Slash was trotting up the wash on his Appaloosa, trailing Larsen's roan. Slash had reset the saddle and scabbard. He rode up to the young lawman and glared down at him.

"That was some kind of a damn tinhorn move!"

"I know," Larsen said weakly, already feeling the fool. "I know it was."

"If you want to kill yourself—that's one thing. But I had to leave the wagon to help bail you out of this jam you were in. I had to leave Jenny alone with the wagon and those killers. There was a good chance that *other* killers were waiting for just that to happen, so they'd have a clear path to the wagon . . . and Jenny."

Slash snapped the words out angrily, lashing Larsen with them.

The young marshal felt doubly stupid and guilty.

Slash fairly leaped out of his saddle, unsheathed one of his pretty stag-butted Colts, pressed the barrel to Larsen's forehead, and cocked it. "If you don't want to live, kid, just give me the word and I'll remedy the situation for you!"

Larsen stared back at the man's enraged, dark eyes. He moved his lips but couldn't form words. He wasn't sure what to say.

"Do you want to live?" Slash asked him.

"Huh?"

"Do you want to live? Simple enough question."

Larsen thought about it. He remembered how relieved he'd felt only a few minutes ago when the killers had been closing in on him. Oddly, that feeling was gone. He'd been happy to see Slash and Pecos sending lead down on his attackers. While he'd been prepared to die, he realized now that he was happy to still be alive.

How could that be? She was gone. Their house and their future . . . their town . . . were gone. Henry was gone. But he, Glenn Larsen, was happy to be alive.

"Yes," he said with some chagrin now, staring back at Slash, nodding. "Yes . . . I want to live."

"All right." Slash pulled the gun away from Larsen's head, depressed the hammer. "Whenever you feel like giving up the ghost again, let me know and we'll cut you loose. No more risking my life or his or the girl's or our chances of getting those killers to Cheyenne. All right?"

Larsen drew a breath. "All right."

"All right." Slash shoved the roan's reins at Larsen and swung up onto his Appaloosa's back. "I sent Pecos back to the wagon, to make sure that wasn't part of the trap. Believe me, he's gonna get his own tongue-lashing. He shouldn't have taken that bait, either. I'm gonna hustle back there to make sure everything's all right. I don't hear gunfire, so that makes me feel better."

Before he could put the steel to the Appy's flanks, Larsen said, "Slash?"

The former outlaw turned back to him, frowning impatiently.

"Thanks for saving my fool hide."

Slash stared back at him. The old outlaw's gaze softened. Finally, a faint smile drew up his mouth corners. He winked, then turned forward and spurred the Appaloosa up the ridge.

CHAPTER 23

That night in the Thousand Delights, Jay set a labeled whiskey bottle on a green baize gambling table in the Wolf Den gambling room and said, "Gentlemen—a bottle of my best bourbon on the house!"

A low roar of appreciation rose from the table of seven poker-playing horse buyers from Omaha. The rotund one with the pinky ring and nicely tailored cream suit, said, "Why, Miss Breckenridge, to what do we owe the honor?"

Thick smoke from his Cuban stogie obscured his large, immaculately coifed and bearded head.

"Your patronage, of course," Jay said, flashing her best winning smile, though the man's eyes, she could tell, were mostly on her corset. "You gentlemen have been visiting here in Camp Collins for a week now, and I wanted to show my appreciation for your business. I do hope that on your next horse-buying expedition to these parts, you'll again consider allowing me and the Thousand Delights to offer you shelter, food, drink, and . . ."

She glanced at the young doxie, Bernadette, who was sitting on the knee of one of the other gamblers—a tall, thin man named Schultz who was just then dealing out another hand of Jackpots.

"And anything else you need to keep you happy, warm, and well satisfied."

The men roared their drunken laughter, exhaled their cigar smoke, and broke into the labeled bottle as they continued their game. Jay glanced once more at the doxie. Her long, creamy arms wrapped around Schultz's thin neck, Bernadette grinned and flashed her all-is-well signal with a single, slow blink of her pretty blue eyes.

Jay nodded, then turned and wended her way through the rollicking Saturday night crowd to the bar and to the coffee cup she'd left there. Her place at the bar was well established, and the clientele always left that gap free halfway down the bar's east side from the stairway at the back of the room, as though it were the throne of a well-regarded— possibly even a little feared?—queen.

After all, Jaycee Breckenridge was, indeed, the queen of her domain.

As she plucked her long, slender black Spanish cheroot from the cut glass ashtray and brought it to her lips, the night barman glanced her way and then walked down the bar to her. He plucked a piece of folded notepaper from the pocket of his red silk vest and set in on the bar between Jay's coffee cup and the ashtray.

"Someone slipped me this note for you earlier, Miss Breckenridge."

"Yes, thank you."

Jay took a drag off the cheroot, sent the plume out high against the backbar, then picked up the notepaper and opened it.

Jay,

> *Please visit me at the freight yard when you can break free. I need to talk to you. I will be up all night. I would go to the Thousand Delights, but I don't think we should be seen together.*

> *Urgently,*
> *Myra*

"Oh, no," Jay heard herself say, quickly folding the note closed.

"Trouble?"

Jay gave a start as she turned to see Cisco Walsh standing beside her, on her right. Her heart hiccupped, raced. She closed her hand over the note and stared in shock to see the town marshal standing just inches away from her. She'd done such a good job of avoiding him for the past three days that for some silly reason she'd thought she'd continue to do so. Her not running into him here had been due in no smart part to sheer luck, she did not doubt.

But now here he was in his fine clothes and neatly trimmed and oiled hair and mustache, smiling handsomely down at her, his eyes on her hand clenching the note. He furled his brows as he returned his brown-eyed gaze to her eyes and said, "I hope it's not bad news. From your expression, however, I'm judging it could be better . . . ?"

"Cisco."

Walsh smiled broadly. "How've you been, Jay? It's been a while. If I didn't know better, I'd wager you were avoiding ole Cisco." He smiled again, his eyes burning holes through her own. She flushed, trying to keep her composure. No wilting lily, however, she summoned back her outrage at the man and said, "You won't get away with it, Cisco. I won't let you."

His smile in place, he said, "Buy you a drink?"

"Go to hell. Let me buy you one." She looked at the barman, the only one still working now after midnight though the place was still doing a hopping business, it being Saturday night. "Burt, a brandy for the marshal. That Spanish one."

"Ah, the Spanish one," Walsh said. "You and I have a history with that brandy—don't we, Jay?"

"How long has it been going on, Cisco?"

"How long has what been going on?"

"How long have you been straddling both sides of the law? Here you showed so much disdain for Slash and Pecos. At least they were honest about who they were!"

"Oh, I don't know. A few years." Walsh raised the glass of brandy Burt had just poured for him. He sniffed the rim, took a sip, then licked the end of his damp mustache.

"Where did it start? Here? Abilene? Surely not as far back as Hayes . . . ?"

"Hayes, Kansas."

"That early?" Jay asked with an incredulous chuff. "That was almost twenty years ago."

"Oh, it was just little things. A little graft here and there. A few dollars now and then to look the other way when the cowhand of some wealthy rancher didn't want to spare him from roundup after he'd busted up a saloon. Maybe fifty bucks on occasion to forget to check the roulette wheel for a gaff. That sort of thing." Walsh sipped the brandy again. "Everybody does it, Jay. Sooner or later."

"You know, Cisco, I guess I'd have a little more under-standing if you hadn't been such an insufferable hypocrite about it. You always made me feel so low for *running*, as you called it, with Pete Johnson and Slash and Pecos. You made me feel like some kind of . . . of . . . ten-cent whore or cheaper. You acted as though if I'd thrown in with you, you'd have reformed me, made me respectable, shown me a better, more upstanding way to live. And now I find it was all bull—"

"Easy, Jay," Cisco said, reaching over and wrapping his left hand around her right wrist and squeezing. He kept smiling, though the smile had grown stiff. "Your voice is rising, in case you hadn't noticed."

She looked down at his hand wrapped around her wrist. The dream . . . nightmare . . . came back to her. Her anger was tempered by apprehension.

Was he, as in her dream, capable of killing her?

"Let go of me, Cisco," she ordered him, trying to keep the fear from her voice.

Still smiling, he pulled his hand away from hers. "Here." He reached into his coat and pulled out an envelope about one-half inch thick. He reached into another pocket and pulled out a small, gilt-trimmed, red-velvet box. He set the box atop the envelope.

Jay arched a questioning brow at the man.

"Take a look," he said with feigned casualness, taking another sip of his brandy.

Jay picked up the box. She knew it housed a ring, but she was still flabbergasted to see the ring inside, nestled on a bed of cream taffeta sprinkled with gold dust. The ring, a diamond surrounded by four small rubies, was almost an exact copy of the ring she now wore on her right hand. Slash's ring. Only, the diamond was three times larger and obviously, even to her untrained eyes, of much better quality than the one Slash had given her.

Chuckling and shaking her head, Jay closed the box, set it aside, and peeked into the envelope. Again, she knew what she would find but was still shocked at the crisp fifty-dollar bills peeking out at her and sending their crisp, leathery aroma pushing up around her.

"My God," she said, brushing two fingers across her temple. "You're actually trying to buy me."

"Take it, Jay." Cisco wrapped his hand around her wrist again, but this time the squeeze he gave it was more beseeching than threatening. "*Marry me*. We'll go to Mexico. I have a half interest in a gold mine down there. A very *lucrative endeavor*, I assure you. You wouldn't believe how much gold those bean-eaters are pulling out of the ground every day for me. We can forget about all this." He glanced around as though at some squalid, back-alley crib. "Down there, we'll start over. We'll start over *together*—two brand-new people . . . married and very much in love."

Jay stared at him, having to remind herself over and over again that, unlike a few mornings ago, she was not dreaming. Or was she? She kept half expecting to blink her eyes and wake up in her bed upstairs with the morning light shining into the room.

Walsh continued. "We'll never have to worry about money again. We'll take care of each other in our old age. We'll be *together*, Jay. You have no idea how badly I want that. It's all I've ever wanted—since Hayes. I've been in love with you for years. You ruined me for every other woman. Have you never wondered why I've never asked for one of your girls?"

"I . . . I guess . . . I always thought you went elsewhere," she said uncertainly.

"Well, you were wrong. I can't imagine being with any other woman except you, Jay. You really and truly have my heart. I am pulling this job . . . this one last job . . . for you. I already have a sizable stake, but when this opportunity came up, I couldn't refuse it. It will give us the extra cushion we'll need for the trip. Extra security."

"Cisco, I know very well why you're taking advantage of that opportunity, as you call it." She paused, stared up at him, blinked. "I heard that part of the conversation, too. Hall knows something about your past. Some dark secret. He's using it against you."

His hand came off her wrist. His face slackened, no trace of the former smile remaining. It was almost as though she'd slapped him across his face. He drew a breath, released it, sipped his brandy. He appeared suddenly so crestfallen that Jay almost found herself feeling sorry for him.

"Cisco, you can tell—"

He turned to her again quickly. "Just know that I love you, Jay. There'll never be another woman for me." He set the ring box atop the money again and slid it closer to her. "Take that. As a token of my love. Please, take it."

"I already have a ring, Cisco." She held up her hand. "Remember?"

He winced as though she'd struck him again. "He can't love you as much as I do, Jay."

"How can you be so sure?"

"I know who he is."

"Yes, well, I thought I knew who you were."

"I'm still the same person, Jay. This doesn't change anything."

"Of course, it does!" she said with a caustic laugh. "It changes everything. If I ever had feelings for you, which I think I did, I don't anymore."

"I'm no worse than him."

"We've been through that. At least Slash doesn't pretend to be anything than what he is, what he's always been!"

On the other hand, she thought with frustration, *he's never declared his love for me, opened his heart to me, with anything close to the fervor that Cisco just did.* Jay shook her head as she gazed up into the lawman's eyes. "Call it off, Cisco. If I really do mean something to you, call it off. Cancel the robbery."

"I can't. It's out of my hands."

"It can't be!"

"It is." Walsh paused, studied her closely, his focus shuttling between her eyes, as though desperately trying to plumb her depths. "Stay out of it, Jay. Forget what you heard outside the billiard room. Forget it for me, but most of all forget it for yourself."

"I can't."

Again, his hand closed around hers. He squeezed again and the threat was back in his voice. Anger blazed in his eyes. "I love you, Jay. I would hate like hell for anything to happen to you!"

"How dare you threaten me here in my own establishment!" Jay jerked her hand from his and stepped back, returning his cold-blooded glare. "Get out. Now. Before I have the bouncers throw you out!"

She'd said that loudly enough for several men and the bartender to have overheard. Faces turned toward her and Walsh. The marshal flushed.

The barman said with concern, "Everything all right, Miss Breck—"

"Yes, it's fine, Burt," Jay said, keeping her gaze on Walsh. "The marshal was just leaving."

"Keep it under your hat, Jay," Walsh said warningly. He stuffed the ring and envelope into his pocket. He threw back the last of his brandy, set his hat on his head, wheeled, and strode out through the batwings. The doors clattered angrily into place behind him.

Jay flushed with embarrassment as several customers continued regarding her curiously. She turned to the bar, her gaze averted, and plucked her cheroot from the ashtray. The bartender set a goblet on the bar in front of her and splashed Spanish brandy into it. "You look like you could use a drink."

Again, she flushed, smiled. "I do, indeed. Thank you."

Burt returned the smile, shoved the cork back into the bottle, and returned the bottle to the backbar shelf. Jay took a deep drink of the brandy, then opened her left hand in which she'd been squeezing the note Myra had sent her. By now it was wrinkled and damp from the sweat of Jay's palm. She opened it quickly, read it again, then refolded it, slipped it into her corset, and threw back the rest of her brandy.

She asked Burt to close up the saloon for her. They closed at two on Saturday, which was an hour away. Jay couldn't wait that long. She had to get over to the freight yard and see Myra about the note.

Her visit with Cisco Walsh had made Myra's note sound all the more urgent.

CHAPTER 24

Slash galloped over a rise and down the north side.

Ahead, the jail wagon remained where they'd left it on the shaggy two-track trail. His heart lightened. Since he'd left the canyon and young Larsen, he'd imagined any number of horrific events, all involving the young schoolteacher and the gang that had come to spring their partners.

Thankfully, that hadn't happened.

Pecos was there now, standing with the teacher a hundred feet west of the wagon.

Wait. Something was wrong.

Slash reined his Appy to a halt, scrutinized Pecos and the young teacher. They were standing close together, and Pecos had his hand around Jenny's waist, lending comfort. The three killers sat slouched in the jail wagon, staring at the pair. Jenny stood with her head down. She appeared to be sobbing.

What the hell . . . ?

Slash booted the Appaloosa into a hard gallop.

"What's wrong," he said, checking the mount down near the girl and Pecos. "What the hell happened?"

Pecos looked sheepish as he patted the girl's back.

Jenny turned sharply to Slash and said, "Nothing. I just let them get to me, that's all."

"What do you mean?" Slash asked from the saddle.

"It's my fault," Pecos said, looking up at Slash. "I never should have ridden off like that. I'm the reason the whole thing happened. Why the kid left and then you had to leave her alone."

"What whole thing, dammit?"

Jenny looked at Slash. She opened her mouth to speak, but then closed it again. Her face was drawn and pale behind the bruises they'd given to her when they so violently ravaged her. A cold stone dropped in Slash's belly.

"What'd they say to you?" he asked through a growl. "When you were alone with them, they said something. What was it?"

Pecos looked sharply at his partner. "Don't cheat the hangman, Slash!"

Slash kept his eyes on Jenny. "What'd they say?"

She sobbed, brushed tears from her cheeks, and said, "They . . . they told me what they were going to do to me once you and Pecos and Marshal Larsen were dead," she said, wiping a fresh batch of tears from her cheeks. "And that's all I'm going to say about it. I will not repeat what they said they were going to do."

"Who? Which one? Or all three?"

"Chaney, mostly," Pecos said, drawing the horrified girl close against him.

Slash turned the Appy and slapped the rein ends against its right hip. "*Hi-yahh, beast—go!*"

"Slash, dammit!" Pecos yelled behind him. "Let it go. It's my fault! What did you *think* was gonna happen when you left her alone, you damned idiot!"

Slash only distantly heard his partner's castigating words.

Rage overwhelmed him. He reined the Appy to a skidding halt beside the wagon and swung down from the saddle. He released the keeper thong over his right-hand Colt and turned to the wagon.

Resting back against the bars on the opposite side of the wagon, the three prisoners stared back at him with their customary silent mockery, faint sneers on their mouths.

"What's the matter?" Hell-Raisin' Frank Beecher asked with feigned concern. "You lose the young marshal? If so, I'm sorry to hear that. It's always sad to lose one so young."

"Shut up, Beecher."

"Oh, all right."

Slash glared through the iron bands at Chaney. "I warned you, you devil."

Chaney snapped his eyes wide in astonishment. "*Now* what I do?"

Slash fumbled the keys out of his pants pocket. He walked over to the rear of the wagon.

"Don't do it, Slash!" Pecos said as he walked toward the wagon from the west, Jenny right behind him.

Slash leaned his shotgun against the wagon, then poked his key in the door's lock and turned the key until he heard the bolt slide back into the door. Leaving the key in the lock, he shucked the right-hand Colt from its holster, cocked it, and aimed it into the wagon as he drew the door open with his left hand.

"Out, Chaney."

"What's this all about?" the outlaw said innocently.

"Out, Chaney. Out now!"

"I don't know," he said, glancing wide-eyed at his two partners. There was still mockery in his eyes, though he was feeling the bite of apprehension, as well. Slash could tell, though the man desperately tried to cover it. "I think

I'd best stay right here. You're runnin' off your leash, Slash!"

"Slash, dammit!" Pecos yelled, stopping by Slash's horse and resting his fists on his hips.

Slash raised the Colt shoulder-high, narrowed one eye as he aimed down the barrel at Chaney's right leg. "Let's see if I can get both legs to match."

"No, no, no, no, no!" Genuine fear flashed in the man's eyes now. "No call for that! I'm comin'! I'm comin'! Just movin' a little slow now, as I'm sure you can under—wait, now . . . *ah-ohhahhhh-geeeeshhhhh*!"

He'd been half out of the wagon, dragging his tender leg, when Slash grabbed the back of his shirt collar and pulled him through the door.

"Oh, for Pete's sake!" Pecos said, appearing resigned to just stand by the Appaloosa and watch.

Chaney hit the ground and rolled, cursing, dust rising around him. Both Beecher and Black Pot lunged toward the door. Slash grinned and slammed the door in their faces. He locked it, pulled the key out, and tossed it to Pecos, who caught it against his chest. He turned to Chaney, who was howling like a stuck pig, half sitting up and clutching his wounded leg.

"What'd I tell you?" Slash barked at him.

"I misremember," Chaney said, sucking a sharp breath through clenched teeth. "What'd you tell me?"

"By the time I'm done with you, you'll remember!" Slash said, burying the toe of his right boot in the killer's stomach.

Chaney grunted and flew back against the ground.

"*Owww! Oh, stop!*" bellowed Black Pot in amused exasperation from the jail wagon. Both he and Beecher watched in bright-eyed fascination through the door.

Chaney sat up again, gasping for breath, holding his hands out in surrender.

Slash walked up to him and thrust his right boot through both hands, burying the toe once again in Chaney's belly.

Chaney fell back, wailing. Slash stayed with him, kicking him in his belly, in his side. When the man was on his belly, Slash kicked him over onto his back again and continued to work on the man's gut and ribs.

"Slash!"

The former cutthroat ignored the girl's pleading cry behind him.

He kicked Chaney over a prickly pear, rammed his boot into his side . . .

"Slash!"

Slash stepped toward Chaney again, drew his foot back, but before he could hammer it forward again, the girl leaped onto his back. She wrapped her arms around his neck. Slash's knees buckled, and grunting fiercely, she drove him to the ground.

Slash cursed and looked at her where she'd fallen ahead of him, just then lifting her head and tossing her dusty hair back from her face. He scowled at her, angry.

He'd fully intended to kick the man to death. The executioner would still have two more to hang. He'd get his pay.

"Slash!" she cried again, hardening her jaws. Her eyes were bright with trepidation.

"What is it?" he said.

"To the west, partner," Pecos said behind him, his voice mild but fateful.

Slash held his gaze on Jenny for another count. She jerked her head to indicate west. Slash turned to see four men sitting four horses atop a knoll maybe a quarter mile away. He rose slowly, wincing against the creak in his knees. Both ex-cutthroats turned to gaze toward the western knoll.

The four horseback riders were silhouetted against the bright western sky.

They sat there for maybe twenty more seconds. Just sitting there. Not moving. One of the horses lowered its head to graze, but the rider pulled its head back up by its reins.

All at once, they neck-reined their horses around and slowly, casually rode down the opposite side of the rise, the horses dropping out of sight first followed by the men, the crowns of their hats disappearing last. A tendril of dust rose above the knoll and quickly faded.

Then the riders were gone and an eerie silence hung over the sun-washed desert.

Slash turned to Pecos. "Where's Larsen?"

"I don't . . ."

Jenny gasped and pushed to her feet, looking around.

Slash strode quickly toward his Appaloosa, preparing to mount again and ride off to look once more for the young marshal, fearing the four gang members—who else could they have been?—had captured him while he'd been kicking the stuffing out of both ends of Talon Chaney.

"No, no," Pecos said, holding up a waylaying hand to Slash. He stared toward the southwest. "Here he comes."

Slash saw the horse and rider then, too, moving slowly toward the jail wagon. The young marshal likely felt worse after the spill he'd taken.

"Thank God," Jenny said, standing beside Slash. Slash sighed in relief. He and Jenny shared a look. "Sorry, darlin'," he said.

She shook her head, offered a wan smile. "I came willingly. I knew what I was likely in for."

Slash kissed her cheek, said, "We'll try to do better next time."

He and Pecos got Chaney back in the wagon. The man was only half-conscious and blubbering, cursing, calling Slash, "Crazy . . . crazy . . . crazy as two coots in a lightnin' storm . . ."

They closed the door and locked it. The other two prisoners merely stared at their jailers in sullen silence.

Slash turned to Pecos with a sheepish sigh, brushing his hands off on his pants. "All right, that was stupid. We both did somethin' stupid. So we're even."

"What you did was dumber than what I did," Pecos said.

By now, Larsen had made it back to the wagon. From his saddle, he said, "I'm the stupid one. Pecos expected me to stay with the wagon. If I had . . ."

"Pecos would've still ridden into their ambush," Slash said.

Pecos whipped an angry look at Slash and opened his mouth for a harsh retort, but Jenny stepped up and held the back of her hand up over his mouth.

"Gentlemen," she said firmly, "what's done is done. Perhaps we'd best get moving before we waste any more time out here . . . ?"

"The teacher's right, you big idiot," Slash snapped, walking around Pecos toward his horse.

Pecos slapped him with his hat.

Late in the afternoon, Slash watched Pecos gallop toward him from the east.

The wagon rocked and rattled, and the geldings' shoes kicked up dust—so much of it that Jenny, sitting beside Slash on the driver's seat—had tied a bandanna over her mouth and nose. Slash held the harness ribbons loosely in his gloved hands. The horses didn't need steering. They knew to follow the trail, and there weren't so many trails out here that they got confused. In fact, this single, two-track trail was the only trail Slash had seen since they'd left Dry Fork that morning. No others except a couple of old Indian hunting trails and buffalo trails had so far intersected it.

A vast lonely landscape out here. A menacing one, under the circumstances.

"Any sign of 'em?" Slash asked as Pecos drew his buckskin up beside the wagon, to Slash's left, and followed along even with the driver's seat.

"Nope."

Slash looked at him with sharp surprise. "*What?*"

"No sign. Not a print. Not a single apple."

"Well, I'll be hanged."

"What's the matter, Slash? Why do you look so glum? That's good news, not bad news."

Slash scratched the beard stubble on his cheek as he looked warily around. The young marshal rode point now, roughly fifty yards up the trail. "I don't believe it."

"Well, I didn't see nothin', and I rode a half mile out in all directions."

"Well, then, they're three-quarters to a mile out. They're doggin' us, all right."

"What makes you think so, Slash?" Jenny asked him, sitting to his right.

"That spider crawling around under my right ear is talkin' to me."

"I don't see any spider under your ear," Jenny said.

"You may not see it, but it's there, all right. Whenever I feel that spider crawling around, I know I got wolves on my trail." He looked to the east, beyond Pecos, to the south, which was straight ahead, and then to the west. He wagged his head and scratched behind his ear. "They're out they're doggin' us. I know they are."

"Maybe those four we seen on the knoll weren't part of the gang." Pecos was building a quirley while he rode loosely in his saddle. "Maybe they was ranch hands just givin' a quick scout. No doubt curious about the jail wagon an' all."

Slash glanced into the cage behind him, through the closely woven iron mesh that fronted the bars so the prisoners couldn't poke their arms through and strangle the driver, or grab a weapon from the driver's box. "Chaney, did you recognize them four on the hill earlier?"

Chaney gave only a guttural curse. He lay on his side on a straw pallet, curled in the fetal position, clutching his battered ribs.

Black Pot and Beecher sat reclining against the cage's rear door, ankles crossed before them. The half-breed was chewing a weed he'd plucked through the side bars from along the trail. "Talon ain't at his best right now. Not after the stompin' you gave him, old ma—er, I mean, Mr. Slash."

Black Pot grinned.

"How 'bout you two," Pecos asked them, hipped around in the saddle to see into the cage. "Did you recognize 'em?"

"Nah," Beecher said, shaking his shaggy head and blowing cigarette smoke out his nostrils. "They were too far away."

"You can bet they were our boys, though." Black Pot drew his thick lips back from his ragged teeth in a seedy smile, his black eyes glinting in the waning sunlight. One long, blueblack braid hung down over his chest while the other one trailed out through the bars behind him. "You can bet your last dollar on that. And I do believe you're right, Slash. They're stayin' just far enough back to keep you guessin', just like you're doin'. Probably just waiting for all the others to join 'em before they make their move."

"If I were you two gentlemen," Beecher said, "I would stop this cart right now and let us out. You let us go, we'll let *you* go . . . as a gesture of our endless appreciation. No harm won't come to any of you. You can just be on your way unfettered . . . get the pretty teacher and the young marshal to Denver all safe and sound."

"Don't go feelin' too smug," Slash warned the killer. "If it looks like they're getting close enough to spring you, I'm gonna shoot all three of you devils through the bars, toss your carcasses to the coyotes. You'd best hope they stay back. Far back!"

"Say, now—that ain't fair!" Black Pot yelled, glowering at Slash through the iron mesh.

"Shut up!" Slash said. He turned to Pecos. "They're out there. Guaranteed."

Pecos drew deeply on his quirley, blew the smoke into the wind, and nodded grimly.

CHAPTER 25

The Thousand Delights's kitchen was quiet and dark, as Jay had expected it would be. Excepting special occasions, she always closed the kitchen, sent the cooks home, and stopped serving food after nine. Most folks were not at the saloon/ brothel/gambling parlor to dine that late, anyway. They were here for sundry other pleasures of the flesh.

She could still smell the lingering delightful aroma of the duck à l'orange she'd put on special earlier that evening, and suppressed a hunger pang. She walked out from the mouth of the stairs and across the rear corner of the dark kitchen. She banged her right knee against a stool someone had left where it shouldn't be, and stopped to suck a sharp breath through her teeth, bending over to clutch the bone in question, trying to squeeze the pain out of it.

She cursed the cook or houseboy who'd left the stool there but was happy when the pain quickly subsided. Limping only slightly, she continued to the outside door and lifted the steel locking bar that was always placed in the brackets once the kitchen was closed, to keep anyone from entering through the rear door. She leaned the bar in the corner by the door, then opened the door and stepped out into the dark alley. She looked around furtively.

Nearly as dark as the inside of a glove out here. It was almost one thirty by now, for after Cisco Walsh had left in a huff, she'd gone upstairs to change into a simpler, more comfortable, dark-colored day dress and black sweater, as well as a black hat so she'd be less visible. The Thousand Delights was probably the last place in town still open except for the seedier hurdy-gurdy parlors out by the now-defunct military fort and the river, so she thought her chances of being seen outside and on the prowl were slim.

She'd intended to take the back way to the freight yard, but she hadn't counted on it being this dark in the narrower alleyways, so she walked around the rear of the Thousand Delights and made her way to the front, her way lighted by the lamplit windows on her right, which she ducked under so no one inside would see her. Being seen by anyone out of doors this time of the night would start the rumor mill churning. By now, half the town probably knew about her blowup with Walsh at the bar. Now she was stealing around outside, dressed in black.

What could she possibly be up to at this unseemly hour? Perhaps heading for a tryst with some mystery man?

Jay didn't know if Walsh had anyone spying on her, but since he'd had the livery hostler watching for her, she didn't count it out. If the crooked marshal knew she was stealing around outside in the dark of the night, he'd likely assume it was on account of the robbery he had planned. Not that Jay knew the robbery was why Myra had summoned her with the note, but what other reason could there be?

When she'd gained the main street, she looked around

to make sure no one else was around or on the saloon's high front veranda, then hurried across the street and, clinging to the dense shadows of the false-fronted façades on that side, made her way east, occasionally weaving around telegraph poles. The broad street was penetrated by the flickering lights of millions of stars awash across the black sky arching over the town, so she had little trouble making it to the northeast side street she'd headed for. She'd seen no one but a couple of stray dogs scavenging for scraps in a trash heap by the Bon-Ton Café.

Turning north on this narrower side street, she slowed her pace. It was darker here, for trees and warehouses blocked the starlight. She didn't want to trip over something and further hurt herself. She'd walked only a few feet, heading north, when she stopped suddenly with a slight gasp and whipped around to face the main street again.

She'd heard something. She wasn't sure what it was, but it had been a stealthy sound. A man-made one. As though someone were stealing up behind her. Jay stared back toward the main street, which she could barely make out in the darkness. It was all so dark here on the side street that she couldn't see much better than in the alley behind the saloon.

She heard it again—a soft, scraping sound. Someone dragging a spur on the ground?

Her heart quickened. Cisco had followed her out here. She remembered her dream, the chilling, suffocating sensation of his hands around her neck, trying to squeeze the life out of her.

"Who's there?" she said, hearing a quiver in her voice.

Silence followed by a shuffling sound.

Louder, putting some anger in her voice, Jay said, "Who's there? Come out where I can see you!"

Silence.

Jay's heart beat faster. Her mouth went dry. She half waited for the flash of a gunshot in the darkness. No, he wouldn't shoot her. Too loud. It would draw others. He'd likely use a knife or maybe, as in her dream, he'd try to strangle her. . . .

"Cisco?" she called, louder, wondering if she should scream for help. "Is that you?" Pause. She moved forward, toward the break between two small, wood-frame grain warehouses. "It is, isn't—" Her voice broke into a clipped scream just before she closed her hand over her mouth.

She stumbled straight backward as a loud growl was followed by a yip, and two short, shadowy figures bounded out of the gap and into her path. They ran past her and into the street—two skirmishing dogs. They appeared to be a large, shaggy dog and a smaller dog with shorter fur. The larger one had something in its jaws, a bone of some kind, and it was teasing the smaller dog with it.

They ran off together, the dog with the bone growling and prancing, and the shorter one yipping angrily and leaping against the larger one, trying to dislodge the bone from its mouth. They disappeared into a gap on the street's other side, and their soft foot thuds and growling and yipping faded as they disappeared.

Jay threw her head back and drew a relieved breath, released it slowly. Her knees were still shaking. She thought for a moment they would buckle and she'd fall to the street. She chuckled and, relief still washing over her, her heart still beating quickly, she swung around and continued walking north.

Just dogs. A couple of silly dogs fighting over a bone . . .

She took three steps and stopped again.

A man had just stepped out of the gap on the other side of the warehouse. This was a man, all right. Not a dog. She could see his silhouetted figure in the darkness ten feet ahead of her. He wore a broad-brimmed hat and a long coat. Something glistened around his middle. A gun. He was holding a gun, aiming it at her.

"Make one sound and I'll shoot," he said softly with quiet menace. "You're coming with us."

That "us" should have tipped her off. But she hadn't been able to override her impulse to turn and run, which she did—right into the second man who'd stolen up behind her. Jay gave a startled "*Oh!*" and pushed away from the man. She backed into the first one, who now stood unyielding behind her. She started to twist around toward him, and as she did, he stuffed a gag between her lips and quickly tied it tightly behind her head, squelching her cries.

She smelled the burlap of a gunnysack as one or maybe both of her assailants pulled it down over her head, turning the night even darker, blacker, horrifying. She struggled madly, her heart really racing now, but there was nothing she could do. They wrapped ropes around her chest and waist, tying the sack over her. They tied another rope around her ankles, tying them together. Then one of them slung her up and over his shoulder.

She'd never been as frightened as she was now, suddenly wrapped and bound like a cut of beef, and carried off like a sack of grain. She couldn't punch, kick, scream, or fight in any way. She was totally at the mercy of her captors. If they wanted to throw her in a river to drown, there was nothing she could do about it.

They carried her off. She could hear the harsh breathing of the man carrying her. He jogged, tripped, almost dropped her—almost fell!—before he righted himself. She heard the other man say, "Careful, Anders!"

"Shut up," Anders grunted, breathing hard again as he ran.

Jay heard a horse give a nervous whicker. Anders stopped.

She felt his hands around her waist, hurting her, pulling her down off his shoulder and then giving her a heave. She landed hard on a rough board surface. Her ears rang with the sudden impact against the back of her head. Pain knifed through her brain. She felt the boards jerk around beneath her.

A wagon. They'd thrown her into a wagon.

Hinges squawked. That sound was followed by the sharp thud of an end gate being closed and then bolted shut.

"All right," one of the men said nervously, keeping his voice down. "Let's go!"

Jay thrashed. Or tried to. They'd tied the bag over her. It came down to just above her waist. They'd tied her ankles, as well, so all she could really do was wriggle around like a worm impaled on a fishhook. She jerked as the wagon bolted forward. It rocked and rattled beneath her, banging her around. She rolled to one side and felt something relatively soft. Possibly a feed sack of some kind. She wriggled around, shoving upward with her heels, and got her head and shoulder far enough atop the feed sack that it offered at least enough cushion to render a braining not quite as imminent as a minute ago.

She struggled against the bindings around her waist but made no headway. Her captors had tied them tight. There was no give in the ropes tying her ankles, either. Beneath her, the wagon rocked, pitched, hammered over chuckholes, and swayed to and fro. She gritted her teeth against the discomfort. Rolling onto her back seemed to make it easiest on her bones. Wherever they were taking her, she hoped it wasn't far. On the other hand, what if they were taking her somewhere private to kill her?

After she'd endured the ride for ten or so minutes, she realized they were in the country. They were heading down a relatively narrow track, moving steadily forward without slowing. That meant they were in the countryside beyond Camp Collins.

How far would they go? What would happen when they arrived at their destination? Who were these men and who had sent them? She wasn't sure why, but something told her they weren't acting on their own.

Cisco Walsh.

Of course. He'd sent them. But how had he known where she was heading? Had he somehow managed to read the note that Myra had sent her? That couldn't be possible. She'd seen him when he'd come into the saloon, and she'd immediately concealed the note in her hand.

A spy. Yes, that was it. He'd had someone spying on her. Maybe the two men driving the wagon. When and if she left the Thousand Delights, they were to grab her and . . .

Do what?

She supposed she was going to learn the answer to that question soon.

Walsh. These men had to be working for Walsh.

Cocooned inside the stinky gunnysack, bound and gagged, she had no option but to endure the misery and the fear that came along with the predicament. It was true. When death threatens, you really do see your life in bits and pieces flashing through the eye in your mind. She saw many scenes from her girlhood on a farm in Nebraska . . . from the time she ran away from an abusive father and made her way to St. Louis . . . from Hayes and Dodge City, where she survived any way she could, ways that she wasn't so proud of now . . . from her first meeting with Pistol Pete, when the charming old outlaw, drunk as a lord, drew her onto his lap after he'd watched her dance in the One-Legged Rooster, and took her under his wing.

When Pete died, she'd been bereft, but she'd pushed on . . . continuing to live in their old outlaw cabin in the San Juan Mountains, giving shelter to Slash and Pecos from time to time when they found themselves on the run, as they so often had back in those days.

Slash.

She was going to miss him. Did she love him? She'd thought until now that she did, but maybe she'd only been fooling herself because she'd wanted to love him, to settle down with him. If the truth be known—and there was nothing like knowing the truth when you thought your life was near its end—she wasn't sure she was capable of love anymore. She'd been through too many ups and downs . . . too many forks in the trail . . . too many men . . . too many disappointments.

Maybe that right there was what had attracted her to Slash. He'd been through the mill himself. If anyone had a solid understanding of the term "ridden hard and put up wet," that man was Slash. He understood her. And she understood him. Deep down, she'd always known it and maybe he did, too, though he wasn't the kind of man who could speak his true feelings.

That's what had surprised her about Cisco. She'd be damned if she really hadn't started to believe him earlier, when he so earnestly and vehemently professed his love for her. She'd damn near fallen for it. But now she was being carted into the mountains—she could feel the wagon climbing and causing her to keep squirming forward to remain on the sack—to possibly be killed for what she'd learned about Cisco's corruption.

The rocking and rattling, the incessant jerking from side to side, finally stopped after what had seemed a long, long journey from town. She knew it had seemed a lot longer than it actually had been, which was probably around an hour, but it had felt like a week. Several times, Jay had honestly thought she would go mad.

Despite that the end of the journey might very well mean the end of her life, she was glad when the wagon finally rocked to a stop and she heard the brake being slid into place. She heard the thuds of the men's boots and their grunts as they leaped to the ground.

Jay tried to speak through the gag, but instead of it sounding like, "Where the hell am I and what do you intend to do with me?" it sounded like a cat being strangled.

"Grab her," said one of the men.

Jay knew it was pointless fighting, so she merely endured the brusque way they pulled her out over the open tailgate. One of them drew her up over his arm again. His shoulder was a hard lump against her belly, making it hard to breath. More jostling as the man carried her. His boots crunched gravel, then thumped on wood. They were rising, climbing steps. She heard a door latch click. Hinges squawked. A door shuddered in a frame.

The man carried her forward—likely through the door and into the cabin or whatever form of shelter it was. If it was a cabin, it was one with a low door, because she felt him duck and crouch a little as he carried her through it. Her left shoulder knocked against something solid—the doorframe, probably—scraping her flesh through the sack. She grunted miserably through the gag.

The man crouched forward. Jay slid off his shoulder to the floor with a *bang!*

Jay grunted and cursed sharply through the gag, though again it sounded like a strangling cat. Stars of pain flashed behind her eyes. One of the men laughed and said, "Jesus, Sully!"

The other man laughed then, too.

There was a loud wooden scraping sound. Then what sounded like more hinges squawked. Another *bang!* as something hard struck the floor, making the whole cabin (or whatever this place was) leap around Jay.

Jay thought, *What in God's name are these two devils up to?*

The question came in the form of a kick to her side.

She rolled to her left. Suddenly, the floor was gone. She dropped like a rock.

She landed on something hard. Bells clanged in her ears. A hot bayonet of pain was driven through the back of her head and into her shoulders. *No*, she thought. *Stay awake! Stay awake!*

But then the gauzy black tar of sleep overtook her, though not before she heard something slam above her and she realized that she'd just been dropped, bound and gagged, into a cellar.

Buried alive.

CHAPTER 26

A shrill cry plucked Glenn Larsen from a shallow sleep.

He sat up, heart pounding, and said, *"Tiffanie?"*

Instantly, however, the current state of his being came back to him. He remembered it all, knew where he was—camped in a grove of pines near a sandy ravine, on his way to Denver.

"No," Jenny Claymore's voice said softly in the darkness. "It was just me, Glenn. I'm sorry I woke you."

Larsen turned to where she lay on the other side of the cold, dark ashes of their fire. As his eyes adjusted to the darkness, relieved only by starlight flickering above the gently swaying crowns of the pines, he saw her sitting up and staring into the darkness, as he was.

"It's all right," he said quietly. "Are you all right, Jenny?"

"I had a dream. A nightmare. I'm all right now."

"Right."

"Are you all right, Glenn?"

Larsen drew a breath, looked around. Slash and Pecos were not in the camp. They were off keeping watch from a good distance away. The jail wagon containing the killers was parked with the horses to the north of the camp. For a short, blissful second, after Larsen had heard Jenny call out, he'd imagined that Tiffanie was still alive. And that maybe there was something he could do to save her. What a warm, sweet, promising feeling it had been. Gone now.

"Yeah," Larsen lied. "I'm all right."

"Yeah." Jenny gave a soft, ironic chuckle. "Me too."

"You thirsty?" Larsen asked her. "I have a canteen over here."

She didn't respond for a few seconds, then said, "Yeah, I guess I could use a sip or two . . . if you have some to spare."

"Plenty."

They'd stopped earlier to fill several canteens at a shallow stream earlier in the afternoon. The water was nowhere near sweet, but it was wet. Larsen rose from his blankets and picked up his canteen, as well as his tin cup. He picked up the flask sitting there, as well. Slash had offered him the ex-outlaw's own private traveling flask to help with the pain in his battered bones. Larsen had never been much of a drinking man, but he had cottoned to the firewater's pain-relieving properties.

He walked around the fire to where Jenny now sat back against a pine. It was a chilly, high-desert night, and she'd pulled two blankets up to her neck.

"Do you have a cup?" Larsen asked her. "Yes, here."

Larsen took her cup, half-filled it with water, the surface of which shone in the starlight. He held up the flask. "Any of this?"

She smiled, shrugged. "Why not? Just a little."

Larsen added a splash of bust-head to the water. He gave her the cup, then poured a little water and whiskey into his own. The truth was, he wasn't thirsty, and he doubted that Jenny was, either. He'd just wanted an excuse to join her over here on this side of the cold fire. He didn't feel like lying over there alone anymore, feeling restless and assaulted with half-formed nightmare images of the night the killers had burned Dry Fork.

"Well," Larsen said, touching his cup to hers and chuckling.

"Cheers."

She snorted a laugh of her own and said, "Cheers." They each sipped, then just sat staring into the darkness.

Larsen turned to Jenny and said, haltingly, "Would . . . you like to . . . talk about it? The nightmare, I mean."

Jenny looked at him, pursed her lips, and shook her head. "No, I don't think so." She looked down at her cup and then at him again. "What about you?"

He thought about it. Then he shook his head. "Wouldn't help, I guess, would it?"

"I don't think so." She sighed and stared at the cold, gray fire ashes. "As I was riding along today in the wagon, I kept wondering if life will ever look right to me again. Like it once was. Will I ever be happy again instead of . . . miserable? Frightened?"

"Yeah," Larsen said, raising one knee and resting an arm on it. "Me too. I can't imagine it. I knew Tiffanie for such a short time, but—this might sound stupid—but I really did feel like I knew her all of my life."

"That doesn't sound *stupid* at all, Glenn." Jenny set her cup down, snaked both of her arms around his, and pressed her forehead against his shoulder. "I know how much she meant to you. I also know how much you meant to her. We were friends, you know?" She smiled up at him. "She told me all about this handsome young man who rode into Dry Fork and stole her heart. She knew it right away— that you were the one for her. The moment you walked into her father's mercantile asking for saddle soap . . . and a job."

Glenn smiled, felt his cheeks warm with embarrassment. "I didn't get the job."

"No, but you got the girl."

He turned his smile on Jenny. "She told you all that, did she?"

"She certainly did."

Larsen drew a deep breath, feeling the air flutter in his throat. "I miss her." His voice threatened to crack.

Jenny pressed her forehead to his shoulder again. "I know. But you're lucky. It never got old or turned bad. You'll have pleasant memories."

"Sorry, Jenny. I mean about . . . you know . . . Malcolm . . ." He could hardly bring himself to utter the man's name.

"Malcolm," Jenny said darkly. "Yes, good ole Dave Malcolm." Malcolm was a businessman from Kansas City who'd bought a ranch north of Dry Fork. He didn't spend a lot of time on the ranch, preferring to remain in Kansas City, but he'd spent several months on the spread the previous summer. He'd spotted Jenny in town one day, looking at dresses for the coming school year, and he'd introduced himself and even bought her a dress against her protestations. Larsen had heard this from Tiffanie. He'd also heard that the rancher, who was a good ten years older than Jenny but quite dashing and well-educated, had become quite smitten with the pretty young teacher. Jenny had become quite enamored of Malcolm. What young woman of paltry means living in a rooming house with two miserly old spinsters wouldn't tumble for such a handsome flatterer? They'd struck up a whirlwind romance, Malcolm even inviting Jenny out to his ranch on occasion.

Eventually, the man got down on one knee in the drawing room of Jenny's rooming house and asked Jenny for her hand in marriage. After a week's deliberation and against her own better judgment, Jenny had told him yes. She wasn't getting any younger and the West was not filled with Dave Malcolms—at least, not for young women like Jenny. Late in the summer, Malcolm went back to Kansas City to "get his business affairs in order"—in preparation for the wedding. It was merely the tedious preamble, he assured her, to the long fantasy of their lives together. He'd told Jenny he'd send for her soon.

But he'd never sent for her.

In fact, she never heard from him again. Whom she did hear from was the man's wife.

Yes, all along, Malcolm had had a wife in Kansas City. Apparently, the wife had learned of her husband's dalliance in Dry Fork from the wife of one of Malcolm's business partners, and she'd taken the man to task for his indiscretion. She'd also written Jenny a threatening letter, calling her a "devious, opportunistic whore and slattern" and threatening that if Jenny ever saw her husband again, Mrs. Malcolm would see that she was fired from her job and never allowed to teach again. She'd be, to quote the letter, which Jenny had read verbatim to Tiffanie, "cleaning outhouses and scrubbing male offal from saloon spittoons and thunder mugs for the rest of her short, pathetic life!"

"Yeah, good ole Malcolm," Larsen said. "The man oughta be thrashed for what he did to you."

"Enough about him," Jenny said with a sigh. "I have enough other miseries at the moment."

"Yeah." Larsen picked up a rock and tossed it into the

brush, wincing at the pain the sudden movement had kicked up in his ribs. "What a damn fool I was!"

"What?" Jenny turned back to him, frowning. "No, you did what you had to do."

"My mistake was ever taking on that job in the first place. I wasn't a lawman. Hell, I was a thirty-a-month-and-found cowpuncher. I had no business wearing that badge."

"That's not true, Glenn. No two men could be expected to win against three demons like those in that cage. You did your best. It's not your fault what happened. I won't let you blame yourself, Glenn. I simply won't let you do it."

Despite the teacher's words, self-revulsion continued to flare inside of the young former lawman. Tears of rage and sorrow dribbled down his cheeks. "The town thought I was protectin' it. *Tiffanie* thought I was protecting *her*. I should have been. Instead, she's gone and—"

"No, I won't listen to this anymore. Look at me, Glenn." Jenny had placed her hands on Larsen's face. Now she turned his head toward hers and stared into his eyes from inches away. A sheen of tears glistened in her own eyes as she said, "Tiffanie is dead. The town is gone. What happened was not your fault. It was evil. We have to put all of that behind us now and move on with our lives. It's going to be hard, Glenn, but I know we can do it. We have to. Do you understand?"

Larsen stared back at her, his eyes two miniature, night-black lakes shimmering with reflected starlight. He placed his hands on her arms, drew her gently toward him. He slid his head closer to Jenny's. Keeping her hands pressed to his cheeks, Jenny slid her head closer to his. Their lips touched.

Their mouths came together.

Larsen wrapped his arms around Jenny. She wrapped her arms around him, returning his kiss with desperate abandon.

Larsen's heart felt as light as a spring kite. God, she felt so warm and tender and supple in his arms!

Suddenly, the town and Tiffanie were gone. Larsen's pain and misery fell by the wayside. There was only him and Jenny Claymore. They kissed each other hungrily, rubbing, caressing, moaning, sobbing—the last two souls alive in the vast, empty universe.

A gun blasted, casting them back into the burning pits of hell.

Ten minutes earlier, Slash was standing at the far northern edge of the camp, fifty feet out from where they'd built the fire. He was smoking a cigarette, concealing the coal in the palm of his hand. His Winchester was cradled in his arms.

The camp was on a hill. It was protected on its southern flank by the deep wash. The hill dropped away on three sides. Ponderosas spiked the hill, offering relative cover and concealment. It was the best place that Slash and Pecos had been able to find to camp for the night. There was no perfect place out here in this mostly wide-open, gently rolling country. Especially with a pack of blood-thirsty wolves on their trail.

They'd done the best they could. They shouldn't have built a fire, but they'd both felt it was worth the risk of the killers spotting the flames to get some hot food and coffee down both Larsen and the young schoolteacher. It had been a long, hard day of travel for them both, and they'd needed sustenance and comfort now at the end of that day.

Besides, there was no way to truly hide the jail wagon. There was no way to travel inconspicuously with the racket the foul contraption kicked up and with as slowly as it rolled along. The killers had followed them easily. They hadn't shown themselves after their initial appearance on the knoll, but Slash knew they were following them. They were laying back, keeping out of sight, letting the menace of their presence work on their quarry, frying their nerves. Also, they were probably waiting for the other members of their gang to arrive.

Then they'd likely effect an all-out assault.

The killers knew where Slash and Pecos's party was camped, all right. The fire hadn't added to the threat.

Now Slash stood with his back to a ponderosa, the quirley smoldering in the cupped palm of his left hand down low by his side. He was watching a slender shadow move toward him up the hill from below.

CHAPTER 27

Had the stalker smelled Slash's cigarette?

Probably. That's all right. If a man or men were near enough to smell cigarette smoke, they were near enough that they needed to die.

Keeping his eyes on the moving shadow, Slash raised the cigarette in his cupped hand. He took a deep drag, blew the smoke out ahead of him, down the slope and toward the shadow angling toward him. He dropped to one knee and flicked the cigarette out away from him.

The quirley hit the ground with a light thump, sparking.

Almost instantly, a rifle flashed and wailed. The flash and the wail came a second time, both bullets tearing up forest duff near where the cigarette had landed. Slash snapped his Winchester to his shoulder, dragged the hammer back, aimed at where he'd just seen the two flashes, and hurled three rounds quickly.

He thought he heard a grunt, but because of his own echoing blasts he couldn't be sure. Instinctively, he threw himself to his left. He hit the ground and rolled twice. He rolled a third time when another rifle opened up, cleaving the air with two bullets where he'd knelt a moment before.

He rolled onto his belly, cocked the Winchester quickly, and aimed and fired from his prone position.

A man cursed. Unmistakable even against the rolling echoes of his own report.

Slash's target fired again. The bullet hammered a tree to Slash's left. Slash triggered two more rounds at the flash. Silence and darkness followed on the heels of the violent crashing sounds and the bright flashes that still flickered on Slash's retinas—quieter, darker than before.

A man dropped to the ground with a crunching thud and a grunt of expelled air.

Again, Slash rolled to his left. He crabbed behind another pine and heaved himself onto his knees. He racked another cartridge into the Winchester's action and peered out around the tree's right side, waiting.

Running footsteps sounded up the hill behind him.

He whipped around quickly and said, "Name yourself!" The running stopped. "Don't shoot, it's Glenn!"

Slash thought he could see Larsen's shadow. "Stay where you are."

"What's going on?" the young man asked, keeping his voice down. "Are they here?"

"Some. I don't know how many. Do you have a gun?"

"Of course."

"Go back to the teacher. Stay with her."

"What about Pecos?"

"He won't give away his position till light and we can see how many are out there. Now get back up that hill and keep your head down. Don't leave Jenny!"

"All right, all right."

Slash cursed and turned his attention back to the slope below him. At any moment he might hear movement or gunfire, and he had to be ready. He had to assume other killers were on the lurk out here and were just waiting for targets. He knew that's what Pecos was thinking over on his end of the camp, to the southwest. He'd stayed where he was because he knew the killers might have the camp surrounded and were waiting to move in from the perimeter, shooting.

He and Slash would have to stay in place, holding their cautious vigils until the killers moved on them or until dawn, whichever came first. Silently, Slash cursed and settled in for the wait. The ground was cold and hard beneath his knees. He lowered himself to his butt and drew his knees up, keeping the Winchester low so starlight wouldn't reflect off the barrel.

He was getting too old for this low-down, dirty business. He'd spent nights like this on the run from posses— long, slow, weary nights in lonely camps in the middle of nowhere, waiting for an ambush. He'd thought he'd left those days behind when he'd hung up his outlaw hat. Old Luther T. Bledsoe sure got the drop on him and Pecos. They could either ride for him or hang. Slash and Pecos might have been better off hanging. Bledsoe gave the two ex-cutthroats all the worst, most dangerous assignments. Why hang them when he could torture them slowly? Slash knew the old, pushchair-bound marshal was getting back at them in the best way he could come up with. Slash couldn't really blame him. After all, it was Slash's own bullet that had put him in that chair. . . .

Bledsoe was probably right now having a good laugh in his sleep, imagining what was happening out here.

Starting out, the job had looked like a summer dance in an old barn by the river. But that was before Slash and Pecos had known the full extent of the situation. Before they'd ridden into a sacked town full of burned buildings and dead people. . . .

Slash had to give a quiet chuckle at that, shaking his head.

He glanced over the shoulder of the hill to his left, where the three lobos likely slumped in the jail wagon, waiting and watching eagerly for their pards to spring them. Slash had known a lot of bad men in his time on the wild frontier, but he'd never met any as bad as those three. He had them cowed for now. They were quiet as church mice and didn't even look at Jenny anymore. They knew Slash was watching, waiting for another excuse to open up the jail wagon door, pull one out, and kick the stuffing out of him.

The cowing wouldn't last, though. When the situation turned dire, their true colors would resurface. Especially if their gang closed in. Especially if somehow they managed to bust out of the cage on wheels. If that happened . . . Well, it just couldn't happen, that's all. Maybe Larsen had a point. Maybe the young marshal should have shot them while they'd slept at Carlisle's. Maybe Slash should just shoot all three right now. Why further endanger the lives of the young woman and Glenn Larsen? They'd been through enough.

On the other hand, killing Chaney, Beecher, and Black Pot would not clear the wolves from their trail. Right now, the wolves were taking it slow and easy, because they wanted to free their pards. Free them without getting them killed. If Slash shot them, they'd move in like lead-triggering lightning to avenge them.

Sure, they would. Slash knew how men like that thought. He and Pecos were in a whole heap of trouble, and there

251 THE WICKED DIE TWICE

was no easy way out. And he had a feeling that things were going to get a whole lot nastier soon before they got better.

He sat in the shadow of the tree, scanning the tree-studded hillside dropping away before him. He kept his ears pricked so that he could, as the old saying went, hear a sleeping rabbit fart. All that he heard, however, were the occasional rustlings of the branches when a slight breeze rose. A couple of times through the night, coyote choirs kicked up a ruckus to the north and then to the east. The din sent cold witches' fingers walking up Slash's spine, reminding him as they did of a wild-assed Apache war ceremony he'd unfortunately been privy to down in Arizona some years ago, when it was still a bloody free-for-all down there. He and Pecos had been on the run, headed for Mexico, when they'd found themselves free of the posse that had been after them but caught in a whipsaw between two bands of bloodthirsty Chiricahua determined to scour the white eyes from their sun-scorched homeland—or to at least bake the pale-skinned interlopers in clay pots over low fires and smile as they screamed.

An owl hooted.

A nighthawk gave its signature cry.

Sometime near dawn there was the piercing cry of a rabbit that had met its bloody end in the talons of some night bird that had likely winged off with it to dine in the peace and quiet of some rocky promontory. There came the soft thumps of many running feet, but Slash didn't even turn to gaze in the sounds' direction, knowing from experience it was just a coyote pack scampering, quick and silent as furry gray ghosts, along the arroyo behind him.

He slept with his eyes open for a time and then the false dawn revealed itself in the east—a faint pearl glow silhouetting the bluffs before it. Birds began their morning songs, growing in volume until, compared to the silence of only a few minutes ago, it was almost deafening. A squirrel scampered up through the dirt and pine needles below Slash, gave Slash the wooly eyeball and then holy hell before dashing up a tree with its bushy tail curled in a snit.

There was enough light now that he could see he was alone out here. If the killers had been waiting for first light to make their move, they would have made it by now. Still, Slash rose and walked around, tracing a broad half circle around his position, just to be sure. He found the second man he'd shot lying on his side, limbs twisted. He was a black man with short hair and long sideburns. Slash recognized him—Creole Green from Louisiana. A former slave who'd taken up robbing Texas trains in the years following the Little Misunderstanding. A bad man. Slash had heard he'd killed passengers for fun, spraying passenger cars with lead while howling like a moon-crazed jackal. Slash had also heard he'd been sentenced to hang in New Mexico.

Obviously, that hadn't happened.

Slash gave a little shudder of apprehension, realizing again just what breed of man was after him and his party.

A magpie told him where the other dead man lay. The long-tailed carrion-eater gave its shrill cries near some shrubs and a small boulder. Slash walked over, and the bird eyed him devilishly, standing atop the dead man's shoulder, not wanting to give ground.

"Get away, you winged rat," Slash growled as he continued forward.

Shrieking its indignance, the magpie with its ridiculously long black tail lighted from the body and swooped up through the pine branches, flashing black and iridescent blue and white in the intensifying dawn light. Slash kicked the dead man onto his back. Pale-blue eyes stared up at him without seeing him. Tight, curly red hair clung like a knit cap to the man's broad head.

Slash didn't recognize him.

"Red Charlie."

Slash had heard Pecos moving toward him. He'd known it was Pecos. He'd recognize that lumbering tread anywhere. No killer would be moving toward him making the kind of noise Pecos was, which wasn't overly loud but loud enough for Slash to know it wasn't a bushwhacker.

"Who?" Slash asked.

"Red Charlie. His half brother was Alpine Billie. Red and Alpine used to ride with their cousins. Can't remember their names. Dead now. Killed by a vigilance committee in Kansas. Red and Alpine got away but got sent to Yuma Pen in Arizona. Alpine died in the pen. Red escaped twice. Can you believe that?"

"Nobody escapes twice from Yuma."

"Red did. The second time was right successful"—Pecos pointed his rifle at the lumpy body clad in broadcloth suit pants tucked into high-topped boots, and a linsey shirt—"as you can see for yourself."

"Not all that successful," Slash pointed out.

"Yeah, well . . ." Pecos looked at Slash. "Long night, huh?"

"Uh-huh." Slash turned and headed toward their camp. "I got a feelin' they're gonna get longer."

"Me too."

Slash entered the camp and stopped. He stared down at Larsen and Jenny Claymore. Arching an incredulous brow, he glanced at Pecos. Pecos followed Slash's gaze to where Glenn Larsen lay on his back and the pretty young schoolteacher lay snugged against him, one arm around him, her head on his chest. They slept entangled together like a couple of baby lambs.

Sound asleep.

Slash turned to Pecos again and pressed a finger to his lips. He thought he'd let the two younger folks sleep another few minutes while he built up the fire for coffee. But just as he stepped forward, Larsen woke with a start. Jenny did, too, both the young man and the young woman sitting up with a gasp and staring in wide-eyed fear at Slash and Pecos.

Larsen reached for his rifle but stayed the movement when Pecos said, "Just me an' Slash is all."

Larsen and Jenny looked from Slash to Pecos. Then they looked at each other sitting so close together, sharing the same two blankets.

"Uhhh," the young man said, flushing deeply, fidgeting around in his blankets.

"Uhhh," the young woman said, also flushing deeply and looking around as though for a burrow she could crawl into.

Slash and Pecos shared another awkward glance before Slash cleared his throat and said, "Uhhh, well . . . uhh . . . s-sorry to wake you . . ."

The moment was so inelegant that Slash was glad when one of the prisoners distracted them from the jail wagon with, "When the hell's breakfast? We're hungry over here, dammit, an' we know you gotta feed us, so git to it!"

CHAPTER 28

Jay listened in horror to the loud scrapes of the table being moved back into place over the cellar door and then to thudding of the boots above her head.

She heard the cabin door close with a raspy thump and a click of the latching bolt. She heard the men's muffled voices outside. She heard the stomps of their boots as they descended the stoop.

Surely, they weren't going to leave her here all trussed up in the cellar! Leave her here to die or to be driven mad as she slowly died all alone here in the darkness!

She pricked her ears, hoping and praying. She could barely hear above the whistling of the blood and the thudding of her heart. But then she heard the drumming of the wagon. Sure enough, they were leaving. She listened in wide-eyed shock, staring into the darkness of the gunnysack, as her captors abandoned her.

The hoof thuds dwindled quickly to silence and she was alone here in the black silence.

Essentially, she was buried alive.

She drew a breath through the gag in her mouth, through her nose, and told herself to stay calm. But instantly, panic overcame her. There was no denying it. Her heart raced and her hands sweat as she struggled against the ropes tying her arms against her body, over the sack, and also binding her ankles together. She wriggled around, grunting and snorting, fiercely trying to loosen the ropes. She quickly grew dizzy as she sucked up all the oxygen in the gunnysack.

She relaxed her body, but not her mind.

Terror flowed in behind the panic, and she squeezed her eyes shut and sobbed.

She wasn't sure how long she'd lain there, bawling against the neckerchief tied over her mouth, so terrified that she thought her heart would explode, when she heard something outside the cabin. Instantly, she stopped sobbing, lifted her head inside the bag, and pricked her ears, listening.

Nothing. Only silence.

She continued listening, though it was hard to hear anything but the thudding of her relentlessly racing heart.

Still nothing. Whatever she'd heard had been her imagination.

Oh, God. Dear God, she thought. *How am I ever going to get out of here? Am I really going to die here in the darkness, gagged and bound in the cellar of what is most likely some abandoned miner's shack?*

No one would ever even find her bones.

A fresh wave of panic was about to overcome her when a tapping sound rose from somewhere above. Again, she lifted her head from the cellar's earthen floor and, pressing her face against the stinky burlap, listened intently.

She heard another soft tap. At least, she thought she did, unless it was only her imagination.

A click. The latch bolt had been tripped.

Hinges squawked briefly. A female voice: "Jay?"

She recognized it immediately. She flopped around and

grunted with a start and tried to scream, to yell, to shout: "DOWN HERE! MYRA, I'M DOWN HERE! OH, FOR CHRISSAKES, PULL UP THE CELLAR DOOR!"

But again, the only sounds she was able to make through the gag were those of a strangling cat.

They must have been enough.

"Jay!" Myra shouted.

Above Jay came the loud scraping sounds of the table being moved.

Hope rose in Jay's chest, tempering her panic. Above her, she could hear Myra grunting as she tried to lift the door. More grunting—fierce, desperate grunting. Jay did not hear the door budge in its frame.

Oh, no. The door was too heavy for her!

Myra stomped around the cabin. There was a clanking sound and then more stomping. The floor creaked over Jay's head. There was a soft thumping sound as Myra toiled against the door. She heard a clank. Myra must have grabbed a tool—maybe a fireplace poker or a lid hook. Hinges squawked. Music to Jay's ears! They were followed by the booming slam of the cellar door falling back against the floor . . . and by Myra's voice, no longer muffled.

"Jay! Are you down there?"

Jay writhed violently, grunting.

"Hold on!" Myra said. "I'm going to light a lamp!"

Boots thudded again as Myra moved around the cabin. Jay remained in a near state of panic, imagining her captors riding back to the cabin and finding Myra here. Unable to stop herself, she continued to fight against the ropes. Faintly, through the gunnysack she watched a light grow. It was like the slow rising of the morning sun.

Nothing more beautiful here in this cold, dark grave!

"Hold on," Myra said. "I'm coming down!"

Jay heard a grunt and a thud as Myra dropped into the hole beside her. Jay tried to tell the young woman that she was tied, but Myra must have seen the ropes already. She said, "Here, here—let me get those."

Jay heard the knife slicing through the hemp. Myra must have had a small knife because it took what seemed forever for her to chew through the ropes. In the meantime, Jay kept listening for the clatter of the wagon. She wanted so much to get out of this hole that it took all of her might to keep from thrashing around violently and making it impossible for Myra to free her.

Myra said, "*There!*" and the ropes around Jay's waist came loose. Jay's arms ached from pinched blood flow, so she was able to help Myra only a little in lifting the sack from her head. Suddenly, fresh air engulfed her and she saw the shadowy figure of the curly-haired young woman kneeling before her, sparsely lit with weak, red light from a lamp perched near the square hole in the floor above them.

Jay grunted against the gag, shaking her head. "Here, here," Myra said. "Let me help."

Myra took the folding barlow knife in her teeth and reached around to untie the gag. When Jay felt it go slack in her mouth, she spat it out and gulped air pouring into the hole from above.

"Oh, God!" she raked out in a mad rush of relief.

"Are your ankles tied?"

"Yes."

"I'll get them."

"Hurry!"

"I will!"

"They might come back."

"Don't worry." Myra lifted her head to stare frankly into

Jay's. "I came armed. If those rascals come back, I'll blow them out of their boots!"

Jay laughed huskily, deeply relieved. Still, she couldn't get out of the hole fast enough. As soon as Myra's knife had chewed through the ropes on her ankles, she rose to her feet. She was very unsteady. The hole was about six feet deep. With Myra grabbing her around the waist and lifting, Jay reached up, nudged the lamp out of her way, and snaked her arms through the hole, planting her elbows to either side. With great effort and much grunting and cursing and Myra pushing from below, she hoisted herself up through the hole and then rolled away from the hole along the floor.

She gained her knees, caught her breath, and then turned to the hole to help Myra. There was no need. The girl leaped upward, thrusting her head, shoulders, and arms out of the hole and then easily hoisted her legs out, as well.

Jay threw herself at the young woman, hugging her tightly, sobbing. "Oh, God!" she cried. "How did you ever find me?"

Myra hugged her back. "I followed you out from town. I'm so glad you're all right, Jay. I wasn't sure what they had in mind."

"You *followed* me?"

"I heard someone around the freight office earlier, looking for me, I think. One of them must have been spying on me, the other on you. When you headed this way, they . . ."

"Right." Jay cursed. "Cisco! He sicced them on us, probably told them that if it looked like we were going to interfere, to step in."

"I think the other one planned to kidnap me just like they did you, but I heard him outside, blew out my lamp, and headed outside by the back door. I hid in the wagon shed. He tried to find me, and when he finally gave up, I followed him . . . to where they grabbed you. I ran back and saddled my horse, and followed you here."

"Cisco," Jay said again, tightly, angrily, shaking her head. "I wonder if he planned to leave me down there . . . forever." She looked into the gaping cellar hole in the floor beside her and gave a shudder. She looked around the small, crudely appointed cabin. "Where are we, anyway? What is this place?"

"We're in Redstone Canyon, one canyon east of Horsetooth Station at the base of Horsetooth Rock. This is Tumbling Box H Range. This must be one of Jason Hall's line shacks, maybe a roundup cabin."

"Figures." Jay glanced at the hole again and hugged herself. "Under the circumstances, it gives me the creeps. Let's get out of here. You said you have a horse?"

"Yeah, my filly is up in the rocks behind the cabin. I wasn't sure if any of Hall's men were still here, so I came up from behind."

"I wonder if they're robbing, or did rob, that gold tonight," Jay said, heaving herself to her feet, wrinkling her nose against the smell of the gunnysack clinging to her like a second skin. "That's why they needed us out of the way tonight."

"Could be," Myra said, also rising and dusting floor grime from her denims. "Or maybe it's still on their schedule."

"In that case, we'd better get back to town and have your boyfriend alert the other sheriff's deputies, maybe form a posse." Jay started for the door, but Myra grabbed her hand, stopping her.

The younger woman's eyes glinted anxiously in the weak

light from the lamp on the floor. "Del's the reason I wrote that note to you asking you to visit me at the freight yard."

"Del is?"

"Jay, Del disappeared. I haven't seen him for two days. Day before yesterday, he said he was going to ride out to Horsetooth Station and tell the station manager what you overheard about the planned robbery, and do some sniffing around Hall's ranch."

"And he never made it back to town?"

Myra shook her head. "No, he's not my *beau*, you understand—we're just *friends*—but I've been worried sick about him. I wanted to talk to you about it, but I didn't think we should be seen together."

"Right, right. Good thinking." Jay stared off, not seeing anything but thinking, worrying. "Poor Del. I hope I haven't gotten him in trouble now, too." She turned to Myra. "Did you talk to the other sheriff's deputies?"

Myra nodded. "And . . ."

"They told me not to worry about it. That they'd look into it."

"And . . ."

"Nothing. No word from them so far." Myra reached out and squeezed Jay's hand again. It was a desperate squeeze. "Jay . . . I have a feeling those two might be in on it . . . right along with Hall and Walsh."

That made Jay's head reel. "If so, what are we going to do?"

"I sure wish Slash and Pecos were here. They'd know what to do."

"I know. But they're not due back for another two days."

Myra opened her mouth to speak again but closed it when hooves drummed in the distance. She and Jay gasped at the same time. The drumming was growing louder. Riders were heading toward the cabin.

"Oh, my God!" Jay said. "The lamp!"

Myra dropped to a knee and blew out the flame, then grabbed her Winchester carbine off the table. "Let's get out of here!" she said, scrambling to her feet and moving through the door. Jay stepped up beside her on the small stoop fronting the cabin. Both women stiffened when they saw the riders—a half-dozen men on horseback— rounding a bend in the trail about a hundred yards to the west. There was a quarter moon, and the pale light gave the riders' shadows definition and flashed off guns and bridle bits. It also glinted off the water off the narrow creek hugging the trail.

"Come on!"

Myra took Jay's hand and led her left along the front of the cabin. Jay hoped the moonlight wouldn't reveal them. When they reached the cabin's southeast side, Myra pointed to a footpath that led down a rocky rise, and said, "My filly's this way!"

"Wait." Jay stepped up against the shack's east side, where its shadow concealed her. "I want to hear what they have to say."

"What?"

"You go on, Myra. I'll catch up to you."

"No way!" Myra stepped up beside Jay and pressed her back against the cabin's wall.

"Myra, please," Jay whispered. "I don't want to get you into any more trouble than—"

"Too late!" Myra placed a finger over her mouth as the riders reined up in front of the cabin only a few feet away from the two women's positions.

Jay's heart thudded heavily. She glanced around the

cabin's front corner. The half-dozen men were swinging down from their horses, one angrily saying, "I don't understand why you didn't kill her. Those were your orders!"

A frigid winter chill swept through Jay to settle at the small of her back.

She'd recognized the man's voice. It belonged to Keldon Reed, the Tumbling Box H foreman.

"I'm sorry, boss," one of the other men said in a faintly wheedling tone. "I just couldn't do it an' Anders couldn't, either. I mean, she always treated us nice at the Thousand Delights, an' . . ."

"So you were just gonna leave her in that cellar to starve to death or die of fright?" Reed gave a caustic laugh without an ounce of humor in it. "You get in there, open up that cellar door, and shoot her!"

"Walsh won't like it, boss," said another man.

"I don't care what Walsh does or doesn't like. We don't take orders from Walsh. We take orders from Hall. Now, get to it, Sully! You'll be doin' her a favor—puttin' her out of her misery!" Jay tensed, heart pounding. Myra must have sensed her trepidation. Standing close beside her, she took Jay's hand in her own and squeezed it.

"All right, you got it, boss."

Jay heard Sully's boots on the porch. She tensed as she heard him go inside the cabin. There was a brief silence. Jay imagined the shock on Sully's face as he stared down at the open hole in the floor. She imagined the dread he was likely feeling right now, knowing he was going to have to go back outside and say:

"Uh . . . we . . . I got a problem, boss . . ."

"Oh, good Lord—don't tell me!"

"Yeah," Sully said, awfully. "Yeah . . . she seems to have gotten out."

"You damn fool!"

A gun blasted twice. A man screamed, dropped.

"Oh!" Jay said with a start. Instantly, she covered her mouth as though to shove the involuntary exclamation back down her throat. No doing. It was out there now.

Had the killers heard it?

"What was that?" one of them said.

Jay turned to Myra. Myra stared back at her, wide-eyed with trepidation.

"What was what?" said Keldon Reed.

"I heard somethin'. Came from that side of the cabin. Sounded like a woman!"

"Well, it's probably her!" Reed yelled. "Get after her, you men!"

Tugging on Jay's hand, Myra bolted out from the side of the cabin. "Come on, Jay! Run! *Run!*"

CHAPTER 29

"See anything?" Pecos asked.

"Right."

"Huh?"

"Haystack butte to the right, maybe a quarter mile," Slash said, jerking his chin in that direction.

They were riding south of the little ranching settlement of Wheaton, along Little Porcupine Creek. They'd skirted the town because they'd seen no reason to bring trouble to innocent bystanders. Wheaton had one old lawman, but neither Pecos nor Slash thought Wilton Dunlop would be much help in their perilous situation. The last thing they wanted to do was get another town burned, its citizens killed and worse.

The two ex-cutthroats were on their own until they reached Cheyenne. They'd swung off the main trail and followed a secondary ranch trail in turn following Little Porcupine Creek as it skirted the settlement's ragged southern edge. A stout old woman in a red scarf had stopped beating a rug on a clothesline to watch them. A dog had run out to chase them for a time, nipping at the wagon's wheels, but it had soon turned and low-tailed it back to the shade of a scraggly cottonwood near where the old woman had been beating the rug.

Pecos turned to follow Slash's gaze to the west. Sure enough, a rider was just then dropping down the far side of the butte over there. Pecos caught a brief glimpse of the man's upper torso and then his shoulders and his black-hatted head just before he disappeared. A little curl of dust spiraled above the crest of the butte, fading quickly on the hot breeze.

"Damn," Pecos said, riding beside Slash sitting on the wagon's driver's seat, crouched forward, the ribbons in his gloved hands. He held a quirley between the index and middle fingers of his right hand, and he took occasional puffs off of it, blowing the smoke out his nose.

Beside him, Jenny Claymore said, "Another one over there."

"Over where?" Slashed asked her.

She turned to gaze through the jail cage behind her and Slash, over the sullen, owly faces of the three desperadoes slouched in the wagon, toward the northeast.

"Yep, I see it," Pecos said.

Another single rider was riding along a low bench another quarter mile or so off the trail. Looking around, Pecos saw yet another rider just then dropping down the far side of a rise to the southeast. The rider's horse switched its tail, and then it and its rider were gone.

Slash lifted his chin and scratched his neck. "Just like a pack of wolves following a buffalo herd. Waiting for dark."

Despite the early-afternoon heat radiating down from the sun and then back up off the pale, bristling ground, Jenny gave a shiver.

Pecos scowled at his partner. "You know, sometimes your colorful way of talkin' gets old."

"Well, ain't that how it seems?"

"I ain't sayin' it ain't how it seems, but do you have to say it like that?"

"I speak the truth, my friend." Slash reached over and patted Jenny's left leg through her skirt. "I'm sorry, Jenny. Pecos's right. Sometimes I get a bad case of the hoof in mouth disease."

"No, you're right," Jenny said, glancing at him and then at Pecos riding just off the wagon's left front wheel. "That's just how it is, isn't it? My father was a buffalo hunter back when there were still buffalo to hunt. He told stories of how the wolves would follow the herds, all spread out, each one waiting for an opportunity to grab a sick one or a calf or maybe . . ."

"One of the old ones," Pecos finished for her when she seemed to think it prudent not to finish the thought herself. "That'd be Slash. His lips might fly a mile a minute, but he's weak and slow. That's what old age and a coming marriage does to a man, I reckon."

Pecos chuckled at that. Not because he'd found what he'd said funny, but because he was nervous and needed a distraction. Maybe he thought Jenny did, too.

She turned to Slash, frowning curiously. "Is it true?" she asked. "Are you getting married, Slash?"

Slash just hiked a shoulder slightly, grumbled, and cast Pecos the quick, furtive wooly eyeball.

Pecos chuckled and said to Jenny, "Slash don't like to talk about it. He don't really like to talk about nothin', when you get right down to it." He winked at Jenny. "Women an' weddin's most of all. Those two things right there scare him worse than a cold pine box in a dark grave."

Chuckling, Pecos rode ahead of the wagon to maintain the point position roughly fifty yards ahead, glancing around to pick out the wolves dogging their trail.

Back in the wagon, Slash could feel Jenny's eyes on him. He could also see that she was chewing her bottom lip, pensive.

Slash took a deep drag off his cigarette and blew the smoke out on a long sigh. "Go ahead."

Jenny frowned. "Go ahead?"

"Go ahead and ask."

She brightened with a smile. "All right, I just will, then." Her smile grew brighter. "Who's the lucky lady?"

"Lucky lady," one of the desperadoes slumped behind Slash and Jenny said through a low chuff. He followed it up with a mocking chuckle.

Slash slid his right-hand Colt from its holster and, without looking behind him, turned the gun over and rested the top of the barrel on his right shoulder. He clicked the hammer back.

"All right, all right!" Chaney said. "Don't get your drawers in such a twist! I was just passin' the time."

"Pass the time keepin' your mouth shut."

"All right, all right!"

Slash depressed the Colt's hammer and slid the piece back into its holster on his right thigh. Keeping his gaze straight ahead, he said, "Her name's Jaycee."

"What a lovely name."

"Jaycee Breckenridge."

"Even lovelier!"

Slash felt himself blush. He hated when he did that. Why did talking about Jaycee make him blush? Talking about the wolves stalking the buffalo didn't make him blush one bit.

"How did you two meet—you and Miss Breckenridge?" Jenny asked.

Slash knew she, too, was just passing the time. Probably wanting to distract herself from the horror of their situation. Normally, he'd probably discourage such personal chinning, but under the circumstances, he thought the gentlemanly thing to do would be to help keep the girl distracted.

"Me an' Jaycee? Hell, we've known each other goin' on ten, fifteen years now."

"And you're just now getting married?" Jenny asked with surprise.

"Yeah, well . . . long story. You see, she took up with a close friend of mine and Pecos. Pistol Pete Johnson out of Dakota." Slash chuckled, fondly remembering Pistol Pete. "Big, fun-lovin' fella, Pete. Ugly as moldy sin, but the women stuck to him like cockleburs on a cur's tale. As did Jaycee," he couldn't help adding with a touch of jealousy. "Pete was killed back five, six years ago now. It was my own damn fault, leadin' the fellas into that box canyon. But, anyway . . ." He shook his head, wanting to swing the conversation back in a friendlier direction. "Anyway . . . Jaycee and I been friends a long time. Only lately . . . in the past year or two . . . we . . . we . . . well, we . . ."

"Fell in love?"

Slash's flush rose so high in his cheeks it blurred his eyes.

"Go ahead," Jenny said. "It's not a dirty word, you know, Slash."

"Oh, I know. Yeah, we . . ."

"Fell in love."

"F-fell in love." Slash felt an embarrassed laugh burst out of him. "That's what we did all right. Sure enough!"

What really amazed him was that he'd been able to say the word and not pass out from overexertion.

"There, that wasn't so hard—now, was it?"

"No." Slash looked at Jenny. His embarrassment was gone. He suddenly felt as though an enormous weight had been lifted from his shoulders.

He loved Jaycee. Why should that be such a hard thing to admit to? He'd done far worse things in his life than fall in love.

"No, it wasn't at all!" He laughed again, louder this time.

He heard a couple of the desperadoes chuckling at him quietly, and he didn't even care.

He turned to Jenny. She'd turned her head to gaze back over her right shoulder at Glenn Larsen riding behind the wagon, keeping pace from about thirty yards back.

She turned her head back forward. She didn't say anything. She stared straight ahead beyond the horses, her eyes cast with thought.

Slash kept his eyes on her. She'd helped him. Why not return the favor?

"You know, Jenny . . . about last night . . ."

She jerked a surprised look at him. It was her turn to blush.

"Especially under the circumstances, you know," Slash said in his slow, resonate Missouri drawl, "it's the most natural thing in the world. Pullin' close, I mean. You and the young marshal."

Jenny drew a deep breath, turned her head back forward. Slowly, a new smile shaped itself on her lips. She turned to Slash, wrapped both of her arms around him, and pressed her head affectionately against his shoulder.

* * *

Riding ahead of the wagon, Pecos suddenly jerked back on Buck's reins.

He slid his hand to the Russian .44 residing on his right thigh. He closed his hands over the pistol's grips but left the piece in its holster.

Roughly thirty yards ahead, three men had just ridden out from behind a boulder to block the trail. They turned their horses to face Pecos. Each man held a rifle with a white cloth tied to the end of the barrel.

"Whoah!" Slash said behind Pecos, checking the two geldings down, rolling the jail wagon to a stop. "Whoah . . . whoah . . ."

One of the geldings whinnied. One of the horses ahead of Pecos answered the greeting whinny with one of its own. The killers' horses looked friendly. The killers themselves, though—and that's who they were, Slash knew, because who else would they be?—looked mean as two bobcats locked in the same privy.

"Tatum!" one of the desperadoes in the jail wagon called to the three newcomers facing Pecos. "How you doin', you old rattlesnake? George! Hidy, Dawg!"

Hell-Raisin' Frank Beecher laughed loudly and yelled, "If you three aren't sights for our sore eyes . . . !"

"Shut up," Pecos heard Slash admonish the jailed killers. He also heard a gun click, which meant that Slash was aiming his Colt at the killers again through the bars.

The middle rider facing Pecos lifted his chin to yell, "Don't worry, fellas, we'll have you out of there in no time!"

The jailed killers did not respond. Slash had cowed

them with his Colt; they knew he was just waiting for an opportunity to blow off another body part.

"I don't think so," Pecos said, keeping one eye on the three men before him, keeping another eye skinned for a possible trap. These three might be raising truce flags, but Pecos didn't trust any of them farther than he could throw them uphill against a Texas tornado.

"We came to talk some reason into you and your partners," said the killer in the middle of the trio. He was short and stocky, and he had long, flowing white hair dropping down from a battered opera hat. His face was Indian dark, deeply tanned and weathered. Pecos thought he was around his and Slash's age.

"Is that a fact?"

"You turn our boys loose before midnight tonight, and we'll let you three fellas and the young lady live. We'll let you just ride on . . . free as jackrabbits. You don't, you'll all be dead by noon tomorrow." He narrowed a hard, cobalt-blue eye and pointed a warning finger straight out at Pecos. "All except the girl, that is." He smiled. "We'll let her live a little longer . . . if you get my drift."

Pecos could sense Jenny's horror on the wagon behind him as anger flared in him and he fired back with: "You come this close again . . . try a single threatening move on us, and we're gonna kill those *boys* of yours. A bullet to each one's head, starting with Chaney, then on to that butcher, Beecher, and that butt-ugly half-breed!"

"I heard that!" protested Black Pot in an ironic tone.

"Shut up," Slash ordered him tightly.

"You do that," said the white-haired man, narrowing one of his cobalt eyes in anger. "And it'll be the same as killin' yourselves, because as soon as you've done it, you'll be dead, too."

"You tell him, Dawg!" Chaney yelled.

"One more word and I'm gonna drill you in the knee!" Slash wailed at him.

Dawg smiled broadly as he looked past Pecos at the wagon. "You boys sit tight. We'll get you out of there. Just wanted to give these civil servants somethin' to think about." He winked, muttered something to the two men sitting to either side of him, then reined his horse off the trail and booted it into a gallop to the east. The others followed suit. All three were soon speck sized as they rode up a distant rise, their dust sifting behind them.

Their hoof thuds dwindled to silence.

Pecos stared after them for a time.

Then he turned his head to look at Slash.

"Better think it over, fellas," Chaney said. "I mean . . . for the girl's sake, if not your own."

Gritting his teeth, Slash drew his right-hand Colt, turned, and fired a round into the jail wagon.

Chaney screamed.

CHAPTER 30

"Hurry, Jay!"

"Right behind you—*ohhh!*" Jay screamed as a bullet spanged off a rock inches to the right of her right foot.

As she and Myra ran down the steep slope east of the cabin where Jay had been caged like some circus lion, the guns of Keldon Reed's men popped behind them. Jay heard the thunder of horse hooves as the half-dozen men gave chase.

"They're coming!" Jay cried as she and Myra reached the bottom of the rise.

"My horse is just up yonder," Myra said, stopping and spinning around. "Keep running, Jay. Up the next rise. My horse is tied up there!"

"What're you gonna do?" Jay asked, pausing to catch her breath.

In the milky moonlight, Jay saw Myra harden her jaws. The young woman's brown eyes flashed angrily beneath the brim of her brown felt hat. "I'm gonna cover you and give Reed something to think about!"

She dropped to a knee and raised her Winchester. "Keep

going!" She pumped a cartridge into the rifle's action and
aimed up the slope behind her and Jay.

Jay wheeled and started running up the next rise, carpeted in fine sandstone gravel and abutted with rocks and
boulders. Behind her, the thunder of horse hooves grew
louder until she knew the men were topping the first steep
rise from the cabin.

She gave a little hitch in her step when Myra's rifle
thundered.

A horse whinnied shrilly. A man cursed. It was followed
by the metallic rasp of Myra pumping a fresh round into
the Winchester's breech and the tinkle of the spent casing
clattering onto the rocks at her feet.

"She's got a rifle, dammit!" yelled one of Reed's men a
quarter second before Myra threw another round at them,
and then another. She fired one more, causing panicked
shouting and a chaotic clattering of hooves up the previous
rise.

Ahead, Jay saw the silhouette of a horse shuffling its feet
nervously where it was tied to a twisted cedar angling out
from the base of a low sandstone ridge capping the rise.
Jay ripped the reins off the cedar. As she did, she heard the
crunch of gravel as Myra ran up the rise behind her, breathing hard.

The shooting had stopped. Jay could hear the shuffling
of hooves and the bellowing of angry curses beyond the
previous rise as Reed's men gathered themselves, angrily
discouraged by Myra's Winchester.

"Climb up on the filly, Jay," Myra said, casting a cautious glance over her shoulder. "I'll swing up behind you."

A sharp flash appeared on the previous ridge. It was
followed by a rifle's wail. The bullet shrieked off a rock

near Jay and Myra, both of whom sucked sharp, startled breaths.

"Where in the hell are we going?" Jay said as she toed a stirrup and swung up into the leather.

"I don't know." Myra stepped onto a rock and then leaped up onto the filly's back, settling her weight behind Jay. "I have no idea what's out here. We'll just follow the trail and hope we can outrun these sons of fork-tailed devils!"

"I hope we can!" Jay said, reining the filly around and putting it onto the narrow trail that appeared to drop into yet another shallow canyon.

Myra racked another round into her Winchester's breech. "I'll cover us from behind!"

"I know you will, honey," Jay said, giving an ironic laugh despite the terror sparking in her nerves and veins. "I know you will!"

Myra had sand—Jay would give her that. In fact, Jay couldn't think of another young lady with whom she'd rather be facing such tall odds.

The moonlight shone on the winding trail ahead. The filly followed it sure-footedly, so Jay gave the horse its head. It could see better than Jay could. The horse thundered into the next canyon, then climbed the opposite side at an angle, following the trail.

As it climbed, Jay and Myra looked back to see the shadows of Reed's men outlined against the starry sky. They were just then reaching the previous rise and dropping down the near side—a long, wriggling snake glistening in the starlight and moonlight winking off tack chains, bits, and guns.

When Jay and Myra gained the next ridge, then galloped along its top, following what was probably an old hunting or prospecting trail, Myra twisted around to her left and raised the Winchester to her shoulder.

"Stick your finger in your ear, Jay!"

Jay did as she'd been instructed. Still, the Winchester's bellow was sharp in that ear, and the sharp tang of gunpowder assaulted her nostrils. Myra's rifle gave another cracking report. Keeping her left index finger in her left ear, Jay watched one of the riders just then traversing the canyon below bound sideways off his horse with a shrill, agonized cry. Moonlight flashed off the rifle the man tossed in the air as he and the horse tumbled into the darkness beside the trail.

The others yelled and cursed.

"Damn," Jay said. "You're good with that thing!"

"Where I come from, a girl had to be!"

"Totally understand!"

The trail dropped again. At the bottom, they crossed a narrow, brush and rock-choked wash, then started up the other side. The filly was blowing hard. Jay could feel the horse's gait become strained. As she glanced anxiously behind, she saw the shadows of their pursuers gaining the previous ridge and start down the near side, hot on Jay and Myra's heels.

"We're not gonna make it, hon," Jay said. "The filly's going to collapse!"

"What's that?"

"What's what?"

Myra stared straight up the slope they were galloping north on. Jaycee looked that way to see a high ridge of rock. It was shaped like a short, tall boat in the darkness. There was something unnatural about its appearance. That ridge was flanked by yet another, steeper ridge.

"Your guess is as good as mine!" Jay said. "Stop."

"What?"

"Stop! We'll make a stand!"

Jay reluctantly reined in the blowing filly. It was hard to stop with men intending to kill you hard on your trail, but she figured it was better to stop when it was Myra's idea rather than the horse's.

Myra leaped off the horse behind Jay. Jay scrambled out of the saddle. Myra spanked the filly's behind with the flat of her hand and then bolted forward toward the tall, boat-shaped ridge.

"Where to?" Jay asked.

"Climb!"

"Oh, boy!"

Jay followed Myra, who began scrambling up the side of the ridge. Jay quickly saw that the ridge was formed of many medium-size rocks. It was a tailing pile from a mine. Mines peppered the Front Range around Camp Collins, and this was likely one of the several abandoned mines near Horsetooth Rock, which Jay could see humping up darkly just over her left shoulder, maybe a mile away.

The formation had gotten its name for good reason. The solid rock escarpment was shaped like three giant horse teeth jutting at the vault of flickering starlight that silhouetted it.

Hoof thuds rose behind Jay.

"Oh, God!" she groaned under her breath.

"Keep climbing, Jay!"

"I'm climbing, hon. I'm climbing!"

She and Myra both gave clipped screams as a bullet cracked off a rock to their left, followed by the screech of a rifle below and behind them. Reed and his men were shouting now as they closed on the base of the ridge. Another bullet slammed into a rock to Jay's right. The rifle wailed angrily.

"Oh, Lordy, Lordy, Lordy," Jay said, scrambling up the rocks and wishing she was wearing jeans like Myra was. Having to escape a kidnapping in the rugged mountains was an occasion for practical attire if there ever was one. A dress of any kind, however fashionable, was exactly *not* the appropriate attire.

More bullets spanged off rocks around her and Myra before they gained the top of the tailing pile. Jay dropped to her hands and knees, keeping her head down as the rifles belched below. Myra swung around, dropped to a knee, and went to work with the Winchester, shooting back down the steep, rocky slope. Jay glanced between the rocks at the lip of the pile, staring down toward the shooters. Myra's first couple of shots scattered the Tumbling Box H riders— black shadows scrambling for cover in the moonlit rocks around the base of the pile.

Myra fired another round, evoking a sharp, shrill curse from below.

Myra pulled the Winchester down and snickered. "Got one!"

She rolled onto her side and reached into a denim pocket for a handful of fresh cartridges.

"Nice shooting," Jay said. "But how long can you hold them off?"

Myra's breathless voice came hard and angry. "Well, I got one or two between here and the cabin. I pinked another one just now, so they're down to probably only two or three operational shooters by now. If the others show their heads, I'll blow them off, and then we'll be dancing over their rotten, no-good carcasses!"

"I don't think so."

Just then Jay had heard a spur chime behind her. She saw a shadow pass through the moonlight over her left shoulder. A tall figure crouched over Myra, jerked the rifle out of her hands. Cartridges clattered onto the rocky ground. Myra cursed, then grunted as the man thrust the rifle's stock out and up against Myra's jaw.

The girl gave a clipped yowl, then flopped onto her back and lay still.

Jay's heart thudded as she lay on her right hip and elbow, staring up as Cisco Walsh turned toward her, his eyes glinting devilishly in the silver moonlight beneath the narrow brim of his brown bowler. He thrust up a hand, stretched his lips back away from his white teeth, and said, "Hold your fire! It's Walsh! I got the situation under control!"

He was glaring down at Jay staring in wide-eyed shock back up at the Camp Collins marshal. "You made a big mistake, Jay. A big, big mistake!"

"Cisco!"

Walsh turned to one of the two other men Jay just realized was flanking him, and said, "Grab the girl. I got this one."

Jay opened her mouth to speak, but fear rendered her mute.

Walsh reached down, grabbed her wrist, and brusquely pulled her to her feet. He stepped behind her and gave her a forward shove. She stumbled away from the crest of the tailing pile. Ahead of her lay a ramshackle log cabin hunched near the base of the higher ridge and roughly a hundred feet away from her, silhouetted in the pearl moonlight. Pale smoke curled from a chimney pipe. The small, low, sashed windows were lit with weak umber lamplight.

Jay realized with a chill that she and Myra had unwittingly wandered into Walsh's outlaw camp.

Out of the frying pan and into the fire, as the old saw went.

Walsh stepped up beside Jay and squeezed her arm. Through gritted teeth, keeping his voice low, he said, "Why couldn't you listen to me?"

"Go to hell," Jay said tightly as one of the other two men stepped up to her right, carrying Myra belly down over his right shoulder, holding a rifle in his other hand. He, too, was heading toward the cabin. He wore a badge on his vest. Jay glanced at the other men walking a little behind Walsh and to his left. That man, too, had a badge on his vest.

"Oh, my God," she muttered.

"You have no idea what you've gotten yourself into, riding out here," Walsh said. "No idea at all!"

"I think I do, Cisco," Jay said with toneless defiance. "Sadly, I think I do."

Hooves drummed. Jay turned to see four riders gallop up the trail that wound around the tailing pile. The riders remaining from the pack of those who'd chased her and Myra from the other cabin horseshoed at the base of the ridge galloped toward the cabin, their dust rising like fog in the moonlight.

Jay glanced at the other two men with her and Walsh, and said, "They're sheriff's deputies, aren't they? That's why they wouldn't help Delbert Thayer."

"Don't dig your grave any deeper, Jay," Walsh said, giving her another shove.

Jay stumbled forward, got her feet beneath her, and swung angrily around to face the marshal. "Where's Delbert, Cisco? Is he part of this, too?"

Walsh stopped. He stared grimly down at Jay, his eyes glinting again like a devil's eyes in the silvery wash of moonlight. "Thayer's dead, Jay. Just like you and the girl, he got too close. And he's feeding the buzzards now for his trouble."

Jay bit down on a knuckle of her right hand to quell a sob. Guilt wrapped its angry black fist around her. She'd gotten the poor boy killed!

Again, Walsh shook his head and gritted his teeth. "Why in the hell didn't you listen to me, Jay? I can't help you anymore. Now you're going to be joining young Thayer, and it's all your own damn fault!"

CHAPTER 31

Well, at least the killers' ultimatum eased the tension a little, Slash thought as he and Pecos positioned the jail wagon in a horseshoe of a mostly dry, sandy wash. He didn't doubt the killers would keep their word and not attack until after midnight. That had made the ride through the long, hot, sunhammered afternoon less nerve-wracking if not peaceful. He and the other members of their party didn't find themselves tensely, constantly scanning the horizon in all directions, looking for signs of the stalking human wolves.

Oh, they were out there, all right, keeping just out of rifle range. But the threat had been postponed. Around midnight and afterward would be the time to start worrying again, and watching for them again . . .

It was a miserable damn country to hold off a dozen savage killers.

The terrain out here, roughly forty miles north of Cheyenne now, was flat and featureless. An endless carpet of green and purple sage, buck brush, and prickly pear swept away in all directions. There were bluffs in the distance that would offer a better, safer camp than the one

Slash and Pecos had ended up choosing now, out on the flat by the wash, but reaching them in the wagon would be a longshot. The terrain was relatively flat, but it was also rough with knee-high sage and rocks, and cut with shallow washes made perilous by deep sand and alkali.

They had little cover here except the wash itself, but they would be easily surrounded and shot to ribbons. Here, they didn't stand a chance. At least the wash offered a slender trickle of water, and they needed water now after the long, hot, miserable day.

Lacking cover from the killers, there was really only one thing to do. Slash didn't even discuss it with Pecos. His partner knew what needed to be done as well as he himself did. They finished setting up camp, building a low fire for coffee and supper, emptying the three jailed killers' slop buckets, and shoving food to the surly-eyed savages through the cracked door. The three coyotes, battered and bloody, smoked cigarettes and glared. Slash tended to them while Pecos stood back, holding his shotgun on the sullen trio. Talon Chaney was even more sullen than before since he was now, like Frank Beecher, sporting only one earlobe, thanks to Slash's bullet through the bars earlier.

When Slash had tended the killers, quickly locking the door again and pocketing the key, he and Pecos set to work cleaning and loading their pistols and rifles. Pecos took special care with his sawed-off ten-gauge, snapping it back together, shoving a fresh wad into each barrel, and snapping the big popper closed.

"What's going on?" Jenny Claymore asked them, casting her puzzled gaze between the two ex-cutthroats.

She and Glenn Larsen had been sitting back against their saddles, eating their bowls of beans and fatback with fried corncakes, the fire's low flames flashing in their eyes as they'd watched the two strangely silent and purposeful older men.

Slash and Pecos looked at each other.

Slash sucked on the quirley dangling from a corner of his mouth as he ran his oiled rag down his Winchester's forestock. "We're takin' it to them."

Jenny and Larsen looked at each other as though waiting for the other to translate.

Pecos translated for them. "The war. We're takin' it to them."

"What're you talking about?" Larsen asked.

Slash shrugged as he glanced around the fire. The sun was down, but a weak green and salmon light lingered over the land. "Look around. We got no cover out here. If we let them come here . . . bring the battle to us . . . we wouldn't have a chance."

"So we're going to take the battle to where they've camped," Slash said.

"You're gonna *what*?" Chaney exclaimed from inside the jail wagon, parked fifty feet to the north of the campfire, near where Slash and Pecos had tied the horses to picket pins.

"Shut up over there or I'll shoot you in the kneecap," Slash said. Turning to Larsen and Jenny, he said, "You two stay here with the wagon. Don't go near it. Remember, they can grab you through the bars if you get too close. Ignore them no matter what they say or do. I'm going to keep the key to the cage with me."

Larsen said, "Listen, fellas, that just sounds crazy to me. You're only two men. Two against a dozen."

"Here, we'd be four against a dozen with damn little cover," Pecos pointed out. "Slash and me have chosen the hand with the best odds. Not that either one is a royal flush. Far from it."

"Two pair, maybe," Slash said with an ironic snort. "Just remember to stay away from that wagon."

"What happens if you don't come back?" Larsen asked.

Slash and Pecos shared a look.

Slash turned back to Larsen and said, "Kill them." He cast his gaze toward the jail wagon. "Throw your saddle on one of the geldings and ride south as fast as you can. We'll likely be able to thin their ranks a little, before . . ."

Again, he glanced at Pecos, who glanced back at him, flushed, then looked at the ground.

"What'd he say?" asked one of the prisoners. It was a whisper, so it was hard to tell which one had asked the question.

One of the others muttered a response too quietly for Slash to hear.

"To *what?*" The exclamation was from Black Pot.

Pecos scowled and said, "One more word from the jail wagon, and I'm gonna let Slash come over there and blow a couple toes off."

A couple of softly whispered curses were the only response. Slash could see the prisoners' slumped silhouettes and the orange coals of their cigarettes.

Jenny looked anxiously up at the ex-cutthroats and said, "How will you ever find them? They could be anywhere out there." She cast her gaze into the thickening darkness beyond the camp.

"We already know where to find them, Jenny," Pecos told her in a gentle voice. "They're camped at the base of a bluff to the northwest. We seen the smoke from their cook fire earlier."

"How can you be sure they're all in one group?" Larsen

asked. "They could be spread out, keeping an eye on us from several different locations."

Slash grabbed his saddle and blanket up off the ground and started carrying the tack toward his horse. "We can't be sure."

"Just a chance we have to take," Pecos said, swinging his shotgun's lanyard over his head and right shoulder, letting the big Richards hang barrel down behind his back. He grabbed his own saddle and headed toward his horse. "Give us a few hours. If we're not back by midnight, shoot the prisoners and light a shuck for Cheyenne."

Since there was no cover out here, and the quarter-moon was on the rise, Slash and Pecos decided to take every precaution to keep from being seen as they approached the killers' camp. They rode northeast, in the opposite direction of the outlaw camp, for a good three-quarters of a mile. They swung east and rode roughly the same distance before swinging to the south for another mile, then west for another mile and a half.

That put them nearly due south of the two bluffs they could see hulking up darkly against the northern sky, roughly a half mile away.

"This is where it gets tough," Slash said quietly, keeping his voice low.

Pecos glanced at him. "What do you mean?"

"We walk," Slash said, swinging down from his saddle.

"Ah, hell."

"Yep."

"You know I hate walkin' worse than bathin'."

"I know, partner, but the hosses would make too much noise. Damn quiet night." Slash dropped his Appaloosa's reins, ground-reining the mount, and slid his Winchester from his scabbard.

Pecos cursed and slid his own rifle from his saddle sheath. "You'd think we could at least get a breeze."

"Don't count on it." Slash removed his spurs, dropped them into a saddlebag pouch. He shouldered his rifle and began tramping north through the sage.

Pecos removed his own spurs, then patted his buck-skin's neck, saying, "Stay now, Buck, and behave your-self," and fell into stride beside Slash.

They walked steadily through the scrub, keeping roughly eight feet apart.

Pecos said quietly, "You got enough cartridges, partner?"

"Oh, I 'spect so."

"You ready to do this?"

"No."

"Yeah," Pecos said. "Me neither."

As they walked almost due north, the two dark bluffs grew steadily before them. The outlaws were camped on the other side of those bluffs. Slash and Pecos were sure of it.

"We climb to the top o' them buttes?" Pecos asked, even more quietly than before as they walked. "That what you're thinkin'?"

"Yep, shoot 'em like ducks on a millrace."

"Sounds easy enough."

Slash stopped. "Wait."

Pecos stopped and looked at him. "What is it?"

"Down." Slash dropped to his knees.

Pecos followed suit, lifting his chin and sniffing. He frowned as he turned to Slash again. "Is that smoke?"

"I think so," Slash whispered slowly.

"They switch camps or what?"

"Maybe they broke up, scattered. Could be they figured we might make the play we're out here tryin' to make."

"In that case . . ."

"We been hornswoggled."

"How you wanna play it?"

"Let's check it out."

Slash dropped to his hands and, holding his rifle in his right hand, sort of dragging it along the ground, crabbed forward through the sage. Pecos did likewise, keeping well to Slash's left. They split farther apart to avoid a nasty-looking patch of prickly pear, then came closer together again when they'd gotten beyond the low-growing cactus.

Ahead, a dull light grew. It was almost the color of a sunset.

It seemed to be radiating up out of the ground.

Slash stopped. So did Pecos.

Slash stared ahead. The light flickered dully, appearing to originate about fifty feet ahead. He glanced at Pecos, jerked his chin to indicate ahead, then, keeping very low to the ground, resumed crawling very slowly and quietly. Ahead the light grew until Slash could see that it was, indeed, radiating up out of the ground. From a wash cut into the prairie at the southern base of the two buttes.

The cut of the wash broadened as Slash crawled up to its edge. He peered down into the cut. The wash was roughly fifty yards wide, maybe thirty feet deep. The fire lay just ahead, beyond a fringe of willows and stunted cotton-woods. The fire appeared small, maybe only a coffee fire, a small blaze to ward off the night's growing chill.

Two men sat around it. They were smoking—Slash could smell the peppery aroma of Durham tobacco—and talking in desultory tones. He couldn't hear what they were saying. They were speaking too quietly. He couldn't get a good look at them, either, through the screen of the growth between him and their fire. They were two blurred, partly lit, partly shadowed figures sitting Indian style on either side of the softly crackling fire.

One of the pair spoke a little loudly to say, "And then she told Ronnie he couldn't have any 'cause he smelled like a dead javelina."

The other man squealed a quiet laugh. "What'd Ronnie say to that?"

"He said 'damn girl' . . ."

The man must have realized he was speaking too loudly, for just then as he continued his bawdy yarn he lowered his voice considerably so that Pecos could no longer hear. That was all right. He wasn't here to eavesdrop on the killer's ribald tales.

He was here for other matters entirely.

He glanced at Pecos, who parted his lips slightly as though to say: "What's the plan?"

Slash patted the breech of his Winchester, then jerked his head to indicate the two men in the wash. Pecos nodded once, slowly. Slash rose to a crouch and dropped first one foot and then the other over the lip of the wash. He moved slowly down the shallow slope. At the bottom of the wash, he waited for Pecos to make his own way down and to stand to his left, holding his Colt's revolving rifle down low, where the firelight wouldn't reflect off its octagonal steel barrel.

Slash canted his head to the left, then to his right.

Pecos nodded, then moved slowly, quietly ahead and swinging left. Slash moved ahead and right, gently nudging the willows and cottonwoods aside. His feet moved quietly on the wash's sandy bottom. Ahead of him, the firelight grew. The two men sat where they'd been seated before.

What in hell were they doing out here? Were they on watch? If so, why the fire?

Maybe just stupid. Maybe they didn't think Slash and his partner would try to sneak up on a such a large and savage gang—two men going up against a good dozen. So they'd built a fire to ward off the chill and were just lounging around out here, against their leader's wishes, chewing the fat until their watch time was up.

Slash continued wending his way through the brush, nearly silently.

The fire and the two men took clearer and clearer shape before him.

CHAPTER 32

Ten feet from the fire in the wash, Slash stopped. He saw Pecos, a large shadow against the moon, quarter toward him on his left.

Slash looked toward the fire. The man on the left sat facing Slash's direction, but he had his head turned toward his friend on the other side of the fire. A Winchester rested across his thighs. He appeared a stout man with an enormous, bearded head. He wore two pistols and at least one knife that Slash could see. The second man was facing away from Slash. Thinner and taller than the other man but just as well armed, he was smoking a cigarette. His own Winchester leaned against his right thigh. A spare cartridge belt lay coiled around the rifle's stock.

They were droning on about pleasure girls they'd known, poker games they'd played and whom they'd played them with, commenting that the reputations of some famous gamblers were overblown.

"Now, you take Doc Holliday, for instance," the man on the left was saying in his high, reedy voice. "I once sat in on a game with him and Wyatt in Dodge City, an' Doc . . ."

He let his voice trail off. Slash had just stepped forward, shoving a willow branch aside with his left hand and thrusting his rifle barrel forward with his right hand. To his left, Pecos stepped forward, as well.

The man facing Slash looked from Slash to Pecos and then back again, tensing. He wrinkled his nose and said, "Holy shi—"

"What is it?" the taller man said, lunging to his feet and whipping around.

He already had the rifle in his hands and was raising it.

Slash pumped two rounds into him with his Winchester.

"Whoa, now!" the other man said, tossing his own rifle aside and raising his hands, palms out. "Whoa, now! Whoa, now! Just *whoa!*"

"Just this, you dog," Pecos said, and fired two rounds with his Colt's rifle.

Both slugs plowed through the man's dusty wool vest and shabby suit coat, and he went stumbling off into the brush beyond a trickle of stream water, howling. Pecos fired two more rounds, and the outlaw tumbled into the brush, quivering as he died.

Slash glanced at Pecos through his own wafting powder smoke. "How dare you insult dogs that way, partner?"

"Yeah," Pecos said. He turned to Slash, frowning. "Hey, what if they weren't part of the gang? What if they were just passin' through or . . . maybe they was cowpunchers?"

"You see any cows to punch around here?"

"No, but . . ."

"Well, I reckon we'll know in about three shakes of a doxie's bell if they're part of our bunch or not."

"Maybe we oughta wager on it. You know—just to pass the time."

"Too late."

"Huh?"

Slash lifted his chin and pricked his ears, listening. He

turned to Pecos, scowling. "I swear, you got the hearing of a deaf old woman!"

"I hear it!" Pecos said, indignant.

Slash heard it, too—men shouting. The shouts echoed in the quiet night.

A horse whinnied.

"I think they'll be along in a couple minutes." Slash peered up the steep, pine-peppered slope on the other side of the wash. "What say you and I climb up yonder and make ourselves comfortable?"

"Yeah, I could use a little rest from all this bustling activity!" Both men ran wide around the fire and the two dead men. Slash stopped, turned back, and tossed a couple of driftwood chunks onto the fire. Instantly, it flamed higher, bolder. Breathing hard, he and Pecos scrambled up out of the wash and then started climbing the ridge at angles, easing the wear and tear on their old ankles, knees, and hips. It was a steep climb. Slash started cussing after three long strides, and he could hear his partner doing the same.

"Shut up over there, dammit!" he scolded Pecos.

"I will if you will!"

After ten strides, Slash thought he was high enough on the ridge for a good view of the wash below. He stopped and dropped to a knee behind a rock. Pecos stopped on his right now as Slash looked down into the wash. Pecos spat. He was breathing raggedly.

"Christ, you sound like a smithy's bellows!" Slash said, hearing hoof thuds now. The outlaws were coming along the wash below and on his right, following the curve of the bluff that Slash and Pecos were on.

"Yeah?" Pecos snapped back at him. "You sound like a gassy horse breaking wind!"

"All right," Slash said. "You got me beat there." He chuckled to himself as he pumped a cartridge into the Winchester's breech, settled his weight mostly on his left knee, rested the barrel on the top of the rock before him, and waited.

He glanced to his right. Pecos knelt behind a ponderosa pine about twenty feet away. The big man had his Colt's rifle raised to his right shoulder and was aiming down the barrel around the ponderosa's right side, also waiting.

The hoof thuds grew louder and louder until . . .

"Here we go," Slash said mostly to himself.

Two figures rode into the edge of the firelight, on the right. Another rider appeared, then another, and another. They rode wide around the backside of the fire, looking around. One man, whom Slash recognized as Dawg by the snow-white hair flowing down from his black opera hat, said, "Why in the hell's there a fire out here . . . ?"

"Hey, look here!" One of the other riders had ridden around the fire and over to the man Slash had shot and who now lay belly down in the brush. He pointed out the dead man and turned to Dawg, who was now flanked by the bulk of the twelve-man pack.

Two other riders had ridden over to the man Pecos had shot. "Another one's here, Dawg," said a man in a low, dull voice, and spat chaw into the high, crackling flames that cast a good bit of orange light over the killers.

It was as though they all just then and at the same time realized they'd ridden into a trap.

"Clear out!" bellowed the white-haired Dawg.

He ground his heels and neck-reined his horse sharply left, but the horse didn't take a single step before Slash's well-placed .44 round blew him out of his saddle. Then all the killers shouted in recognition of the whipsaw they'd ridden into and started yelling and desperately reining and spurring their mounts wide of the fire, but not before both

Slash and Pecos hurled a veritable rain of lead down upon them. Slash yelled like a wild lobo as he aimed and fired and pumped the Winchester's cocking lever, ejecting the last spent rounds, seating fresh and blowing yet another killer out of his saddle.

When Slash's Winchester clicked empty, he set the rifle aside, rose from his knee, and ran down the slope, palming both of his stag-butted Colts. He continued his fusillade with the two .44s, which leaped and roared in his hands, flames lapping from the barrels.

Whooping and howling like a moon-crazed coyote, he saw in the right periphery of his vision that Pecos also stride quickly downslope, tossing away his rifle and lowering his right shoulder to swing the Richards around in front of him. Most of the riders were already on the ground, either dead or wounded and trying to scramble toward the cover of darkness beyond the fire. Trouble was, the blaze was so large that its sphere of flickering light was broad—so broad that the few who did make it to the edge of it did so with lead inside them, and sliding down the sides of their screaming, buck-kicking horses.

Pecos entered the Richards into the melee.

KA-BOOM! thundered the wicked twelve-gauge, evoking at least one shrill, girlish scream as the double-ought buck tore into a man trying to gain his knees near the base of the slope. The buckshot chewed into his chest and flipped him over backward and straight into the fire.

Screaming with maniacal agony, he bounded back to his feet inside the fire and ran out of it and across the wash, in the opposite direction of Slash and Pecos. He was a literal human torch rocketing across the wash and lighting up the darkness back there to reveal several wounded riders who'd made it into the cottonwoods and willows before their wounds had taken them down.

KA-BOOM! spoke the sawed-off again.

KA-BOOM! KABOOM!

Slash emptied both pistols quickly, then dropped to a knee to reload. When he'd ejected all the empty casings and replaced them with fresh cartridges from his shell belt, he rose again to his feet, thrust both revolvers straight out before him, and clicked the hammers back.

He couldn't find a target. A half-dozen men lay within ten feet of the fire, which had spread due to the human torch's having run to the south, setting dead brush aflame. More men lay beyond that ten feet, and they were more in shadow than light, but none seemed to be moving.

Scratch that. One was moving straight down and out from Slash's position, and slightly right. The man cursed as he pushed himself to his hands and knees. As the man turned his head toward the slope, his eyes glowing demonically in the orange light of the fire, Slash aimed his right-hand Colt and drilled a bullet through the man's forehead.

The man flopped straight back against the ground and jerked his boots a little as his ghost abandoned him in favor of loftier lodgings.

"You see any more?" Pecos was on one knee to Slash's right, aiming his own big Russian down the slope and sliding it back and forth and up and down, looking for a target.

"No," Slash said. "Let's head down and take a look."

Slash started moving carefully down the steep slope, edging sideways, sort of half facing Pecos, for better balance on the sharply dropping terrain.

Pecos yelled, "Dammit, Slash—behind you!"

Slash wheeled so suddenly that both boots slipped out from beneath him. As he dropped butt-first toward the slope at an odd angle, a gun flashed to his left. As he hit the ground on his ass, he saw the bullet that had been meant for him tear Pecos's hat off his partner's head.

Pecos jerked the Russian around and fired two times quickly, both bullets plowing into the hatless man in the red-and-white checked shirt and brown vest who'd been hiding behind a ponderosa. Now the man stumbled straight back against the tree with two startled grunts, one for each chunk of lead that shredded his heart.

Back pressed against the tree, he looked down at the twin holes in his chest, side by side, and said in a breathy, bewildered voice, "Well . . . I'll . . . be . . . *damned* . . . !"

He dropped to his knees and fell forward on his face.

"Dammit, Slash!" Pecos glared at his partner.

"Ah, don't get your drawers in a bunch!" Slash sat up, wincing at the pain in his tailbone. "I think I just broke my—!"

"Look at that!" Pecos reached for his hat and held it up, poking a finger through the hole in the crown. "That bullet was meant for you, dammit!"

"Better your hat than my ticker!"

"I'm not so sure about that," Pecos said, stuffing the topper back on his head. "I bought this hat new last Easter!"

"I'll buy ya a new one!"

"Yes, you will!"

Slash gained his feet again and made his way even more gently down the slope, wincing at the pain in his posterior. Cursing about his hat, Pecos walked down the slope, as well. He'd reloaded his shotgun and was aiming the Richards with his left hand while aiming the Russian with his right hand, looking cautiously around for a still-kicking desperado to shoot.

The fire had died down to half its previous size. The

flames that had been spread by the burning killer were mainly just smoke and cinders now, for there wasn't enough dead brush on the other side of the wash to fuel much of a blaze. Slash couldn't see the human torch himself, but he was mostly likely one hell of a crispy critter by now, lying against the wash's far bank.

"Well, I'll be damned," Pecos said after a minute had passed and neither he nor Slash had spied any movement around them. Only dead men's eyes staring glassily in death.

"We cleaned up well, partner."

"I think one or two might have gotten away on their horses, but they won't be back. Not with as much lead they're hauling. Probably won't live to see the next sunrise."

"Well, I'll be hanged." Slash chuckled and lowered his Colts, depressing the hammers. "We got 'em." He looked at Pecos, grinning delightedly. "I do believe we got 'em. We're in the clear."

Pecos smiled and wagged his head in disbelief. "Looks like!"

"If you weren't so damn ugly, partner, I'd waltz over there and plant a big, wet kiss on your mouth!"

"And get a bullet for your trouble!"

A gun popped, muffled with distance. Both men turned toward the southeast.

The gun popped again, then one more time. The reports echoed hollowly.

Slash swung toward Pecos, his eyes suddenly sharp with apprehension. "Those shots came from our camp!"

"Ah, hell!"

Both men broke into a run across the wash, heading for their horses.

CHAPTER 33

Jenny sat very close to Glenn Larsen, staring into the flames of their small fire. She held a cup of coffee in her hands. She'd draped a blanket around her shoulders, against the night's building chill. Larsen had an arm wrapped around her. He, too, stared into the fire, though she knew that his mind was with Slash and Pecos, as was hers.

Occasionally, she glanced over at the jail wagon hunched menacingly in the darkness, just beyond the reach of the firelight. She could see the three dark figures inside, hunched like caged pumas. Now she saw the umber glow of a cigarette being drawn on, the pale wisps of smoke slithering into the air around the smoker's head.

She knew the prisoners' eyes were on her. They were watching and waiting, hoping that Slash and Pecos did not come back. Hoping that their gang would come for them instead.

And then . . .

Jenny shuddered.

Glenn turned to her. "Are you all right?"

She drew her mouth corners down, nodded.

"I know," Larsen said softly, pressing his cheek to her temple. "I'm worried, too."

"Will we be able to outrun them?"

"Yes." Larsen spoke firmly. "We'll do just as they said. If they're not back by midnight, we'll saddle up and ride south. We should make Cheyenne by midnight."

"On only one horse?"

"It'll be tough, but we can do it."

"They'll run us down. They won't let us escape. Not them . . ."

Larsen squeezed her gently, drew her closer to him, said more firmly, "We're gonna make it."

"Slash and Pecos . . ."

"They'll make it, too."

"They're two against a dozen, Glenn."

"I know, but . . ." He snorted a wry laugh. "There's just something about those two old cutthroats."

"If you two lovebirds could take a break from all your googoo talk, we could use some coffee over here. It's a cold night." That had been Frank Beecher. Jenny had become all too familiar with their individual voices.

"Go to hell," Glenn said. "You had your supper, now just smoke your cigarettes and keep your mouths shut, or I'll come over there and give you the Slash treatment."

"Don't you think it's a little early?" That was Black Pot.

Larsen frowned curiously at Jenny, then turned to the jail wagon and said, "What?"

"For you two to be gettin' all cozy," said Gabriel Black Pot in a mock admonishing tone. "Don't you think it's a little early for that? I mean, good Lord, Marshal, your wife—"

Larsen stiffened and closed his right hand over the

grips of Henry's Colt. "Shut up about her! You shut up! If I hear one more word—"

"Glenn, don't!" Jenny reached up to place a calming hand on his cheek. "They're just trying to get you riled. Don't let them." She turned to the jail wagon and raised her own voice with menace and felt oddly pleased as she did, feeling a little of the murderers' own dark power. "In an hour or so, they'll probably be dead. They're not worth getting riled up about."

One of the killers cursed softly. She thought it was Chaney.

Larsen relaxed. He turned to her. "I know. You're right." He lifted his cup to his mouth, then lowered it and looked into it, frowning. "I'm dry. Time for a fresh pot, I think."

"I could use some more," Jenny agreed. "I'll get—"

"No." Larsen placed a hand on her knee. "My turn. I'll get the water. Just remember not to go near the wagon."

"No, I won't."

Larsen smiled, then rose stiffly, still aching from his sundry injuries. He grabbed the coffeepot, then tramped off into the darkness, heading into the dry wash east of the camp for water. Jenny sat back against the ponderosa before which she'd spread her blankets. Worry was a lion inside her. She was tired of the ache in her belly. It was like being stabbed and having the knife twisted.

She stared over the fire's flickering flames and the wavering tendrils of gray smoke, wondering, silently praying for Slash and Pecos's success. . . .

Distantly, a gun belched. A fusillade of gunfire followed. Jenny gasped, tensed. She'd turned her head to stare toward the southwest but stopped when one of the outlaws cursed sharply, and said, "Ah . . . ah oh, say there—*problem over here!*"

Jenny turned toward the wagon. Something glowed on the ground on the wagon's right side, within roughly two feet of the wheeled jail. Gray smoke rose from the glow.

Louder, Chaney said, "Oh, hello, li'l miss—need your help over here. I dropped my cigarette!"

The glow grew. A couple of finger-size flames rose from the dark ground, sending more smoke into the darkness. The men were moving around in the wagon now, Beecher saying, "Good God, Talon—what the hell you tryin' to do? *Roast* us in here?"

"Damn!" exclaimed Black Pot, sliding back on his butt, away from the fire on the wagon's east side. "Come on, girl—put the fire out before it grows any bigger! With the dry brush around here, it ain't just gonna roast us. It's gonna roast you an' the young marshal, too!"

Tethered nearby, the horses whickered edgily.

Jenny rose, trembling, watching the flames grow before her eyes.

"Get over here and put that fire out, dammit!" Talon Chaney wailed. "We ain't gonna be the only ones burning alive, dammit!"

Jenny's heart kicked in her chest. She glanced behind her and into the wash. She couldn't see Glenn. The stream was a good hundred yards away. He probably wouldn't be back for another couple of minutes.

She turned back to the fire. It had doubled in size over the last minute. Soon it would triple. The killers were right. A blaze out here, with all the dead fuel around to feed it, would turn into a raging dragon in no time.

The prisoners were lurching around in the wagon, coughing and cursing and urging Jenny for help.

She grabbed two blankets off the ground and strode quickly toward the blaze.

"You fools!" she scolded them, looking at the wagon and then at the building fire, gauging the distance between the flames and the wagon. She couldn't get too close to the wagon. The fire might be a trick. Still, it had to be doused.

She stepped up to the east edge of the flames and whipped the blanket at them. She doused a couple, but she was too far east. She couldn't get at them all. She stepped forward by inches, wanting to stay as far from the wagon as possible while still reaching the flames.

Again, she whipped the blanket at the fire. She whipped again, again . . . again.

She vaguely heard Glenn Larsen yell, "Jenny, no!"

She pulled the blanket back once more, cocking her arm for another assault on the flames, but something had grabbed the blanket. Too late, she released it, realizing that one of the killers had reached through the bars and grabbed the end of it and had jerked it back toward him.

Now Jenny was falling toward the wagon over the ground the fire had charred and from which small flames still leapt.

"Nooo!" she screamed, and fought to break her momentum as the dark wagon loomed before her.

A hand grabbed her hair and viciously jerked her head against the wagon. Her scalp on fire with pain, she twisted around, putting her back to the wagon. A cold horror turned her belly to stone when she felt and smelled a thick, muscular, sweaty arm hook around her throat and slam her head and shoulders back against the bars.

"Hi, little honey," Talon Chaney hissed in her ear, his eyes red, like a demon's eyes. *"Miss me?"*

The cold horror inside of Jenny now froze her insides. She tried to scream, but the man had drawn his arm taut across her throat. She could barely breath, much less scream. Flames from the fire licked at her ankles. She could hear her own strangling sounds as she placed both her hands on the man's bulging arm, trying to pry his grip loose to no avail. The man's arm had the strength of iron, and she couldn't work even a little slack in it.

She leaned backward at an awkward angle, her butt only a couple feet off the ground. She hung there from the man's arm, strangling, her vision dimming, her hearing muffled by the hammering of her heart inside her head. She looked straight out away from her to see Glenn Larsen run toward her, his eyes wide with horror and reflecting the orange light of the leaping flames.

"Let her go!" he shouted, aiming his revolver at Chaney on one knee above where Jenny hung from the side of the wagon, struggling to keep her legs away from the flames, the stench of the burning brush making her eyes water.

"Lower the gun or I'll snap her neck!" Chaney shouted.

As if to demonstrate, Chaney jerked Jenny's head to one side. She gave a garbled wail, which died suddenly as her windpipe was pinched entirely off. She struggled weakly, her strength dying as her consciousness faded. The tension left her body, and she hung slack now from Chaney's arm, staring up at the killer grinning over her now, face pressed up taut against the bars.

She was totally helpless. Totally at the mercy of the crazed killer in the jail wagon.

"No!" Larsen said. "Don't hurt her! I'm lowering the gun! I'm lowering it!"

"Get us out of here!" Beecher shouted.

Black Pot yelled, "Hurry up, young lawman, or Talon's gonna rip her head clean off her shoulders. He can do it, too. I seen him rip a head off a grown man my size. He'll rip hers off in two rings of a doxie's bell!"

"I don't have the key!"

"Shoot the lock!"

No, Jenny wanted to call to Glenn. *Don't do it. Don't set them free. They'll kill me, anyway, and they'll kill you, too.* But she had no strength to give voice to her pleas. Her vision was growing dimmer, fading slowly to black. She could barely hear what the men around her were saying beneath the thunder of her blood in her ears.

She could sense Glenn's terror and frustration. It was almost like their souls were already bonded through grief and misery. She knew he felt he had no choice but to shoot the lock in the door and set the killers free. He likely knew what would happen when he did, but he had no choice. By not doing so, Chaney would snap her neck like a kindling stick, and he couldn't let it happen.

He couldn't lose another woman he loved so close on the heels of the first one.

He'd lose Jenny, anyway. Still, he had to open the door.

Don't do it, Glenn. Please, don't do it, Glenn. Let them kill me, then shoot them all!

She flinched only slightly when she heard the shot. She felt the reverberation of the blast, as well as the bullet hammering into the door lock. There were two more blasts, two more sets of reverberations through the jail wagon's bars.

Suddenly, Chaney's arm released Jenny's neck. She felt her butt hit the ground. The violent jarring radiated all through her. She lay only one-quarter conscious for a time—she wasn't sure how long. She was aware of shouting and a violent commotion around her. A hand grabbed her arm, jerked her into motion. She winced at the pain in her shoulder.

Someone was dragging her.

She rose from unconsciousness like lifting her head out

of a dark lake, and saw Chaney dragging her by one arm. He was limping on his wounded leg, but he was laughing and hollering while the other two were milling wildly around the fire, kicking through gear, likely looking for a bottle.

Jenny looked behind her. The fire was out, the charred brush only smoking. Only one man was slumped in the dark wagon now, obscured by smoke. She knew it was Glenn because she recognized the bereaved voice calling to her, *"Jenny! I'm sorry, Jenny! I'm so sorry, Jenny! I should have shot you! I'm sorry, Jenny!"*

She returned her gaze to Chaney, who was just then dragging her into the firelight. A gun was wedged behind the waistband of his trousers, over his belly. She yearned for it but knew she had no chance at it. She was nearly as weak as a corpse.

"Don't use her all up, now, Talon," Black Pot said, sitting back against a tree and tipping a bottle to his lips. "Save some for me an' Hell-Raisin' Frank!" He gave a loud, victorious whoop and drank.

"The boys should be along soon," said Beecher as Chaney released Jenny's arm and she slumped beside the fire. "They might want some, too!"

Chaney stood straddling Jenny, staring down at her with that devil's grin on his face once more, his eyes still red with reflected firelight. "I make no promises."

He dropped to his knees and started to lower his head toward Jenny's.

She had no idea how a rock suddenly got into her right hand, but there it was. Not only that—and no one could have been more amazed than she herself at what happened next—but she found herself swinging the rock savagely up and to her left. It smacked against Talon Chaney's left temple with a thudding *crack!*

Chaney's head jerked sharply to one side. He sagged backward on his knees.

"Ouch!" he cried, reaching up with both hands, clamping them both over his head.

When he pulled his hands away, saw the blood on them, he stared down at her again, another lusty smile flickering in his eyes and shaping itself on his mouth. "Why, you purty li'l devil!"

He frowned as his gaze dropped to the Colt revolver in Jenny's hands. She'd grabbed it out from behind his waistband. Again, she had no idea where she'd summoned the strength for such an action. Maybe it was the raw energy leeched from the horror of knowing that the misery she'd known before, while the town was burning and these three were savaging her in the smoky streets of Dry Fork, would be nothing compared to the horror she was about to experience if she didn't do something impossible.

She looked at her own right thumb cocking the Colt's hammer. It was as if the thumb belonged to someone else entirely, a much calmer and stronger person whose soul had invaded her body, and she was merely watching this person cock the gun.

Chaney's smile grew brittle, and the red light left his eyes. They turned flat and dark with fear. "Hey, now, you silly little thing." He reached for the gun in Jenny's hands. "Give me that, you—"

The gun bucked and roared. Flames blossomed from the barrel and spread to Chaney's shirt. Instantly, Jenny smelled the sickening stench of gunpowder and burning flesh and scorched blood. Automatically, she fired again, and Chaney flopped backward against the ground, screaming, flames lapping at his shirt.

Through her own wafting powder smoke, Jenny saw the other two killers bounding toward her, cursing and yelling. Jenny extended the pistol again . . . again cocked the weapon . . . and fired at Beecher, who stopped in his tracks and looked down in shock and horror at the hole in his belly, and started yowling.

Black Pot lunged toward her on her right.

Smoothly, coolly, almost with the abandon of a stone statue, Jenny turned and felt the Colt again leap in her hands, roaring, flames stabbing toward the big, dark head of Black Pot, which snapped back on the man's shoulders as the bullet ripped into his forehead, two inches above the bridge of his long, broad nose. She watched without emotion as his eyes rolled back in his head and he fell backward without breaking his fall.

Slowly, purposefully, she pushed herself to her feet.

Beecher was down on his knees, holding his arms over his bloody belly. He was glaring up at her, cursing her. Jenny smiled grimly at the man—though it was not really her smiling but this other much cooler, calmer, cold-blooded woman who had invaded her body—and raised the revolver. Her grin broadened as she drew the hammer back and aimed at the howling man's head.

"Nooo!" Beecher shouted.

"Oh, yes," Jenny said.

The bullet caromed into his wide-open mouth and exited the back of his head, painting the ground behind him red. He fell back over his boot heels and lay kicking like a scarecrow in a windstorm.

Jenny stepped back away from the fire. She looked at the three dead men. A strange serenity had fallen over her.

She turned slowly to see Glenn Larsen staring at her through the bars of the jail wagon, a bar in each hand, his eyes wide in shock.

Suddenly, the night spun. Vaguely, Jenny heard the rumble of hoof thuds.

She started to turn, but then her head grew light, her knees week. They buckled and she fell into the arms of Slash Braddock. He gazed down at her, smiling reassuringly, closing his hand over the smoking Colt in her own hand, gently pulling it away from her, dropping it.

Pecos galloped up behind him and leaped down from his buckskin's back.

"I got ya, darlin'," Slash said. "I got ya, darlin'." He picked her up in his arms, and she'd never felt so warm and secure before in her life. "All's well. All's well . . ."

And she knew that finally it was.

CHAPTER 34

Cisco Walsh kicked the cabin door open and shoved Jay so hard through the opening that she ran stumbling inside, fell, and rolled up against the cabin's back wall.

"What do you want to do with this one?" asked the man behind Walsh, who held Myra over his left shoulder.

"Inside," Walsh said.

He stepped aside as the big man, who Jay now saw wore a five-pointed deputy sheriff's star, carried Myra over to where Jay lay on her hip and elbow near the cabin's back wall. The man stopped, smiled nastily down at Jay, then lowered his shoulder. Myra rolled down his arm and dropped to the hardpacked earthen floor with a thud.

The girl gave a loud groan and a sharp curse. The tumble seemed to snap her back to consciousness.

Jay reached for her, hardening her jaws and sharpening her eyes as she glared up at the hulking deputy with a round, fleshy face in which his small eyes were set too close together. "You damned brute!" She switched her gaze to Walsh, who was stepping into the cabin now, removing his hat and tossing it onto the table. "Damn you, Cisco!

You killed Delbert Thayer!" She felt her voice breaking on the boy's name. *"How could you?"*

Myra turned to her, eyes widening with shock. "What . . . ?" the girl gasped.

"I'm sorry," Jay said. "He . . . Delbert . . ."

Myra half sat and swung her head with her bloody mouth to Walsh. *"Murderer!"*

"Shut up. You two are the ones who killed him. I might have pulled the trigger, but I wouldn't have had to if . . . Well, what's done is done." Walsh stood by the table, reaching up to, with insolent casualness, rearrange his hair with one hand as he stared grimly down at Jay.

By the light of two burning lamps, she saw the dark malevolence in the man's eyes.

Voices rose from outside the cabin. Quick footsteps sounded. The door was jerked open and another man walked in—a slender, mustached man in a crisp gray Stetson. Long sideburns peppered with gray framed his long, pale, angular face with cold gray eyes. The end of his long nose was touched with red from the cold and the wind. He wore two pistols on his hips, beneath a hip-length corduroy jacket. He had a bandanna wrapped around his right hand, and he was squeezing that hand painfully in his other hand against his belly.

As he did, his teeth showed in a straight white line beneath his neatly trimmed mustache. He fairly seethed with rage.

"What'd you bring them in here for?" Keldon Reed asked Walsh, switching his angry gaze from Jay to Myra and back again.

Walsh stared grimly down at the two women. Myra sat on her butt beside Jay, sobbing into her hands for the murdered Delbert Thayer. "We're gonna keep them in here till the job's done," the outlaw marshal said.

"Like hell we are!" Reed strode forward and buried his right boot in Myra's side. The girl screamed as she slammed back onto the floor and rolled onto her side, facing away from the man and drawing her knees up, gasping.

Jay reached for Myra and cursed the man shrilly.

"She killed one of my men, wounded another, and damn near blew my hand off!" Reed held up his bloody paw to show Walsh, then drew a revolver with his right hand. "I'm gonna kill them both!"

"No, you're not." Walsh had already drawn his own revolver. He aimed it at Reed's head and cocked it. "I told you not to kill them, and I meant it."

Reed wheeled toward Walsh, jaws hard with rage. "Hall wants them both dead!"

"Hall doesn't run this show!"

"He sure as hell does! And don't forget the dirt he has on you, Marshal!"

"Dirt or no dirt, without me, he wouldn't be able to pull this job. I'm the one who learned about the run. No one else knows about it except the company who mined the gold and the stagecoach company shipping it!"

"You're outgunned, Walsh." Reed laughed caustically and glanced at the two deputies flanking him and at the half-open door beyond which three of his own men stood in the darkness, staring in. They had their hands draped over the butts of their holstered guns. "I mean, you're badly outgunned!"

"Maybe. But I could drill a bullet through your head right now." Walsh narrowed an eye as he aimed down the barrel.

That seemed to take the starch out of Reed's drawers.

He glared back at the Camp Collins marshal, flushing. He glanced at Jay kneeling beside Myra, caressing the injured girl's back soothingly. Myra was sitting up now, her lower lip bleeding. Jay returned the man's cold gaze before he turned his head back to the lawman. "They'll talk, Walsh. You know they will."

"It's my decision. Now get the hell out of here. We have a stage to rob in two hours. Your boss is likely waiting for you at the other cabin. It's time to get into position."

"What about you?"

"I'll be right behind you."

Reed held his gaze for another fifteen seconds, then stepped quickly around him and stomped out the door in a huff. The two big deputies flanking Walsh turned to leave, as well, but they stopped when the lawman said, "Not you two. You're going to stay here." He glanced at Jay and Myra. "With them."

"What?" said the larger of the two beefy, cow-eyed men. "You're going to stay here and keep an eye on them. Get rope. Tie them."

When the deputies had found rope hanging from the wall of the cabin cluttered with old airtight tins, tack, and odds and ends of mining paraphernalia, they each tied Jay's and Myra's hands behind the women's backs, and then they tied their ankles.

"Now, get out but stay close. You'll stay in here with them until I return."

The deputies shared an oblique look, shrugged, and stepped outside. Walsh kicked the door closed behind them, then turned to the two women sitting with their backs to the soot and cobweb-covered rear wall from which rusty mining implements hung and on which a moldering old bobcat skin was stretched.

He gestured toward the potbelly stove hunched before him, in the center of the shack. A table lay to the stove's right, opposite the side of the cabin Jay and Myra were in. "Can I offer you ladies a cup of coffee?"

"Go to hell, Cisco!" Jay shot back at him.

"How are we supposed to drink coffee with our hands tied behind our backs, you murdering moron?" Myra fired at him, as well, her eyes narrowed furiously.

Walsh drew a deep breath, nodded. "Good point." He walked forward. "Look, Jay—I'm sorry." Glancing at Myra, he said, "I'm sorry for that little tap, young lady."

"It was more than just a tap, and you had no right to kill Delbert, you low-down, dirty—"

"All right—I'm sorry about Thayer! I'm sorry I struck you! I didn't know who you were. I saw Jay, and I thought perhaps her cutthroat pal had thrown in with her out here, acting like heroes." To Jay again, he said, "You could've just stayed out of it, you know. Young Thayer would still be alive if you had. It's none of your damn business!"

"When the law breaks the law and there's no one else around to know or to try to stop it, it's my business. It's any citizen's business. The law has to be on our side, the side of good. Otherwise . . ." Jay shook her head, glowering at the man who'd now dropped to his haunches before her and Myra. "What is it he has on you, Cisco? What's the dirt?"

Walsh drew a breath, lowered his head, and again ran a hand through his hair as though he couldn't leave the barbered mop alone. "I knew Hall in Texas before I came here. He was a money man down there with an interest in ranching. He came up here about a year after I did. He knew a dirty little secret of mine. Only, well . . ." He looked down in chagrin. "It's not so little." He gave Jay a level look. "In Abilene, I got a woman . . . a young woman from a good family . . . in the family way. I was going to marry her. I really didn't want her to give birth to an illegitimate child. I really didn't. I didn't want her to have to carry around that terrible reputation because of my own indiscretion, but . . ."

He let his voice trail off and released another burdensome sigh as he looked around the room as though for the answer to his failings.

"But . . ." Jay prodded him.

"I left. There you have it. I left. After the baby was born, I pulled out. I'd been dragging my feet on getting hitched." Walsh sighed. "She was a good woman, too. Decent and caring. A good, simple, small-town girl. A churchgoer. Lived by the Golden Rule . . . till I came along and she fell for me. Couldn't help herself, she said. And I took full advantage. But after all was said and done, I just couldn't see myself married to her, raising a child in Abilene with a simple small-town gal when I had such higher aspirations. I didn't want to be pinned down by a family. Not then. I was younger, you understand. This was twelve years ago. So I ran."

"It's a terrible thing, but it happens, Cisco," Jay said. "And it was a long time ago."

Walsh looked at her again directly. "She turned alcoholic. She hanged herself in her bedroom in her family's house. But only . . ." He drew a breath and closed his eyes, steeling himself. "But only after she'd smothered the little boy, when he was five years old."

"Ohh," Jay breathed out in shock.

"I gambled with Hall back in those days, before I fled Abilene. He knew all about what I did. When he came here and couldn't get his ranch off the ground . . . not where he wanted it to be . . . he turned to robbing stagecoaches coming down out of the mountains, hauling bullion to the local banks and the railroad. He needed an inside man to help his operation run a little smoother. He had that dirt on me, and if I didn't agree to throw in with him, he threatened to go to the newspapers with the story . . . to ruin my name. He even has an ambrotype of me an' the girl, taken before we were to be married . . . with the baby. Could you see that splashed across the front pages of the local newspapers?"

"You might have just pulled out," Jay remarked. "God knows you're accustomed to moving around the West, Cisco."

"I wanted to stay here. I'm tired of running, sinking taproot after taproot. Besides . . ." Walsh wrung his hands together. "I didn't want you to know, Jay. I would have been so ashamed. And I *am* so ashamed. I love you, and I honestly thought you would marry me."

Jay glanced at Myra, who returned her hopeful gaze. Turning back to the marshal, who appeared near tears, Jay said, "If you love me, Cisco, let me go. Untie us."

He looked back at her, expressionless at first. Then he offered a grim smile and a single shake of his head. "Can't, Jay. I'm sorry."

"We won't tell," Jay lied.

He laughed at that. "Of course, you will. I can't have anyone finding out. I need time to get to Mexico, and I don't want bounty hunters trailing me for the rest of my life. They'll look for me even south of the border. I'm gonna live high on the hog down there in my old age. You could have, too, Jay. It didn't have to come to this. I can't risk going to jail. You know what happens to lawmen in jail."

"So you're just gonna kill us?" Myra said, her voice taut with anger. "Just like Delbert . . . ?"

"Yes, I'm afraid so. Don't worry. Not yet. Not here. You deserve better. I'll take you off alone, into a ravine, and give you each your sendoff. Just me. No one else around to see. That's how I did Thayer. It'll just be the three of us. I owe you that, Jay. A respectful killing."

"You're mad," Jay said, narrowing her eyes, studying him closely. "You've been driven mad by greed. You've been driven to *murder* by greed!"

"Maybe," Walsh allowed, nodding, tucking down his mouth corners. He reached out and gently placed his hand on Jay's left cheek. "And by love."

She shook her head, recoiling at the killer's touch.

"Love will do it, too, Jay. Unrequited love. You see, I just can't see allowing you to marry that . . ." His mouth twisted into a bitter expression. "That old scalawag and outlaw, Slash Braddock."

"Scalawag? Outlaw?" Jay gave a shrill, ironic laugh. "Slash is three times the man you could ever be! You're nothing but an expensive haircut and an empty suit! A cold-blooded, murdering snake!"

Walsh's face turned red. He snapped his right hand back behind his shoulder and had just started to swing it forward, toward Jay's face, when a grunt sounded from outside the cabin. There was a heavy thud as though of a body hitting the ground.

A voice said, "What the . . ." Another thud followed by a sharp, *"Oh, ah!"*

A heavier thud as a body hit the ground.

"What the . . . ?" Walsh rose, wheeled, and strode toward the door. He closed his hands over the grip of the Colt in the holster on his right hip.

Before he could pull the gun, the door burst inward with a thundering *boom!*

Walsh froze as a frightening visage stepped through the door—a specter in the night.

CHAPTER 35

The crouched figure, appearing half-man, half-beast—
a giant coyote, maybe—stepped quietly into the cabin,
both arms raised to the right, holding something in the
thing's hands over its right shoulder, just off that ear.

The figure was like a coyote ghost belched out of the
night—wiry, filthy, sweating, seething with anger. The
ghost was badly disheveled, wearing a soiled pin-striped
shirt and suspenders and baggy broadcloth trousers, both
knees torn, stuffed into the high tops of mule-eared boots.
A bloody bandage encircled the top of the specter's coyote-
like head with a long, thin nose and pinched up eyes. Thin
sandy, sweaty hair trailed down over the bloody cloth.

Jay blinked as she more closely scrutinized the new-
comer, felt her lower jaw drop.

She turned to Myra. The girl's own jaw was sagging,
and both eyes were growing wider. She and Jay yelled at
the same time, *"Delbert!"*

"Thayer!" Walsh said in horror. "What in God's
name . . . ?"

"God didn't have nothin' to do with it, you fork-tailed
demon. You ugly, dry-gulchin' sidewinder!"

Delbert stood six feet from Walsh. Jay now saw that what the young man held in his hands, cocked and ready to fly, was a slingshot. Young Thayer canted his head to his right, aiming the rock-loaded scrap of rawhide, attached with cow gut to the forked wooden handle, at Walsh's head.

He showed his buck teeth as he seethed out, "You left me in that canyon to die, didn't ya? Or maybe you *figured* I was dead! Well, I *wasn't* dead. I was playin' possum, 'cause while folks might like to laugh and make light of me, like you and them two deputies out there nursin' split skulls, I'm smarter than I damn *look!*"

"Oh, Delbert!" Myra sobbed into the hands she was clamping over her mouth, tears of joy runnin' down her cheeks and over her hand.

"Hah!" Delbert laughed bitterly, his eyes spitting bayonets of raw fury at Walsh. "I'm back from the dead, all right. Delbert lives! Ya see, ya stupid fool, *Marshal Walsh*, any kind of a head wound bleeds profusely. Even a small nick like the one you gave me. It threw me from my saddle, all right, but I lay there playin' possum till I heard you chuckle and ride away. *Yaring-tailed polecat! Copper-riveted dunderhead!*"

Delbert shifted his boots on the earthen floor as he glared with challenge at Walsh. The marshal still had his hand wrapped around the grips of his holstered Colt. The two men faced each other, crouching like pugilists frozen in midmotion.

"Go ahead and de-leather that smoke wagon, Walsh! Go ahead! You don't think my aim is true? Or maybe you think bringin' a slingshot to a gun battle gives me the short end of the stick!"

That was what Walsh must have thought, all right.

In the next second, the marshal whipped the gun out of its holster. There was a creak of rawhide and gut as Delbert loosed the rock. It thumped against Walsh's forehead just as the man's hogleg cleared leather.

Walsh wailed and dropped the pistol. He clamped both hands to his forehead, stumbling backward. Dropping the slingshot, Delbert stayed on the man, pulling his own six-shooter from the soft leather holster on his belly, clicking the hammer back and thrusting it hard against Walsh's chest. Walsh stumbled over his own feet and dropped to the floor, falling hard. Dust and grit rose around him. He landed in front of the wide-eyed women.

Delbert dropped to a knee and pressed the barrel of his cocked old Remington against the outlaw marshal's forehead. Walsh raised his hands in supplication. Delbert's sharp-featured face with its long nose and blue eyes was still flushed deep red with rage as he glared at Walsh's, whose own face was now twisted in pain and terror.

"How dare you dry-gulch me, you criminal! How dare you hurt my girl an' Miss—"

Young Thayer stopped himself and turned a shade even redder as he glanced sheepishly at Myra and said, "I mean . . . Miss Myra an' Miss Breckenridge."

Jay glanced at Myra, who smiled, then tucked her bottom lip under her upper one, suddenly wistful.

Delbert cleared his throat self-consciously, then switched his narrowed, enraged eyes back to Walsh. "I oughta feed you a pill you can't digest right here an' now for doin' something that low-down an' poison mean. I heard how you was gonna kill these ladies. I had my ear pressed against the back wall there. I heard the whole thing . . . before I stole around an' beaned both of those post-stupid deputies with my old slingshot. Yessir, Walsh, I oughta turn you toe down an' kick you out with a cold shovel. Give me one good reason why I shouldn't!"

Jay cleared her throat, hesitant to intervene in the young man's castigation of the outlaw marshal, since he seemed to be airing his spleen over a good many injuries even above and beyond Walsh. "Uh . . . Delbert?"

"Yes, Miss Jay?"

"The others left to meet Jason Hall and hold up the bullion run. Don't you think we should tie him up and . . ."

"Don't you worry yourself, Miss Jay. Nor you, hon . . . I mean, Miss Myra." Again, Delbert's flush deepened. "I got it all taken care of."

"What?" Walsh blinked up at the enraged young deputy, suddenly curious.

Keeping his eyes on Walsh, Thayer said, "Before I rode out here the other day to hunt me some outlaws and warn the Horsetooth Station about an imminent holdup, Uncle—er, I mean *the sheriff*—wired me from Santa Fe an' said he was headed back on the next flyer. Well, after you dry-gulched me, you low-down dirty dog—with my apologies to dogs—and I spent two days tryin' to clear my head and track down my horse and then heard shootin' that drew me over here, I ran into the sheriff his ownself. He's leadin' a posse out from Camp Collins—a good twenty men. They'll be layin' for you and Hall at Horsetooth Station, armed for bear!"

Young Thayer cackled wickedly and shoved his coyote face down closer to Walsh's. "Oh, I guess you won't be there, will you, Marshal? Since you're here and I got you dead to rights! Hah!"

Jay turned to Myra, and the two women shared a delighted, much-relieved smile.

Then Myra turned to Thayer and said, "Del . . . honey . . . ?"

Thayer jerked his head to her, his face turning as bright as Christmas morning. "Yes, Miss Myra?" he asked eagerly.

"Since you got that poison-mean, low-down dirty dog—with apologies to dogs—dead to rights, could you maybe tie him up now and cut me and Jay loose? We haven't had any blood to our hands or feet for a good half hour."

Young Thayer stared at his beloved. Jay thought that if his heart had been a bird, it would have flown out of his chest and burst into song. "Why, sure, sure. Sure, I will, honey!"

EPILOGUE

"Gentlemen, I feel the need to apologize one more time for my unpardonable crime of cheating the hangman," said Jenny Claymore.

"There ain't no need," Slash said.

"No need at all," Pecos agreed. "We'll send him a few bucks for a bottle and a cheap doxie."

"I don't know what came over me."

"Hell, it was goin' over Slash nearly every hour. If you hadn't finished off them three curly wolves, Slash would've blown off so many of their body parts there wouldn't have been anything left to hang in Denver!" Pecos chuckled as he glanced around at the first shacks and shanties moving up around the four riders as they passed the old army outpost and rode into the outskirts of Camp Collins.

Two days had passed since Slash and Pecos had culled the outlaw herd down to nothing but the outlaws' horses, two of which now carried Glenn Larsen and Jenny Claymore. Jenny had finished off Chaney, Beecher, and Black Pot, so the last leg of their journey to Cheyenne had been a whole lot quieter and less laborious—what with their being no more extra mouths to feed and slop buckets to empty.

They'd spent the night in a nice hotel in Cheyenne, after indulging in long, hot baths at a Chinese bathhouse, then hopped the train earlier this very morning for the Camp Collins station, out on the flats east of town. The loot the outlaws had stolen from the Sundance stage had been turned over to Sheriff Hank Covington in Cheyenne, who had bristled at seeing the two ex-cutthroats still kicking and appearing very little worse from their recent wear.

Slash and Pecos had convinced Glenn and Jenny that they might find an easier time starting their lives over in Camp Collins, which was smaller and more sedate than the bustling cosmopolitan cow town that Denver had grown up to be. Besides, in Camp Collins, the pair—who were, indeed a pair now, though they were still shy about it and hadn't formally announced themselves—could take advantage of Slash and Pecos's connections, few as there were.

They'd even offered Glenn a job as hostler or teamster for their freighting company until he could find a more permanent vocation. They'd also offered to stake them to rooms in Camp Collins's finest hotel, the Horsetooth Rock Inn, directly across the street from Jay's House of a Thousand Delights saloon and gambling parlor, until they could find more permanent housing of their own.

"Yes, but I got you in trouble with your boss," Jenny pointed out.

They were entering the Camp Collins business district, which was growing quiet this late in the afternoon, nearing five p.m. with the shadows growing long across the broad, dusty main street sandwiched on both sides by tall business façades and stitched along its north side by telegraph poles and their sagging wires.

"Oh, don't worry about ole Bleed-Em-So," Slash said,

reining his Appy around a stalled lumber dray. "He's just sore he don't have no one to hang."

"He's also chafed that we're still kickin'," Pecos added.

"Ain't that the truth?" Slash chuckled.

"He threatened to dock your pay, though," Glenn Larsen said as he looked around at the shops and offices lining the street.

Whoops and hollers were already issuing from the local and relatively new opera house the quartet was just now passing and before which a good dozen horses stood tied to three hitchracks.

"Ah, he was just blatherin'," Pecos said, referring to the cable Bledsoe had sent to him and Slash in Cheyenne, in response to the cable they'd sent the marshal announcing that due to circumstances beyond their control, he would have no outlaws to hang. "He knows if he docks our pay, we'll just put in for the reward money the dead outlaws have on their ugly heads, and we'd come out better in the long run. He'll pay us. He wants to keep in good with his old ex-cutthroats because he's got no one else to take on his dirtiest assignments, and he enjoys torturing us so much!"

"You're right there, partner," Slash said, chuckling.

Jenny reined her chestnut to a stop and turned to regard a secretarial school housed in a tall, narrow brick building sandwiched between the Western Union office and a grocery store.

"What is it, Jenny?" Glenn said, reining in his own mount.

Ahead of the pair, Slash and Pecos did likewise, turning back to regard the younger folks.

"Look there," Jenny said, pointing at a pasteboard sign in one of the school's two front windows. " 'Tutors needed.' "

Glenn smiled at her. "Surely you don't want to apply for a job already, Jenny. We just pulled into town."

Jenny returned his smile with a winning one of her own and flicked her hair back with mock haughtiness. "I feel fresh as a flower. I had a long bath last night, and I haven't powdered this pretty new outfit Slash and Pecos bought me with too much dust." They'd bought both her and Larsen full sets of new duds in Cheyenne yesterday afternoon. "I look presentable, don't I?"

"I'll say you do!" all three men said at nearly the same time, meaning every word.

"Well, then . . ." Jenny slipped smoothly down from her saddle and extended her reins to Glenn. "Wait for me?"

Beaming, Larsen stepped down from his own horse's back and accepted her reins. He lowered his new Stetson from his head and held it over his heart, giving a courtly dip of his chin. "It would be my honor."

"Good luck, Miss Jenny." Pecos doffed his own hat to her.

Slash said, "Good luck, darlin'. I know you'll get the job. Any gal who looks and talks good as you is a lead-pipe cinch!"

Jenny winced, flushed a little. "Um, yeah . . . that would be 'Any gal who looks and talks as *well* as I do,' Slash." She flashed him a tolerant smile.

"See what I mean?" Slash said, chuckling.

When he and Pecos had said goodbye to the pair and made plans to meet later for supper, Pecos turned to Slash. "Well, partner, looks like we're on our own."

"It does, indeed. Shall we wet our whistles?"

"Capital idea. Any place in mind?"

Pecos grinned at his partner.

Slash scratched beneath his chin as he gazed off, pretending to laboriously consider the question. "Well, I reckon I was sorta thinkin' maybe the Thousand Delights."

"You *were*?" Pecos said, feigning shock. "The *Thousand Delights?*"

"Yeah, I was thinkin' maybe we should go over and get a drink at the Thousand Delights."

"There wouldn't happen to be a raving red-headed beauty you're sparking over that way—would there, Slash?"

"Oh . . ." Slash chuckled, feigning incredulity as he spat over his left stirrup and ran a hand across his mouth. "I don't know, I reckon there might be." He booted his Appy forward. "There just might be, at that."

"Well, what the heck, then?" Pecos spurred his own mount up beside Slash. "I reckon we can get the low-down on what's been happening around here while we been gone, too. That may or not be interesting."

"In this lazy town?" Slash said with sarcastic chuckle. "I doubt if anything more interesting happened around here than a drunk miner or two broke out some windows in one o' them cheap parlor houses down by the river."

"Yeah, I gotta feelin' you're probably right, Slash. Nothin' much interesting ever happens around here. Not that I'm complainin', but it does get a little boring from time to time."

"Purely, it does," Slash agreed. "Purely, it does."

Keep reading for special excerpt....

BLOOD IN THE DUST
A HUNTER BUCHANON BLACK HILLS WESTERN

by William W. Johnstone
and J. A. Johnstone

*The greatest Western writers of the 21st century continue
the adventures of Hunter Buchanon,
a towering mountain of a man who made his name
as a Rebel tracker in the Civil War.
Now he and his coyote sidekick Bobby Lee are trying to
forge a new peaceful life in the Black Hills, Dakota.
But they'll have to fight to the death to keep it . . .*

THERE'S COYOTES IN THEM THERE HILLS.
Ex-Rebel tracker Hunter Buchanon is down on his luck.
He lost his family's ranch in a fire. He lost his gold to a
thief. And he just might lose his fiancée—a beautiful
saloon girl named Annabelle—to a stinking-rich rival.
But Hunter's not ready to give up just yet. He's got a
temporary sheriff's badge, a long-range plan to rebuild
his ranch, and his loyal coyote Bobby Lee by his side
to make things right. Too bad it all goes wrong—
when Annabelle gets kidnapped . . .

The mayhem begins with a stagecoach robbery
in the Black Hills town of Tigerville.
It won't end until Sheriff Hunter Buchanon gets back his
girl and his gold—on a long, dusty trail
of blood-soaked vengeance . . .

Look for **BLOOD IN THE DUST.** *On sale now.*

CHAPTER 1

"That coyote makes me nervous," said shotgun messenger Charley Anders.

"You mean Bobby Lee?" asked Hunter Buchanon as he handled the reins of the rocking and clattering Cheyenne & Black Hills Stage, sitting on the hard, wooden seat to Anders's left.

He spoke through the neckerchief he'd drawn up over his nose and mouth to keep out at least some of the infernal dust kicked up by the six-horse hitch.

"Yeah, yeah—Bobby Lee. He's the only coyote aboard this heap and that there is a thing I never thought I'd hear myself utter if I lived to be a hundred years old!"

Anders slapped his thigh and roared through his own pulled-up neckerchief.

"No need to be nervous, Charley," Hunter said. "Bobby Lee ain't dangerous. In fact, he's right polite." Buchanon leaned close to the old shotgun messenger beside him and said with feigned menace, "As long as you're polite to Bobby Lee, that is."

He grinned and nudged the shotgun man with his elbow.

"If you mean by 'polite' give him a chunk of jerky every

time he demands one, he can go to hell!" Anders glanced uneasily over his left shoulder at Bobby Lee sitting on the coach roof just above and between him and Buchanon. "Hell, he demands jerky all the damn time! If you don't give him some, he shows you his teeth!"

As if the fawn-gray coyote had understood the conversation, Bobby Lee lowered his head and pressed his cold snout to Anders's left ear, nudging up the man's cream *sombrero.*

"See there?" Anders cried. Leaning forward in his seat and regarding the coyote dubiously, the shotgun messenger said, "I ain't givin' you no more jerky, Bobby Lee, an' that's that! If I give you any more jerky, I won't have none left for my ownself an' we still got another half hour's ride into Tigerville! I gotta keep somethin' in my stomach or I get the fantods!"

Hunter chuckled as he glanced over his right shoulder at Bobby Lee pointing his long snout in the general direction of the shirt pocket in which he knew Anders kept his jerky. The coyote's triangle ears were pricked straight up.

Hunter gave the coyote a quick pat on the head. "Bobby Lee understands—don't you, Bobby Lee? He thinks you're bein' right selfish—not to mention womanish about your *fantods*—but he understands."

Hunter chuckled and turned his head forward to gaze out over the horses' bobbing heads.

As he did, Bobby Lee subtly raised his bristling lips to show the ends of his fine, white teeth to Anders.

"See there? He just did it again!" Charley cried, pointing at Bobby Lee.

When Hunter turned to the coyote he'd raised from a pup, after the little tyke's mother had been killed by hunters, Bobby Lee quickly closed his lips over his teeth.

He turned to his master and fashioned a cock-headed, doe-eyed look of innocence, as though he had no idea why this cork-headed fool was slandering him so unjustly.

"Ah, hell, you're imagining things, Charley," Hunter scolded the man. "You an' your fantods an' makin' things up. You should be ashamed of yourself!"

"He did—I swear!"

A woman's sonorous, somewhat sarcastic voice cut through Anders's complaint. "Excuse me, gentlemen! Excuse me! Do you mind if I interrupt your eminently important and impressively articulate conversation?"

The plea had come from below and on Buchanon's side of the stage. He glanced over his left shoulder to see one of his and Anders's two passengers poking her head out of the coach's left-side window. Blinking against the billowing dust, Miss Laura Meyers gazed beseechingly up toward the driver's box. "I'd like to request a nature stop if you would, please?"

Hunter and Charley Anders shared a weary look. Miss Meyers, who'd boarded the stage in Cheyenne a few days ago, was from the East by way of Denver. Now, Hunter had known plenty of Eastern folks who were not royal pains in the backside. Miss Meyers was not one of them.

She was grossly ill-prepared for travel in the West. She'd not only not realized that the trip between Cheyenne and Tigerville in the Dakota Territory took a few days, she'd not realized that stagecoach travel was a far cry from the more comfortable-style coach and buggy and train travel to which she'd become accustomed back east of the Mississippi.

Here there was dust. And heat. The stench of male sweat and said male's "infernal and ubiquitous tobacco use." (Hunter didn't know what "ubiquitous" meant but he'd been able to tell by the woman's tone that it wasn't complimentary. At least, not in the way she had used it.)

Also, the trail up from Cheyenne into the Black Hills was not as comfortable as, say, a ride in an open chaise across a grassy Eastern meadow on a balmy Sunday afternoon in May. Out here, there were steep hills, narrow canyons, perilous river crossings, the heavy alkali mire along Indian Creek, and, once you were in the Hills themselves, twisting, winding trails with enough chuck holes and washouts to keep the Concord rocking on its leather thoroughbraces until you thought you must have eaten flying fish for breakfast.

Several times over the past two days, Miss Meyers had heralded the need for Hunter to stop the coach so she could bound out of it in a swirl of skirts and petticoats and hurl herself into the bushes to air her paunch.

So far, they hadn't been accosted by owlhoots. They'd even made it through the dangerous country around the Robbers' Roost Relay Station without having a single bullet hurled at them from one of the many haystack bluffs in that area. Nor an arrow, for that matter.

Indians—primarily Red Cloud's Sioux, understandably miffed by the treaty the government had broken to allow gold-seeking settlers into the Black Hills—had been a problem on nearly every run Hunter had been on in the past year. He'd started driving for the stage company after his family's ranch had been burned by a rival rancher and the man's business partner, his two brothers murdered, his father, old Angus, seriously wounded.

He wanted to say as much to the lady—a pretty one, at that—staring up at him now from the coach's left-side window, but he knew she'd have none of it. She was a fish out of water here, and in dire straits. He could see it in her eyes. She was not only road-weary but world-weary, as well.

Though they'd left the Ten Mile Ranch Station only twenty minutes ago, after a fifteen-minute break, and would arrive in Tigerville after only another ten miles, she needed to stop.

"Hold on, ma'am—I'll pull these cayuses to a stop at the bottom of the next hill!"

She blinked in disgust and pulled her head back into the coach.

"Thank you, Mister Buchanon!" Charley Anders called with an ironic mix of mockery and chiding.

"Now, Charley," Hunter admonished his partner as the six horses pulled the coach up and over a low pass and then started down the other side, sun-dappled lodgepole pines jutting close along both sides of the trail. "She's new to these parts. I reckon you'd have a helluva time back East your ownself. Hell, even in the newly citified Denver!"

"Yeah, well, I wouldn't go back East. Not after seein' the kind of haughty folks they make back thataway!" Charley drew his neckerchief down, turned to Hunter, and grinned, showing a more-or-less complete set of tobacco-rimmed teeth ensconced in a grizzled, gray-brown beard damp with sweat. "She's hard to listen to, but she is easy on the eyes, ain't she?"

They'd gained the bottom of the hill now, and Hunter was hauling back on the ribbons. "I wouldn't know, Charley. I only look at one woman. You know that."

"Pshaw! You can't tell me you ain't admired how that purty eastern princess fills out her natty travelin' frocks! You wouldn't be a man if you didn't!"

"I got eyes for only one woman, Charley," Hunter insisted. Now that the mules had stopped, the dust swirling over them as it caught up to the coach from behind, Hunter set the brake. "You know that."

"Yeah, well, sounds to me like it's time for you to start lookin' around for another gal. Sounds to me like you an' Annabelle Ludlow are kaput. Through. End-of-story." Charley narrowed one eye in cold castigation at his younger friend. "And you got only one man to blame for that—yourself!"

Gritting his teeth, Charley removed his dusty *sombrero* and smacked it several times across Hunter's stout right shoulder. "Gall-blamed, lame-brained, cork-headed fool! How could you let her get away?"

Hunter had asked himself that question many times over the past few months, but he didn't want to think about it now. Thinking about Annabelle made him feel frustrated as all get-out, and he had to keep his head clear. You didn't drive a six-horse hitch through rugged terrain haunted by desperadoes and Sioux warriors with a brain gummed up by lovelorn goo.

He climbed down from the driver's boot and saw that Miss Meyers was trying to open the Concord's left-side door from inside. She was grunting with the effort, her fine jaws set hard beneath the brim of her stylish but somewhat outlandish eastern-style velvet picture hat trimmed with faux flowers and berries.

"I'll help you there, ma'am."

She looked at him through the window in the door—a despondent look if he had ever seen one. She was, how-ever, a looker. He couldn't deny that even if he had denied noticing to Charley. He felt a sharp pang of guilt every time he looked at this woman and felt . . . well, like a man shouldn't feel when he was in love with another gal.

"It's stuck," she said, her voice toneless with exhaustion.

"I apologize." Hunter plucked a small pine stick from the crack between the door and the stagecoach wall. "A twig got stuck in it somehow, fouled the latch. I do apologize, ma'am. How you doing? Not so well, I reckon . . ."

As Hunter opened the door, she made a face and waved her gloved hand at the billowing dust and tobacco smoke. "The smoke and dust are absolutely atrocious. Not to mention the wretched smell of my unwashed fellow traveler and his who-hit-John, as he so colorfully calls the poison he consumes as though it were water!"

Hunter helped the woman out. He glanced into the carriage to see the grinning countenance of his only other passenger—the Chicago farm implement drummer, Wilfred Farley. The diminutive, craggy-faced man with one broken front tooth and clad in a cheap checked suit— which seemed the requisite uniform of all raggedy-heeled traveling salesmen everywhere—raised an unlabeled, flat, clear bottle half-filled with a milky brown liquid in salute to his destaging fellow passenger's derriere, and took a pull.

Hunter gave the man a reproving look, then turned to the woman, removing his hat and holding it over his broad chest. "Ma'am, let me apolo—"

"Will you please stop apologizing, Mister Buchanon? I'm sorry to say your apologies are beginning to ring a little hollow at this late date. My God, what a torturous contraption!" She looked at the coach's rear wheel and for a second, Hunter thought she was going to give it a kick with one of her delicate, gold-buckled, high-heeled ankle boots.

She thought about it for a couple of seconds, then satisfied herself with a chortling wail of raw anger and tipped her head back to stare up at the tall, blond-haired, blue-eyed jehu hulking before her. "And must you continue to call me ma'am?"

"Uh . . . uh . . ."

"How old are you?"

"Twenty-seven, ma'a . . . er, I mean, Miss Meyers." At least, he hoped that was the moniker she'd been looking for. If not, he might end up with a swift kick to one of his shins, and in her state of mind, even being such a light albeit curvy little thing, he didn't doubt she could do some damage.

"Now, see—I'm younger than you are. Not by much, maybe, but I am young enough that you can feel free to call me Miss. *Miss Meyers.* Not ma'am. For God's sake, don't add insult to injury, Mister Buchanon!"

"I'm sorry, Miss Meyers, it's just that you seemed older . . . somehow." *Wrong thing to say, you cork-headed fool!* Backing water frantically, Hunter said, "I just meant you *acted* older! You know—more mature! I didn't mean you *looked* older!"

He'd said those wheedling words to her slender back as, fists tightly balled at her sides, she went stomping off into the brush and rocks that littered the base of the ridge wall on the west side of the stage road.

"Don't wander too far, ma'am . . . I mean, Miss Meyers!" he called. "It's easy to get turned around out here!"

But she was already gone.

CHAPTER 2

Hunter stared after the pretty, angry woman.

Something nudged his right arm. He looked down to see Wilfred Farley offering his bottle to him, and grinning, his thin, chapped upper lip peeled back from that crooked, broken tooth.

"No, thanks. If that's the stuff you bought at the Robbers' Roost Station, it'll blind both of us."

"Pshaw!" Farley took another deep pull. "Damn good stuff, and I see just fine."

"That's how Hoyle Gullickson lost his top knot." Charley Anders was climbing heavily down from the driver's boot, his sawed-off, double-barrel shotgun hanging from a lanyard down his back.

"What?" Farley asked. "Drinkin' his own skull pop?"

"No—brewin' it." Anders stepped off the front wheel and turned to face Hunter and the pie-eyed Chicago drummer. "He sold it to the Sioux. Several went blind, and the others came back and scalped him."

Farley looked at the bottle in his hand as though it

had suddenly transformed into a rattlesnake. "You don't say . . . ?"

Hunter snorted softly. He knew the story wasn't true. Hoyle Gullickson had lost his top knot when he'd been out cutting wood one winter and was set upon by four braves who'd wanted whiskey.

Gullickson had refused to sell to them because he'd already done time in the federal pen for selling his rotgut to Indians, and he wasn't about to risk returning to that wretched place. Incensed, the braves scalped him, so now he wore the awful knotted scars in a broad, grisly swath over the top of his head, making any and all around him wince whenever he removed his hat, which he loved to do just to gauge the reactions and turn stomachs.

Charley Anders, however, preferred his tall-tale version, which he related often and usually at night around some stage station's potbellied stove to wide-eyed pilgrims in his and Hunter's charge.

Hunter glared at the drummer. "I thought I told you not to smoke around that woman, Farley. And to stay halfways sober."

"Kills the time," Farley said with a shrug, raising a loosely rolled, wheat-paper quirley to his mouth and leveling a defiant stare at Buchanon. "I offered to share my panther juice with her, but she turned her nose up. That offended me. So I got the makings out and rolled a smoke."

He pointed his bottle toward where the woman had disappeared in the rocks and brush. "That pretty little bitch can go straight to hell."

"He's got a point, pard," Charley said, reaching through the stage window. "Give me a pull off that, Farley. I could use a little somethin' to cut the dust."

"I thought you said it'd blind a fella!" Farley objected sarcastically.

Anders jerked the bottle out of the drummer's hand and swiped the lip across his grimy hickory shirt. "I been drinkin' the rotgut so long I'm immune to blindness by now." He stepped back and started to take a pull from the bottle. As he did, a rabbit poked its head out from between two shrubs roughly ten feet off the trail.

Hunter, who'd been looking around cautiously, wary of a holdup and also starting to get a little worried about the woman, had just seen the gray cottontail pull its head back into the shrubs. Bobby Lee gave a mewling yip of coyote excitement, leaped from the roof of the coach onto Charley Anders's right shoulder to the ground.

Charley jerked back with a startled grunt, dropping the bottle.

Bobby Lee plunged into the shrubs between two boulders, then shot up the ridge, hot on the heels of the streaking rabbit, the rabbit and the coyote darting around the columnar pines.

"Damn that vermin!" Charley wailed, clutching his right shoulder with his left hand. "He like to have dislocated my arm! What gall—using me as his damn stepping stool! Has he no respect?"

Hunter snorted a laugh. "That's what you get for being so tight with your jerky, Charley."

"The bottle! The bottle!" wailed Wilfred Farley, pointing at the bottle lying on the ground between Anders and Buchanon. "Good Lord, you're spillin' good whiskey!"

Hunter crouched to pick up the bottle. There was still an inch or two of rotgut remaining. Not for long.

Grinning at Farley, Hunter turned the bottle upside down. The whiskey dribbled out of the mouth to which dirt and pine needles clung. The liquid plopped hollowly onto the ground.

Farley was flabbergasted. "Good lord, man! Are you *mad*?"

"Jehu's rules, Farley." Hunter tossed the bottle high over the coach and into the trees and rocks on the other side. "No drinkin' aboard the coach."

"You're sweet on that gal!" Farley shook his head in disbelief. "You must like a gal who runs you into the ground with every look and word. Me—I got some self-respect. No purty skirt's gonna push Wilfred Farley around!"

"Speakin' of purty skirts," Anders said, staring off toward where the woman had disappeared. "What in the hell's she doin' out there—knittin' an afghan?"

Hunter glanced around, making sure no would-be highwaymen were near. He didn't like standing still here on the trail like this, making easy targets. It was always best to keep moving between relay stations, as a moving target was always harder to attack than one standing still in the middle of the trail with good cover all around for would-be attackers.

Hunter stepped forward and called, "Miss Meyers? You all right?"

No response.

"We'd best get movin', Miss Meyers!"

Hunter took another couple of steps forward, then stopped again, concern growing in him. "Miss Meyers?"

He didn't want to call too loudly and risk alerting anyone in the area to their position. He and Anders were carrying only two passengers, but aboard the stage they had ten thousand dollars in payroll money, which they were hauling to one of the many mines above Tigerville.

Hunter glanced back at Anders, scowling his frustration. Anders shrugged and shook his head.

"I best look for her," Hunter said. "Charley, stay with the stage. Keep a sharp eye out. I don't like sitting out here like a Thanksgiving turkey on the dining room table."

"You an' me both, pard," Charley said behind Buchanon, as Hunter stepped off the trail and walked into the rocks and brush littering the base of the western ridge.

Hunter pushed through the brush, wended his way around rocks. "Miss Meyers? Time to hit the road, Miss Meyers!"

He saw a deer path carved through the brush. It rose up a low shoulder of the ridge. Hunter followed it, frowning down at the ground, noting the sharp indentations of the heels of a lady's ankle boots.

As the path turned around a large fir tree, the indentations of the lady's heels became scuffed and scraped. Amidst the scuff marks was a faint print of a man's boot.

Instantly, Buchanon's hand closed around the pearl grips of the silver-chased LeMat secured high on his right hip in a gray buckskin holster worn to the texture of doeskin. He clicked the hammer of the main .44-caliber barrel back and, his heartbeat increasing, the skin under his shirt collar prickling, he continued following the scuffed trail.

The prints led up and over the rise then down the other side, through tree shadows and sunlight. Somewhere ahead and to Hunter's right, a squirrel was chittering angrily. That was the only sound.

Hunter continued forward for another fifty feet before he stopped suddenly.

Ahead, a man crouched between two aspens. He seemed to be moving in place, making jerking movements. He was also talking in a heated but hushed tone.

Hunter could see a second man—or part of a second man—on his knees on the other side of one of the aspens. Hunter could see only the man's boot soles and the thick forward curve of his back clad in a blue wool shirt. This man, too, was making quick jerking movements.

He seemed to be holding something down.

Hunter stepped to his right, putting the left-most aspen between himself and the crouching man. He moved slowly forward, both aspens concealing his approach from both men before him. As he moved closer to their position, muffled cries blazed into the air around him.

Muffled female cries.

Hunter stepped behind a tree. He peered around its left side. From here, he had a clearer view of the two men and of Miss Meyers on the ground between them, partly obscured by tree roots humping up out of the forest duff.

The man on the right knelt by the woman's head, leaning down, holding her head against the ground with both of his hands pressed across her mouth. Miss Meyers was kicking her legs out wildly and flailing helplessly with her arms, making her skirts flop and exposing her pantaloon- and stocking-clad legs.

Thumping sounds rose as did the crackle of pine needles and dead leaves as she thrashed so desperately, her cries muffled by one of her assailant's hands. The kneeling man laughed through his teeth as he held the woman down, his brown-mustached face swollen and red.

The other man, tall and skinny with long black sideburns and a bushy black mustache, had pulled his pants down around his boots and was opening the fly of his long-handles, grinning down at the struggling woman.

"Hold her still, Bill. Hold her still. I'll be hanged if she ain't as fine a piece o' female flesh as I—"

Leaning forward, exposing the evidence of his craven lust, he grabbed Miss Meyers's ankles and thrust them down against the ground. Leaning farther forward, he slid his hands up her legs from inside her dress, a lusty grin blooming broadly across his long, ugly face with close-set, dark eyes set deep beneath shaggy, black brows.

The man clamped her legs down with his own and reached for her swinging arms, grabbing them, stopping them as he lowered his hips toward the woman's. He stopped abruptly, turning his head sharply to see Buchanon striding toward him.

The man's eyes widened in shock. "What the . . . *hey*!"

Hunter had returned the big LeMat to its holster and picked up a stout aspen branch roughly five feet long and about as big around as one of his muscular forearms—as broad as a cedar fencepost.

It made a solid thumping, cracking sound as he smashed it with all the force in his big hands and arms against the black-haired man's forehead. The branch broke roughly a foot and a half from the end. As the would-be rapist's head snapped sharply back, his eyes rolling up in their sockets, the end of the branch dropped with the man into the deep, narrow ravine behind him.

The other man cursed and leaped to his feet, his amber eyes as round as saucers and bright with fear.

"No!" he cried as he saw the stout branch swing toward him.

He tipped his head to one side, raising his arms as if to shield his face. Buchanon grunted as he thrust the branch down through the man's open hands to slam it against the man's left ear, blood instantly spewing from the smashed appendage.

"Ohhh!" the man cried as he hit the ground.

Buchanon stepped forward, raising the club again, rage a wild stallion inside him. Only the lowest of the lowest gut wagon dog did such a thing to a woman. This man would pay dearly—and he did as Hunter, straddling the man's flailing legs, smashed the club again and again against the man's head. After the third or fourth blow from the powerful arms and shoulders of the big, blond, blue-eyed man standing over him, the man's cries faded and his flailing arms and legs lay still upon the ground.

Hunter raised the club for one more blow but stopped when the crackle of guns rose from the direction of the stagecoach. His heart shuddered. He hammered the second rapist's head once more, then kicked the still body, the dead eyes staring up at Hunter in silent castigation, into the ravine.

It landed with a thump near the other carcass.

Hunter whipped around, crouching and drawing the LeMat from its holster, facing in the direction from which guns blasted angrily and men shouted.

Connect with  Us

Visit us online at
KensingtonBooks.com
to read more from your favorite authors, see books
by series, view reading group guides, and more.

for sneak peeks, chances to win books and prize packs,
and to share your thoughts with other readers.

facebook.com/kensingtonpublishing
twitter.com/kensingtonbooks

Tell us what you think!

To share your thoughts, submit a review,
or sign up for our eNewsletters, please visit:
KensingtonBooks.com/TellUs.